Takers: Apocalypse in Eden Book One

Horror meets mysticism. A fast moving, bloody, and dark book—with some awesome musical references.

Seekers: Apocalypse in Eden Book Two

This is book II in a series that will keep you glued to the pages. Lock the doors and get ready to read.

Chems

A blue zombie and a kid named Billy … This would be a kickass movie. More please!

Yeah, but I Didn't

Timely coming of age story. Profound and brutally relevant.

Telephone Road

Intense, dark, gritty, and real. This author never disappoints.

All For Love

Wonderful story. Pulls at every fiber of your being. An everyday tale of the horror one woman goes through for love.

Stevie-girl and the Phantom Pilot

Stevie reminded me of a young Katniss Everdeen.

Stevie-girl and the Phantom Student

I loved Stevie and Jase in Stevie-Girl and The Phantom Pilot, but I love them even more in The Phantom Student.

Stevie-girl and the Phantom of Crybaby Bridge

As a kid I always had a fondness for Nancy Drew and the Hardy Boys, and things-that-go-bump in the night. The Stevie-girl stories have that same feeling of mystery and wonder.

Stevie-girl and the Phantom of Forever
If you need a new book series for your middle schooler, check out this one!

Stutter Creek
This story grabs you around the neck with a tight grip and doesn't let go.

Lilac Lane
The whole package. A surprising and brilliant read.

Copper Lake
Best scary book I've ever read. More Stephen King than romantic suspense.

The Remains in the Pond
Only five stars because ten wasn't an option.

REMAINDERS

Also by Ann Swann

The Apocalypse in Eden Series
Takers
Seekers

Yeah, But I Didn't

REMAINDERS

APOCALYPSE IN EDEN BOOK 3

ANN SWANN

WordCrafts Press

To Mike Parker, Publisher, Wordcrafts Press
Thank you for your patience as I endeavored to wrap
up this trilogy. Jack and Snake are some of my favorite
characters of all time.

Perhaps I wasn't ready to leave them.

CHAPTER ONE

What now?

"Head for Denver?" I asked.

Dad shook his head. "Gran and Gramps are gone."

I stared straight ahead, a solid hard lump in my throat. "How did they die?" I tried not to picture my gentle, always smiling grandparents hanging from the oak in their front yard.

"They must've been in the garden when the sound came." His voice quavered. "At least they weren't flayed. The elderly were the first to go, it seems. Just like the virus before this."

I thought about that. Elderly. Infirm. Maybe children. Not the strongest members of the human race. *Culling the herd*, Carlos would've said. Did say, more than once.

Maybe I could examine that idea with Dad later. But it would have to wait. We now had several people traveling with us, and if we weren't going to Denver, I wasn't sure where we were headed.

Sam had pulled Marla's body from the tow truck and busied himself cleaning out the cab. He wanted to drive it as far as possible. It ran on diesel, so it might be harder to fuel up.

Dad sat in the shotgun seat beside me. Faith and Snake were with eight-year-old Milo in the back seat of our new Chrysler—silver this time—and Drew and Trina had just pulled their Nissan Pathfinder up beside us so we could talk across the gap.

We were all waiting on Sam.

He finished cleaning the cab and then moved Marla's body off the road into the ditch. Only then did he walk back toward where we were all parked and ready.

None of us mentioned burying the murderer, Marla. We needed to be shed of this place as soon as possible.

"Cleaned the cab the best I could with limited water," Sam said as he walked up. "Maybe we should stop and get that Cadillac if you have some extra gas for it."

"Sure," I said. "And we'll get more fuel. But I forgot your punch tool. We'll have to pick up another of those handy little things."

Sam nodded and leaned against the car.

In the distance, the winged Turqs kept watch. Every now and then we would hear one whistle down like a missile. Then a sky hole would open, and the blackness would fall. It seemed as if the Turqs were arrows from the sky. They would spear the enemies, make them bleed, and then the dark rain would whoosh down and gather them up.

From where we sat, it appeared the black sludge had cleaned up all the bodies, both Takers and humans. Except for the ones inside the Cheyenne Mountain Complex. We had no way of knowing what happened in there. The one glimpse I'd had inside the mountain had been so horrific, I hadn't waited around to see more.

But there must've been other survivors. We'd seen several vehicles start up and head back toward the highway. I figured we'd catch up with them down the road.

"Hey, Dad," I started to say, "did you see many survivors—

But Dad had started talking first. "When I didn't find you in Texas," he said. "I went on up to Denver, hoping you'd made your way there. I was so frantic to locate you, I didn't even take time to bury Aunt Edna." He looked away, but not before I saw the moisture in his eye. "That still haunts me."

I touched his hand. "It's okay. We buried her. Besides, I had the same plan. To look for you at Gran and Grampa's house. I just got sidetracked a time or two."

He clasped my fingers. "I want to hear all about it. Especially about those guardian angels you call Turqs." His grip tightened, then released. He'd been through so much, as a captive of Marla and the Takers. "I still can't believe those flying Turqs used to be Takers, the same monsters that are killing everyone."

I thought back over the last few days. "Chaos reigns. I don't know who said that. But I do know one thing, it feels true now." I looked at his scarred face and skeletal body. "I want to hear all about your time when we get a chance. Especially when you were with Marla and the others."

"It was Cade," he said. "He rescued me, kept me alive as best he could. Right there at the end."

Glancing at the road, I said, "Cade again. He turned out to be quite a hero." *Just like Thad,* I thought. *Except I should have known better. I'd known Cade all my life.*

No, my subconscious said, *you can't feel guilty about Cade. He did what he had to do, and you did what you had to do. Someone shot at us on the highway. Someone in his group. That was not just my imagination.*

It was true. Cade could have come with us at any time. But I wouldn't let Faith ride with him and Hal. I'd vetoed that in a heartbeat. And afterward, he'd changed. Stuck closer to Hal instead of us. As if I'd somehow betrayed him.

Am I my brother's keeper?

Dad spoke again, interrupting my reverie. "I don't think Cade knew what was happening at first." He touched the red marks around his neck. The rope burns from where Marla had tied him like an animal. "I had traveled from Denver with a group that got sprayed. We couldn't help ourselves after that. Then Cade came along. He was with Marla and a wiry kid with a foul mouth. They had these hard hats and plastic face shields, so they didn't get the spray." He hesitated. "I wanted to beg Cade for news of you, but that spray made it difficult to think, impossible to talk."

I failed him. Cade. I should have made him come with us, should have forced him. But I didn't tell Dad any of that. Instead, I said, "I'm glad he saved you. I don't know how he fell in with Marla. I only met her the night I left Eden."

Dad nodded. "When Cade saw me, he pulled me out of the group in front of the entrance and managed to keep me alive until I came back to my senses. That's when Marla found out I was your dad." His eyebrows went up. "She said you killed her boyfriend, but I didn't believe that."

"You're right. I didn't kill him. But she blamed me because I wouldn't let her take Mom's pain pills out of the medicine cabinet."

Dad patted my knee. "Good job, Wayward Son."

We smiled at each other. "I still can't believe it," I said.

He gave my knee a little back and forth shake. "I knew that wasn't your skull in the ashes." He closed his eyes. "There were two women walking in our neighborhood, looking for bikes to ride or cars that would start."

My stomach fell. "You're kidding me."

Dad shook his head. "One of them told me what happened at our house the night you were there. They said they were the ones who had dozed off and let the candle fall over. Caught the drapes on fire."

So at least Thad was honest about that. *But why hadn't he gone back and picked them up? The first Chrysler, the white one, supposedly belonged to Mo's daughter.*

I forced those thoughts out of my head. "So that's when you went to Aunt Edna's. But why didn't you—"

"When they said how you had taken off in the night, on your bike, I knew you were headed there. I had already found Mom's car in the underground parking at the library. After I found her." His throat muscles worked overtime as he spoke, as if he had to swallow his sorrow with every word.

I couldn't speak. I couldn't have spoken for all the money in the world.

Finally, he continued, "After finding Edna on the porch, and no trace of you, I began to have doubts. I talked myself into thinking maybe it *was* you in the ash, and the women were just trying to cover it up. I was so distraught about finding mom, and Edna ..." He glanced away. "I think my mind started playing tricks on me. I didn't even go down in the silo to get supplies."

"It's okay, Dad." I recalled the horrific message scrawled on concrete in the Quonset hut. *Was it there, or in my head?* "You were alone. You didn't have all the help that I had."

He laughed, but it was tinged with sadness. "I want to hear more about your help. And about your journey."

"And I want to hear what happened to the two women. They were good to me. But we'll have plenty of time to chat on our way to wherever we're headed." I laughed a bit. A good feeling. One of hope. "Where *are* we headed?"

"Any place but here," he said. "Any place but here." He almost grinned, a bit of the old pirate curling up one side of his mouth.

Drew leaned over and spoke into the gap between his SUV and our car. "I say we find some tropical isle. A place untouched by all this. A place with good food. Lots of fish, maybe some bananas and coconuts." He held up Trina's skinny arm. "Something that will put some meat on these bones." He glanced toward the backseat at his son. Milo was asleep with his arm around Snake's neck. The dog didn't seem to mind at all.

I wondered why we hadn't seen other kids, but that would be another topic for the road. For our first campfire.

Sam and Faith spoke almost in unison. "It's not tropical—"

"—but the silo still had a ton of food."

"Jinx," Faith said.

I saw Sam stick his pinkie finger in her window so she could hook hers around it. "You owe me a Coke," he said.

She laughed and hooked her pinkie around his. "I will gladly pay you Tuesday," she quoted an ancient Popeye cartoon, and it endeared her to me all over again. "Or when we hit up the next 7-Eleven." She paused then added, "Whichever comes first."

Sam grinned. "I'll hold you to that, young lady." He straightened to his full, Jack Reacher height and turned toward the tow truck.

"On the Road Again," cued up in my head. Even Willie Nelson agreed it was time to go. "I believe Dad is right," I said. "Any place but here." When I glanced at Faith in the rearview mirror, she nodded.

I put the Chrysler in gear and headed south. I didn't think there were any tropical isles within driving distance from Colorado, but at least we were going somewhere.

Suddenly, "On the Road Again" felt like home.

CHAPTER TWO

Telepathy

The landscape had not changed much while we were at Cheyenne Mountain. "Where is everyone?" Faith asked as we tooled along in the Chrysler. "I mean there were lots of survivors at the entrance. I saw them leaving in cars and trucks, like us. Where'd they go?"

I let my gaze rake the landscape. "I don't know—"

Dad spoke up, his fingers massaging his temple none too gently. "Most folks have been in hiding since the rip. After that fiasco, they probably went right back underground."

I thought back to my harrowing time in the school basement, hiding in the thick dark like a scared rabbit while the Takers crashed into our hometown on silvery strings of poison. Eden, Texas. My hometown. The perfect place to live. Until now.

"You're probably right," I agreed. "I hid down in the school basement. I guess we were all underground somehow, right?"

Milo, who had elected to continue traveling with us to be close to Snake, said, "We were down in the cellar of the old gangster house when the big sound came."

He said it so matter-of-factly, it almost slipped right past me. "Gangster house … you don't mean The Bitty Sloan House?"

Milo nodded.

I felt a goose walk over my grave, as my gran would've said.

"I've been there, too," I told him. "Which is kind of odd when you think of it." My mind zipped back to our time in New Mexico.

"I met a man named Carlos there." My eyes sought Faith's eyes in the rearview again.

"We *knew* him," Milo said. "He was our Realtor."

"Dear Carlos." Faith smiled sadly. "One of the best people I've ever met. Did you say y'all were in the cellar when the rip occurred?"

Milo nodded again. "Was Snake with you when you were there, Jack?" His tough, little boy hand rested on the dog's broad back. Snake rolled his eyes up to the boy's face when the boy rubbed his neck.

Now it was my turn, but I wasn't sure my voice would work properly. Such an amazing thing, this coincidence. Such a hard time, the loss of Carlos, and before him, my complicated old friend, Thad. "Yep," I said at last. "We both knew Carlos. In fact, we became good friends with him. Like family—" I could see moisture on Faith's cheek when I glanced at her reflection again.

I once read that coincidence is just God doing things without being asked. I wondered if those were Faith's thoughts, but I didn't have time to examine them.

"What happened to Carlos?" Milo asked. "Why isn't he here?"

I caught Faith's eye again. *Do I tell him the truth?*

Her direct gaze made me think, *yes.*

I plunged ahead. "Carlos isn't here anymore because—" I was about to tell him how Carlos had died but Milo cut in, thinking aloud.

"He was my friend. And he was there when that black stuff ate Mama. But when we left that big house, he stayed."

I waited to see if he would elaborate on the death of his mama, but he didn't, and I was leery of prying since his dad and sister were not riding with us. If the poor kid had a meltdown, I wanted them nearby. So, I let it ride.

"After y'all left, I guess we came along," I said. "Me and Snake and a man named Thad." I felt the prickles tighten up my skin again. "Seems like another lifetime already."

Dad laid a bony hand on my knee, just for a second, and I came out of the past. I patted his fingers to let him know everything was alright. *Guess Milo wasn't the only one in need of comforting.*

I cleared my throat. "Where have y'all been since then, Milo?"

The little guy shrugged. "We stay in some caves. Sometimes we go through stores and stuff, looking for food, but at night we always go back to this one big cave and camp out there. Daddy says it keeps us safe."

"Makes sense to me," Faith said. "Dawk told me he was going to check out Carlsbad Caverns if he got the chance. This was back when we were traveling through West Texas together." She laughed a little. "Carlsbad is in New Mexico, not far from the Texas border. But after that, he said he was also going to try Alaska. See what was happening there."

I matched her laugh. Alaska was a long way off. New Mexico was a lot closer. "Carlsbad Caverns, huh? We've been there a couple times."

Dad nodded. "Your mom loved that place."

"Yeah," Milo said. "Carlsbad? That's what Dawk called it, too."

I glanced in the mirror again. It felt like a new form of communication.

Faith's eyes were as big as saucers. "You know a man named Dawk?"

Milo giggled. "Dawk, with *A W*. He always said that, so people wouldn't think he was a real *D-O-C* doctor." He laid his cheek on Snake's flat head. The dog let out a doggy sigh. "I liked him," the boy added. "But he wasn't jokey and fun like Carlos. Dawk was serious. He didn't say, *Put up your dukes, mijo.*" The kid tried to make his voice growl the way Carlos must've done.

For a moment, an ache like a bad tooth took over my memory and transported me back to an elegant old farmhouse and Carlos collapsed on the floor holding a teddy bear and a wallet photo of his little girl. The one who had run outside with her mother to see what the terrible killing sound might be.

"That's him alright." My voice cracked. "Always called me *mijo*, too." I swiped the memories out of my eyes and clenched my teeth to prevent new ones from rolling down my face.

Dad suddenly found much interesting scenery outside his passenger window. I appreciated that, but I couldn't keep my eyes from straying back to the rearview mirror to check Faith's reaction.

She didn't appear to be thinking about me at all. Her gaze was focused on the top of Milo's head. In addition to the news about Carlos, she'd heard something else that surprised her. "Did the man called Dawk come with y'all to Cheyenne Mountain?"

"No," Milo's tone was thoughtful. "He told my daddy he was going to some place with a military base." He stopped talking and resumed petting old Snake, counting the numerous twisty scars he could feel under the dog's tawny fur.

Faith met my eye in the mirror. *Dawk*, I could almost hear her say. *He's talking about Dawk, my first traveling companion.*

An unfamiliar feeling invaded my thinking. *Jealousy?* Maybe. Maybe I'd already claimed Faith in my head. Caveman style. A teenaged caveman.

Don't be an idiot, Jack. Dad didn't say it aloud, but that thought found its way into my head, too.

We didn't speak anymore. I wasn't sure if Faith wanted to talk about her friend, so I let it be—just like the death of Milo's mama.

Being out in the open countryside again, away from the chaotic battle scene at Cheyenne, I finally felt my bones settle back into their places. The crowds at Cheyenne Mountain had smothered me even before the monsters set in on us. I was small town, just a kid, knew everyone or thought I did, until the rip. I thought I knew how to handle everything, until it was over. Then the shakes always set in. The internal, self-doubt, question-everything-that-happened, shakes.

Dad looked my way.

Could he hear my thoughts?

Back at the mountain's covered, tunnel-like entrance, we'd encountered a nightmare of strangers, monsters, and death. Out here, nothing but wide-open space and my own small caravan, Dad riding shotgun beside me. The difference was wonderful but jarring. How could the other people disappear as if they'd vanished into thin air?

I glanced at Dad. I *still* had to look over at him every now and then to convince myself he was real. And then I'd take stock of the rest. Faith and Milo keeping Snake company in the backseat. Drew and Trina in the navy-blue Nissan Pathfinder behind us. Sam in the giant tow truck behind them.

Carlos was badly missed. And Turq—both forms—the original turquoise-shirted gray creature, and the beautifully winged, bullet-shaped angel, the one we had taken to calling Turq 2.0 or sometimes just 2.0.

To be honest, I missed the original Turq the most. He'd been a protector in both forms, but the first one had also been something of a companion. A silent companion. I laughed internally at my own joke. The further we got from Cheyenne, the further we got from Turq 2.0 and his flock of angels. It felt wrong, but I didn't know what else to do. We had to keep moving. Of that, I was certain.

As we drove, we encountered mile after mile of scattered wrecks and red rocks piled up along the sides of the highway. Knowing the rocks, some the size of small boulders, must have rolled down from the mountains during the rip kept my attention sharp most of the time.

When we did have a clear stretch of road, I couldn't keep my mind from wandering to the girl in the backseat.

Faith grew more amazing by the mile. The supernatural stuff seemed to have left her now, as if she only channeled it under duress, or maybe when she was near a certain Turq of the 2.0 variety. Could that be it? He had power, no doubt about that. I recalled the healing cocoon in which he'd wrapped Dad and Snake … had Faith been wrapped as well? I couldn't rightly say. Already, as with most fantastic events, things were growing fuzzy. Like wings blurring the horizon.

When that idea crossed my mind, I leaned out the window to check the sky. We hadn't seen Turq—or any terrestrial Takers either, for that matter—since leaving the Cheyenne Mountain area, but I had a feeling the good ones were still around somewhere. Fighting the Monster-Takers in other places, perhaps. I had many theories about the two kinds of Takers, the winged angels, and the gray sin-word cannibals.

Now that I'd glimpsed inside the mountain, momentarily, I came to believe people *were* behind a lot of the sorrow we'd encountered. At least as far as the rounding up of survivors. My own dad had been delivered to the mountain by a human—an evil human—for whatever reason. *Maybe the government is using us as collateral in some extra-terrestrial takeover,* I thought. That felt true. Or at least possible.

I tried not to study my dad, but I couldn't help myself. His head was leaned back, mouth slightly open like an old man, seemingly sound asleep. *He's been through so much,* I thought. But before my mind could take me down that rabbit hole, I overheard a snippet of Faith's conversation with Milo in the backseat.

"Did Dawk say which military base he was going to?"

I watched in the mirror as Milo shrugged, blinked. "Somewhere near here, I think." He yawned, and his eyes closed. He leaned over a bit.

Faith arranged herself to better accommodate the sleeping boy. Soon, Milo had snuggled under her arm like a chick under a wing.

Smiling into the mirror, I whispered, "You should nap, too."

She nodded, having already rolled up her jacket and stuck it beside her head like a pillow. "Only if you promise to let me drive later, so you can do the same."

"That's a promise," I agreed. I heard myself, and it sounded grown up, worrying about other's needs that way.

Feeling another new unfamiliar feeling, I laid my arm along the open window to better appreciate the rush of air on my skin. At times like this, I missed my head-tunes, the songs that had guided me across the land right from the beginning.

Now that Dad was right beside me, the music seemed to have stopped. I tried forcing our song, "Carry on Wayward Son," but it didn't quite work. It no longer came out as a full-on musical production; instead, it came across as a simple memory. One I'd have to sing to hear.

It felt like losing another old and trusted friend. Not as bad as losing Carlos or Thad or Cade—not even as bad as the emptiness I felt after Turq morphed from a turquoise-shirt-wearing Taker into the amazing winged being—but it did feel like a loss nonetheless. In fact, the loss of both the music and the Taker had been palpable. I'd felt it in my fingers, and I'd felt it in my toes.

A snippet of the old Troggs song, "Love is All Around" blipped across my brainwaves. It was on Dad's Moldy Oldies playlist. "I feel it in my something …" I sang inside my head. "I feel it in my bones …" No, those weren't the correct lyrics. But they were similar. At least, I thought they were. Again, it was only a memory, not the actual song.

I beat a light rhythm on the steering wheel with my thumbs. "Carry on …" I tried under my breath. *Nothing.*

After a few moments, I gave up, internally recited The Lord's Prayer, threw in a few Hail Marys, and then allowed my mind to wander across the rushing, mountain-framed land.

The sky was milk-blue, the color of that thin, no fat stuff my mom used to buy. It never looked right on cereal, and after I complained she went back to buying whole milk just for me. "I guess you don't need to watch your fat intake yet," I recalled her saying. "But don't drink my no-fat kind." She showed me where mine would be kept, in the fridge door, and where hers would be kept, on the second shelf. I remembered laughing and telling her I'd try to control myself.

When I felt moisture in my eyes, I steeled my face, didn't let them fall. But I couldn't steel my mind. *I miss you, Mom.* A quick flash of her turquoise sweater invaded my head and I quickly turned that aside and thought of how we'd found Faith in the locker room at the high school.

Yes. That was a much better memory. Nevertheless, Simon & Garfunkel's old song, "Sound of Silence," beat inside my skull like a trapped moth inside a summer-night window screen. Try as I might, that screen wouldn't seem to open so I could let it fly. It stayed there, like an idea entombed in amber. Seemed my mom-memories were going to play out whether I wanted them to or not.

Once again, the classic song was little more than a memory. Mom had loved what she called "the poetry of those lyrics." But I still couldn't understand why, now that I had found Dad, my conscious was blocking the actual music while seeming to allow me to wallow in her death.

Like the memory of the day—not that long ago—when I'd pulled up Disturbed's version of "The Sound of Silence" on my phone. I'd thought it would shock her, this modern version, but she ended up singing along. Enjoying it.

"Just goes to show, good poetry is good poetry," she'd said. And then she'd smiled in her librarian's secret way. As if she knew things I didn't and probably never would.

It's true, I thought. *She knew so much more than I ever will. Like how it felt to die.* I smashed that thought aside and ran through the entire song in my head, the lyrics surprisingly easy to remember—*good poetry, right Mom?*—and then I stuck my face into the slipstream and let the warm wind soothe my hurting soul.

"I love that song," Faith whispered from the backseat.

My eyes flew to the rearview. "What song?"

"The one you're thinking of. "The Sound of Silence"." She waited a moment. "Or am I completely wrong?" She laughed, ready to be embarrassed.

Hesitating, wanting to be certain I'd heard correctly, I said, "You can read my mind?"

Faith half-smiled. "Same wavelength, I guess." Her gaze held mine in the reflective glass. "Only some things come through. Either that, or you have a lot of blank space up there." She smiled to let me know she was joking.

"Seriously," I said. "Is it only music you get? Only songs?"

Faith looked away, out the window, as if deciding what to admit, or perhaps just thinking back, trying to recall. "Maybe," she said. "I'm not sure. Maybe that's it."

I hope that's it, I thought. *'Cause if she gets it all she'll know what I'm thinking about her. And that would be downright humiliating.*

"Can you hear mine?" she asked.

That brought me back. "No. Not now."

She nodded.

"But before I got to Cheyenne, when I was trying to catch up to Marla and the Takers, after they took you and Sam, I could hear you calling me. Telling me to hurry." I looked up again, to see if she believed me. "It was the same once we were there, and I couldn't locate you in the crowd. You called out to me, in my head."

Faith nodded. "Yes. Same wavelength. For sure."

I caught movement in my side mirror. "Sam's motioning me to pull over." I slowed and put on the blinker to let Sam and Drew both know what we were doing. Near the edge of the highway, we rolled to a stop.

Out of habit, I scanned the skies and pale horizons for any sign of danger. Seeing none, I stepped out of the Chrysler and waited for Sam to come alongside.

Both Sam and Drew pulled up. Sam got out and came to the car.

Shading my face against the noonday sun, I waited. "Everything okay?"

Sam stretched his muscle-bound six-foot five-inch frame one shoulder at a time as he walked from the truck to my window. "Got an idea we're being followed. Y'all sense anything weird?"

I immediately latched onto the way he said sensed instead of see or seen. As if the supernatural happenings were becoming old hat to all of us.

Faith opened her door quietly so not to wake Milo, but she didn't emerge, just sat, open to the still air. "Ever since we left, I've had a creepy feeling on the back of my neck."

No one asked what that meant. Everyone understood it was either clairvoyance, or good old, amped-up, everyday intuition.

Drew got out of his blue Nissan and came over, Trina right behind him. Snake did not move. He seemed to take his new job as little-boy-pillow very seriously.

"I don't feel anything," I said. "But I trust you and Faith." I had a flash of Cade memory. "Wish we had some of those old walkie-talkies like some of us had back in the day."

From the front seat, Dad chimed in. "Would they work, I wonder?"

"You got me." I leaned down and dug in the console for one of the paper maps we'd taken from the jack-knifed semi-truck when

Thad and I were traveling together. "I've kept this map through it all. Even remembering to get it out of my first Chrysler." I displayed it reverently. "Let's see what town is coming up."

"Are we going back to The Bitty Sloan House?" Trina asked.

I shook my head. "We've already passed the cut off. Could've been a place to spend the night, I guess."

Trina hugged herself. "*Should* we go back there?"

Drew's face had taken on the look of a mask. "I don't know." He glanced at the kids, but the pain in his eyes told a broader tale. "Rose. The memories …"

I knew what he felt. My library-mom-memory still haunted me even after I let it out to walk around the campfire that night. The group had absorbed part of my pain that evening, that much is true. Carlos, Turq, Sam, and Faith. I know they did.

Maybe they had needed it, too. We each shared our pain in different ways. I figured Drew and the kids would share their pain, in time. "Look here." I pointed to a place on the map. "The turn off for a place called Verde is coming up soon. That could be a good place to recoup."

"Look at the sky," Faith murmured. "Kinda cool green and warm turquoise." Her eyes sought the horizon. "You know, blue turquoise represents male energy and green turquoise represents female energy." Her voice had gone all singsong again, the way it did sometimes.

I waited for more explanation, but none came. Instead, what came were images of dancing and chanting and Native American type ceremonies.

Not quite understanding, I let my finger touch the place on the map, as if that might make things clear. "Verde means green. It might be an interesting town. Maybe we could find some food and a place to hole up for a night." I looked at Sam and suddenly I knew we were both thinking of the camp at Palo Duro Canyon where we'd been overrun with Takers. They'd killed Carlos there, and kidnapped Sam and Faith.

"I never want to go through that again," Faith said.

My hand had absently slipped down to my thigh, the one

where a bullet had grazed me. The one I'd had to cauterize with a butter knife to stop the bleeding.

"Nope," Sam said, still stretching first one arm and then the other up and over the opposite shoulder, elbow in palm, push, push. "Let's avoid that if we can." He grinned, and I was once again reminded how lucky we were the big man was on our side.

"Anyone know how to tell if a place has a basement or cellar? I don't think we can afford to drive around looking for doors set into the earth." He glanced down at Faith, still sitting in the car with the door cracked open. "We'd run out of gas—"

"I think if a house is set up off the ground, it probably has a crawlspace," I said. "Maybe we need to be in the Midwest, you know, what my mom always called the breadbasket." I pictured white farmhouses set in the middle of green and gold patchwork fields. In my head, I heard a song called "Fields of Gold." My dad said Sting wrote the song after he married his wife, and they bought a house beside a field of barley. Something in the way the wind blew across the fields led him to write the song.

I was delighted to hear the music, even if was simple background noise in my mind. I wondered if Faith could hear it this time, but what she said next led me to believe otherwise.

"That's where the real farms will be, all right," she said. "But I think we'll find plenty of canned stuff in big warehouse markets and distribution centers. Dry goods, too." Her expression was still thoughtful. "I don't think there are enough survivors left to clean out all the canned food." That bold statement fell into the air between the lot of us like the proverbial lead balloon.

"Besides," she continued, wandering into the conversational void she'd inadvertently created, "doesn't every town have a fallout shelter in the basement of the courthouse or Police Station where we could sleep?"

"Yes," I said, remembering how I'd often thought the same thing. I pictured my hometown of Eden. "And hospitals and libraries—" I waited for Mom's turquoise sweater to make an appearance, and it didn't disappoint, but it was no longer a dagger pain when it came, just a melancholy ache. "Churches, too, maybe."

"And along with police stations there are sheriff's offices and military bases where we can look for more ammo. Even Amy Surplus stores for those walkie talkies."

"Since the ambush, when we learned it wasn't only the monsters we had to look out for, we've done our best to avoid enclosed places, except for the silo. And I'm pretty sure even it had suffered a cave-in or something."

"Slow your roll, kids," Sam said. "Those will be the first places people look. And even if there aren't millions of survivors, we've already learned that it's not only the good guys, like us, who survived." He almost grinned, but this time it turned to a grimace. "We will need to be extra careful going into any enclosed spaces."

"After what we've seen," Drew said, "I heartily agree. But so far, the kids and I have been blessed with good guys." He looked around the group. "Really hated to hear about Carlos, though."

That dropped a caul over the group once again.

"You're right," Faith said. "We can't let our guard down. Not for a minute."

"Anyone hungry?" Milo piped up from the backseat.

Everyone laughed, glad for the distraction.

Snake hopped over Faith and landed on his tiptoes outside her door. I popped the Chrysler's trunk lid and strolled around to the back. "I don't know about y'all, but I'm getting a little tired of crackers and Slim Jims. Let's see what we've got left."

"I wouldn't mind some fresh meat," Sam said.

Drew nodded. "I guess the best we can do is hope we find a working freezer somewhere."

"Stranger things have happened," Milo added, cracking them all up again.

"I was hoping for something to shoot at," Sam replied. "Or maybe even a creek with a fish or two in it."

That took me by surprise. We'd seen evidence of rabbits and gophers, even a fox once, or so we thought. We could eat those. And what about snakes? They live underground. In West Texas, where my little town was located, snake was listed on some menus.

Especially around the town of Big Spring where the annual rattlesnake roundup was held each year.

I looked at Sam with new eyes. "Let's talk about this hunting and fishing thing."

He nodded. "I have ideas …"

Again, we all laughed, as if anything different was good.

CHAPTER THREE

New old friends

After everyone had a snack and potty break, another exercise in new world problems, the little caravan prepared to get back on the road. But not before Sam scanned the horizon behind us again.

"I feel it, too," I said. "Wish we still had your field glasses and all the other survival gear you had in the Jeep."

"And the other weapons," he added. "I'm just thankful I found these in the Caddy." He indicated the machete and shotgun he'd found in the out-of-gas car.

Drew loped back to his SUV and dug around in the back seat, coming out with black binoculars on a sturdy lanyard. "Never fear. Milo's dad is here!" He handed over the expensive looking field glasses after taking a second to scan the horizon himself.

"Awesome," I said, using that word my English teacher used to call a trash word because in her opinion it was so overused it should be thrown out.

I did a careful 360° scan of the area. Nothing but mountains and the odd wreck here and there. In the far distance, I could see another vehicle going the same direction we were. Quite a distance ahead of us. I assumed it was one of the survivors that had left before we did.

But since the black sky sludge always rained down on injured or dead Takers, at least we didn't have to contend with their corpses. *How nice. Chalk one up for the invading forces.*

I took a breath, willed my mind away from the negative

thoughts, and focused strictly on the positive. Sometimes it was the only thing I could think to do. Despair lived at my edges, now. Maybe a real man wouldn't feel this way, but most of the time, I still felt like Pinocchio, just hoping-to-be-real boy. Even that thought was bittersweet. *Pinocchio* had been one of my mom's go-to books at story time in the library.

Skimming the area once more, I thought, *If not for the wrecks, we could be traveling through a cutout paper collage.* My eye admired the mountains we were leaving behind. Snowcapped Pike's Peak towered in the near distance. We hadn't gone too far from the Cheyenne Complex yet. Could some of the survivors be trailing us instead of leading us like the one vehicle ahead?

I handed the glasses to Sam. He took them and examined the scenery exactly as Drew and I had done. "Maybe some movement behind us, coming. Hard to tell." He handed the glasses back to Drew. "Good field specs. No brand or markings, though. Army surplus?"

"Nope. Took 'em right out of a downed helicopter south of the Bitty Sloan house." His usual smile thinned away as he spoke. Obviously not a great memory. "Tell you all about it tonight when we stop. If it's of interest." He nodded toward Trina. "Kids can tell you most of it. Saved their old dad's life, that's for sure."

"Definitely of interest." Faith's voice layered over mine. We didn't just finish each other's thoughts, we spoke them word for word sometimes.

"Here's the deal," I said, wondering if Faith was thinking the same thing. "Do we wait and see who's coming up behind us, hope they're friendly, or do we hightail it on to our destination?"

Dad spoke up from his open window. "What *is* our destination?"

I'd thought he was still dozing. "Undecided," I admitted. "Drive south is all I know, back toward Aunt Edna's silo where we know there is food."

"We could probably do that," Dad said. "But it seems like a step back. I know we don't *need* to go on to Denver now, but I've read there's an entire complex of tunnels beneath the airport there. Some articles insist it's a giant military bunker or installation of some sort. Might be worth investigating."

Sam nodded. "Conspiracy theories, maybe. But we're so close, why not see for ourselves? Especially considering the activity of drones and helicopters and governmental types around Cheyenne mountain. I once heard a podcast that put forth the theory that there are tunnels beneath the airport that go all the way to the Cheyenne complex."

"I read about that," I nodded. "Besides, we all need to see Blucifer, the cursed horse statue that killed its maker, right?"

Faith and Trina looked at each other, and I sensed something pass between them.

"Sur-r-r-e," Trina drawled, "we definitely can't miss that." She giggled a bit. "I can't believe we had to choose between checking out the airport and checking out the mountain, and we chose the mountain." She smiled, to let us know she could joke, too. "But seriously, those helicopters were weird. And the gray monsters …"

Toward the end of her unusual little speech, Trina's voice had grown a little dreamy, the way Faith's did on occasion. As if she were speaking to herself, inside her head. She glanced toward the empty road. "I don't feel like the monsters are marching behind us, though. I don't hear the shushing-feet-sound, do you?" Her slightly unfocused eyes sought Faith's, as if they'd shared an instant, unquestionable connection.

"No," Faith said. "I haven't heard or felt that energy since the battle *at* the mountain." She also sounded as if she might be listening to some other voice or background noise. Like me with Sting's "Fields of Gold." Then she continued, "I do sense something though. Something not quite human."

A small voice from beside the Chrysler asked, "Are they all dead? The monsters?"

Drew half-turned at the sound of Milo's voice. It was a hard question. But Drew didn't shrink from it. "Well, son," he pulled Milo to his side. "We think there are more monsters out there. You remember how many we saw on the way here, right? But we know how to deal with them now." He looked at old Snake. "And we've got new friends to help us."

Faith stood, one hand shading her eyes, staring at the highway behind us. "May I see those field glasses?"

Drew handed them over. Snake began to rumble.

Faith gazed through the binoculars. "There's a vehicle coming from the direction of Cheyenne Mountain. Do we wait?"

Sam turned to his big truck and started the engine. He'd changed his mind about getting the Cadillac. Once he began driving the tow truck on the highway, he realized it was much more utilitarian than a luxury car, even if it was harder to fill with fuel. It also had *two* tanks, and much bigger ones at that. It's what we'd wished for back at the canyon the day we were ambushed, and every time we'd come upon a pile-up of wrecked cars blocking our way.

All at once, every one of us turned our attention to the road. Now we could both hear and see the vehicle approaching. It was a white van, which is probably the reason we'd had trouble seeing it in the distance. White disappears against a glare.

"Dawk," Faith said. "I swear that's my old friend behind the wheel." She stared harder, her head thrust out toward the road, field glasses still glued to her face. "Who's that with him, though?"

The oversized white van covered the distance soon enough. A solid looking vehicle, its sides were graced with high, thick windows.

"Looks like a prison van," Sam said.

"I don't know about that, but it's Dawk, that much I know." Faith's voice was hard to read. "He has a monster with him. At least one. I can see glittery red eyes. Sense that alien feeling." Her voice fell. "I don't underst—"

Adrenaline shot through my veins as the Snakeman pressed against my knee. "It must be our Turq," I said. "Or at least one like him." I *knew* I liked the sound of the man called Dawk when Faith had spoken of him earlier.

I started toward the van as it coasted up on the middle line nearby. My new Spidey senses—the ones always on the lookout for danger—took note of the fact that he made certain to park far enough away so we wouldn't be able to block him in if he wanted to leave.

A springy-haired man stepped out of the driver's side. His movements were smooth, purposeful.

To my surprise, Snake strolled over to the middle line, waiting to greet him as if they were long-lost acquaintances. *Maybe he knows him through his connection to Faith.* The thought seemed strange but plausible. I didn't question it.

The man adjusted wire rimmed glasses—the kind that turn dark in the sunlight—further up on his sharp, hawk-like nose. Then he took a backpack, strapped it onto his back, closed the driver's door and strode around to the rear of the van. In one quick move, he pulled open one side of the heavy double doors and sprayed a misty cloud of vapor into the back of the van using a flexi-hose attached to the pack.

Snake retreated.

I was reminded of our exterminator back home.

"He just sprayed some Takers." *Or were they Turqs?* My voice sounded incredulous even to my own ears. Now I knew how others felt when they had come upon Carlos and me with Turq and Snake. Shock to the system, most definitely.

"Joy Juice," the man said, shutting the doors and jiggling them to make certain they were secure. "A chemical deterrent to having my head taken off at the shoulders." His voice sounded sharp, intelligent, jovial, the tone of it grasping each syllable of his words like the powerful downward curving talon of a bird of prey. Or maybe it was his beak-like nose that gave me that idea.

He knelt to Snake's level and held out his palm. I was not surprised when Snake solemnly placed his paw there. The man didn't shake the paw, simply held it for a few seconds, as if they were communing.

While Snake introduced himself to the stranger, I counted three bald gray heads and three sets of garnet insect eyes visible through the high narrow windows of the van. The letters CDJ were stenciled on the bottom of the door. *Bet those are bullet proof windows,* I thought. *They'd almost have to be bullet proof in a prisoner transport van.* From the little I could see, none of these Takers appeared to be clothed.

"Joy Juice," I echoed. "To bliss them out. Just like Cheyenne." That got Dad's attention. He'd pulled himself out and leaned against the open door of the Chrysler, one hand shading his eyes from the glare.

"Who is it? One of Marla's bunch?" A note of alarm edged his words.

"No, it's just—"

The gangly man whose joints seemed to be fastened to his body with loose connectors, like an old-fashioned doll, crossed the pavement directly toward Faith. "My friend!" he cried. "So good to see you."

Faith hugged him and patted Snake at the same time. "Great to see you, too, Dawk. How was Alaska?"

He grinned and looked away. On his face, an earnest look, like that of a little boy on a scavenger hunt. "Haven't got that far, yet."

Faith touched the backpack questioningly. "What is all this? You've got monsters in your van, and you're keeping them docile with this spray?"

I expected her to finish with, "Are you with *them* now?" Instead, she said, "What gives?"

Dawk looked back at the van, and for a moment I was reminded not of a little boy but of a genius scientist from my old favorite YouTube series, *Dr. D's Adventures in Dimensions*. But then the moment passed. This guy was nothing like Dr. D except for the crazy hair and wire rimmed spectacles.

"I see you've met Snake," she smiled at our furry friend, then glanced at me. "And this is Jack," Faith stepped over to take hold of my elbow. "Jack, this is Dawk—"

"Good to meet you." I held out my hand the way Dad had taught me to do. "Faith told me about you. One of the few survivors she trusted."

Dawk shook my hand. His grip was strong, certain. There was nothing iffy about the man other than his loose-jointed gait. I immediately trusted him, too.

"Jack." He held onto my grip for a second longer than I intended.

I got the feeling I was a bug under a microscope, but I also had a good feeling about him. "Come meet my dad and the rest of the crew."

He laughed, right out loud. "Oh, I know most of them already." At that cue, Milo shot out of his dad's shadow and hooked his arm around the new guy's waist.

"Hey, my man!" Dawk's tanned face was split by a genuine grin when Trina stepped forward and latched on to him from the other side.

"Why are those monsters in that van?" Trina asked, echoing Faith's question without preamble.

"Captured them outside Colorado Springs," he said. "A huge platoon of Grays—I don't know what else to call them—had just been sprayed by a giant drone. But the drone crashed right afterward, and I was able to get these three guys and some more of the Joy Juice, too." His mouth turned down at the corners for a moment. "It was really odd the way they just let me shove them in the van."

He cleared his throat, then continued, "The funny thing is, I'd just liberated this van and this pack from Supermax prison yesterday." He patted the strap of the backpack. "They had a trashed-out lab right there on the premises. Picked up a few other things there, too. I think, subconsciously, I knew I would need them."

We nodded. Intuition, of course.

"Anyhow," he jerked his chin toward the van. "I wanted one of the clothed ones, too, since they seem so different, but I didn't see any with this bunch."

My mouth fell open as my mind prepared to shout, *No! Leave the Turqs alone!* but Faith intervened by leaning forward and thumping the side of his backpack. It sounded tough, solid. "Hard plastic," she said. "Why doesn't the juice burn through? I saw it burn and melt faces if sprayed incorrectly."

"It's the polypropylene plastic," Dawk said. "Used for containing all kinds of acids. One reason they can use the PVC pipe to spray it from the drones." He smiled, and I got the impression he was used to explaining things. "But I still don't know who is behind all this, the spraying, or the creating. I think it's the military because … well, because who else would know all this stuff?" He stroked a small patch of whiskers on his chin, deep in thought. "I just need to take these apart and see what makes them tick."

"Does it still seem like they're a figment of someone else's imagination, made up, and then made real?" Faith asked.

Dawk grinned, ducked his head. "You remember that, huh?"

Faith nodded. "I hoped it was so ..."

I shifted my feet and rubbed my own chin—no real whiskers there, yet—as I processed his plan to dissect the Takers. It was a good idea. Take one apart, see what they're made of. He'd even given me the idea that the spray could be used for self-defense rather than just as a weapon. I half expected a song to filter through that thought, maybe give me an inkling as to the nature of all this nonsense. But none came.

On top of all the weirdness, it also felt odd to see the kids clinging to Dawk's sides like little monkeys. "It's amazing how you guys all know each other. I've heard how you and Faith traveled together way back at the beginning." I glanced at her to make certain I was saying it right, then I continued. "But man, all these connections are kind of surreal, aren't they?"

Drew laughed, watching his children interact with their new old friend. "Yeah, it is kind of a strange tale." He glanced at me, at Dad, and at Dawk. "It's all strange, the way we all filtered through The Bitty Sloan House, met up with Carlos, found Jack's notebook."

Faith said. "As if that house is a magnet or—"

"—a portal," Trina said.

"Yeah," Milo added. "Maybe a weird way station like in *Harry Potter*."

I thought of how each of us had made contact, somehow, with the old gangster's house in New Mexico. *Six degrees of separation*, I thought. And finally, a song laced my thoughts together.

Amazing grace, how sweet the sound

"Yes," Faith murmured. "Exactly."

My dad held up two thumbs as if to say, "I hear it, too."

My mind reeled. *Is everything connected now?*

CHAPTER FOUR

Portal

"One thing I don't understand," I spoke directly to Dawk and Drew. "If you guys were all at the house together, how did you become separated?"

"Simple," Dawk said. "But sad. After the loss of Rose..." he glanced at Drew as if seeking permission to mention it.

Drew didn't say a word, so Dawk continued. "I felt a compulsion to check out the airport." He seemed to wait for someone to add more information, but when no one said anything, he went on. "When we all left the Bitty Sloan House, I felt the need to go on to the Denver Airport and the bunkers beneath."

He glanced down at his feet as if deciding how much more to reveal. "To be honest, I thought since the US and Canadian government had revived NORAD at the Cheyenne complex during the pandemic, I'd be able to start at the Denver Airport and follow those rumored tunnels from there right back into the heart of the mountain complex. Be there when Drew and kids arrived."

Dad chuckled. "I've read about those supposed tunnels."

Dawk glanced at the sky as if thinking again. "There wasn't much left of the Denver airport. Someone hit it. Hard."

That made perfect sense to me.

"But you didn't tell them what made you want to go to the airport," Drew said.

Dawk shrugged.

"After seeing helicopters in the sky, I figured they had to be connected to military somewhere nearby. That and those multi-colored aurora lights made me decide it was time to stop milling around and start trying to figure things out."

We all nodded. Rather than simply trying to survive, it was nice to find someone who seemed to be taking an investigative approach.

"The lights seemed to be stronger around the airport," Dawk said. "Shimmering lights. I figured it was…" he looked at Milo and Trina. "A portal." The corners of his mouth turned up again, as if he'd said the word just for the kids.

Sam had remained quiet, taking everything in. Now he spoke up. "My question is why?"

We all turned toward him. I thought he was asking why this had happened, or why we seemed all connected, but he wasn't looking at us, he had never taken his eyes off the van. "Why do you have *three of them* captive? Why not just one?"

Dawk looked at the van. "I not only need to find out what makes them tick," he said. "I also need to determine if they are all identical inside. Like robots."

"You gonna experiment?" Milo loosened his grip on the man's waist as he looked up at his face.

"Investigate," Dawk said. "We must start somewhere. If we want to come out on top."

I was glad he didn't say if we want to *survive*. In my head, that's what he meant. But was he talking about cutting up Takers and Turqs?

"There's just one thing," I said. "The clothed ones that you mentioned really are different. They've turned. Gone through some kind of metamorphosis, you know. Or they might be in the process of morphing—anyhow, they're the good ones."

I hesitated, realizing he might not know about Turq and all he had done for us. "We had one traveling with our group at first. He wore a turquoise shirt." I nodded toward Snake and the scrap of turquoise fabric still tied on his collar. "He saved my life. More than once. Dad's, too. Even Snake's."

Dawk looked at his van again. "That puts a new spin on things, doesn't it?" His forefinger stroked the chin patch. "I had myself convinced they were all just killing machines. Cyborgs or something."

I nodded. "Same here. Until the one in the turquoise shirt literally yanked me away from another one that was attempting to stab me onto a tree branch."

Suddenly, the man was speechless.

Milo and Trina were, too. But Drew spoke up. "We weren't all the way to the Cheyenne Mountain entrance when we met Sam." He directed a thumb toward the big guy. "But we did see some flying things that were so incredible we simply stopped the Nissan and stared in awe."

"That was Turq 2.0," I said. "After he morphed." I sifted through my recent memories, recalling the strange scene in the cottonwoods. "But I guess I should say all of them were Turqs in the flock. There are lots of them now. Flocks of angels is how I think of them. They saved us at Cheyenne, too." I tried to keep my voice flat, manly. "Anyway, all that aside, we can't forget the main thing. If you try to dissect them, cut them open in anyway, you'll bring down the black rain."

Nods all around. "Right," Dawk said. "That's why I didn't just do it beside the road. That sludge." He looked up at the sky. "I don't see too many of those sky rips hereabouts, and that seems both good and strange. As if they didn't fall through here like they did back in Texas, and around The Bitty Sloan house in New Mexico."

The rest of us glanced up, also wondering.

"Anyway, I'd like to capture and contain some of the sludge, too. If possible." He paused. "Amazing stuff, it falls as a liquid, devours the gray creature completely, then changes to a seemingly organic lifeform—with wings." He laughed and shook his head. "You know, it's almost like metamorphosis in mid-air. The way the insect dissolves whole bodies on the way to becoming its next incarnation." His voice changed, as if he'd suddenly became aware of his scholarly tone. "So, you call the big grays, Takers?"

I nodded, a little thrown by his sudden change of direction. But apparently, he was still on the same thread, just thinking out loud.

"And then the locusts, or whatever they represent, ascend back into the heavens as if nothing has happened."

"What do you mean, *whatever they represent?* Sounds like you don't think they're bugs at all."

He shrugged. "In regular life, locusts emerge as one thing, then morph into another." His voice took on the professorial tone again. "The egg is laid in a frothy liquid, then the wingless nymph emerges, the liquid hardens to a protective shell and eventually wings appear—"

"Wow," Faith said. "When you put it like that, there are similarities."

I rubbed the back of my neck. Standing out here in the sun was getting old. "So maybe some smartie took all these ideas, sped them up—"

Sam said, "The black sludge reminds me of tobacco juice, you know, the kind grasshoppers use to defend themselves?"

"They do have some of the characteristics of locusts, what you all might call grasshoppers." Dawk touched his chin, again, making me wonder if the scruff was a new thing, or something that simply occurred from time to time, like moss on a tree.

"Grasshoppers? Seriously?" Trina didn't disguise the disbelief in her voice. Probably didn't know how.

Dawk stared at the van. "Yes. Grasshoppers—also known as locusts—go through phases. They're hatched in pools of frothy liquid. Then they come out wingless, nonflying, unfinished—"

"Yes," Faith breathed. "Exactly like the first Takers rising from those weird silver puddles. Unfinished. But *hungry.*"

Nods all around. "Grasshoppers are always hungry."

"Then they grow and change to full grown adults with the ability to fly—"

"Turq can fly now, too," I said. "And I saw him go through his metamorphosis in the woods. Faith saw it as well." I looked to her for confirmation.

"Absolutely amazing," she said. "But it was different from these, I mean the murderous ones. He didn't kill and eat everything in sight. He is an angel. Saved us all."

"Especially me," I said, again.

"And me," Dad agreed.

"All of us," Sam said, as if he couldn't reiterate the fact enough.

"And not just then," I said. "It began way back before then, come to think of it, he was also at The Bitty Sloan house." I recalled the image of the turquoise-shirted Taker trudging across the burning prairie toward us. The big fire burned in the canyon below the buffalo jump, and I'd just found Carlos lying beneath a sticker bush, his skin charred from the battle. Then Turq came walking out of the mess like a turquoise vision. "No doubt about it. He was good. From the beginning," I said. "From the start."

"I saw him at the big house, too," Milo said matter-of-factly.

In my head I wondered how that jived with Dr. D's idea of Purgatory. Why would someone with a good heart and soul wind up in Purgatory? Didn't unsullied souls go straight to Heaven?

"Jack?" Faith's voice.

I looked up. "Sorry. Thinking about Turq. Man, I really miss that—*guy*."

She laughed. "I know. He was easy to like. Never spoke, never had an opinion, never needed anything. Sort of like a life-saving-robot-bodyguard."

I understood her meaning. He was easy to grow attached to because he never asked for anything in return. Not even food or water. "Yeah, never needed or asked for a thing." I glanced at Dawk. "He was sort of like a blank person. How does a living organism never need sustenance of any kind." *And why am I suddenly deferring to this guy as an expert? Just because he says he's going to find out what makes them tick doesn't mean he knows more than the rest of us.*

"That's one of the things I hope to find out," Dawk said, as he unconsciously smoothed an errant shock of hair away from his glasses. I imagined it bothered him no more than a worrisome gnat, but it seemed his hands need to do something to help him think. Or help him share. He seemed on the verge of something more. Some telling or some asking, perhaps.

"I'm going to find a good lab," he said. "I was a research student back in the real world, so I kinda know what I'm looking for.

And there are several military bases in Colorado, so I feel certain I'll find what I need." He laughed. "*All* those conspiracy theories can't be wrong."

"We saw a back entrance at Cheyenne," Faith said. "Did you check it already?"

Dawk nodded. "It was bombed. No longer an entrance nor an exit." He shifted the backpack a bit. "I have a theory about gene splicing and AI robotics. Cyborgs in an insectile, hive-type sense. So many characteristics of insects—" He stopped and shifted the backpack again, looked at them as a group.

The white-hot sun beat down. I wondered how long before he needed to spray the Takers again.

"And yes, even the self-defense tobacco spit." He looked at Sam. "But the dark sludge. It comes down to grab them, take them away, repair them, even defend them, perhaps."

"That may be a little bit of a stretch," I started to say.

He laughed good-naturedly. "I don't mean there's a giant grasshopper sitting up above us, spitting juice every time there's an injury." His grin widened a bit. "I just meant perhaps some super science-types were developing all these animalistic attributes in super-charged ways. Like the pheromones and the hive mentality—"

"And the metamorphosis," Faith added.

"And maybe they added some fishy genes, too."

They both looked at me askance.

"Hagfish slime." I started to explain more, just one of my theories about the electronics-killing slime, but then I stopped. *Did it really matter? At this point, all questions seemed moot.* Let the man called Dawk dissect a few—as long as they aren't wearing clothes—and see what he learns.

I shrugged. "What do I know? Anything's possible. Most days I feel lucky to get my shoes on the right feet." I wasn't sure why I said that. It came to me on the breeze. I looked at Faith. It seemed like something she would say. Maybe because she was looking for shoes when we first found her. Did she put those words in my head? And if she can do that, can I do it, too? *Hey, Faith, I thought at her, ask Dawk—again—if any of those Takers had clothing on, like our old friend Turq when he first started out.*

Faith smiled. "Hey, Dawk …"

He looked her way.

"Were any of these Takers wearing clothes when you took them captive?"

The gangly man shook his head, grinned again. I was a little bit amazed at how easy it had been to put that thought in her head.

I was also amazed at how strong and white Dawk's teeth were. They appeared to be perfect. It made me remember all the times I'd gone to sleep without brushing mine, even though toothpaste and toothbrushes were free for the taking.

"These three Takers, as you call them," Dawk said, "were definitely not of the *domesticated* variety." His tone sounded nearly jovial again. "I'm still trying to wrap my head around the idea that you guys were able to observe the metamorphosis. Sounds almost spiritual, but in a scientific way." He touched his chin. "Wish I could've seen it."

"After the chaos at Cheyenne, I wondered if they had all changed at once. I mean, there were a ton of angelic bombers helping us out." I studied Dawk's eyes behind his wire-rimmed glasses. What would he think if he knew Faith had asked him exactly what I'd sent her in a thought. *Does he know about this new level of communication?*

Dad spoke aloud. "The spiritual realm is one of our unseen dimensions." His gaze floated from me, to Faith, to Snake. "We've all been touched by it now. Seen it. Been saved by God's angels. It's all real. Dissect the Takers if you need," his gaze floated to Dawk. "But don't forget we're all God's creatures."

Everyone looked toward him, then. Even Dawk. I expected to see the shape of a cross glowing at the base of Dad's throat the way it always had with Carlos, our previous religious guide. But if there was any mark, his head was turned in such a way I couldn't see it.

I wanted to stop right there and discuss this new topic with my dad. We'd never been a religious family, but apparently being enclosed in those miraculous, see-through wings had changed all that. What did he mean we're all God's creatures? Dissect them but don't hurt them?

That made no sense, they were our enemies, they would eat us alive without blinking one of those freaky eyes.

But that conversation would have to wait. First there was this matter of Dawk and his captives. "Maybe you'll discover the source of those internal tattoos at least," I said. "You know the words changed before the creatures morphed." I glanced at Faith. "Although, to be honest, Turq's words were always changing." I glanced at the white van, and my hand fell to Snake's head. He had just reappeared beside me.

He and Milo had been examining the faded edges of the highway where the wild grass had begun to creep up from the bar ditch to reclaim the asphalt. Minute cracks in the pavement were also giving way to vegetative growth.

Snake pressed against the outside of my thigh. "There's my good dog," I muttered, surprised he'd left Milo's side for a moment.

I stroked his head and was only slightly amazed when my fingers discovered the shape of a cross in one of his recent scars. The one on the back of his neck. "Carlos," I said. But no one heard me. Except maybe him and Faith. And my dad.

The tune to "Amazing Grace" began to rise in my head. "Amazing Grace, how sweet the sound." *Someone* is *always listening. Is it you, God? Or just the universe? Or are you one and the same?*

Does it really matter? Dad asked.

I don't think so, Faith replied in our heads. *I don't think it matters at all.*

CHAPTER FIVE

Gone

If Drew or Sam, or even the kids heard our short thought conversation about God and the universe, they did not chime in. But Dawk did. Not about religion, or even about the tests he was hoping to perform. "Guess I'd better get on down the road," he said, "if I'm going to explore some more military bases and find a good lab." He pushed at his glasses. "I only stopped because I sensed Faith was here."

The only reason? Sensed Faith? How does that work? I wanted to question him, but before I could, he continued.

"Yeah, that didn't come out the way I intended." He smiled a tanned, friendly smile. "Getting out of the conversation habit, I think. Or maybe I've inhaled some of the Joy Juice myself."

We all laughed at that. But to be honest, I wondered how he could avoid it.

Nope, Faith spoke inside my head. *That's just Dawk. Says whatever he's thinking. I like that about him.* The words stopped for a moment. *That bluntness kept me alive at first. Taught me how to run and how to hide.*

I glanced at her and nodded, remembering how she'd made it all the way from Lewisville in Central Texas to Eden in West Texas all on her own. Still ... this telepathy thing was going to take a little more getting used to.

Hey, I pushed the words at her. *Do you communicate with Dawk this way, too?*

She smiled but was saved from answering when Dawk said, "Okay, gotta go get these things to a lab somewhere." He looked up at the calm, bleached-white sky. "I would go back to Cheyenne, look for another way in, like you said, but that change back there. That's a little spooky."

We all glanced back at the reflective arc of colors swirling around the top of the mountain behind us. We wanted to think they were regular northern lights, but not one of us seemed truly convinced. Even I, who had never seen the northern lights, knew better.

Dawk continued talking. "Anyhow, I hope the grays don't reach a tolerance level on the Joy Juice. I'd hate to be trapped in that sardine can with 'em if it wore off suddenly." He thrust his chin toward the van, an aww-shucks laugh escaping his lips.

But the image in my head wasn't anything to laugh at. Not at all. Three Takers trapped in a van when the juice wore off? I recalled the body parts in the basement locker room at Eden High where we'd found Faith.

"Maybe not such a good idea, traveling with them."

"Or dissecting them," Faith said. "Why not go ahead and bring the sludge down, let them go back to wherever they came from? Better them than you."

Every one of us nodded agreement to that statement.

Dawk paused. "We need to know what they're made of."

"The sludge will come," I said. "No matter where you are when you slice into them—"

"Did it come down when they were injured inside the mountain? Anyone know?" His voice sounded sharper than before, but I didn't take offense. It was a legitimate question.

I thought back to what I'd seen through the narrow gap between the entrance doors at Cheyenne. The massive doors had been closing, crushing humans by the score, and the automated collaring machine, like the turnstile at the dry cleaner, had appeared to be "one size fits all," but of course the metal collars had not fit them all. When the machine clamped the collars around the necks of the Takers and their human prisoners, blood had flowed, both human blood, and Taker blood, that clear fluid filled with words.

I tried to recall if any black rain had found a way inside after the Taker's had spilled their own sin-word-filled fluid along the cave's wide corridor.

"No," I said, at last. "I don't believe it did."

Just as the electromagnetic pulses of energy couldn't penetrate the mountain, neither could the insectile-pheromone-signals of the injured Takers bring down the sludge.

Dawk was right.

I clamped my lips together before any other words could escape. I don't know what I would've said, but it probably wouldn't have been helpful.

Faith laughed, covered it behind her hand.

She *can* read my mind, I thought. *She can.*

She nodded slightly, more giggles bubbling behind her hand.

Well, I don't know about all this—

It's all good, she thought back at me. *All good.*

I couldn't think about Dawk and his problems anymore. I was too busy examining every thought I'd ever had about Faith, checking them with my embarrassment-meter. And that added a new worry *… is everyone on the same wavelength? Like the hive mentality I'd been entertaining where the Takers were concerned?*

Time for my own investigation. *Hey! If you can hear this, say yes out loud.*

Only Faith murmured, "Yes." And then she smiled at me. *We'll figure it out,* she thought back at me. *We'll get the hang of it. We're just learning as we go.*

And then a strange new idea occurred to me: Evolution. *Directed evolution.* Someone is causing us to change right along with the Takers, causing us to be able to read each other's thoughts … to hive-up—like insects.

Once again, Faith nodded. *I've thought the exact same thing. I just didn't want to sound crazy by saying it out loud.*

Then she paraphrased a quote from Darwin that made me sit up and take note. *It's not the strongest species that survives, it's the species that's most responsive to change.*

CHAPTER SIX

Changeling

As we were all standing there, chatting, inside the van the Joy Juice was wearing off. A muted *c-r-a-a-c-k* grabbed our attention, and we all turned our eyes back to the van just in time to see one of the Takers push out the bulletproof window. Strong gray hands grabbed the sides of the window frame and bent them outward. In seconds, all three were coming out.

Dawk rushed forward, spraying them with his pack.

One Taker fell to the ground, overwhelmed.

"Get in the car!" Sam yelled, wielding his machete.

We raced toward our vehicles just as he sliced his blade across the chest of the nearest monster. Clear blood and black words jetted from the wound. I couldn't read most of the words, but I did see one: **SURVIVE** was spelled out big and bold, the letters wriggling on the hot surface of the asphalt.

The kids scrambled into the back seat of the Chrysler as Sam and Drew ran for their vehicles. Snake headed into the midst of the fight as always. Snarling and snapping, his pit bull jaws closed on the leg of the injured Taker just as the third monster burst completely free of the van.

Dawk stood his ground, spraying, spraying, spraying until his backpack was empty. I worried he would spray Snake, but somehow the big dog avoided the fall out.

And then it happened.

The sky split open, black sludge rained down, and the injured

Taker was enveloped within seconds. Fortunately, it had dragged itself far enough away that none of us were in danger of being engulfed by mistake.

In the Chrysler, Milo and Trina hit the floor. They were taking no chances.

"Jack!" Faith yelled my name—I couldn't tell if it was in my head or in the air—just as my dad tossed me Carlos's shotgun. I pulled the trigger almost reflexively.

Boom!

The nearest Taker went down, but only momentarily. I'd hit him in the shoulder, not the head.

A second sky hole opened.

And then the strangest thing happened.

The first sprayed Taker, the one on the ground, began to rise. He wasn't injured, just loopy and docile from the spray. It freaked me out when he came crawling toward us, one hand extended as if asking for assistance. He wasn't clothed, just *different*.

I looked at Sam. He had traded his machete for his shotgun as well. We both leveled our guns at the Taker's head. For the first time since all this began, I gazed into the face of the monster, and it did not look away. The multi-faceted garnet eyes locked on mine and even Snake backed up.

I'd thought it was the Joy Juice keeping Snake at bay, and perhaps the juice is what made the monster seem more human, but one thing it couldn't account for was the outstretched hand that now sported regular human-type fingernails. Wiry black hairs sprouted from each knuckle.

My gaze sought Sam's. "Are you seeing what I'm seeing?"

His eyes were on that one reaching hand just as mine were. "They aren't supposed to have fingernails," he said. "They never had anything on their fingers. Not even Turq."

I nodded. The blue-bright day grew suddenly cloudy.

The black sludge had cleaned up both injured Takers, the one Sam had swiped with the machete and the one I'd shot. Now the sludge changed, breaking off into individual locusts which buzzed in a flock back up into the wounded blue. They aimed at the wavering sky hole like a living arrow. The crawling Taker continued to hold his hand out toward us in supplication. The words beneath his translucent skin swam uncertainly beneath the membrane of his face, his skull, and his shoulders.

Fascinated, I watched as one of the words appeared inside the thing's bicep. *SURVIVE*, the word read again. *LIVE*, another read.

How could I possibly kill it now?

Answer: I couldn't.

Sam and I watched in amazement as the unmarred Taker got to its feet. I looked down. Sure enough, all ten of the thing's toes were now delineated with toenails, knuckles, the works. I glanced up at Dawk to see if he was looking, but he had dashed around to the other side of the van, climbed inside, and appeared to be trying to refill the Joy Juice backpack from a second container in the passenger seat.

The Taker finally rose to its full height, towering over me, and even over Sam.

"We have to go back to the Bitty Sloan house," Milo said.

"Carry on, son," Dad's musical-voice layered over Milo's.

And then a new song edged out Kansas. It was Tracy Chapman, "Give Me One Reason." *I get it,* I said in my head. Dad was telling me to carry on as usual, and Faith was telling me to wait for proof, just one *reason*, to stay and let the thing live.

I hope you're right, I thought back at her, but then a new song-thought flew out of my head toward her—toward them all, I suppose—and it was without my foreknowledge at all. The song-thought was "Come Together," the ancient Beatles tune with the strange, strange lyrics.

For a moment, that shocked even me, until the meaning became apparent. Standing before me, dark hairs sprouting from every knuckle, from its head, even on the calves of its gray legs, stood a new kind of Taker. Not a Turq, not even a Turq 2.0—No. This was a new species, an evolving species, a *hybrid* species indeed.

No wonder Dawk wanted to dissect it in the lab. And no wonder Dad was saying it was one of God's creatures. It was changing, somehow.

"Carry on, Wayward Son," wove into my thoughts again.

Carry on how? I flung the question back at my dad who was near the Chrysler, keeping watch over the two kids. *How? How do I carry on?* I didn't know if he'd hear that thought, or not. I sent it subconsciously. A habit, almost, an extension of our musical communications.

As I debated, I saw the thing raise both new-looking hands to the sides of its head. Ears had begun to sprout there like smallish, gray cauliflowers unfolding into something new and completely different.

Sam kept his shotgun leveled on the thing's chest.

My weapon had fallen to my side during the song battle inside my skull. I couldn't believe I'd wished for the return of the music. *Had I really missed this chaos?* I glanced up at Faith standing near Drew and his SUV. Yes, I had. I *had* missed it.

I lowered my defenses completely as "Come Together" took complete control of my brainwaves.

Snake whined near my knee. My hand went to his head, soothing him. "It's alright," I murmured. "I think it's gonna be alright." Even those words sounded like a song, but one I couldn't quite place. Some band made up of several famous guys including Tom Petty and Roy Orbison. Maybe Bob Dylan.

I smiled at the garnet-eyed Taker-face, watching in disbelief as a slight trickle of clear fluid escaped from one of its new ears, leaked onto the side of its neck, dribbling down as the external hearing organs continued to unfold, as if the thing had sprung up from the soil in a very different kind of garden.

Is that pheromone fluid leaking from the Taker's new ear?

Faith's question was barely formed when the silvery line of liquid reached the thing's shoulder, and a new bout of dark rain shot down from the sky, covering the monster from head to newly-formed toes in shiny, black sludge.

In seconds the thing was gone and buzzing black insects were breaking off the edges of the opaque shroud, winging their way back up to the sky just like the flock before them.

In a moment, all that was left of the changeling-Taker was a tiny black shadow where the thick, oily rain had briefly touched the ground around its feet.

I felt my mouth hanging open, felt my eyes bugging out of my awestruck head. Now all that was left of the three in the van was … nothing. Nothing at all. As if they were never here.

"Damn," Sam said. "That's efficient."

"Echo that," Drew said.

"Come Together," continued to play softly in the back of my mind. "Did you guys see it changing?" I turned to Faith. "Did I imagine those ears?" My hand went to the side of my head, rubbing, feeling, helping me think.

Dawk came around the front of the damaged van, useless sprayer still in hand. "I missed it," he said. "I missed my opportunity." His voice cracked. "I'm going on to Colorado Springs, to the other military installations. To their labs." He rubbed his face roughly, no more patting at the soul patch on his chin. "No. I'm going all the way to Europe, to CERN. That's where many important discoveries have been made. There'll be people there. People figuring this thing out."

Alarmed at the sudden change in his demeanor, I said, "Can you even get to Europe?"

He looked at us as a group, but when he spoke, I felt he was talking more to himself than to us. "Maybe I should just go to Cambridge. Dr. Zhang's lab. CRISPR. Gene splicing experiments." His eyes skated across us. "Or maybe The Army Research Lab in Maryland."

His speech grew more erratic. "It's all coming true. Every bit of it." He rubbed his mouth. "We just saw the most amazing example of self-assembly imaginable, had it right in the palms of our hands." He opened his palm, looked at its emptiness. "And now it's gone. And I didn't even get to test my invisibility theory."

Faith and I both said, "Invisibility?"

"Like Harry Potter?" Milo chirped.

"Like a Stealth Bomber," Dawk replied, seemingly brought back to the present. "Like, I think that translucent gray skin makes 'em invisible. Organic weapons, you know, their orders uploaded right into their life fluid, just under their skin."

His eyes said we should all have figured this out already, but he went on anyway. "Invisible until damaged. When their fuel-fluid leaks out, their blood so to speak, it gives them away so the black sludge can find them and take them back. Recycling at its best."

"Whoa," Drew said. "If that's right, and now they're changing, it must be on purpose. That's means there are two factions at war here, and we're just caught in the mid—"

"Yes!" Dawk interjected. "That's why I must go. If we're going to conquer this new world, live with these changelings, and whatever else is coming, it's imperative we learn all we can about them."

"But Dawk," Faith's soft voice brought him around. "Even if you capture more, you can't dissect them, that's their death knell. You said it yourself, that's what calls down the dark rain."

"Of course." He mumbled what sounded like, "It's one more thing we need to understand."

It was obvious we were not on his wavelength. He seemed to be forming his hypotheses in real time. "I just need to observe them long enough to figure out how to cause them to change without triggering that self-destruct signal. Maybe in an enclosed environment like the van, but stronger." He hefted his pack and strode back around the front of the vehicle. It appeared he'd forgotten about the rest of us.

"Hey, Dawk?" Faith called.

He stopped. Smiled, as if embarrassed. "Sorry. You wanna come with?"

She shook her head, kindly. "I just want to say, be careful, wherever you're headed. Take care of yourself."

He nodded, set the closed pack in the passenger seat, barely glanced at the broken window and damaged shell of the van, then started it up and drove on down the highway.

We were left dumbfounded, scratching our heads in wonder. *That's a scientist,* I thought. *Determined to find out what's going on.*

Or die trying, Faith thought back at me.

We stood around our vehicles, ready to head out again, but the feeling had changed. We'd all seen the Taker with the ears and fingernails. He'd been different.

"Should we talk about it?" I asked.

Milo looked at me out the side window. The black rain had scared the kids. They had not reemerged. We all moved closer.

"We need to go back to The Bitty House," Milo said again. I looked at him through the window, really paid attention. The trembly tone of his kid voice told me he was speaking about something important. Important to him, at least.

"Why go back?" I asked. "The house burned, it's just a shell, now. Only the cellar rooms were untouched."

"That room at the top of the stairs might still be there—"

A Tom Petty song about a room at the top of the stairs ghosted through the group, any other time I would have thought it was only in my head, but now, I knew better.

I pictured the old house in my mind. Yes, part of the shell had been left standing after the firenado swept through, but the third floor?

"What is it about that room?" Faith asked.

"It was watery," Trina said. "The ceiling moved like waves on the beach."

Drew nodded. "Carlos was there, too. It's where we found your notebook, Jack."

Snake whined. I glanced down at him, thinking he was acknowledging the mention of his old friend, Carlos. *Wait,* I felt like an idiot. *Snake can't hear. Is he picking up our thoughts as well?*

As if in answer, he strolled over to the Nissan and hopped in the backseat. *Crazy dog, what's he up to?*

I scratched the back of my neck. "Watery?"

"Like some kind of portal," Sam said. "We were all drawn to it at one time or another."

"A way station," I said, glancing down at Milo, thinking about Harry Potter. And about how the Bitty House drew us all together. Still, something about the idea of water struck a chord in my head.

Dad spoke up for the first time in a while. "How do you mean, watery?"

I looked at him. His eyes were healed, his scars, too. He looked a lot like the man who'd grilled all those backyard steaks and let me sip the foam off his beer when Mom wasn't looking.

He returned my gaze. *I'm beginning to remember that guy, too.*

I grinned. *What d'ya think about this telepathy thing?*

It's odd, isn't it? As if we can direct our words and feelings to one or even to more than one. I remember how you thought of hive mentality earlier.

I nodded, and he continued, *I don't mean to alarm you, but I wonder if we aren't becoming like a hive or even a pod, like dolphins or whales.* In his voice he said, "There's a theory, about water. The Pacific, to be exact. Off the west coast, near San Diego—"

That got Sam's attention. "Camp Pendleton?"

"Possibly," Dad said.

Drew nodded. "The Marine base there. Navy fliers tracked UFOs skimming along beneath the water, mocking them, mirroring them—"

"I remember those videos. Seems like they came out during the pandemic." I looked at Dad. "We decided they declassified all those reports because they wanted to take our minds off our virus-problems."

"*Chinese* virus problems." That was Sam again. "Now I wonder if it could have been someone else using the Chinese lab at Wuhan." His gaze seemed to peer toward the disappearing van this time. "The Chinese lost a lot of people, too. Probably more than we know—"

"Because they locked down all their media access—"

He nodded. "Nevertheless, it could have been an unseen force, and they didn't know it, either."

"You mean some alien-types using a human-created virus against all of us?"

Sam shrugged. "Maybe. Or maybe they're using viruses to speed up those changes we just witnessed on the Taker." He scratched his head, as if he'd had a hat on and just removed it. "I mean, it would be smart to use what's available instead of trying to bring a dangerous weapon with you, right?"

I shrugged. Drew nodded.

"But now we'll never know," he continued. "I'm with your dad, though, Jack. Why not go on to the Pacific?" He pointed toward the sky. "We know *something* extraterrestrial is going on. Whether it's being generated from someone here on earth, or someone *out there*, I have no idea. I thought about going with Dawk, but he took off like a shot. Guess it wasn't time for me to fly after all."

Dad and I looked at each other as the old REO Speedwagon song floated into our heads. *That makes me wonder ...* I sent the thought to Dad. *If they use our available weapons and modify them with our current characteristics, even our animal characteristics, does that mean they're here to take over, or are they simply directing this evolution for some other reason?*

Oh, boy of mine, my wayward son—the Kansas song came, it did not disappoint—*I wasn't thinking all those deep sciency thoughts at all.* Dad smiled. *I was simply thinking I'd like to see those waves near San Diego for myself.*

An old guitar intro cued up in my head and Dad grinned. I recognized the long, beautiful intro to "Hotel California" by the Eagles.

I gave him a thumbs up. *I wouldn't mind that either.*

From the corner of my eye, I saw Snake hop back out of the rear door of the Nissan. Like all of us, Drew and crew left the doors open in case they had to leap back inside suddenly. "What have you got there, boy?"

My four-legged buddy stopped beside my knee; an old spiral notebook held carefully between his teeth. "What is this?" I asked, removing it gently.

"That looks like your notebook," Trina said. "The one we found at the Bitty Sloan house." She glanced back at the Nissan. "How did Snake know?"

"I think he's on our same wavelength," I mumbled, thumbing through my own written words. "I mean he was at the Bitty Sloan house, too." My eyes skimmed the pages. "It's funny, but it seems to me the more people join our little group, the stronger our telepathy becomes."

Faith and Dad agreed. Sam, too. The others were newer so maybe they didn't have as much experience, yet.

I stopped on several pages in the notebook. It appeared I'd

written a lot more than I remembered. Observations about all that had happened, about my injured arm, about the Takers, and Turq, the one who had saved me, about finding old Snakeman, and page after page about Thad and the mess that had occurred at my house in Eden.

I'd also written a lot about Carlos, the one who had turned out to be such an amazing friend, about how we'd started the firenado and drove the horde of Takers off the cliff we called The Buffalo Jump. I even mentioned how the house itself had barely survived. And how we had returned with Turq to the well in the basement so Carlos could heal from his burns and Snake from his own broken leg.

"Wow," I said, skimming again. "I don't remember writing half of this." There were bits of songs, and scraps of poems—nod to Dad *and* Mom for exposing me to a wide variety of writings— and there was an entire section devoted to how Snake and I had discovered Mom's body in the comparative religions room in the library she'd loved so well.

By the time I neared the end of what could almost be considered a memoir, my eyes were brimming with unshed tears. Not only for myself, but for my whole, entire world. Even the part about finding the red mustang at Dad's old high school brought a bittersweet feeling of nostalgia. I continued skimming until my eye caught up on a group of words like a bit of river-trash caught up on a spiky branch.

I've found a portal …

I'd written the words and underlined them so hard the point of the ink pen had scratched through the top page into the one beneath.

It was in the room at the top of the stairs. I wanted to go through it, but after the fire, it was gone. There must be others, somewhere.

I read the words aloud. At least I think I did. Everyone crowded around me, reading over my shoulder, Milo pulling my forearm down so he could see the words, too. "A portal," he said. "I knew it. But maybe it was closing when we got there. It was a point of light. So tiny, and wavy."

Shaking my head, I said, "I never wrote those words. I don't remember that at all." My eyes sought Faith's, then Dad's. "How can this be?"

Faith spoke first. We'd gone back to speaking aloud for some reason. "I've heard of automatic writing. Spirit writing, so to speak—"

"I've heard of that, too," Dad said. "I thought it was usually doodles or unreadable letters and numbers. Like code."

Milo was shaking his head. "You did write it. For us. For now." He smiled up at me.

Out of the mouths of babes, crossed my mind. "What do you mean?"

"Somehow, you knew we were coming, so you wrote the first of the notebook for you." His forefinger ruffled the edges of the already-read pages. "Then you wrote this last part for us." He looked at the group members. "For now." His hand went to Snake's head, then around his thick neck.

So … does that make me a prophet?

Faith nudged me with her elbow. *Labels don't matter anymore. Was I a prophet on the mountain? Or when I appeared to you in the middle of the road with Marla?*

We were thinking only to each other now. *I guess you're right. It doesn't really matter. I guess it's just onward now, right.*

"Carry on Wayward Son" drifted through our words. "Onward Christian Soldier" came in behind it.

Maybe there's another portal, Faith thought. *You said even Carlos thought so.*

I had no answer to that.

CHAPTER SEVEN

Onward

In light of the notebook information informing us that the portal room was gone, the entire group agreed there was no use in going back to the Bitty Sloan house.

"San Diego, then? The coast? Those underwater UFOs?"

Dad laughed. "Oh, wayward one," his voice stayed jovial. "If you look on that map of yours," he nodded toward the Chrysler, "you'll see that we were headed there all along. It isn't far off the beaten path."

My face must've belied my confusion. California was at least a thousand miles.

"I guess we'd better hit the road, Jack," Faith said. "And don't stop at Verde or pass go."

I grinned at the old song-pun and Monopoly reference. "Well, all right," I flung one of Dad's own Buddy Holly quips into the mix. "I guess I can't dispute evidence written in my own scrawl, can I?" I tried to sound more confident than I felt, but in my head, I couldn't help thinking, *This is weird. Very weird. It seemed as if our almost meeting at the Bitty Sloan House caused some kind of ripple. Closed the portal, perhaps. Or did I do that by starting the firenado?*

It is weird, Faith echoed. *But then again, weird is obviously our new normal.*

On the heels of that, I flung out a message to Dawk. *Change of plans. I hope you can hear me. Our little band is going to break off here, take a different path. Head to the west coast, San Diego, California to be exact.*

Faith clapped her hands. The others smiled. "I think everyone in the group got that message," she said.

In my mind, I pictured Dawk touching the patch of whiskers on his chin, deep in thought. Then we all heard, *Yes. Yes. Good idea. Take the cutoff to Four Corners, that will get you on the right path. I will join you after I check out the rest of these Colorado bases.* He hesitated, and I thought we'd lost the connection. *I'll see if I can capture some more creatures. CERN was just a momentary lapse of reason. I can't get to Europe. Not anymore. Not yet.*

"Maybe I *should* have gone with him," Sam said aloud. "I'm itching to see the military bases." He shot me an apologetic glance. "I need to come with y'all, though. We've been through thick and thin together so far. But this guy has me completely intrigued. What *is* our military doing?" He shook his head. "After what we saw at Cheyenne, I think Dawk is right. They must be doing something. Maybe *they* made the black sludge."

No one had a reply to that, although in my heart, I knew our military didn't create the sludge. It was so otherworldly it had to be from God.

We all loaded back into our vehicles. Trina and Milo stayed in my backseat along with Snake—they were as drawn to him as he was to them—and Dad returned to his usual spot in my passenger seat. I had a moment when I wondered if Faith would be hurt that there seemed no room for her, but I needn't have worried. She climbed into Drew's Nissan after only a moment's hesitation.

Okay. Truth? That did give me a pang of jealousy. I mean Drew wasn't *that* old. Not quite as old as my dad anyway. Was he? I mean, why didn't she ride with Sam? He'd been with us longer.

My eyes stayed glued to the rearview mirror until I heard a slight giggle in my head. *Faith?*

Yes, Jack. And the reason I didn't ride with Sam is because the Nissan seems much more comfortable than that old tow truck, wouldn't you say?

I grinned. *Okay, I'm an idiot.* I sent her the words. *I didn't know it would be like this.*

Silence from her for a moment. Then, *Didn't know what would be like this?*

I debated lying, then decided, why bother, the girl reads my thoughts like I used to read stuff on my tablet. *I didn't know this is how it felt to want to be with someone all the time.*

She giggled again.

Man, I *loved* that sound.

It's kind of nice, isn't it?

It is, I sent back. *It certainly is.* The word *love* slipped into my thoughts even though I'd been trying to avoid it. I was just a kid. Love was for grownups, right? I was infatuated, my mom's word, or I had a crush, my own word, but it wasn't about love, was it? At our age?

She giggled again, and I thought about nudging her, making her answer everything she'd just heard, but then I decided not to press my luck. I still couldn't believe I'd even *thought* the word. Then it occurred to me that she probably just heard all that, too. *Geez.*

After that little exchange, driving was a breeze. Just being alive, having my tribe around me, Dad, Snake, Faith, Sam, even the kids and Drew, having my little crew—*especially* Faith—filled me with euphoria. With a feeling that even in our desperate circumstances, the world was still a good place. God was still with us.

Where'd that thought come from? Carlos, you here, too?

Silence, no actual words from anyone, but there was a sudden shifting of the light. A tinge of turquoise at the horizon, and a feeling of turquoise in my—

Jack?

That was Faith.

Yes? I replied.

I keep forgetting to give you back the lump of turquoise that fell out of Carlos's hand that day. I have it in my pocket.

Seriously? I thought we buried it with him in the woods.

No. It was lying on the earth where it had fallen from his hand. I picked it up and put it in my pocket, but I keep forgetting to give it to you.

I glanced at the sky, half-expecting to see a sign in the clouds. *It's okay,* I thought back at her. *You keep it. Carlos belongs to all of us.*

From between the kids in the backseat, Snake whined.

When I glanced at him in the rearview mirror, the dog's brown marble eyes bored directly into mine. I'd swear there was a new level of understanding there. I mean, I hadn't even spoken aloud.

As we drove out of the mountains, we passed a billboard advertising the Four Corners monument. Pulling over, I fumbled my paper map out of the console and looked it up. Of course, I'd heard about it. The famous place where the states of Colorado, New Mexico, Utah, and Arizona form a near perfect junction. *The only right angles in America,* someone thought at me. I didn't know if that was true, but it was definitely the place Dawk told us to go.

My mind whispered. *Why are none of these important landmarks in Texas?*

Faith laughed in my head. *Not everything is about Texas, Jack, no matter how much we natives think it should be.*

Even in my thoughts, I felt embarrassed. She was right, of course.

What do you think about Four Corners? I asked.

I think it's about time we started following the signs, don't you?

CCR tuned up in my mind. "Down on the Corner," blared right out.

You must be right, I replied, chuckling in my own head. *Do you hear the music?*

Faith hummed along. *Does that answer your question?*

I nodded, and that was that. We were going the Four Corners route to San Diego, California. I didn't know exactly how long it would take us to get there, but thanks to my dad and my old friend, Thad, I knew how to use the paper map to figure out the distance.

Looks like two or three days, Faith whispered in my mind. *What do you think?*

Stunned, I muttered. *Can you* see *my thoughts as well as hear them?*

Yep, she replied. *I can see the map you're looking at in your head. Of course, I can't figure the mileage exactly, like I could if I was holding it—Dawk taught me how to read one in those first wild days on the run—but I suppose I can guess-ti-mate pretty well.*

I glanced down at the map unfolded loosely beside me on the console. *Yeah,* I replied. *I think two or three days is a very good guess-ti-mate.*

But it turned out we would get there much quicker than that, we just didn't know it yet. The multi-colored skies traveled with us, much to our delight. Then CCR started playing again, and this time, everyone began to sing or hum along.

It seemed everyone knew a few words or at least the tune. Dad belted out the part about "Willy and the Poor Boys," and Sam chimed in with a few lines about "all the people" gathering to watch someone they called "a magic boy." Since we were in three separate vehicles, all singing the same version of a classic rock song—and we could all hear each other—the hive theory took on new meaning.

Hive theory, yes, Faith said. *Clairaudient is another word; except I've never heard of everyone being able to hear and see each other's thoughts the way we can.*

Clairaudient? That's a new one on me. But if you say it's a real deal, I believe you. I turned the concept over and over in my head. *So, this isn't a new thing?*

Faith's laugh tinkled.

In that moment, I would have believed anything she told me.

I have no idea, really. She laughed again. *Until this all happened, I was just a chubby teenage girl worrying about starting high school in the fall.*

It seemed odd to be having what felt like an intimate conversation with everyone listening in. But then someone took up the song again, and that ended that.

We wound up singing Creedence Clearwater Revival songs almost all the way to our destination.

CHAPTER EIGHT

Food

A couple hours after we met Dawk, we began to encounter heavier traffic. I say that jokingly—some of Cade's dark humor—because of course I'm talking about wrecked cars and trucks. We still hadn't run across anymore survivors. Not yet.

I'd say they lit out for the territories, Dad chimed in, out of the blue.

Faith and I both laughed. We'd been driving along, throwing ideas back and forth in our heads, avoiding the elephant in the car which was, what do we do when we get to San Diego?

And that's when we saw Sam pulled off beside the road.

What's this? Faith asked.

Straight ahead, off to the left, the tow truck sat idling on the grassy median. Sam stood beside it, peering across the double lanes.

Dad said, "What's going on?"

I let my foot off the gas, and we eased up beside Sam. *If there was any sign of danger, he wouldn't be out of the truck, right?*

"Hey, Jack," he spoke into my open window with a grin across his face. "Do you still have the keys to that food trailer?" He glanced back across the road.

There it was.

I could hardly believe it. Barely visible, tucked behind a thick stand of chunky trees, sat Aunt Edna's old stock trailer. Marla and her misted-Takers—the ones that were sprayed with Joy Juice from the drones—had stolen it from us when we were camped at Palo Duro Canyon. The same place the evil witch killed Carlos, shot me in the leg, and kidnapped Sam and Faith.

And led us to my dad.

Opening the Chrysler's console, I was thrilled to find I *did* have the old horsehead key fob with all of Aunt Edna's keys attached. It was right there with the old photo of Dad and Aunt Edna when they were kids.

Putting the gear shift in PARK, I debated turning off the engine before stepping out. I couldn't do it. Too many times we'd had to dive back in and take off in a mad dash to escape the horde. I had to leave it running. "Man. I can't believe it!" I tossed Sam the keys, and he stepped over the rumble strip, headed to the trailer.

"We won't even have to bother about going in search of more food if everything is still inside," he said.

I agreed. I remembered canned hams and cans of Spam and other made-to-last foodstuffs Aunt Edna had been storing in the missile silo. Even MREs from military supply stores. Or maybe one of those online prepper survival companies.

After seeing the silo, I decided she had turned prepper, as if she'd known what was coming. But that couldn't be right, or she would've been here with us instead of being stuck on a branch of the old live oak beside her front door.

Rubbing my forehead, I recalled how Sam and Turq and Faith had helped me bury her in the field near her home.

"How's it look?" I asked as Sam unlocked the padlock and swung the door open.

Drew pulled up alongside us in the Nissan. We could hear classical music coming from the open windows. I shaded my eyes, wondering if I was having an auditory hallucination. Radio was kaput. Even satellite radio was no more, this was the first actual music I'd heard.

"Hey!" I yelled. "Did you find a radio station?"

Drew pushed a button on the dash, and a CD slid out onto his waiting fingertips. "Just my traveling music. Vivaldi. Beethoven. Bach. Mozart. Can't believe they all survived with us. Kept the CD case under the seat. Old school. Bit of normal." His eyes smiled, but it didn't match the nonchalant shrug. "This one's Vivaldi." He held up the CD he'd just removed. The afternoon light winked off the silver disc and streamed across the road.

My dad, the music teacher and player of all instruments, craned his head around. "Any room for passengers in there?"

I looked at him. "You're throwing over your wayward son for Vivaldi?"

He laughed heartily. "No, for Mozart." He held his hands up in a *sorry* gesture. "And Beethoven."

I ducked my head and glanced inside. "Any hip hop in there? Or pop? Maybe some old rock or country?"

Drew shook his head. "All classical. Music to soothe the savage beasts." He laughed out loud. "Don't worry, I know it's really the savage breast, but beasts always seemed way more appropriate when we were on car trips."

I thought of how I'd tried to stay awake when I was driving across the prairie, alone. Doing my best to stay awake the night the Takers, under Marla's command, raided our camp. No classical for me, no thanks.

"Check this out." I inclined my head toward the trailer. "Look what Sam found." He stood beside the trailer, seeming to analyze the lock.

Faith clapped her hands. "Can you believe it?" She climbed out of the passenger seat to stand beside Snake and me. He'd followed Milo out as soon as I opened the car door. Dad stayed in the shotgun seat. Drew put the Nissan in park, but he didn't turn off the engine, either.

"What is it, exactly?" Drew asked as he climbed out. Milo didn't wait to hear. He scrambled across the rumble strip and across the bar ditch to where Sam stood.

Snake followed.

Trina got out and stood near the shoulder of the highway, indecisive.

"I can't believe it," I told them. "That's the trailer we brought from my Aunt Edna's missile silo way down in Texas. We filled it with non-perishable food and water and all kinds of stuff. Marla and her evil cohorts stole it from us when they killed Carlos—"

"And kidnapped me and Sam," Faith murmured.

I nodded. "Y'all go on over and see what's in there, if you want." I looked at my dad in the front seat of the Chrysler. "I'll be the lookout." Smiling to let them know I didn't expect any reply, I said quietly, "Just remembering how they ambushed us back then makes me think we'd better always have someone on guard."

Drew nodded. "Things can sure change quickly, can't they?" An indescribable look of sadness crossed his face, and I knew he was thinking of his wife and the mother of his kids.

"Yep, circumstances can go south in a hurry, and after everything Dad has been through, I don't want to leave him alone for a second. You know he was also taken and held by Marla's bunch."

We both glanced at Dad in the Chrysler. He looked much better now, but he was still mostly skin stretched over a bony frame. Turq 2.0 had healed his vision, and he no longer had the massive chemical scars on his face, but he was still alarmingly thin, and somehow, *different*.

I tossed the horsehead key fob to Sam. He examined the choices and then chose the correct padlock key on the first try. He pulled open the doors with only a slight creak. Milo scrambled right inside. Moments later, he emerged from the trailer with a huge grin and a bag of Cheetos. In his other hand he had a bottle of berry flavored Gatorade.

He made it all the way back to the shade beside our car before he sat down and ripped into his snack. Snake sat beside him.

Milo stuffed three cheese puffs into his mouth, then gave one to Snake. "Don't worry, boy," he said, wiping his orange fingers on his jeans. "We've got some beef jerky, too." He lifted one hip and reached back into his back pocket. "Dad said the other day if I had one, I had to have the other." He rolled his eyes, showing the deaf dog the package of jerky. "Even in the apocalypse he says we have to eat our protein." He stuffed another Cheeto into his mouth and crushed it with his tongue.

A look of bliss crossed his young face.

"Good snack," I said. "Snake loves jerky and Cheetos, too."

Milo grinned and wiped his orange fingers again.

"You want something?" I asked Faith.

She nodded. "Let me get it. That juice looks good. Be better cold, but beggars can't be choosers." She stepped across the rumble strip, then hesitated. "What can I bring you and your dad?"

"Gatorade would be perfect. And anything to eat that isn't crackers or jerky." I laughed. We'd survived many days on peanut butter crackers, jerky, Slim Jims, and water. They were just so handy. Right beside the register in every convenience store we encountered. I always intended to search those stores more fully, but almost every one of them had a corpse or two waiting to be discovered. Funny how dead people took away a boy's desire to get food, even if he thought he was starving.

Faith laughed. "Maybe there will be apple trees somewhere."

"Right. Maybe we'll become happy wanderers. Texas for pecans, California for grapes and walnuts, Washington for apples, then way down south to pick peaches in Georgia."

She nodded. "And oranges in Florida."

I thought of all the dead birds. *Who knows what will become of fruit trees. What about the bees needed for pollinating all those fruit trees?* I pushed down that worry. Too negative for this moment. One thing I'd learned in my short stint of being a survivor, negativity does no good. For anyone.

There are inground dwelling bees, too, remember? Faith thought. *I think they're called solitary bees.*

That was true. They were all over Texas. I didn't know about other places, but I assumed so. *Thing is,* I said, *are they pollinators? Are all bees pollinators?*

Let's Google, Faith joked. *When we come to the next library, that is.*

I laughed. She was right, of course. I found myself actually looking forward to a leisurely trip to a library—not the one where my mom lay in perpetual state—just any library where we could research some of the stuff we thought we knew but didn't.

In a moment, Faith came back followed by Sam and the others. We all had bottles of juice or water along with cans of fruit and pre-packaged trail mix. There was more beef jerky, and in Sam's case, several tins of Vienna sausages. He fished the tiny franks out of the pop top cans with his Swiss Army knife. Everyone seemed to be munching on chips or Ritz crackers as well.

Dad ate and drank more than anyone. It was obvious how starved he had been. When he spied Sam's Vienna sausages, his eyes lit up. Sam gave him his own tin, then went back for another when that one was done.

"Guess we need to take a vote," I said.

Everyone looked at me. I was leaning against the Chrysler where Dad sat with his door open and legs out. He had his feet on the ground and appeared comfortable.

Drew had opened the cargo area of his Nissan so the kids and Snake could sit in there with the gate up.

The rest of the group leaned against the vehicles or sat on the hood. It felt almost like a picnic. "Should we hook it to your truck?" I asked Sam, indicating the food trailer with a tilt of my head.

"I've been thinking about that," he said. "But I think it'd be best on one of the other vehicles in case I have to hook up to something to pull it out of the way."

I nodded. "That makes sense."

Drew said, "I'm all set for towing with the Nissan. I'll be glad to pull it."

"In that case," I said. "I say we move on down the road in search of a place to spend the night."

Everyone agreed, and within minutes we were busy stowing everything away—all except the can of peaches I'd found—and getting ready to head out.

"I wonder how they lost control of it," I said to Sam and Faith, the only two who had been there when the trailer had been taken.

"After seeing what went on with the three Takers Dawk captured, I can just imagine the same thing happening to whoever had tried to make off with it."

"That's right," I said. "The Takers needed to be sprayed almost continuously, didn't they?"

Dad raised a hand. "I can attest to that," he said. "It was

ongoing. Which is why I couldn't function other than walking and breathing—and barely that."

Sam cleared his throat, waited until everyone looked his way. "I say we get on with it. Just keep driving. I'd like to see the Grand Canyon again, if possible." He grinned. "I think it's somewhere in between here and San Diego." He scratched his chin. "But I could be wrong. I was, once."

We all laughed.

"Before that, maybe we can find a place to hole up for a few hours, better to arrive fresh, not exhausted." His eyes automatically scanned the sky. "We can make more plans after we're rested."

Everyone nodded. "It's not far to the cavern system from here," Dad said. "It stretches for miles, you know. And it probably would be a place to regroup, and plan."

I looked at the man who'd been my beacon, my rock, for every moment of my short life. He looked different, weary, yet tough, and his voice sounded different, raspy and rough, but his words were as true as they'd ever been. They went right to the heart of things. "Dad's right. Sam and Dad, both." I slurped a peach slice into my mouth from a pop top can. "We have to have a plan, a goal."

I thought back to the first days after the rip when I had to force myself into action by formulating minute-to-minute goals like "find a flashlight," or "get home, find Mom and Dad." Just traveling the few blocks back to my house from school had required a plan. One of my first.

When I thought of all the things I'd endured, that all of us had endured, my mind nearly collapsed under the sheer weight of it.

"That's settled, then," Faith said. "Onward before it gets too late."

Everyone nodded. Even Milo, who once again sat with his arm around Snakeman's thick neck. I watched as he fingered the ragged scrap of turquoise still fastened to the big dog's collar. It was all that was left of the original Turq before he morphed into the winged Turq 2.0.

As if bidden, the whir of wings came to my ear. I shaded my eyes, searching the sky. *Turq, is that you?* I flung the thought question out into the ether. I knew he would hear it if it was meant to be heard. What I didn't know was how, or if, he would respond.

My hand sought the back of my neck to quell the prickles. I'd felt them since leaving Cheyenne. As if someone, or something, followed us. Just other survivors, probably. But still—my hand rubbed and rubbed.

Overhead, I thought I heard it again. In my mind, it was easy to envision Turq 2.0 and his flock, looking out for us, shielding us, guiding us, perhaps. It made me feel a lot more comfortable out on the open road. I hoped I wasn't imagining it.

CHAPTER NINE

Cliff dwellings

We drifted through the afternoon and evening, a vagabond caravan, until the sun barely peeked over the horizon. "Time to settle in for the night," I said. "It's still a long way to San Diego. But I wouldn't mind seeing the Pacific again. We'd only been once when I was still young enough to enjoy Disneyland."

"I remember that trip," Dad spoke up. "My, wasn't that day warm?" He clucked his tongue like an old schoolteacher. "But that was way north of San Diego, up near LA."

"Yes, it was," I laughed. "But the ocean was so chilly at Huntington Beach. I remember you bought a giant pink and orange beach towel for like twenty-five bucks just to have something to wrap around me. Mom nearly had a fit—"

My words dried up as something came to my attention. I pointed at a large roadside sign directing drivers toward the exit for The Rio Grande National Forest. "Looks like a good place to set up camp for the night."

"Should be a park map at the visitor center," Dad said. "If we get lucky, we may find a cave or cabin to sleep in."

Faith said, "The visitor center itself might be a good place to camp, if nothing else."

Drew agreed, and we all took the exit into the national park.

There were cars and corpses all up and down the park trail roads, and the beautiful trees around the visitors center were rife with wind chimes made of the flesh-stripped bones of humans.

"I don't think I like this place," Milo said as we made our way around the sad vehicle-tombs leading up to the building.

"It's ugly and spooky," Trina echoed.

"Fortunately, there's a huge park map right there." Sam pointed to a tall plexiglass-covered map near the front door. "Let me look it over. I think I see a symbol for caverns."

"That sounds cool." Milo perked up. "And if not a cave, then maybe at least a river."

I peeked at his thoughts and saw him and his sister playing at the edge of the water on a muddy bank. It looked pretty good to me, too.

Drew got out of the Nissan to look at the map with Sam. I climbed out, too. There were several caverns marked on the map, but only one near where we were. "Think we can find the entrance in the dark?"

The thick forest made the sunset speed up, hiding colorful rays amongst the branches only to have them peer out a little further down the road. Like the spokes on a pinwheel seen from faraway. Threatening to plunge us into darkness at any moment.

"Doesn't look too bad," Drew said. "I say we try. I wouldn't mind having a solid wall at my back to get a good night's sleep."

"We can take shifts staying awake," Sam said.

I nodded and sealed the deal. We drove on through the open entrance gate, and within minutes, we were seeing signs directing us toward the cavern system. But before we got there, Faith said, "Jack, look up on that ridge."

I craned my neck to see where she was pointing. Some sort of long rectangular openings peeked through the bushes higher up the mountain.

"What is that?"

"Could they be cliff dwellings?" Dad asked.

That struck us all into silence until Milo said, "What?"

Trina said, "Can we go. Let's go up there. Look, there's a little road. It doesn't look far at all."

We were following Sam through the park, but he must've heard all the conversations because his brake lights came on, and he stopped and got out. We pulled up, and he leaned into the car. "Cliff dwellings? We could stay there, right?"

"I think so. I wonder if these are like the ones built by the ancient Pueblo people way back in the 1300s." Cade was right, I was a walking encyclopedia, thanks to my mom. "They're sort of like apartment caves."

"Solid wall at our backs, that's all I care about," Drew said, walking over from where he'd pulled up behind us.

"Sounds good to me. Let's turn around and take that trail," I said. "Can you get up there with the trailer?"

Drew said, "You bet. Wouldn't it be great if they had a water well there somewhere? Like at the Bitty House?"

"I don't know if they had wells. Seems I read they used reservoirs and cisterns."

"Maybe we'll get lucky, then," he said.

For once I had to disagree. "Think we might want to stick with our bottled stuff for now. Unless there is an actual well." The thought of drinking water that had been in open outdoor storage didn't seem like a good idea. I thought of all the slivery slime that had fallen from the sky when the Takers first came.

But then I also remembered bathing in streams and rivers, so I really had no argument other than the fact that cisterns are still water opposed to rivers and streams which are made up of flowing water.

"You never know," I replied, not wanting to sound like a smarty pants. "This is all new to me."

We made it up the short road easily and parked down below the dwellings. To me, they looked mostly like a row of unfinished adobe walls punctuated with dark windows. The only difference was how they were built in and under the overhanging rock cliffs.

"They're absolutely amazing," Drew said, climbing the short ladder to access the first level of dwellings. "I know these have been preserved as history, or whatever, but man. Seems like the Native people could just walk right out of there—" He ducked his head to peer into another part of the dwelling, which could be accessed by a different ladder going down into a large open room with a fire pit near the wall.

"Look, Dad," Milo scampered up to peek into another. "How many rooms are there?"

"There could be dozens," Faith said. "Hundreds, even." She shined a tiny flashlight into the dark recesses of the sandstone rooms. "It *is* like an apartment complex, isn't it? Here's another firepit. At least I think that's what it is. Looks charred, anyway."

We all spread out in the long, low, sandstone dwellings. "They are amazing," I said, walking around, examining everything in the pale shafts of light falling in from the remains of the sunset. "These look like places to sit." I placed my hand flat into a hollowed-out chair carved into one wall. There were several around the rounded room.

"So, these must be sleeping platforms, then." Faith stood beside longer, rectangular platforms along the back wall. "There would be lots of blankets, maybe some sort of grass-filled mattress pads. To make the beds more comfortable."

"I wish we could see all that stuff," Trina said. "Woven baskets for their grain and stuff they hunted and gathered."

Her dad looked at her in awe.

"Wikipedia," she said. "I had to do a report for history last year." She reached up and almost touched the ceiling. "They weren't very tall people. The men only about my height, and the women rarely got over five feet tall." She smiled. "Poor Sam and Dad."

Everyone noticed them, then. Hunched over to move into the covered parts of the dwellings.

I reached up to touch the ceiling. I had plenty of room. I laughed at myself. One thing I had learned on this horrible journey was that size didn't matter nearly as much as the ability to think and plan. And pick up an equalizer.

After we explored the rooms as much as possible, we all brought some food, water, and bedding up the first ladder and down the second one into the main room. We could look down on the vehicles if we wanted. *But we shouldn't carry up too much stuff,* I thought. *In case we need to leave in a hurry.*

Even though the place was unique, cut into the side of the sandstone cliff that way, I wasn't convinced of its safety. I'd never stayed in open air dwellings unless it truly was out in the open, camping. Everyone having to go up one ladder and down another made me nervous.

I hear that, Faith said, inside my head. *It might be difficult to get out if we have to leave all at once.*

I hadn't realized she was listening, but I hadn't tried to hide my thoughts, so I should have known. At least I didn't have to worry about Snake. I'd wondered if he could handle the short ladders, but he proved more than adept with his oddly dainty paws that sort of tiptoed everywhere.

"Seems pretty secure here," Sam said. "But I'll take first watch, and in case we need to leave quickly, I'd be the anchor, and y'all would just hand up the kids if need be."

No one argued with that. "I'll take second watch," I said. "And the same rules will apply while I'm on guard." I hoped we wouldn't have to put the plan into action, but better safe than sorry.

It took a while for us to get settled with our canned food and our tiny fire in the firepit. "Is this what they called a *kiva?*" Trina asked, running her hand across the rough sandstone of the pit. "I can't remember if it means the fire circle or the entire round room."

Faith shrugged. "I'm not sure, either. It just amazes me that this whole place is still livable after so long."

"Maybe they remade it for the tourists," Milo said. "You know, the way they do dioramas and stuff for museums." He also ran his hands over the rough sandstone walls. The texture was impossible not to touch.

We heated cans of porky beans—Dad's silly word for them from my childhood—popped open some of the small cans of Vienna sausages, and added some canned corn.

Sam, Drew, and the kids chose to try the MREs, what Sam called Civilian Style—as opposed to the military versions—and they turned out to be excellent. Pop-Tarts, chili, spaghetti, and even some candy along with a flameless heater and spoon with wet nap. "These are not bad," Drew said. Milo nodded, mouth full, and even Trina and Faith agreed.

Even though we had the tiny flameless heater, we were glad of the pit fire after the sun disappeared. Not only because of the deep darkness, but also because the autumn nights in Colorado get chilly in a hurry. We broke out some of Aunt Edna's shrink-wrapped blankets from the stock trailer. Drew still had some in his Nissan, too.

"This is cozy," Faith murmured after we'd all finished eating and picked out our sleeping spots. Dad and I were near each other on large flat platforms against the back wall. Faith and Trina were near each other on platforms of their own. Everything was sand colored in the faint glow of the rising moon showing through the ladder opening and the high, narrow offset window.

From our vantage point on the slope of the mountainside, in the underneath of the cliff rock overhang, the landscape view was as grand and relaxing as any painting.

But Milo wasn't ready to go to sleep just yet. "I'm glad we aren't going back to the Bitty House," he said. "I liked it there until they killed Mommy." He was on a lesser platform near Drew and the fire. He sat up, as if he'd unnerved himself.

Trina crossed the small space and hugged her brother. "We never have to go back there," I heard her whisper. Then she looked at Faith, Dad, and me in turn. "Y'all didn't know my mom, but she was kind of awesome. What happened to her was wrong. It was really bad." That's when the tears began to flow.

I had a feeling they had been stored up awhile.

Faith inched over beside her and held her gently, while Milo snuggled up to his dad who had opened his arms. Snake moved in between them, and I got the idea he wanted to comfort them all.

"This reminds me of when we first met Sam," I said. "We had a campfire going then, too."

Sam took the hint. "It was pretty close to the beginning," he said. "And Jack and Carlos, Snake and Faith, and even ol' Turq, accepted me right into the group." He cleared his throat, and just like that night outside the Yucca Motel back in Eden, he began to make a pot of coffee in another enameled pot. This one from Aunt Edna's trailer.

Déjà vu all over again, I thought, quoting Yogi Berra in my head. "That was the night Sam told us all about his granny and what happened to her during the first rip. What some people call the EMP."

"Did it help?" Drew asked, looking at Sam. "To talk about it, I mean. Did it help to talk about it, because let me tell you, it still doesn't seem real, what happened that day. It's like a nightmare that won't fade away."

"It does help," he said. "How about you, Jack? Faith? Did it help to tell your stories?"

I nodded, but to be honest, I didn't think I'd told all of mine. I wrote most of it in the journal though, so that was good enough for me.

"I had to write it *and* tell it," Faith said, treating me to a sudden memory of her sitting by the campfire that night, reading from her own small, battered notebook. It was easy to remember how her voice went all story-teller-singsong as she read.

"Yeah," I said. "It seems to help us all, and to be honest, I'd like to hear how you guys were connected to Carlos and the Bitty Sloan house. If you don't mind."

The group echoed my sentiment. Oddly, though, when Drew began to speak, it was not storytelling around a fire, as it had been with Faith and Sam. This seemed more like a shared memory-movie or even a storyteller tale in my mom's library. One of those being told in third person, from a narrator's perspective.

As the story unrolled in our collective consciousness, I found myself glad the kids fell asleep quickly. Some of Drew's memories of his recently lost wife were not exactly G-rated. I was thankful Faith couldn't see my face in the fire shadows. No doubt, my cheeks were reddened on more than one occasion.

CHAPTER TEN

Drew and family—Before the rip

From the road, the old house looked ancient. As if no one had lived there for a hundred years. Rose turned her head as they drove past. "Did you see that?" Drew's palm was still on her thigh. They'd been holding hands like teens up until then. It had been a wonderful trip to the lake.

"See what?" His voice was lazy. He'd been lost in thought as he drove. Thoughts about how long it would take to get the kids bathed and tucked in so that he could get his wife alone.

"That house on the hill," she said, her voice holding just a hint of impatience. "How could you not have seen it? The thing was huge, a veritable mansion." Her voice went all dreamy. "A gingerbread mansion." She nudged him and unbuckled her seat belt so she could turn around more fully. "Go back, just, you know, back up or something."

That got Drew's attention. He allowed the car to slow, but he didn't brake. "Back up? Why? What's so special?"

Still twisted around in her seat, Rose said, "It's difficult to see now." A stand of cottonwoods crowded the corner of the intersection like sentinels; their branches touching overhead, tree-swords held high. "I think it had a For Sale sign out front, sort of hidden in the weeds."

Drew looked in his mirror. The empty road stretched behind them, but he didn't really want to wake the kids just to look at some creepy old house. They couldn't possibly afford it anyway. Not a *veritable mansion* or any other kind.

All he had on his mind was getting home before the kids woke up, then getting them into their cozy little beds so he could get his wife into their cozy big bed.

"Come on," Rose urged. "Turn around. *Please?*"

"But—"

"It'll only take a second. I just want to look at it."

In the dim moonlight, with her face turned away, Drew could not read her expression, but then he thought, *Oh well, why not? It'll only take a minute.* So, he shrugged and gave in.

They'd had such a great day he didn't want to ruin it by denying her a glimpse of whatever had caught her eye. "Alright, hon," he said, slinging his arm over the back of the seat so he could look over his shoulder. "We're going back. Just for you." He winked at her and made certain nothing was behind them, and then he backed down the service road in reverse. He was pretty sure they wouldn't be able to see much even if the house was for sale.

In another moment, he had the blue Nissan Pathfinder evened up with the start of the hilly driveway leading up to the old house. Sure enough, a red, white, and blue FOR SALE sign leaned precariously in a patch of tall grass.

Drew backed up a bit more and then pulled in nose-first so the SUV's headlights lit up the eerie scene. "Well, there it is." He turned to face Rose, but to his surprise, she had climbed out already.

"Hey—" He shoved the gearshift into park. "What are you doing?" He started to get out, too, but he didn't want to leave the kids sleeping in the backseat on this deserted stretch of road.

"Rose!" He stood half-in and half-out of the driver's door, his right foot on the running board, his left foot on the ground. "Rose Marie *Branson*," he hissed across the roof in her direction, trying to keep his voice low enough to avoid waking the kids, but loud enough to get her attention.

It didn't work.

Rose continued toward the house as if in a trance. She hadn't closed the door; she'd simply pushed it barely shut with her hip.

For a second, Drew stood there, admiring her shapely backside illuminated in the vehicle's headlights, then he gave up, stepped all the way out, and dashed around the hood. He caught her by the arm, his fingers digging into the crook of her elbow.

Pulling her around to face him, he said, "Honey, what're you doing? I don't think we should go up there in the dark. What if the owners still live here?" His eyes followed her glance toward the house. "Or what if there's a dog, or something?" He had visions of Cujo, lurking beneath the porch.

She glanced at him, then at the house.

It appeared deserted. The long, humpy, driveway rose steeply and then curved slightly, so it was difficult to be certain. There appeared to be some minor problems, peeling paint and such, but it was hard to tell. Some folks lived with problems, especially if the house was up for sale.

Drew peered at it again. In the moonlight and the car's headlights, all the windows appeared intact. *At least there's that*, he thought.

"There's no one here," Rose gestured toward the massive front porch. "It could be grand, don't you think?" She let her gaze drift from the house to her husband's face. "Don't you?"

Drew felt a strange unease in his gut. "Yeah, sure." He looked at the old house again. "With a couple million bucks, maybe."

Rose giggled uncharacteristically. She never giggled. Rose was a belly-laugher, not a giggler. Especially after a couple margaritas. "Come on, Drew. A little paint, some nice landscaping, I think it would look as good as new." She started forward again, pulling away from his grasp as if by accident.

Drew had seen enough. "Dammit, Rose. What are you doing?" He glanced back at their Nissan, idling behind the bright headlights with his most prized possessions snoring softly inside, unaware. *What had come over her?* He couldn't believe she was walking away from him in the darkness. Surely, she wasn't planning on walking all the way up there. The drive was long and humpy, and that curve could hide anything.

"Mom?" Eight-year-old Milo stuck his curly head out the window, rough little schoolboy fists rubbing at his sleepy eyes. "What's Mama doing?" His gaze followed her silhouette as it moved up the hill in the darkness. "*Mama?*" His voice went from sleepy to strident in an instant.

Drew hurried back and leaned inside the car. "Hey, buddy. It's okay. Don't wake your sister."

Rose stopped, the sound of her son's voice grabbing her attention like an audible beacon. She gave the house one more glance before she turned and headed back down the bumpy drive to her waiting family.

When she turned, the rubber stopper holding the straps of her flip-flop between her toes popped out of the base, and her foot burst free. She'd split the rubber around the stopper when she turned so suddenly.

Reaching down, she picked up the remains without stopping. The fine red dust of the dirt driveway puffed out from beneath her bare foot with each step. The car's headlights were like spotlights on a stage. Suddenly, she cried out.

Drew patted his son's arm and dashed to his wife's side. "What is it?"

"Blew out my flip flop," she laughed. "Then stepped on a sharp stone." She climbed back in the passenger seat, only slightly embarrassed. "At least it wasn't a pop top."

Drew stifled a laugh as Rose turned to soothe Milo's uncertainty.

"Jimmy Buffet would've been proud it wasn't a pop top," Drew whispered as he rounded the front of the vehicle, still holding in his laughter at the song reference and the look on his wife's face when she'd held up the mangled flip flop. He knew a laugh now would not earn him any favors back home.

He slid back inside behind the steering wheel.

"What was it, Mama?" Milo asked.

"Just a bit of silliness," she said, patting his arm the same way his dad had done a moment earlier. "You go back to sleep. Your old mom thought she saw a mansion on a hill." The giggle came again. "But my flip flop fell apart." She glanced at her husband. "Maybe Daddy will bring us back in the daylight sometime."

Drew laughed. "We'll see." He backed out of the entrance to the driveway and steered back toward the interstate. For the life of him, he couldn't understand what had come over his wife. Rose was usually the picture of reason.

The rest of the drive home was uneventful. He passed the small sign that read:

Exit here to visit historic
Kansas, New Mexico

Drew thought, *No thanks. That's the last time I take an unfamiliar short cut.*

But it turned out all right. Milo went back to sleep and Trina never woke at all.

CHAPTER ELEVEN

Rose

The next morning, Rose was not ready to leave her comfy tangle of bedclothes, but the garbage truck came. *If we had that big old mansion,* she thought, *we would probably have to pay a private company to come and pick up the trash. Or haul it to the dump ourselves. It wouldn't be a city service, that's for sure, not way out there in the country.* She allowed her mind to wander for a moment longer. *If we had that place, the kids could have another dog. Hard to believe it's been over a year since we lost dear old Argus the Wonder Dog.*

She headed into the kitchen, still daydreaming, relishing another day off from her teller job at the bank, leaving Drew snuggled into a big snoring lump under the big, embroidered quilt. Nothing woke Drew. He pulled the blankets up over his ears and slept like the dead.

Rose stretched and yawned, thankful there was no school today. The kids had finished up the school year last week. They always got out before Memorial Day which usually meant a three-day weekend filled with fishing and grilling at her parents' home at Copper Lake. Which was exactly what they'd done yesterday. Burgers and steaks and sweet corn on the cob. The kids swam and the men fished, and she and her mom had solved all the world's problems over tall glasses of sweet iced tea on the wide lakeside deck.

It had been a wonderful visit.

She and Drew always breathed a sigh of relief when summer

rolled around. Oh, she knew the kids would be bored soon. They were so busy during the school year with sports and choir and art, it wouldn't be long at all before they began to get on each other's nerves. But vacation was already planned. A trip to Galveston and a few surf lessons. It was something new. Something they had never done.

It was something to look forward to.

Rose thought about the kids. Even though her work was interesting—she knew almost everyone in town through their bank accounts—becoming a mom had opened her eyes to a type of joy she'd never even dreamed about.

She was so proud of her kiddos. Trina was the singer. She dearly loved her middle school choir. And she definitely had the first-born attributes all the parenting articles said she would.

Milo was the baby. Named after her grandfather, he was a tough little guy who loved superheroes and baseball. On the other hand, he also excelled in art. He had such an eye for detail. When he drew a housecat, he made sure you knew it was a cat by the long tail and whiskers. If it was a lion, he focused on the mane. He had just finished third grade, but even as a kindergartener, when he'd brought home his classroom drawings, Rose never had to ask what the pictures were, the way she had with Trina.

Unfortunately, he was also well on his way to earning pest-of-the-year award from his big sister. They fought and argued like civil war enemies forced to share a country called home. Rose lost patience with them, frequently. Drew, on the other hand, was usually able to jolly them back to good humor with a joke or simply by picking one or the other up and carrying them around like a sack of laundry.

Her husband was a great dad. They'd had their problems as most married folks do, even separating for a few weeks due to his football betting and her propensity for retail therapy, but once they'd gone to a financial counselor and truly learned that money doesn't grow on trees—and frugality is not a bad word—they had turned a corner. Now they were both acutely aware of how close they'd come to messing everything up.

Drew was a hard worker; that wasn't a problem. He loved his career with GreenEnergy, manufacturers of wind turbines. Even so, when Rose thought of sharing her children in some ridiculous, every-other-weekend custody arrangement, she felt faint. Literally heartsick.

She quickly changed her ways and insisted he do the same. Soon, they were crawling out of debt, slowly, but surely.

Now, Rose felt certain her little family was stronger than ever. And the kids seemed to be doing great.

She made her way to the kitchen, thinking about nothing more than how delicious it felt to have a free day with the family. No work, no school, no sports, no practices.

Once in the kitchen, however, the day took a small left turn when she grabbed the old Mickey Mouse juice glass, the one Drew had bought for Trina on their trip to Disneyland, and accidentally banged it against the counter, knocking a chip out of the rim.

Rose held the glass up to the light. Not a big chip. *Shouldn't have hurried*, she chastised herself. The glass wasn't a total loss, but a chip is like a magnet; once one happens, others will follow. *I should just chunk it*, she thought, but she couldn't do it. She loved that little memento from their long-ago vacation. Later, she would reflect on that morning and wonder if that chip was kind of an omen. As if a piece of their Disney-esque innocence had already been lost.

Rose tried to shake the weird feeling by starting preparations for a big family breakfast. As she assembled the ingredients for veggie omelettes, Drew came up behind her and pressed his front to her backside. Even after twelve years, two kids, and many issues of trust, their bodies still met in all the right places.

"Watch out old man," she turned her head for a kiss. "You'll have me wanting more, more, more—"

He laughed, popped a grape tomato into his mouth, and then snuzzled her neck as if they were teens again. When he made as if to scoop her up and head back to the bedroom, Rose resisted good naturedly.

In the back of her mind, she couldn't help wondering how long the kids would sleep. *Better not chance it this morning*, she thought.

Little did she know it would be the last time she would ever have to worry about that sort of intimacy issue.

Marveling at how wonderful things had been between them of late, she sent up a silent thanks to whatever supreme being was in charge. It truly felt as if they were experiencing the early days of their marriage all over again.

Now they would be free to focus on the kids and have a family life like they'd had before. Preferably in the country so the kids could have plenty of room to roam and play.

Rose suspected that's why Drew agreed to return to the old house. She could hardly wait until tomorrow. *I guess it's true,* she thought, *things really do happen for a reason.*

CHAPTER TWELVE

Carlos

The real estate agent's name was Carlos Ramirez. He had agreed to meet them at the old house around two that afternoon.

"I'm excited!" Rose said, stepping from the shower.

Drew leered at her. "I can take care of that, if you're up for a repeat." He tugged at the corner of her towel.

"Silly boy," she whipped off the towel and flung it at his face, racing back into the bathroom clutching her bra and panties. "Don't make promises you can't keep."

"Tease!" he called after her. Then he made his way into the kitchen to start a simple, cereal breakfast. No omelettes this morning. They had a mansion to inspect.

After the sleepy-eyed kids got awake enough to understand what was in store for the day, they enjoyed a quick meal, then climbed back into the Nissan to go and tour the old house from the night before last.

Even though Trina had never awakened the night her mom blew out her flip flop, they told her all about it, and before long, they were all singing "Margaritaville" in as good a humor as Rose could ever recall.

Soon, both kids were hungry again. Drew looked at his watch, amazed at how fast the morning had disappeared. He glanced at Rose, then shrugged. "I could eat," he said. "How about you?"

She matched his shrug and laughed. "Let no good sandwich go uneaten, right?" It had been a running joke between them for as long as they'd been together. Neither of them ever turned down a meal request when the kids were hungry. "Beats candy," they always reasoned.

Drew grinned and pulled into the parking lot of a Subway sandwich shop on the edge of town. "Don't unwrap them yet," he instructed, an idea forming in his head.

He'd seen a little rest stop on the way to their destination. Quite attractive as he recalled. Before long, they were pulling into a shady parking space.

The spontaneity thrilled the kids. They loved the least little surprise.

"This weather is beautiful," Rose said. "Great idea, hon." She treated him to a smile that took him right back to their college days.

And she was right. The weather was amazingly fresh and temperate for late May. Not too hot, yet. Not by Texas standards at least.

They spread their meal across a cement table and dug in. After they ate their subs, Milo and Trina chased each other around the grassy setting like wild beasts, growling and shrieking with laughter.

"It feels like the neverending holiday, doesn't it?" Rose put the last bite of sandwich into her mouth, chewed, and swallowed. "Just think what fun those two could have at that old mansion with all that room to run." She licked dark maroon flavoring off her fingertips, thought of all the horrid virus germs she might've just ingested—Covid not the least among them—and crumpled up the barbecue flavor chip bag before tossing it at the nearby trash can.

"And who, knows," she said, getting up to retrieve the rapidly uncrumpling bag that had bounced off the rim. "Maybe we'll get lucky, and the house will be *super* affordable."

Drew shook his head. "Be careful what you wish for. Super affordable probably means super fixer-upper, and I'm not much of a carpenter." He smiled. His lack of handyman skills was legendary.

Rose couldn't keep the awe from her voice when she said, "Yeah, but on the phone, the Realtor said it's on the *historic register*."

Just as she finished speaking, a loud clap of thunder spanked the sky and sent the kids scurrying back to the table. Glancing up, Rose said, "I don't recall any thunderstorms in the forecast."

"Neither do I," Drew agreed, gathering up the remains of the meal as he spoke. "Nevertheless, we'd better head for cover." He sniffed the air and rubbed at the back of his neck. A chill wind had crossed the rest area as surely as if a fan had been pointed their direction. "That's quite a breeze," he said. "Might be some hail coming."

Rose corraled the kids, and together they all dashed toward the Nissan, Drew veering off to stuff the rest of the trash into the garbage can on the way.

"Guess we'll head on to the old house, it's closer than home and we can park in the garage if it does begin to hail." He started the engine and looped around the drive-through to get back on the highway.

They barely made it to the big house before the storm hit.

The driveway from the highway to the house was rough, red earth, rutted, not well maintained. Rose held on to the Pathfinder's grab bar. "Was the driveway this rough last time?"

Drew laughed. "We didn't go up very far that night. You blew out a flip-flop, remember?" He looked off toward the west. "I didn't know about that, though." He pointed out the window. "I knew it sat on a hill, but a cliff?" He glanced at Rose. "I don't like the idea of Milo and that cliff."

Rose didn't like the look of it either, but now was not the time to discuss it. The storm was coming fast.

Drew drove straight up the bumpity drive. It veered to the right at the last moment, and there stood a man just inside the open garage motioning for them to hurry. They drove directly under the three-story house into an underground garage.

When they got out of the Nissan, the man pulled the overhead door all the way down, and now he stood at the top of a set of cement steps leading through a regular interior door into the kitchen. "*Vámanos*," he urged. "*Hurry*. Storm looks like a bad one. Any reports of tornadoes?"

"Nothing on the radio," Drew replied. "But did you have a look at that sky?"

The man nodded. "I wasn't sure if you guys would make it or not. Sky looks like *poison*."

Sure enough, in the short time it took them to drive from the rest area, the sky had gone from lazy-days-of-summer blue to pus-filled cyst yellow-green.

"It *does* look like poison," Rose said.

Another clap of thunder sent them all scampering up the cement steps into the kitchen.

The gentleman closed the door behind them and held out his hand. "Carlos Ramirez, your Realtor. Pleased to meet you, Mr. and Mrs. Branson." He glanced at the kids. "Pleased to meet all of you."

Rose liked the way he acknowledged the children. She also liked the twinkle in his brown eyes and the gold cross at his throat.

"Thanks for coming out. I think you will really be amazed at this old house." Carlos's voice faded as a sonic boom of thunder rattled the windowpanes. He laughed self-consciously. "Anyway, I can't think of a better place to begin this little tour than down in the secret tunnels." He rubbed his palms together like a late-night horror movie host.

"Secret tunnels?" The kids looked at each other. "Let's go!"

Carlos grinned. "I hoped you'd say that." He led them straight down the back staircase from the kitchen into the basement, which came complete with a hidden water well.

The family could not believe their eyes. "A water well, in the basement? But why?" Trina was completely perplexed. They all were.

The Realtor smoothed his thumb and forefinger across his generous upper lip. "This house once belonged to the famous outlaw, Bitty Sloan."

"That old bootlegger from the Prohibition era?" Drew was astounded. "The one who ran illegal booze all over New Mexico and into Colorado?"

Carlos nodded vigorously. "He had a water well dug down here to keep folks from knowing how much water he was using— just like that Levi Coffin house up in Indiana. You know, the one that was called the Grand Central Station on the Underground Railroad?"

He looked at them as if they were certainly every bit the history buff he was, but when they didn't respond, Carlos continued,

"Well, anyhow, Levi Coffin—the station master—had a water well in the basement of that Indiana house so folks wouldn't know how much water they were using to help out all the freedom seekers who passed through their home."

His voice dropped to a whisper. "But the hidden well isn't the only neat thing about this old mansion." He moved a large chest on wheels and pressed a hidden panel in the wall. "Take a look at this."

A door slid open soundlessly.

Milo and Trina exchanged open-mouthed glances. "Can we go in?"

"Of course." Carlos produced a large flashlight. "There are electric lights," he flipped a switch, and the tunnel was lit by hanging bulbs. "But with this storm brewing, I thought we'd better be prepared."

Rose glanced at her husband, a look of consternation marring her features. Drew just shrugged and followed the children into the gloom.

Another *boom* shook the air as Carlos disappeared into the tunnel. "This goes even deeper. We'll be safe further down." He shined the flashlight onto a darker rectangle of wall that turned out to be another door leading down a short series of old steps. "In here is a storage room where some of the booze was kept."

The air was redolent of hops and barley and something sweet. To Drew it smelled like heaven. "How many of these storage rooms are there?" He reached for the rough rock wall to steady himself, his equilibrium suddenly wonky.

"Half a dozen," Carlos said. "This one even has a few kegs and barrels still intact. Aside from bringing in beer, they also made something called Sugar Moon, which was moonshine made from sugar beets."

"Whoohoo!" Drew laughed. "What a great place to ride out a storm." If he'd been hesitant about the old house before, the tide had just turned.

Then the hallway door slammed shut between them and the kitchen.

Trina squealed, Milo jumped, and Rose gasped and yelled,

"What's that awful *noise*?" She covered her ears with her hands as the room filled with thrumming vibrations so strong they might have stopped their hearts had they been out in the open. "It sounds like a bunch of marching bands," Rose yelled.

"I think it's a tornado!" Drew shouted.

The sounds were so loud they could barely hear each other.

The lights went out and Carlos thumbed the switch on the flashlight. "We can go back up as soon as it's ov—"

The ground began to shake. The marching bands rose to a crescendo. Milo clapped his hands over his ears and fell to the floor.

Carlos yanked the heavy storage room door shut as Trina fell to her knees beside her brother. She clasped her hands over her ears, too.

Rose groaned as her knees gave way, and then she was on the floor, attempting to scoop her children to her breast and keep her own ears covered at the same time.

Drew gathered them all into a huge embrace as Carlos collapsed beside them, the flashlight hitting the dirt floor with a goodbye wink.

The house shook and the ceilings rained dirt down upon their heads, but the old stone walls held even though the vibrations were so severe a couple of eighty-year-old kegs fell over and burst open. The rich smell of ancient beer permeated the closed-up room and quickly sank into the earthen floor.

The five of them huddled in a pile until Milo finally crawled out of his parent's embrace. "The beer spilled," he said.

Drew sat back on his heels. "Everyone all right?"

Trina's voice shook. "I don't know." She sat up but didn't let go of her mother's hand.

"Where's that flashlight?" Drew asked.

The Realtor moaned. "What happened?" His voice was no longer jolly and kind, now it sounded confused, muddled.

Milo came up with the flashlight and gave it to his dad. Drew flicked the switch on and off, and it came back on.

"Thank God," Rose breathed. "I was afraid we were going to have to find our way out in the dark."

Carlos moaned again.

"Hey, man." Drew shined the light toward the other man. "You okay?"

Carlos held his ears. When he took his hands away, one side was smeared with blood.

Drew shined the light toward him. "Did you hit your head?" He moved toward the Realtor cautiously.

"I don't think so," Carlos replied. "But that *sound*." He grimaced. The expression was especially pronounced in the unsteady beam of the flashlight. "One of my eardrums is whistling," he said. "Like wind in there."

Drew looked at his little family. "You guys okay? Ears hurt?"

One by one, they took stock of each other and found no injuries.

"I think we're okay," Rose said, standing. "It was just so sudden. Was it a tornado, or an earthquake?"

"I don't know. We'd better go up and check it out," Drew said. They all looked at Carlos to see if he would lead them. But he seemed in no shape. Drew took him under the arm and helped him stand. "Can you make it?"

Carlos stood shakily. "Yeah, maybe. I—I think so." He put one hand over his left ear and swung his other arm around Drew's neck. "My balance is not so good."

Together, they hobbled to the door.

Drew hesitated, his hand on the large brass knob.

"What is it?" Rose asked.

Her husband shook his head. "I don't know. Fear of the unknown, I guess." He grasped it and pulled it open before he could give in to the doubt that wanted to overtake him.

The tunnel was filled with fine dust floating through the air.

"Pull your shirt up over your mouth and nose," Rose told the kids.

They followed Drew into the tunnel—thankful they could only go one direction—and trudged back up the short staircase.

The sliding door was right where it should be. But Carlos couldn't find the hidden panel that opened it again.

"It seems to be stuck," he mumbled, one hand still covering his ear.

Drew pounded the wall where he thought the panel should be. "Vibrations probably knocked it out of whack."

"After all these years?" Rose's voice was incredulous. "Surely this place has withstood a million storms over the last century." She pushed the kids behind her and stepped up beside her husband. "You guys are not looking in the right place."

Just as she said it, Drew's fist connected with the correct spot, and the pocket door sprang open with a whoosh. "Wow, good way to lose a finger," Drew said.

He ushered everyone out onto the basement landing, then he led the way up, supporting Carlos beside him. "Up we go," he said. "Into the kitchen." And up to see what kind of damage might have been done. He didn't think it had lasted long enough to be a tornado, but then, he'd never actually been in a tornado before, so he couldn't rule it out.

"Maybe it was that thing they call wind shear," Rose said, reading his mind like always. "You know, a down draft or something—"

"I think it's called a down*burst*," Milo corrected his mother gently.

"Yeah, that," she agreed.

They entered the dusty upstairs one behind the other.

"Look!" Trina whispered.

A multitude of people-shapes were visible outside the cracked and broken windows. They seemed to be going somewhere, all headed in the same direction.

"What the hell?" Carlos and Drew stepped up to the window at the same time. Their view was of the side of the house. They could also see part of the driveway.

"Are they soldiers?" Carlos asked, shaking his head slightly, still experimenting with his balance and the noise in his head. "The National Guard or something?"

Drew shook his head. "Naked *gray* soldiers?"

Milo ran to stand beside his father. "Naked? I wanna see. What are they doing? Why are they naked? Where are they—"

"Slow down, son," Drew said quietly. "This doesn't make sense. Those guys aren't soldiers, not our soldiers anyhow. They look like, they look like, like—"

"Aliens. Or robots," Carlos finished. "Automatons. I read that in a book once. Automatons. Yeah." He gazed out again. "See how they all have the same shape and they're moving almost exactly the same?"

"Where did they come from?" Rose asked. "The *storm?*"

"Wasn't really a storm, I don't think." Drew's face appeared drawn, almost as gray as the shapes outside the window. "Look at the sky. It's so strange. It shouldn't be this dark. It's only afternoon."

Rose went to the front window. "Oh, my God! Drew, look. The sky is *torn.*"

Everyone rushed to the front windows, their shoes crunching broken glass as they came. "Watch out," Rose cautioned, throwing her hands out to catch anyone who slipped. All the windows were broken.

Further away from the house, the sky bled sour yellow light and thick, silver rain. The droplets fell in poisonous looking splotches that hissed as they struck the ground.

"Oh, dear Lord," she prayed. "What is this?"

Puddles formed beneath the ragged places in the sky. From the shiny puddles, the naked, gray creatures continued to arise, steaming as if from afterbirth, pulling themselves out of the wetness fully formed, yet featureless.

When they turned their identical heads toward the house, bright, maroon-colored eyes studied everything, taking in their surroundings through multifaceted lenses like big garnets stuck in their flat, unfinished faces.

As the people in the house watched through the broken windows, small groups of the creatures marched past. "Mama," Trina breathed. "What are they?" She hadn't called her mother *Mama* since she was in kindergarten.

Another of the things arose with a watery hiss and turned toward the house. As it grew closer, the tiny band of people inside could see odd blue-black words pulsing beneath its wet, gray, skin. *Torture, kill, destroy.* The words—some much darker than the others—rose and fell beneath the translucent skin, appearing and disappearing again and again. Roiling inside out tattoos.

Rose fell back from the window and stumbled over an over-stuffed armchair. "Please, don't let it come in." Her face mirrored the terror in her voice.

Frozen in disbelief, the others watched as the thing continued up the hardpacked drive toward the front of the house.

"It's gonna get us!" Milo shrieked.

Drew picked the boy up and crushed him to his shoulder. "Daddy's here. Nothing's going to get us."

"Back to the cellars," Carlos cried.

He turned toward the kitchen and the back staircase, but the Branson family seemed entranced by the movie-like creature marching steadfastly up the narrow drive.

"Wish I had my old shotgun," Drew murmured.

That seemed to break Rose's paralysis. She grabbed Trina and yanked at Drew's shirt. "Let's go!" She rushed to follow Carlos who only swayed a little bit, one hand still covering his aching ear.

CHAPTER THIRTEEN

Drew

They all managed to get back into the cellar without incident. But after an hour passed, Drew said, "This is not going to work. We can't stay down here from now on."

They sat in stunned silence for a few more minutes, then one by one, they began to come up with theories about what they'd seen, why the electricity never came back on, and why none of their cell phones would work.

The kids were convinced the world had been invaded by aliens from another planet.

Rose said she thought they were all suffering from mass hysteria, that perhaps they had inhaled something when the barrels fell over and split open—in this very room—and that there was really nothing out there at all. And for a moment, that made more sense than anything. After all, who knew for certain what was in those barrels?

But then Drew and Carlos began to discuss the notion that the beings were invaders from another *country*, not another planet. "We know what we saw," Drew insisted.

"Yeah," Carlos said, still holding his ear. "Automatons created in a lab by some place like Russia, China, maybe North Korea." He sounded halfway apologetic when he said it, but considering all the backbiting that had gone on between the superpowers, especially after the Russian invasion of Ukraine, it really wasn't much of a stretch.

For years, Russia had touted its satellite capabilities. Maybe the ripped-open sky was some sort of space weapon. Take out only specific satellites, reprogram the rest and turn them against us. Even CGI special effects could be beamed down from above.

After a bit, Drew took Rose by the shoulders and spoke directly into her face. "I'm going to get in the Nissan and drive out of here." He watched her eyes to see if she understood what he was saying. Her idea about mass hysteria alarmed him. They needed to be on the same page. Not in denial. "I can't just sit here, guessing, any longer."

Rose nodded. "Of course. Of course." She glanced at the kids. "We're coming, too." Now her glance took in Carlos as well.

He smoothed his thumb and forefinger over his top lip again, as if there once was a mustache there. "I don't know," he said. "I rode my Harley down here. It's in the garage." He glanced at the cellar door. "I'm not certain I can ride it out through that pack of creatures though."

"You'll ride with us," Rose said. "C'mon, kids. Hold my hands. Follow Daddy and Carlos."

Drew still had the flashlight.

He opened the heavy door leading out of the storage room, led the way back up to the hidden kitchen door.

This time, he didn't pound the walls.

They all stood silently, uncertain what might be on the other side of the sliding pocket door.

"What if one of them—"

Drew shushed Milo gently. Then he pulled the SUV keys from his pocket and gave them to Rose. "I'll go out first, make sure the coast is clear. You and Carlos get the kids to the car and—"

"Wait, wait," Rose said, shaking her head. "That's not right. Let's just go back down and wait for someone to come. You know, the Army or National Guard or something, like you said. Like in the movies." Her eyes were large in the dim light. "Even in mass hysteria, someone always comes to the rescue."

Drew dropped a quick kiss on his wife's forehead, glad she could joke even in the face of unknown danger. "No one knows we're here, remember. This is a vacant house." He waited for that information to sink in.

"Someone from Carlos's company—" she began.

"Independent," Carlos said. "My only listing." He ducked his head in shame. "I'm just getting started."

Rose drew in a deep breath and squared her shoulders. "Okay. Nissan it is, then." She took her son and daughter by the hand and prepared to rush through the door as soon as Drew gave her the sign. "Don't let me drop these," she whispered to Trina as she pressed the key fob into their conjoined palms.

Drew said, "Ready?"

When she nodded, he popped the wall in the correct spot, the door slid open, and he rushed them directly into the empty first floor kitchen.

"Clear!" he said.

They hurried down the cement steps and into the garage.

Carlos's Harley leaned against the far wall.

Rose didn't hesitate. She opened the driver's door on the Nissan Pathfinder—the closest door to the stairs—and pushed the kids inside. At the last second, she wondered if one of those things could be hiding in the back seat, but it was too late to worry, her children were already climbing over the seat to huddle in the corner.

She crawled in after them as Carlos, still holding onto his left ear, manually raised the garage door with his other hand.

Drew leapt into the SUV, took the keys from Rose, started the engine, and shoved the gearshift into reverse.

Carlos got the door up just as the rear of the vehicle reached it.

Drew stepped on the brake, Carlos yanked open the back door, fell in beside the kids, and they careened down the drive in reverse.

"Watch out!" Rose cried.

At the top of the drive, they knocked into one of the creatures and down it went, head bursting beneath the SUV's tires.

"Oh, *Drew!*"

She turned to the back seat, snatched at the front of the kids' clothing, and shoved them into the floorboard behind her. "Stay down!"

The monsters were everywhere. Most were walking in formation just like before, but a dozen more were simply milling about uncertainly.

Drew yanked the wheel sharply as another one appeared directly behind them. The SUV skated past, barely clipping the thing's legs with the rear bumper. Still in reverse, the Pathfinder flew up and over the humpity place where the drive connected with the service road.

For a moment, they were sickeningly airborne.

"Hold on!" Drew yelled, twisting the wheel, somehow maneuvering the solid vehicle onto the blacktop. In the rearview mirror, he could see the torn flaps of sky fluttering in the vibrating air.

"Damn," he muttered when the vehicle back slammed down. "Everyone okay?" He continued down the service road in reverse, swerving back and forth to avoid the milling monsters.

As he slowed to cross the shallow bar ditch and avoid a knot of the naked grays, his foot began to judder up and down on the accelerator. The result of too much adrenaline, he thought. He had to deliberately clamp his jaws together to keep from laughing out loud. Driving in reverse, they seemed to be going *toward* the bad spots, rather than away.

We're in a freaking video game. Avoiding monsters in a family sized SUV I have to drive in reverse to save our lives. Maybe Rose was right! Maybe it is mass hysteria. He ground his teeth together and continued to steer to the best of his ability.

Most of the things seemed to prefer walking on the pavement so Drew kept to the wide bar ditch or the grassy median to go around them. The majority didn't seem to notice the Nissan, but every now and then, one would turn its blank face in their direction and stare at them with those gemstone eyes.

When that happened, Drew would have to force himself to look away. He would force himself to focus on driving, and to the feel of his family surrounding him inside the car. If he didn't focus, his mind tried to skew sideways, as if on the edge of a dark pit, or deep well like the one in the basement of the old house—a black place where their usual reality no longer took center stage.

He shook his head and focused on utilizing the backup camera. All across the road, pools of slime were drying to crusty lace.

When they were at least a mile past the initial downpour, he finally felt safe enough to stop and put the gear shift into Drive. Rose allowed the children to sit up in the seats, and that's when they began to comment on all the stalled cars dotting the highway.

"Don't look too closely," Drew said. "I think the storm, or whatever made the holes in the sky, killed the people driving those cars." He didn't see anyone outside the cars. There weren't that many on the road in this remote area.

Rose turned around in her seat as they passed a smaller SUV that appeared to have a driver slumped over the steering wheel and a couple of smaller heads barely visible in the backseat. "Shouldn't we stop and check on them?" she asked. "What if they're just hurt?"

Drew shook his head. "Going on intuition here," he said. "I don't think anyone survived that killing noise unless they were deep underground, the way we were."

He knew his wife wanted to argue. She'd never turned her back on a child or person in need in her entire life. But he was driving. There would be no stopping.

Turning away from the Bitty Sloan House, they made it all the way into the small town of Kansas before they saw the first mutilated bodies. That's where they also found another batch of gray-skinned creatures with inside-out tattoos and multifaceted eyes that seemed to see everything and nothing.

Drew drove carefully, avoiding more remnants of silvery birth-puddles drying on the asphalt main street. Directly overhead, another sky-rip fluttered, its torn edges unable to conceal the poisonous yellow-green light illuminating the depths of a blackness far deeper than that of the old well.

"Look at the highlines," he murmured. "Coated with that silvery slime, and the sky, all those holes in the sky." He craned his neck to see upward, but when he glanced at his wife, the tears running down her face alarmed him, so he stopped talking and just concentrated on avoiding the creatures milling about.

As they drove past another stalled vehicle, they saw one of

the monsters drag a body from the car and drop it as if it had lost interest for some reason. Drew wanted to comment on the floating tattoos clearly visible, but he didn't want to alarm his family any more than necessary.

When Rose saw the first body hanging from a tree, being devoured by the jagged silver teeth of one of the pulsating creatures, she said, "That isn't real." Even so, she smashed the kids down into the floor again. This time she didn't let them back up.

Her eyes met Drew's and fourteen years of marriage-language passed between them in a single glance.

It can't be, her eyes said.

It is, his replied.

All over town, creatures trudged along, dragging people by their hair, or by their heads. Bodies of animals and birds lay everywhere, but only the living people were being dragged through the streets. Only the living were being stabbed onto tree branches and sign posts. Only the living. The dead were all untouched.

As they continued through town, Drew said, "What are they? Did you see their tattoos? All those awful words about killing and destroying? So, why aren't they bothering *us*?" He'd told himself he wasn't going to comment, but he couldn't seem to help it.

"Look," Carlos pointed out. "Everywhere the sky is torn open, people are lying dead. It's as if the tearing kills them, and then the creatures stand around and wait on other people to come outside to investigate. That's when they grab them."

They could see the logic of his views. Otherwise, everyone would be dead already.

Rose dried her face with her palms. "So, they aren't bothering us because we were safe inside and didn't run out into their trap?"

"Mo-o-m," Trina whined. "What's going on? Can't we get up? I'm getting sick down here … the *fumes*."

Rose allowed the two kids onto the seat again.

"Ohhh," Milo said. "Look at all the dead birds—and dogs."

Trina began to cry. "Is everything dead?"

Just then, they passed a creature pulling the skin off a living victim.

"What's he doing?" Milo squirmed around in his seat to watch. "Mom, what's that thing doing? I don't—" He turned his head just in time to throw up all over the floormats.

In the mirror, Drew saw the thing dig its fingers into the meaty skinless belly of its victim. Even through the closed car windows, they could hear the screams of agony.

"Don't look!" Rose insisted.

Too late.

Trina threw up as well.

Carlos groaned and covered his mouth with the neck of his shirt.

"Oh my God," Rose cried. "I think I'm going to be sick, too."

Drew drove around more dead bodies and moaning victims with a wild glint in his eye. "I thought if the end came in my lifetime, it would be an organized assault with lasers or nukes or some shit." He clenched his teeth and gripped the steering wheel tighter as a creature turned to stare at them. "I never dreamed it would be this haphazard, hit or miss *mess*." He jammed one hand into his hair. "Look at them! Mostly they don't even seem to know we exist—they only go for the ones that are already helpless, but not dead."

"They *are* robots," Carlos said. "They have to be!"

"Are robots in Revelation?" Rose muttered.

No one answered. Drew drove around another monster and headed toward his parents' rural home on the other side of town.

Along the way, they passed several trees covered with dripping people. The sound of screaming, moaning, *dying* victims was more than he could bear.

Rose crawled into the back seat with the crying children. Carlos crawled into the front passenger seat. Rose found some car cleaning rags in the cargo area and cleaned up the nastiness as best she could. She threw them out the window, something she wouldn't have done for a million bucks before this.

As soon as she was settled, both kids pressed their faces into her shoulders, hands over their ears again. Her face was the chalk white of a Halloween specter. She clutched her children tightly to her sides.

Drew turned on the radio in hopes of drowning out some of

the horrific sounds, but all he got was nothing. He punched the button for the CD player and Vivaldi's "Summer" blossomed into their ears. The stormy violin music drowned out the cries of the people being flayed and eaten alive.

Every few minutes, Drew consciously took stock of where his hands and feet were and what they were doing. His right foot wanted to smash down onto the accelerator with all its might; his hands gripped the molded plastic steering wheel so tightly he thought it might crack. His jaw ached from the constant clenching of his teeth. From the corner of his eye, he could see Carlos. The man's tanned face was splotched with red. Some of it was blood from his ear.

When they drove past The Tiny Tots Daycare, he steeled himself for what he might see lying in the yard or stuck onto playground equipment, but it was blessedly empty. Closed because of the holiday weekend.

Driving on, Drew finessed the SUV around stalled cars and knots of creatures. *Thank God the Pathfinder isn't low to the ground,* he thought as he went up on sidewalks and accidentally drove over dead bodies lying here and there. Everything had happened so quickly he hadn't had time to think about the horrors occurring all around them. People dead, people being stuck onto tree branches and fence posts, screaming—

He snapped off the CD player when they reached the outskirts of town.

"It's so quiet away from town," Carlos whispered. "I can't believe the world is ending like this."

Drew shook his head. "It's not ending," he said. "We're still here." He caught Rose's gaze in the rearview mirror. "There are lots more people, somewhere."

She looked into his mirror-eyes. "After we check on your parents, let's head to Copper Lake and see about mine."

Drew nodded. "We'll check Carlos's family, too." He looked at the Realtor again. "Just tell us where to go."

"Yes," Carlos said. "We're going the right direction. Yellow Bend. My wife and daughter. I need to get there, not thinking clearly. Please. Let's go."

Drew nodded. "God. What a weapon."

Carlos didn't say anything, but later, he would tell them he agreed, this must be the newest weapon from somewhere. "Extra-terrestrial or man-made right here on earth," he would go on to say. "Doesn't matter, it's high tech in a B-movie sort of way."

He cleared his throat, examined the sky. "Do you think more are coming?" He glanced at Drew. "I mean, can you go any faster? Yellow Bend is at least an hour the other side of Copper Lake."

CHAPTER FOURTEEN

Rose

Drew's parents were fortunate. The force of the universe ripping open killed them in their front garden. They had been weeding the flowerbeds. His father still clutched a trowel in one hand. His other hand was pressed to his chest.

His mother had fallen face-first into her beloved petunias.

Drew gasped when he saw his mom like that. Then a harsh bray of sorrow burst from his chest, and he reached out and turned her over, wiping a clot of dirt from the corner of her mouth with his thumb.

He closed her eyelids and gathered her into his arms. Visions of Christmas cookies and game day snacks and spit-finger touch ups of his cowlicky hair on Sunday mornings flooded his mind.

The kids didn't get out of the car.

Rose tried to keep their eyes turned the other direction. The only dealings they'd had with death—until now—had been the passing of their beloved old dog, Argus, who had died of heart failure.

"Here," Drew opened the back door of the SUV and thrust the garden hose inside. "Drink. Wash out the car, whatever." His eyes were wild. "Carlos, I need your help." He didn't wait for an answer.

The Realtor exited the vehicle cautiously.

Drew turned on the water hose, and a rush of tepid water poured forth. Rose took it, stuck her lips into the flow, then offered it to the children. After quenching their thirst, she tried to eliminate the smell from the SUV. Both kids climbed into the front seat while she was doing it. Neither of them looked at what their dad and Carlos were doing.

After a few minutes, the water stopped. The water well pump was electric. The water in the storage tank was now gone, and there was no electricity to pump more. Gravity had done all it could.

That seemed to frighten Rose as much as anything. No electricity, no running water, no life-as-we-know-it. She tried to hide the tears of panic building behind her eyelids again. One more thing and the dam would burst. Maybe she wouldn't be able to plug it next time.

She murmured, "There's a water well in the basement of the old house. Was there a bucket attached to that pulley?" She wasn't speaking to get answers. She seemed to be formulating a plan.

While Rose worried about water sources, the men carried the bodies of her mother-in-law and father-in-law into the house and tucked them into their bed. She got out and followed them partway into the house, but not far enough to let the children out of her sight. They were all running on pure instinct—act and react.

"When this horror show ends," Drew's voice cracked. "I'll come back and bury them properly." He later told her he'd been amazed at how lightweight his folks were. As if age had already prepared them to fly away.

Carlos pulled the comforter up to Mrs. Branson's neck and made the sign of the cross. It appeared his mind was just coming around to reality. As if the tuba sounds in the cellar had damaged his hearing and maybe something else. Maybe thinking of his wife and child ignited a fire inside him. Or lit a fuse. He suddenly seemed ready to explode, his hands and eyes in constant movement.

Drew's face was slick with tears, his eyes streaming without pause. "C'mon." He plucked a set of keys off a cup hook hidden in the closet behind his father's good suit. "Gun cabinet," he said, leading the way down the hall to the den. "I'm not sure what's going on, but I know we need all the protection we can get."

Rose let the men gather the guns while she went back to the car with the kids.

There were two shotguns, a deer rifle, and several boxes of shells to go with them. They also had a couple of handguns his folks had bought for protection after they retired.

Gathering all the weapons, with help from Carlos, Drew stopped in the doorway and surveyed the scene in the front yard.

Now that his parent's bodies were gone, everything looked serene—except for their old beagle, Snoopy. His body lay half-in, half-out of the shadow of the rose bush. Dead birds also dotted the lawn, and he even saw a dead squirrel at the edge of the garden.

He and Carlos looked at each other.

"Looks like this thing is killing the animals, too."

"We were underground," Carlos said. "Think that's what saved us." His glance fell on the squirrel and the garden. "Rabbits live underground. Maybe there will be rabbits, somewhere."

He and Drew loaded the guns and ammo into the cargo area of the Pathfinder. Drew saved one shotgun and a box of shells and put them in the front passenger seat.

A plan had started to form in his mind.

He backtracked to the kitchen, retrieved all the plastic grocery bags he could find, and loaded up every bit of canned and boxed food he could carry.

He emptied the freezer and refrigerator as well.

Carlos came in to see what was keeping him, and without a word, he went through the house and gathered as many pillows and blankets as he could carry.

He avoided the master bedroom, but he did take all the towels and washcloths from the guest bath. As a last thought, he laid a thick towel on the counter and added all the toiletries he could carry. Shampoo, soap, conditioner, shave creme, and Band-Aids. Then he opened the medicine chest and scooped out all the old people's liniments and salves—plus the prescription bottles he found there.

Both men were playing by ear. Neither knew for certain they would need all or any of this stuff; they just had a vague notion that things might grow scarce. Better safe than sorry.

At the car, they handed the kids all the pillows, blankets, and towels. They accepted them wordlessly. The groceries went into the cargo area where the guns and ammo were stored.

Before he got into the driver's seat, Drew went back and retrieved the red five-gallon gas can from the garage. He was a little worried about how they would get gas for the vehicle if the power was off everywhere.

He used his pocketknife to cut a length of garden hose, which he used to siphon gasoline from his dad's old Chevy right into the gas can. He'd never had to get fuel that way before, but he'd heard about it, knew other guys who had done it, but when he put his lips to the end of the hose and sucked, the first cold, acrid mouthful of gas hit the back of his tongue, and he began to cough and sputter.

Drew yanked the hose out of his mouth losing precious liquid all over the ground before coming to his senses and sticking the thing into the gas can, hawking and spitting on the ground until all the taste and all his saliva was all gone.

It was only when he'd picked up the hose to cut it to a manageable length, that he realized he hadn't turned off the water faucet, the flow had just quit on its own.

That gave him a moment's pause, just as it had Rose. But Drew didn't stop to mull it over. He just screwed the lid on the gas can and hurried back to the SUV.

The container went into the cargo hold along with the other things they'd gathered. The hold was now packed to the ceiling with all the odds and ends. At the last second, he ran back and retrieved the length of hose—in case they had to get more gasoline on the road—then he locked the door of the house and closed the garage.

"On to Copper Lake," he said. It was a small resort town about eighty miles away. Rose's parents had bought some land, built a small cabin, and retired there a little over a year earlier. It's where they'd spent the Memorial Day holiday just a couple days earlier.

"Maybe it will be a safe place," Rose murmured as they headed out. "Maybe they are okay."

Drew heard the desperation in her voice, saw the despair in

her eyes. He felt the helplessness that only a husband and father can feel when he can't fix things for his family.

She reached across the console and took his hand. Carlos had somehow wound up in the backseat with the kids. He closed his eyes and leaned his head back.

Milo shifted one of his pillows onto Carlos's lap.

The man smiled and stuffed it behind his head gratefully. Milo took his other pillow and placed it on Carlos's knee, laid his head on it, and closed his eyes.

"Guess I'm not the only one who's wiped out," Carlos murmured, patting the boy's back to let him know it was okay.

A single tear slipped from the corner of Milo's eye. It pooled in the curve of his nostril, but Milo didn't seem to notice.

Drew turned the CD player back on, and Vivaldi's violins moved into "Spring" as they headed toward the interstate and the tiny camping and resort town of Copper Lake.

Turned out the lakeside resort town pine trees made excellent people-hangers.

The creatures went from low-hanging branch to low-hanging branch, bleeding and eating their fill.

It appeared the entire population of the village now hung from the trees like sides of beef in an open-air slaughterhouse.

Drew was worried his wife might have a stroke. She couldn't seem to look away no matter how horrific each scene unfolded as they drove down Main.

"Cover your eyes," he instructed as they neared her father's cabin several miles outside town, up a mountainous road.

Even before they turned into the drive, Drew could see that her parent's fate was the same as his had been. "Thank God they didn't suffer," he said, imagining them stabbed onto pine branches and left to bleed out like so many of the townspeople.

He drove past the driveway a bit, just as he'd done at the Bitty Sloan house that first night, so he stopped at the edge of the drive and shoved the Pathfinder into reverse. In his mind he was already gathering her poor parents, tucking them into their bed the way he'd done his own, but as he was visualizing exactly what needed to be done, something changed.

He pressed his foot down on the accelerator.

Nothing happened.

Gazing out the passenger window, concentrating on the bodies of his in-laws in the yard, Drew hadn't noticed the knot of creatures under the shadowed trees near the front of the vehicle.

When he jerked his head around to see what had hung them up, he saw that two of the amorphous creatures had simply stepped out of the dense copse of pine and grasped the Nissan's right front fender. He pushed the gas pedal harder, a knee jerk reaction.

The vehicle didn't move.

Spam in a can, Drew thought. *Just Spam in a can.* He tromped the gas. The SUV's tires bit into the gravel road and churned up white dust that made it even more difficult to see what was happening.

Rose uncovered her eyes and screamed.

Carlos's eyes flew open.

Two more creatures were headed their way.

Adapting, Drew thought. *Learning how to catch the live ones. Us.* He handed Carlos the box of shells and the shotgun he'd placed at Rose's feet.

"Hurry," he clicked the button to make sure all the doors were locked. *Like it would matter once they figured out that they can simply punch through the window and pluck us out.*

Trina and Milo rose from their little nests and began to scream.

More and more creatures appeared out of the forest. Their skin-words pulsed faster the more agitated they became.

"My window!" Carlos yelled.

Drew pushed the button to lower it.

Carlos stuck the shotgun out and fired at the two holding the front fender.

Both things fell back. One was missing an arm, the other half its head. Cloudy word-filled fluid gushed out of the creature's wounds.

"Go!" Rose squealed.

The blanket of dust grew thicker as the tires dug in and the trap was broken. The Pathfinder shot backward as if propelled from a cannon of dirt.

Creatures began to come after them, their elbows bent at forty-five-degree angles, their knees rising and falling in piston-like rows—*automatons*, Drew thought, *just like Carlos said. They don't run, but they hurry in tandem.*

He crushed the brake, slapped the gear shift from reverse to drive, spun the steering wheel to turn onto the highway, and careened back down the mountain and onto Main Street, turning the other direction at the corner. Heading out of town.

Behind them, a thick mass of black liquid oozed out of one of the sky-rips. It slithered to earth and enveloped the injured creatures before dissolving into buzzing, black, locust-like-insects that winged their way right back up into the broken sky, sealing the edges of blue behind themselves in a dark, raggedy scar.

Once the humans were safely outside town, the creatures thinned and seemed to disappear. "What the hell was that?" Drew said.

He slowed his speed to conserve gas.

The five of them threw out ideas like loud confetti, everyone talking, no one listening.

Rose wanted to go back and make sure her parents were dead, not just hurt. Drew assured her they were gone.

The kids wanted to go home, Rose wanted that, too. But Carlos quietly told them he was going on to Yellow Bend.

Drew noticed the man's fingers tighten their hold on the shotgun, but he didn't think anyone else noticed. He wasn't certain Carlos even realized it, but in his place, Drew knew he would go to extremes to check on his wife and kids, too.

He told Rose and the kids they would go home after they took Carlos to check on his family the way they'd promised.

No one argued.

Carlos's fingers relaxed. It was only another hour to his place. Maybe less since there was no traffic. "We can't be the only ones alive," he murmured. "We *can't* be."

Drew wanted to ask if his house had a cellar, or basement, but he didn't want to raise the tension level inside the SUV. It was high enough already.

"What were those insects?" he asked instead.

In a dreamy voice, one hand touching the crucifix and the other still on the shotgun, Carlos replied, "Locusts ... like in Revelation. It is said that God will send a plague of locusts to devour everyone who doesn't have the seal of the Lord upon their forehead."

He did not tell them that the mentioned locusts were said to be like winged horses, with hair, tails, and breastplates. Locust-horses who served a named king. Perhaps Carlos forgot that part, or possibly he just wasn't processing things the way he usually did.

Drew wondered, again, if the sounds that had brought them to their knees had done something else to Carlos besides affect his hearing. He seemed *out there* now. But then, why wouldn't he be a little wonky? It's a wonder any of them could string two words together.

"Hey," Drew said. "I'm not very knowledgeable about religion, but I do feel we were safer in the cellar of the old house. "Maybe we'll get Carlos's family and go back there, try to figure out what we're going to do next—"

"We're bound to find places that haven't been touched by this," Rose said.

Drew nodded. "I think so, too. But if even the satellite radio has been knocked out, along with every other radio station, then I don't know. I just don't know."

"We have to go back to the tunnels," Rose said.

"Yes," her husband agreed. "If they come again, and we are outside," he let the idea sink in. "We'll wind up like our folks." He thought that idea would hurt more when he said the words, but surprisingly it didn't. In fact, it was almost a relief to know they hadn't suffered like the others they had seen.

Milo's voice was barely more than a squeak. "Why do some people die right away?" he asked.

Drew shook his head. "It's only my theory, but I think if you are outside when the sky rips open, force is so great it just stops your heart, disrupts the electrical signals or something." He looked at his son. "At least it seems to be painless." *Maybe we should try to make sure we are outside when that happens. At least then we might not be mutilated and hung up to dry.*

He looked at his eight-year-old son, the one who was tough on the baseball field, but tender where everything else was concerned. *I can't tell him why we should die outside. Before this, the greatest thing he had to worry about was whether he might get a new glove for his birthday.*

Within the hour, they were pulling up to the rural home Carlos shared with his young wife and daughter. It was a few miles outside Yellow Bend, New Mexico. They passed a sign giving the actual distance, but Drew didn't pay much attention. Carlos told him exactly where to go, where to turn.

When they pulled into the drive of the neat white house outside town, Carlos opened the door before the car had even come to a stop. He dashed up the porch steps and into the house without a word or backward glance.

Drew looked at his wife as if searching for some protocol for the situation. But her eyes held no answers. Both their gazes searched the green yard for signs of a young woman or child. There were no bodies.

"I'd better go see—" Drew started to say, but he was interrupted by the slap of an old-fashioned screen door from the rear of the house. In the eerie silence of no traffic, all other sounds carried supernaturally clearly.

Drew opened his car door just as a guttural scream tore apart the silence.

"Nooo," the voice cried. "Addie, my *Addie*. Please God, no."

When Drew rounded the corner of the small home, he saw Carlos doing his best to gently wrest a small body off a broken tree branch. The tip of the branch protruded below the child's collar bone. With a cry of horror, Drew ran to help.

Rose clapped a hand over her mouth. "Oh, my God," she uttered. "Oh, Drew—"

Drew looked around at his wife's shocked face. "Bring blankets," he commanded. "Hurry!" His voice went up a notch, "But not the kids. Don't bring the kids back here."

Rose backed away, eyes wide, hands still clasped across her mouth. She could see that Drew and Carlos were doing their best not to hurt the poor damaged body any more than necessary. But there was so little left. Only thin strips of flesh and tangled strands of dark brown hair clinging to the shining narrow bones.

The child's mother lay beneath the tree. Her remains appeared to have slipped off the downward facing branch after the monsters had flayed the flesh from her bones.

After a moment, it occurred to Rose that Carlos might have seen his wife first. He might have yanked her off the broken branch and then spied his daughter nearby.

Rose put a hand to her stomach and willed herself not to retch.

The kids wanted to know what was going on.

"Just lock the doors and stay still until I come back." She grabbed two blankets from the stack Carlos had brought from her in-law's house. "I'll be right back—"

"What is it, Mommy?" Milo pleaded. "Why are you crying?"

Rose smoothed her fingers across her cheek, surprised to find it wet with tears. "It's Carlos's family," she said. "They didn't make it."

She ran back to the edge of the woods with the two blankets. The men had both bodies down and Carlos cradled them in his lap as he sat on the ground.

Drew took a blanket and knelt beside him. The smell of the remains was strong. Drew thought this must be the smell of death—bloody, dark, sickening. Beneath it was another smell he couldn't identify. He thought it must be the odor of the damp black soil beneath the leafy trees.

But as he took the small body, to wrap it in the blanket, Drew couldn't help noticing that what he thought was rich black soil was mostly a deep layer of dead insects and birds. *They must have been knocked right out of the trees,* he thought.

Rose helped him wrap the child. Then she placed the other blanket across the body of the woman Carlos held. She also had dark brown hair—what was left of it—but even now Rose could see how entire tufts of it had been ripped out, right out of the scalp in the few places where it still clung to the skull. Her intestines glistened in the dirt. Rose turned her head to the side. "I'm sorry," she said. "So sorry, Carlos."

He didn't look up, didn't seem to notice. He simply tucked the edges of the blanket around his wife's tattered form and pressed her even closer to his chest.

CHAPTER FIFTEEN

Some invisible line ...

They helped Carlos bury his loved ones in the loose soil of the flower bed his wife had filled with spring flowers only a few weeks earlier. It didn't take long.

Milo and Trina were allowed to come and help pat the earth into place when they were finished. Drew said a prayer, but Carlos could not join in even though he gripped the tiny gold cross at his throat the entire time Drew spoke.

After the prayer, Carlos went to the Nissan, climbed into the back seat, and closed the door. He did not go back inside his house.

"I wonder if I should go inside and get some clothes for him." Rose glanced down at herself. She felt dirty even though she hadn't touched either of the bodies. Carlos and Drew, on the other hand, were both sticky with blood and redolent with gore.

Drew went to the SUV, opened the door, and spoke with Carlos. Their conversation was too low for the others to hear.

Rose pulled her own children close, saying a silent prayer of thanks that they had not been made to suffer such agonizing deaths. What had started out to be a hopeful real estate excursion had turned into a nightmare from which they could not escape. Rose thought back to the picnic in the roadside rest area on the way to the Bitty Sloan House. She couldn't believe it had only been a few hours earlier.

Drew strode over. "He said we were welcome to anything in the house." He glanced at the neat little dwelling. "I'll just run in

and get a couple of shirts and jeans or whatever I can find for him."
He shook his head. "Later, we'll go to our house for more clothes."
He felt his teeth clench. "But right now, I'd feel safer going straight
back to the old Bitty Sloan House."

Rose nodded. "I thought that strange feeling I had when I
first saw the house meant that we should own it." She looked at
her kids, then glanced toward the fresh graves in the flowerbed. "I
never dreamed it would save our lives."

Drew's head snapped up. "Thank God, you talked me into
that viewing." He turned toward the three-step porch. "I won't be
but a minute."

He waited, but Rose and the kids didn't move. Drew gave
his wife a tiny push toward the Nissan. "Go on, now. Get in the
car." He waited to make certain they were going. Then he turned
and cleared all three steps in a single bound. "I've got one of those
feelings right now," he muttered to himself. "It's telling me we need
to get back to that old house as soon as possible."

He pulled open the storm door, stepped inside—ignoring the
shower of shiny flakes of dried slime that drifted down from the
door frame when he pulled it open—and went straight down the
hallway to the largest of the two bedrooms.

Inside the closet he found several pair of pressed blue jeans
and corresponding button-down shirts. He grabbed two of each,
then turned and scooped t-shirts, socks, and underwear from the
nearby bureau before rushing out. The walls had begun to close
in around him. They hadn't seen any more of the monsters since
his in-laws' home, but he knew they were out there, and now, he'd
seen what they did to people.

Drew resisted the urge to go through the kitchen cupboards in
search of food, instead, he hurried back to the Nissan Pathfinder
where Rose and the kids appeared to be trying to comfort Carlos.

He opened the back door, handed Carlos a clean t-shirt and
jeans, then went back to the rear of the vehicle and stowed the
rest in the overflowing cargo area. He'd left the back door open on

purpose. Now, he watched as Carlos stepped out, looked down at himself, and suddenly began to yank off his clothing.

Drew was proud of his family when they all looked the other direction.

In moments, Carlos had changed his clothes and left the others in a heap beside the car. Drew handed him a bottle of water they'd taken from his parents' home barely two hours earlier.

Carlos took the water, bent over at the waist, and poured the liquid over his head. It sluiced down his face when he straightened again. "Thank you," he said. "I can't believe—" his gaze roamed back toward the flowerbed, then toward the broken trees. "I can't—"

Drew put his hand on the Realtor's shoulder. "I'm so sorry, man."

Carlos nodded, then he stepped over his pile of filthy clothes and got back into the rear seat with Milo and Trina.

Drew closed the overhead gate and rounded the corner of the Pathfinder. He could see the two kids patting Carlos on the arms and shoulders. As he crawled into the driver's seat, he glimpsed Milo push the pillow back into Carlos's lap. The grieving man took it and leaned over to kiss the top of Milo's head.

Drew blinked away tears as he put the Nissan in Reverse and backed out of the driveway. He watched the neat, white house grow smaller and smaller in his rearview mirror. The fresh graves were visible until a dip in the road made them disappear.

Several miles on, Rose took his free hand and held it in hers. She didn't release it until the Bitty Sloan House was in sight. When they slowed to go around stalled vehicles, Rose no longer glanced their way, nor did she mention stopping to check on possible victims. She'd had her fill of death and gore. Or so it seemed.

As he drove, Drew noticed how this part of New Mexico was bordered by tall pine forests, but the trees did not encroach upon the highway. These forests seemed polite, as if giving travelers their space. Nevertheless, he could see broken branches hanging down. He could see bodies on the ground below the branches, but not many. Most of the dead were still in their cars and trucks. He understood that some killing force had stopped them in their tracks. What he didn't understand was why some folks had been pulled out and hung in the trees while others had not.

They passed the exit to Yellow Bend, going the opposite way this time, but once again, they didn't take it. They weren't going into town. They were going back to the big house outside Kansas, that odd place that had saved them.

Every now and then Drew glanced at Carlos in the rearview mirror. He'd been afraid the man was going into shock at first, but so far, he seemed to be hanging on. Milo had squeezed up against him before falling asleep. Drew thought perhaps the human contact was helping to keep them both grounded somehow.

It wasn't until they were back in Kansas that he noticed the slime that had birthed the monsters had now dried to a crinkly sheen on everything. He recalled the dust-like flakes that had showered him when he opened the door to Carlos's neat white house. He ran his fingers over his scalp, ruffling his own dark brown hair, hoping he wasn't covered with the alien stuff. But he didn't have time to contemplate, the old mansion came into view with the sun setting behind it.

"Any other time, I would be begging you to stop and let me take a picture," Rose said, gazing at the fiery display of color on the western horizon. "Can you believe nothing works? No phones, no radio, nothing?"

Drew nodded. "And yet the sun is setting the same as always. I wonder if life goes on in other places?" He switched on the radio again, to make certain nothing had changed. It was still deafening silence and nothing more.

"Maybe the sun won't rise tomorrow," Rose said. "Maybe this is really the en—"

Drew squeezed her fingers, causing her to stop talking and look at him. He cut his eyes toward the back seat without turning his head.

She got the message. No use spelling out the worst-case scenario for those little ears back there. Whatever would happen would happen whether they worried about it or not. Rose squeezed his fingers. *At least we're all together,* the gesture seemed to say.

After skirting the same half-dozen wrecked vehicles as before, they drove up the bumpy, rutted drive to the old mansion's garage door. Carlos got out of the back seat and ran to raise the overhead. Halfway there, he paused to stare at the flaming sky. Drew wondered what he was thinking. Was he cursing God for the suffering of his family?

Even as they watched, Carlos raised his gold cross to his lips, kissed it, and made the sign of the cross as if he'd just said a prayer.

Drew saw Rose shiver. The man's faith in the face of what he'd just experienced was difficult to fathom.

After kissing the cross, Carlos strode to the garage and raised the door. Drew drove the Pathfinder straight inside, and Carlos closed it behind them.

The connecting kitchen door stood open at the top of the cement steps.

Drew tried to recall if they'd left it that way. He thought it odd they would leave it wide open, but they'd been in such a hurry to get away, he couldn't rightly say.

Nevertheless, something about it disturbed him. He shot a glance at Carlos. "Did we leave it that way?"

Carlos shrugged, but neither of them said what they were thinking. If anything was in the house, they would deal with it. Half an hour after they'd left his house near Yellow Bend, Carlos had loaded every gun. Then he'd begun quietly instructing Rose and the kids on how to use each one. Drew thought it might've been his mind's way of coping with the horror of finding his wife and child slaughtered like that.

Telling Rose and the kids to stay put for a bit, Drew and Carlos scouted the interior of the house. They found nothing. Apparently, the things didn't stick around if they found no human flesh in need of devouring.

Drew shook his head when that thought hit his brain. *Have I gone over? Crossed some invisible line between sane and insane? Am I really locked up in a strait jacket in a padded room somewhere?*

CHAPTER SIXTEEN

Rose

After they unloaded the car and brought everything inside, Rose and Drew took the kids and followed Carlos back down to the cellar tunnels. They snacked on some of the packaged food they'd brought, more for something to do rather than to stave off hunger, and then they cautiously settled in for the night.

"I feel safe down here," Rose said. The others nodded and continued making their pallets with pillows and blankets. They all slept near one another in a loose group, the kids snuggled up between their parents, Carlos just at the edge. She never thought they would sleep, but then Carlos began to murmur The Lord's Prayer, and it soothed them all. By the time he'd said it through a couple more times, interspersed with a few Hail Marys, Rose realized he was reciting the Rosary.

In the night, Rose awoke several times, certain she'd heard something trying to get inside the cellar. Each time she awoke, she would find Drew sitting up, watching. He would pat her and hug her and let her know everything was all right.

The last time she woke, Rose found that Milo had silently made his way closer to Carlos. He'd wrapped himself up and wiggled around until his back was as close to the Realtor as he could get. She couldn't believe her little boy was so empathetic to their new friend's devastating loss. Maybe losing both sets of his grandparents that way had made them partners in grief.

Maybe it has made us all partners in grief, she thought.

After another hour of dozing in and out, she convinced Drew to close his eyes and allow her to keep watch for a while.

It wasn't long before the others began to stir. Soon, they were all awake and anxious to make their way back upstairs to begin the arduous task of securing the broken windows. In some unspoken agreement, the three adults had decided the Bitty Sloan House was now their communal home. At least for the time being.

They crept out of their cellar bedroom like little mice, as quiet and meek as possible. Everything they'd experienced the day before came back to haunt them on their short trek through the tunnel and up the stairs to the kitchen. At least it seemed that way to Rose. Her flesh was a mass of goose bumps and her mind a whirl of gory images.

After what they'd recently witnessed, the lovely many-windowed drawing room and parlor appeared to be much less secure than before.

After a short discussion, they began to work feverishly, gathering wood and objects with which to cover the doors and windows.

"Do we need to board-up those on the third floor?" Rose asked. "The view is incredible; we can see if anything is coming for miles and miles. And I don't see how those things could get in way up there." She swiped sticky bangs off her forehead. Without the draw of air through the living room, the heat had become nearly overwhelming.

Drew halted in his efforts of dismantling the dining room chairs. They were using anything and everything they could find to nail across the windows and doors. "I think we need to leave those third-floor windows open to let in some air. What do you think, Carlos?"

"Si," he agreed. "Maybe even the second floor?"

Rose shook her head. "Those monsters are tall. I don't like the idea of them being able to even *almost* reach those windows. I mean if one got on the roof of the porch—"

"I see what you mean," Carlos said. "Thank God I found this coffee can full of old nails down in the basement—"

"Why is it sometimes called a basement and sometimes a cellar?" Milo asked, sticking the head of a ten-penny nail between his lips the way Carlos did.

The Realtor stopped and looked at his little buddy, then shrugged. "I don't even think about it. They're both underground, so I just say whichever one comes to my mind."

That seemed to satisfy Milo who took up his hammer and began to pound away at the nail he'd been holding.

After a couple more hours, all the downstairs windows had some sort of wood nailed over them. There had been a stack of two by fours in the garage, and a sheet of plywood, but Rose thought it was too thin. She'd begged Drew to reinforce it with the two by fours and bed slats from the antique beds. Of course, he'd complied.

They'd also resorted to using the legs from the tall bar stools that had been in the dark and cozy wet bar. But using furniture legs had been tough. The nails weren't long enough to go through the sturdy legs, so they had to drive them in at an angle and then bend them over the curve. It was tricky. And it took twice as many nails.

In her head, Rose also gave thanks to God for sending them to this crazy house with the safe tunnels in the basement and the life-saving indoor water well. Now she added her thanks for the red Folger's can full of ten-penny nails.

She never asked why they were being made to suffer this horrendous invasion. Rose had been brought up to believe stuff happened, and you dealt with it. Her folks had been like the furniture legs and bed slats—sturdy, and no nonsense. She let the tears roll down her face again when she thought of them. And then she gave thanks once more that her folks hadn't been made to suffer the way so many others had suffered.

After the first-floor windows were done, the whole crew moved up to the second floor. "Now, we will only come and go through the garage," Rose said. "Right?"

"That's right," Carlos replied. "Feels a little claustrophobic, but what else can we do?"

Rose nodded. "Reminds me of that old black and white zombie movie, *Night of the Living Dead*." She shivered. "Even though it was in black and white, it terrified me—"

"These things might be futuristic zombies. They move like robots, eat flesh, they're hard to kill—"

"—umm, hey, buddy," Drew indicated Milo with a tilt of his head.

The boy's eyes were way too large for his face.

Carlos got the message. "Sorry, man." He opened the large chest of drawers and started dismantling the long front pieces for wood to nail across the second-floor windows.

Drew clasped his shoulder. He didn't seem to know what to say.

"There are a lot of windows in this house," Trina said, plopping down on a second-floor guest room bed. Her hair stuck to the back of her neck, and her brother had smashed her finger between two boards. She stuck the end of the injured digit in her mouth, tears drying on her cheeks.

Rose shot a sympathetic look at her daughter, then stood in front of one of the few uncovered windows. "I really think they've all moved on." Her expression was hopeful.

"I don't know about that." Drew's face was harder to read in the remaining light. "Better safe than sorry, I say."

Carlos pressed his lips into a thin line. "I'm not sure either. But I feel better with everything nailed." He inclined his head toward the downstairs. "I found a long wrench and jammed it in the garage-door roller. Nothing will come in through there. Of course we'll have to unjam it to drive out later."

He picked up an old-fashioned candle in a tin holder. "These were part of the staging." A shadow of emotion crossed his face. "Man. Everything, gone in an instant. We didn't know how good we had it." His voice grew fainter toward the end of his sentence. Then he shook himself, more like a shiver. "Anyhow, I'm sure glad all this stuff is here. Maybe there are some more candles around." He cleared his throat and swiped at his face with the side of one hand. "It sure is dim in here, without the light from the windows."

"We'll go through the pantry and cupboards," Rose said. "I think I saw a lantern." She turned toward the door as the two men rallied themselves and began to nail the drawer parts over the window. "Hey," she said. "You also had a big flashlight when we were down in the cellar."

Carlos nodded, nails sticking out of his clenched lips like spiky quills. "Yes ma'am," he mumbled. "We had it when we came upstairs. After that, I'm not sure."

Drew paused; hammer poised above a nail. "I brought it up, didn't I?"

Carlos nodded.

"I remember bringing it, and then there was such a shock when we opened the garage door." He was obviously thinking back, trying to recall what he'd done with the big light. "It must be in the Pathfinder somewhere. I can't imagine I would've just laid it down."

He drove in another nail and picked up his shotgun. "Think I'll keep watch up here tonight," he said. "I can see out through the gaps, and I won't need a light. It might attract them—like moths." He handed Trina his hammer. "I'm going out to look in the Pathfinder, anyway." As he walked out of the room, he murmured, "Looks like we're going to be here awhile."

The flashlight was not there, but Drew did manage to give the floor mats a more thorough cleaning with dish soap and a pan of water. Rose had been delighted with those gleaming pots and pans hanging on the old-fashioned wrought iron rack over the kitchen island. Drew had simply been amazed at how much detail had gone into staging the place before putting it on the market.

Eventually they all ventured back down to the cellar kitchen and the good, deep well. After everyone quenched their thirst, thanking God for the cold water and the bucket. Rose glanced at her husband. "We were destined to find this house. Remember how it pulled at me when we drove past that night?"

Drew nodded. "As if you were entranced."

She nodded, realizing she and Drew had basically had this same conversation in the car, but needing to repeat it for Carlos's sake anyway.

They were snacking on the packaged foods again, along with some Carlos had brought for the upstairs kitchen. "I had planned to stay here a few days," Carlos told them. "I had another couple of people scheduled to look at the house after you guys. I figured it would also look good, for the staging, you know."

He hesitated, then admitted, "I'd also been told the smell of fresh baked cookies could help sell a home." His glance fell to the floor. "It seems so stupid now."

Rose patted his shoulder. "I don't like to think we were all saved for a purpose, when so many were not, but you just should have seen how this old place grabbed my attention the night we took a wrong exit and wound up passing by."

Carlos touched the gold cross at his throat. "I used to believe in exactly those sorts of things." He made another little throat clearing sound, a ragged noise in the stone-walled cellar. "I'd even convinced myself that this old place was God's way of saying I was on the right track with my new real estate career. It hadn't been that great so far." His shoulders went up and down as he filled another dipper from the bucket at the well. "But I don't know now. I can't see how losing my wife and daughter that way serves any good purpose."

Milo grabbed the man around his waist. "We never know the reasons why," he said. "We're not supposed to know. We're just supposed to do. Isn't that what the Bible always says?"

Carlos broke down. Crumpled to the ground like an ancient scarecrow down from the post. He couldn't seem to say anything. He didn't have to. Milo followed him right to the dirt floor, arms about the man as if he could somehow hold him together.

They wound up in an odd embrace, the older man sobbing, the younger boy just holding him around the neck.

"And a little child shall lead them ..." Rose murmured.

Carlos roused himself a bit. "That's from the book of Isaiah," he said. "Thank you for reminding me." He clutched Milo to his chest and kissed his forehead making the sign of the cross with his other hand. "I've been trying to hold on to my faith. God bless you, my friend," he whispered to the boy.

They both stood and Milo went about getting himself a drink as if nothing had happened.

Trina's eyes were wide in the lamp light.

Drew appeared uncomfortable.

No one knew what to make of the sudden well of empathy embodied by the little boy. To Rose, it felt as if her son—this child of her own womb—had become someone else. She took Drew's hand the way she always did for strength. Or comfort. "Are you sure you want to stay upstairs?"

Drew shook his head. "No, I've changed my mind. I don't want to leave y'all alone. Not for a minute."

The night passed quickly. They were so exhausted they all slept as if entering hibernation.

Rose was thankful there were several distinct rooms in the cellar. They used one just for a bathroom. It wasn't ideal, but they'd found a couple more buckets, and it was better than trying to go upstairs in the middle of the night.

The next morning—they could only tell it was morning by looking at Milo's watch, his pride and joy—they all sat up and looked around, somewhat surprised by their surroundings.

"I'm hungry," Milo said, stretching.

Trina nodded. "Me, too." She dug around in the tote bag her mom had brought from the SUV. "Here's some nuts and muffin thingies."

"Thanks," Milo took the package of muffins from his sister's hand.

"I actually brought eggs and bacon," Carlos said. "But with no power, I'm afraid to cook them. How fast do those things go bad?"

Drew shrugged and stretched. "Even if they haven't gone over yet, I'd be afraid to build a fire. The smoke might attract the monsters." He looked at the ceiling, as if he could see through to the upper floor.

"Right," Carlos agreed. "Who knows where they are or what makes them come?"

He sounds so defeated, Rose thought. And then, as if reading her mind, Milo went to sit beside him, offering him a mini blueberry muffin without a word.

After a few minutes, Rose addressed the elephant in the room. "So," she began, "what is our plan? Are we going to live here from now on or go out and see if the rest of the world is intact?"

"We have to go," Trina said. "This can't be all that's left—" She glanced around at the stone walls and dirt floors of the cellar.

Rose looked at her young daughter. *If my memory is correct, she's about the age Anne Frank was when they had to go in hiding from the Nazis. How awful. And then they were discovered and murdered anyway.* "Maybe Trina's right," she said. "Hiding may be what saved us in the beginning, but we aren't equipped to stay here forever, are we?"

"We could go into the little town of Kansas. See what we can get from the grocery stores," Drew said.

Images of shredded bodies and bloody sidewalks flooded Rose's mind. "I guess so. Do you think it's safe?"

Drew looked at the stout door, wondering if it was safe to even open it. "Do we really have a choice?" he asked. "I mean, you guys could stay down here while I go into town." He glanced at Carlos. "Or the two of us could go—"

Rose held up one hand. "No. Uh-uh. I can't imagine being stuck down here in the dark, not knowing if you're safe. Besides, you aren't going to leave us alone for a minute, remember?"

"Right, right. That's right."

Carlos stood, crossed himself, kissed his small gold cross. "I'm ready." He tousled Milo's hair. "Let's do this thing."

"C'mon," Milo said. "We're burnin' daylight!" He quoted an old John Wayne movie. He was a giant fan of The Duke. Used to watch the old movies on TV with his gramps.

Trina stood and shook out her blanket. "I won't mind a little daylight," she said. "I'm already tired of the cold dark." She pulled her blanket around her. "It doesn't even feel like summer down here. Not even *spring*."

Rose thought back over the last few days. School had barely ended when the world caved in. No wonder the girl couldn't recall if it was summer yet. Technically, it wouldn't start until the third week of June, but in their little corner of the world, spring turned to summer in the blink of an eye.

"All right," she said, pulling her fingers through her wavy hair. "Let's make a little plan. Dad will go first, with us following behind—"

"No offense, Ms. Branson," Carlos said. "I think I'd better go first." He stepped up. "We'll make sure nothing is in the tunnels, then straight up the stairs to the first-floor kitchen. We can peek out the window-gaps on all sides of the house. Make certain the things really have moved on."

Rose nodded, then clasped his forearm. "Sounds like a good plan, but please, call me Rose. I mean, we're family now, right?"

Carlos patted her fingers with a sad expression. "Yes," he said. "Yes, we are."

They trooped up the stairs like kindergartners in a choo-choo line.

Drew couldn't believe how late it was. The morning sun had already climbed high into the sky, too high to see through the slats and scraps they had nailed over the windows. "We really slept, didn't we?"

Rose nodded. She'd held onto the hem of his shirt the whole way up through the tunnels, through the secret door, Carlos in the lead, and up the rough stairs into the kitchen. "God help us, this makes me think of a scene in that old movie *Signs*. Remember that old alien movie with Mel Gibson and River Phoenix?"

"Joaquin," Trina said.

Rose looked at her.

"It was Joaquin Phoenix, not River," Trina said. "I think he died before I was even born."

How do you know so much, Rose wanted to ask, but she knew how. Both her children were sponges. If they ever read anything, it stuck with them. That included movie credits, Wikipedia articles, you name it. And *Signs* was one of their favorite movies. Just the right amount of scary.

Still didn't quite explain how she knew about River Phoenix's untimely demise, but now wasn't the time to delve into that. Everything had been available on the internet until a couple of days ago. *How will we get by without it? How did we before?*

"I can't see the side of the house from these windows," Carlos said. "The garage blocks that side. Maybe if I go upstairs, I can see from the second or third floor."

"Good idea," Drew said. He checked the front and back doors to make sure they were still secure, then the lot of them traipsed up to the second floor, and then the third. At each window, they stopped and peered out.

"I don't see anything," Rose said. "Except those fluttery places in between the puffy clouds."

"They are puffy, aren't they?" Milo replied. "Like everything is okay. Like nothing even happened."

"Trompe l'oeil," Trina said. "Fake but so real you can't tell. Like some major artworks." She shrugged, seemingly embarrassed by her knowledge.

"I don't know where I come up with these things. Our art teacher mentioned it one day. Showed us photos of works that were two dimensional but appeared 3-D because they were painted using trompe l'oeil style." She chewed her lip. "The teacher said it means *trick of the eye* in French."

"I know what you mean, hon," Rose said. "A type of illusion. Now they've got deep fake. That new AI thing. Disgusting. Nothing real anymore." She glanced at one of the sky rips. The edges seemed to flutter constantly. "But if those are fake, they sure are good fakes."

Then she thought, *Nah, those monsters are not fake. Fake monsters don't rip people apart.* As for the big blast of sound and energy that ruined all the cars and electronics, she'd read about EMPs—electromagnetic pulses—before. Nothing new there.

And with all the known hypersonic weapons the ever-changing Axis of Evil had, and all the nuclear bombs and other unknown weapons of mass destruction, this didn't really surprise her. Rose had always been a pragmatist, just like her husband said. What surprised her more than anything was the speed with which it had happened. That, and the supernatural attraction she had felt toward this old house.

It had saved their lives, of that, she had no doubt.

But why?

She thought of the flashes of empathy she'd seen in Milo. Of course, she knew her children were special, gifted in many ways, but was that why they had been spared? No. She wouldn't believe that. All children were special. That was a given.

"It looks like they've moved on," Carlos said, his tone flat, as if he didn't really care one way or the other.

"Yeah," Drew agreed. "I can see everywhere except that one spot directly in front of the garage." He looked again. "It's impossible to see straight down." He began to pull the drawer pieces off the window. "Man," he said. "We nailed these up *good*."

"What are you doing?" Rose stilled his hand.

He shook her off, but lightly. "Going out on the roof so I can make sure it's clear before we drive outta here."

Rose placed her hand on his arm again. "That sounds dangerous. Let's go on down to the garage. I'm sure we can see or at least hear them if any are milling around out there."

Drew looked at Carlos.

"It's a steep pitch," Carlos said, referring to the slant of the old roof.

Drew stopped pulling at the boards. "Maybe you're right. Why would they be right there? They would be trying to get inside, wouldn't they? Not just hanging around, waiting."

He turned toward the door. "I guess it's time. Everyone jump in the Nissan as quickly as possible just like before. When Carlos opens the big overhead, we're taking off. We'll come back here after we get food and supplies unless we think of something better. Everyone on board with that?"

They all nodded.

Except for Milo. He stood at the window, one hand on the board his dad had been pulling on. Milo tested it with his own hand, surreptitiously.

"Come on, son," Drew called. "We stay together, move as one."

Milo peered out through the gap. There was nothing to see but endless prairie and blue sky dotted with those puffy clouds.

CHAPTER SEVENTEEN

Tragedy

When Carlos removed the wrench blocking the overhead roller, the monsters were right there. He'd barely begun to raise the door when strong gray nailless hands grasped the bottom of the door and sent it crashing upward.

Rose had been holding the Nissan's door open so Carlos could hop in, but now she ran at him, grabbing his arm, screaming at him to, *Come.*

Carlos tore toward the Nissan and flung himself inside, but Rose seemed frozen, the whooshing of gray feet suddenly loud in the silence.

"Mom!" Milo screamed. "*Get in.*"

Huge gray hands reached for Rose.

Carlos launched himself from the backseat, shotgun in hand. Everyone heard the *cha-chunk* as he racked a shell. Trina lunged over the seat, intent on going for her mom.

Carlos drew down on the reaching monster.

Ka-Boom!

The blast rattled the metal door and the monster flew backward, halfway outside, a gaping wound appearing in its chest. Cloudy fluid flew from the thing's wound, spewing black letters, opening a sky hole, bringing down the rain. The monster rolled over and dragged itself toward Rose, across the garage floor, intent on its mission.

Trina lunged forward again, determined to get her mom. Drew grabbed her shirt as a second gray creature entered.

Outside, dark rain whooshed, hitting the ground in a shiny, solid torrent, flowing across the drive and into the garage, licking up letters as it came. The stuff belched across the injured monster, shoving it forward just enough to let it latch on to Rose's sneakered foot.

"Drew!" she screamed, finally turning.

Shoving Trina aside, Drew plunged onto the scene, but the monster held her firm, its own feet and legs already gone inside the thick black syrup. Now it was a torso with arms and a huge hole in its chest.

"Help me!" Rose shouted, kicking at the thing with her free foot.

The monster grabbed that foot as if it had only been waiting. It wrenched her down to the concrete floor allowing the gelatinous substance to flow up and over Rose's feet and ankles. She screamed in terror.

Drew grabbed her arm, shouting to Carlos, "Give me the gun!"

Carlos ignored that and fired a blast into the growing crowd of monsters at the door, then he clawed out the spent shells, shoved in two more from his pocket, and ran right up to the half-prone creature, placing the gun directly against the thing's bald gray head.

"Don't hit Rose!" Drew screamed. He pulled on his wife's arm and hands as hard as he could. Her face had gone as gray as the monster, her eyes huge, bulging. Bright red splotches of panic dotted her cheeks.

Milo and Trina screeched at their father to, *Do something*!

The blackness swallowed the grasping creature's torso and arms. It flowed over Rose's legs and halfway up her body. Now, the monster was all gone except for its head and shoulders.

Rose's shrieks echoed off the concrete floor and metal doors. She no longer said words, now it was one long syllable, like a teakettle building to a boil.

Eeeeeeee Eee Eee!

Carlos fired and the black gel leapt over the injured monster's head enveloping both it and Rose in a single gush. Drew fell backwards onto his hands, shock blanching his face of all color. The kids tumbled out of the backseat, grabbing their father, pulling him away.

The gel flowed back toward the door as more and more creatures appeared in the driveway.

An unknown man came running toward the open garage. He'd just crested the small rise at the bend in the drive.

No one had time to worry about him.

Carlos aimed and fired into the knot of monsters coming from the west. Cloudy liquid flew as Drew grabbed Milo and Trina and stuffed them back into the car. "Hold on tight," he commanded, revving the tame engine.

Carlos fired one more shot to distract the black gel toward the wounded things outside.

The monsters scattered, doing their best to avoid the dark mass, which had doubled in size and spread out across the drive and the garage floor sending out narrow tongues of gel in search of the injured, lapping up the dark, still-wiggling words even as it washed across the concrete in a black wave.

Carlos fired his last shell into a creature that appeared out of nowhere. The thing fell inward, wiggling black letters leaking from its head. The thick gel whooshed toward it in a wave, cleaning up the cloudy fluid in record time.

Drew drove over the body, knocking another one out of the way in what seemed a tiny miracle. "C'mon," he shouted.

Carlos fell into the open back door, broke open his shotgun, and shouted, "Go!"

Drew hit the gas, and then let his foot off the accelerator when he saw the man at the top of the hill. He couldn't believe the guy wasn't hiding or going the opposite direction. *Heading right toward us,* he thought. *Is he insane?*

From the backseat, he heard Carlos rack another shell, ready for whatever came next. "See this man?" Drew shouted. "When I get to him, open the door."

Carlos grunted in reply. But the instructions were unnecessary. As they drew even with him, the man grabbed the door handle and slung himself into the front passenger seat. The one where Rose should have been.

"Thank you, kindly." His voice was surprisingly even. "I didn't know if I was going to make it or not." He sounded unconcerned, even though his breathing was short from his dash up the hill. "Name's Dawk," he went on. "Spelled like hawk, with a W." He held out his hand as if for a shake.

Drew shot him a sideways glance. His children were sobbing in the backseat, probably in shock, and the man was making small talk. "We've got to get the hell out of here," Drew said, maneuvering the SUV from side to side to avoid ruts on the hilly drive.

Dawk, dark blond hair slightly wild, turned to look out the back window. "I don't know what y'all did back there, other than the shotgun, but the aliens are leaving. They're heading away from the house across the prairie."

Carlos turned around, too. "He's right. They're all leaving."

Drew slowed, looked over his shoulder. The kids' tears had been reduced to sobs. They clutched each other like little koalas, eyes like holes in their pale, shocked, faces. "They *are* leaving," he said, looking around at Carlos. "Should we go back? We've already boarded up the windows and we've got the well down in the cellar."

"Yeah," Carlos said. "And from the third floor, you can see for miles."

Drew nodded.

The new guy said, "I've read about the Bitty Sloan House." He turned back to the front. "That's why I was headed there. That water well in the basement sounds ideal, the perfect place to hole up, figure things out. I've been haunting libraries in every town I pass through, especially the local history rooms. They tell about all the old places in their towns. Those with basements and water wells."

He smoothed his spiky hair down. Touched a patch of whiskers on his chin. "There are lots of places like that if you know where to find them." He jerked a thumb over his shoulder. "Right down the road, there's a greenhouse, and a horse farm." He shrugged. "I would've checked closer, but I just grabbed a few veggies and came on. Something seemed to be driving me toward the big house."

His glance took in the mansion. "I've come all the way from Southeast Texas. These creatures are everywhere. The sky is shredded there, too. No radio, no satellites, nothing. Just a lot of dead bodies, and a few wandering remainders, like us."

Carlos craned his head toward the rear window again. "Maybe we should go back and make some real plans." He glanced around the area. "Seems a bit foolhardy to rush out with no real plan or destination in mind." He looked at Dawk. "We were just going to make a grocery run. See what we could find, then return."

Drew came to a complete stop and turned the SUV around. His shoulders were tense, his fingers clutched the wheel in a death grip. "Those things just killed my wife." He swallowed hard and grasped the steering wheel tighter. "My kids are falling apart. They also killed Carlos's family and my parents and my wife's parents." He inhaled, shakily, one breath away from a break down. "I'm sure you've suffered some of the same things. Until now, I thought we were the lucky ones." He lowered his foot back to the accelerator, rubbed his forehead as if something in there needed to be wiped away.

He absently allowed the Nissan to wander back up the hill, muttering, "But then they got my Rosie."

The kids' sobbing filled the car. Carlos tried to comfort them, his own loss fresh, still weeping.

The big house loomed over the drive, welcoming them back into its embrace. Drew drove into the still-open garage. There was no sign of the black, gelatinous mass other than a greasy-looking stain on the concrete floor.

"I want Mama," Milo wailed.

Trina hugged him closer. "She's gone, Milo. She's gone."

Carlos climbed out of the backseat, shotgun at the ready. "I'm going to search the house before we go in." He strode to the overhead garage door and yanked it down. The new man helped. Drew opened the door to get out of the car, but he couldn't seem to put his feet out onto the concrete where Rose had just died.

"Carlos, I—" He wanted to say, *I just can't put my feet down and act like nothing happened.* But then he thought of how Carlos had been forced to bury the grisly remains of his own wife. And his little girl.

Carlos stared at him. "You don't think we should search the house?"

Drew took a deep, ragged, breath and forced himself out of the Nissan. He opened the back door to help the kids out. He'd driven as deeply into the garage as he could, so they didn't have to step exactly onto the shadowy area where Rose had been enveloped.

He tucked a child under each arm, pressing them to his sides the way he'd seen Rose do so many times. The sobbing had lessened, but their faces were masks of disbelief, still wet with tears.

They were halfway up the steps to the kitchen door when the sound of helicopters reached his ears. He turned and looked at Dawk across the garage, and then he rushed the kids all the way up and into the house where he could see through the slats covering the windows.

The light outside was broken into chunks as a flock of black helicopters headed toward them from the east. Drew had to strain his neck to see them as they passed directly over the house. The noise rattled the boards covering the windows and the glasses stacked in the cupboard.

"They're low," he muttered. "Maybe they know we're in here."

"Are they here to rescue us?" Milo asked.

"Maybe it's the Army," Carlos said. "Where are they going?"

By now, it was apparent the helicopters were just passing over. They were not landing. They didn't even seem to notice the big house on the hill. The noise shook the earth. It filled Drew with hope and, inexplicably, with fear.

For a moment, everyone stood with their eyes pressed to the slender spaces between the boards. In the far distance, something caught Drew's eye.

The aliens, he thought. *Such a huge gray block I thought it was just a shadow on the land. Didn't even see them until they began to move.*

He coiled his fingers into a fist and peered through the center. Now that he was looking for it, he could just make out the rippling motion of the constantly moving internal tattoos.

As they drew closer, he saw one of the aliens stop. It stood motionless, like one of the Easter Island monoliths, its blank face pointed skyward, eyes glittering in each stray shaft of rising light.

Then the helicopters were gone, and the sky was clear except for a thin ghost of last night's moon. Drew tried to imprint that image onto the backs of his eyelids to block out his own internal tattoo, the horror-movie image of his Rosie, stuck and screaming on the floor of Bitty Sloan's garage.

One by one Carlos, the kids, and even the new guy, backed away from the windows. But not Drew. He couldn't tear his eyes away from those slender spaces between the boards.

He gazed at the marching, milling horde. "Look at them. At first, I didn't even see them. Now they look like they're waiting for someone to yell action." *Of course, they're waiting on directions from … someone. Whoever is directing them. Then another idea struck. Maybe the "directors" are also behind the black gel. An entity created just for cleaning up all the remains because if they don't, we might be able to examine them and learn something.*

His heart began to pump faster as the idea took root. *Remains might give us a clue as to what they are, where they came from. No remains. No evidence.*

Clean it up like a crime scene. Leave no clues behind. Then another thought occurred. *The helicopters aren't looking for monsters, they're right there, a huge block of them. The helicopters are looking for us. We are the rest of the remains that need to be cleaned up.*

He was about to voice his ideas to the group when a huge boom erupted from the direction of the cliff. Carlos immediately covered his head and ears. "Is it another *rip?*" He yelled so hard his voice cracked.

Trina squealed and grabbed Milo, hauling him to the floor.

"Oh, my God," Drew breathed. He yanked away a weaker board. "I think it's the helicopters."

Carlos and Dawk rushed back to the windows.

A tremendous ball of fire rose from the direction of the cliff. "Ohhh," their voices blended into one long tone of disbelief. "They crashed?"

Drew looked back at the monolithic monster that had been

staring after the 'copters. The air rippled. Had it somehow made them crash with lasers from its eyes like some old sci-fi movie?

He visored his hand to shade his vision, then looked around for someone to confirm what he thought. "Did those monsters cause the crash?" His fingers massaged his temples again. *What just happened? Maybe my theory isn't legit after all. Not cleaning up remains at all.*

Trina began crying openly, hands shielding her face. Milo had worked his way out of her grasp and joined his dad and the other men. "What are we going to do?"

They all watched the column of gray as it turned toward the canyon where the helicopters crashed. "Look at them," Carlos said. "Going to check for survivors." His voice was harsh. It made Trina wail louder.

Drew shot him a scathing glance for scaring the kids even more. "I'm sorry, man," Carlos said. "But *look.*"

"What d'you think happened?" Drew murmured. He slid an arm around his daughter to quell her shaking. "How could they just crash like that? The things can't reach them up there, in the sky."

"Why not?" Carlos demanded. "They came out of the sky so maybe some more came through or opened one of those holes and we just can't see it. Hell, maybe something jammed the choppers' signals and made them go down instead of up." He grabbed the small gold cross at his throat and kissed it, made the sign of the cross on his chest as well.

The kids stared at him in horror.

He softened his tone. "Or maybe they just ran out of fuel or something. They could be amateurs—you know, not even experienced pilots. The updraft from that canyon could have knocked one into the other and started a chain reaction that brought them all down."

Drew remained silent.

"I have a thought," the wild-haired man said after a few moments. They all looked at Dawk as if they'd completely forgotten about him. "Now would be a good time to start planning," he said, "while the things are headed away from the house."

Drew nodded. He wanted to ask the man how he'd gotten here so fast. All the way from East Texas. But those were questions for later. "Let's get some food and water, talk while we can."

He looked at his pale-faced children. "We need to stay hydrated. And discuss where we go from here." He knew he wasn't making complete sense. How could any of them make sense after what they'd just experienced?

His built-in guilt gauge refilled itself of its own accord. Went straight to the F for Full. *It should have been me in that garage. I should have been outside the car in harm's way, not my Rosie. Not the kids' mother.*

Carlos started toward the kitchen. "You know what we've got to do first, don't you?" His face was immobile, resolute.

Drew dragged the sides of his hands across his face to scrape away the pain. "We've got to search the entire house. Make certain." He glanced at his traumatized children. *Make certain they're safe. Just do that for now. Worry about the fallout from all this later.*

Carlos didn't say anything for a long moment. "I think so. Yeah. I think we're safe, but it does seem strange how that one kept looking up. Gave me the willies, I don't mind saying."

"Yeah," Drew said. "Just make sure we're safe. Better safe than sorry."

CHAPTER EIGHTEEN

Third floor

After the search, a reverse of the choo choo train with Rose only a few hours earlier, they wound up back in the kitchen. The house appeared safe. No lurking monsters.

Once they reconvened and drank glass after glass of cool well water, Dawk pulled a few battered veggies—tomatoes, green onions, a bell pepper—out of his voluminous pockets. "My contribution." He placed the colorful treasures on the table. "From the greenhouse. I accidentally broke the door glass trying to get it open. Probably need to fix it soon. Keep out the bugs."

He glanced around. "We also need to learn how to plant and grow. Maybe get some books. We'll need this knowledge when we start our new communities."

"Glad you have hope," Carlos said. "My abuela could grow anything down there in Mexico. Her shelves were lined with canned food—in jars, you understand—that's something else we need to learn how to do." His voice softened. "My wife, she knew how. She knew everything, all the old ways like Abuela." Features twisting in pain, he added, "I wonder if I have any family left?" As always, his fingers found the cross at his throat, caressing it as he spoke.

The kids were busy opening chips and didn't seem to be paying attention, until Trina said. "Glad you have hope for what?"

Drew's heart jumped in his chest. He kept his hands busy pouring water over the cherry tomatoes and green onions Dawk had brought. "Hope for an end to this mess, sweetie. There's always hope. We'll make plans, figure out where to go—"

Trina didn't seem to accept that. "Dad. They're aliens. They're here to take over. What are we supposed to hope for?" She stopped, seemingly shocked at the way she had spoken to her father in front of everyone.

But he didn't scold her, so she continued, "How can a whole thing, even a robot, just appear out of nowhere and start grabbing people?" She gulped air, swallowed. "How do we have hope with those monsters around, and that black stuff that ate Mom?"

Drew caught her in his arms as she crumpled.

She buried her face in his chest. "Maybe it's CGI," she said. "Green screen stuff, and we're all just special effects."

Her dad held her close. He suspected he was the only one able to hear that last statement. And it was a good one, not that he believed they were all in a movie, but maybe the monsters *were* cyborgs. After all, the astronauts were already using a 3D printer on the International Space Station to replace and repair plastic parts. That made it seem entirely possible for someone else to use a 3D printer to make a cyborg-monster.

But that black gel? No. He'd seen it cover Rose. It was organic. Evil, sci-fi, return-of-the-Blob, organic.

Dawk stepped forward to lay a gentle hand on Trina's shoulder. "I believe if men can conceive it, they can create it."

"I think it's the universe," Milo said. "It sends that black stuff to take out the monsters, but it got Mommy by mistake." His shoulders slumped. "Like when I tried to throw the rubber bone for Argus once and hit him in the eye instead. Just a bad, stupid, accident." His voice fell off, matching the slump of his shoulders.

Dawk put his other hand on Milo's shoulder. "That could be it, alright. We are all made of stardust. Each of us our own little walking-talking universe."

Drew thought he was misquoting Blake's famous poem "Auguries of Innocence," or doing a mashup of that poem with the old Crosby, Stills, Nash & Young song about Woodstock. For a moment, the old song wafted through his skull. It was before his time, and he didn't know all the words, but he knew enough of the melody to recognize it, and for some reason, it gave him chills. As if an unseen doorway had cracked open somewhere.

Rose? Is that you, Rosie? Sending me a message? Telling me every-thing is all right? Tears flooded his eyes, tears of relief this time. It was a good feeling, a calmness. *There is an afterlife. This proves it. I guess.*

He swiped his wet face with his forearm, unashamed. He wanted to tell the kids he'd just received a message from their mom, or at least from their mom's new universe, but something stopped him. Maybe they weren't ready yet. Maybe it wasn't even true.

"I'm going up to the third floor to get a better view," Drew said.

Carlos nodded. "We still need supplies."

He trailed Drew up the stairs, Milo directly behind him, Trina following like a little slender shadow, quiet, with a hiccupping sob every now and then. Drew didn't know what he was doing. He just needed to keep moving, not stop. If they stopped, he would be forced to deal with the last image of Rose all over again.

They inspected the view from the second floor, glancing through the slats covering every window. Drew recalled how Rose had insisted on covering the second-floor windows, and he almost sobbed from pain.

The sound of Dawk's voice saved him. "A tremendous view," the man said, pushing his wire-frames up a little higher on his nose.

Drew got the impression he wasn't praising the view for its lookout value, but more for its aesthetic value. He tried to see it through that lens, and it *was* amazing, the stretched white clouds dreamy, the sand-colored prairie a perfect foreground leading to the deeper reddish-brown of the canyon running out the other end, away from the behind-the-house drop-off of the cliff.

"It is beautiful," he said, expecting someone to agree with him, but the room had gone silent. Dawk had disappeared.

Alarm bells jarred his senses. "Dawk? Carlos? *Kids?*"

No answers. Just silence.

He dashed from the room back to the landing, past the other

painting-worthy view out the end-of-hall window, and straight up the short flight of stairs to the other bedroom, the one tucked up under the eaves.

And there they stood. The bunch of them. Shoulder to shoulder, staring up at the ceiling where a point of light shone, pencil thin, through a hole in the apex of the gabled roof. The beam of light arrowed down to the floor directly in front of their feet.

"Look," Milo said. He acknowledged his dad's presence, but he did not take his eyes from the origin of the light. "What is that, Dad?"

Drew stepped closer. "A hole in the roof?" He found he could not look directly at the place where the light came in. When he tried, everything blurred, and he was forced to look away. "It's bright." His hand went to his eyes to shade them.

A cloud passed over the hole in the roof and both the beam of light and the spell it had caused, were momentarily broken.

Trina was the first to move away. She stumbled to the narrow bed and sat down, but something grazed her leg. Something poking out from under the thin mattress. "What's this?" she said.

Almost as one, they moved toward her across the tiny room. She pulled out a spiral notebook. On the cover it simply read *Journal—After the Rip.*

The handwriting was neat, a forward-leaning print almost as easy on the eyes as a good cursive. "Who's is this?" she asked. "Did this person once live here?"

Carlos shrugged. "It's possible. I know the *historical* details of the place, you know, Bitty Sloan and all that, but I don't know much about the modern families who made their homes here."

Trina opened the cover and saw the date. "This is dated a few days ago. It says *After the rip,* as if it had already happened." Her voice shook. "And look, she pointed to the first paragraph. It says he's only fourteen, barely older than me. It must be some kind of fiction. A short story, or something." She continued to scan the page. "Wait—this doesn't make sense. It says he's writing from the road because the creatures invaded his hometown of Eden, Texas."

She sought her father's eye, confusion evident on her young

face. "How could this be if *the rip*, as he calls it, happened to us yesterday, in this same exact house?" She closed her eyes. "Or was it the day before? I'm getting mixed up."

"Me, too," Milo said. "Something in the way this room sways—"

Drew's gaze fell on his son. "A time slip," he said. "It must be a time slip." He almost quoted the old Beatles song, "Something in the Way She Moves," because it reminded him of what Milo just said.

But Milo wouldn't know that song. Drew barely knew it himself, and only because of the Beatles channel on Sirius satellite radio. He shook his head. He'd never uttered the words *time slip* before. Not ever. But the room did seem to be canted, a bit. Swaying.

Or was it the sudden snippets of music invading his thinking that kept making him feel off balance?

"Look at the ceiling," Carlos whispered, rubbing his ear and his temple with his free hand. His other hand rested on his cross. His expression was one of puzzled confusion.

They all gazed upward.

Where the pinhole had been, the ceiling lines wavered like foamy ocean waves crashing along a painted shoreline.

"Interesting," Dawk said, stroking the patch of beard on the point of his chin the same way Carlos stroked his gold cross. "You're right, Drew. It must be some sort of time-space anomaly. When the creatures burst through, something had to give. Our physics don't seem to be holding up anymore."

"If they were even right to begin with," Milo murmured. "Don't scientists discover new junk all the time?"

Drew looked at his son. He'd never heard *him* speak that way either. Something about this room. "Come on," he said. "Time to exit stage left, I think." He shook his head. *I'm speaking in musical references and cartoon catch-phrases. Maybe that's the universe coming through, too. Rosie, ae you with me?* He got no reply other than Easton Corbin repeating, "Are you with me? Are you with me?"

He touched his head. That was not a song he knew or recognized, not even a little bit. It unnerved him. He closed his eyes, fought for control, and then motioned for his son and daughter to follow him.

They melted back downstairs, single file, him in the lead in case there were any surprises.

"Anyone else feel sick?" Trina asked when they got to the bottom.

"Queasy," Dawk said, one hand on his midsection.

Everyone nodded. "Like motion sickness," Carlos said. "I really want food now. At least some crackers to settle the belly."

"We've got those," Drew replied. He stopped in front of the kitchen window. The slatted sunlight climbed his tall form like a ladder. "I still want to go into town for supplies."

Trina laid the spiral notebook on the kitchen counter. "It says this kid was here, but he wrote the date as next week. He describes the gray monsters and the black rain and then he said there was an awful fire and now he's gone to Cheyenne Mountain in Colorado. With a man named Carlos and a dog named Snake."

We all looked at Carlos, our unspoken questions spearing him like daggers.

"Cheyenne Mountain Complex. That's NORAD," he said. "Guess I'm supposed to go there."

"That's where I intend to go," Dawk said. "After the Denver Airport, that is. Maybe we should all go."

Carlos laid one hand on the notebook Trina had placed on the counter. "I don't know." He looked at his hand, rubbing the cover of the notebook as if it had grown warm. "Maybe I need to stay here for a while longer." His fingers ruffled the edges of the pages, but he didn't open them.

And he didn't try to explain any further. There was no need. It was obvious his mind was made up.

Drew nodded. "It's safe here, in the basement downstairs." He didn't look at the kids. It wasn't fail-safe. Nothing was, it seemed. "I think I'll drive into that little town. Kansas. Look at the farm and greenhouse on the way." He nodded at Dawk, acknowledging what he had said.

"I'm going with you, Dad," Trina said.

Milo glanced up from his snack. "And me."

Drew nodded again. "Of course." He looked at Carlos. "You are welcome to come. We will bring you back and stay the night if you want. Decide more tomorrow."

Carlos drank from a glass of water before he answered. "Thank you for the offer. I'd better wait, see what's what." His other hand still rested on the notebook. "I may need to open the garage door again."

No one knew what to make of that, but Drew said, "That sounds fine—"

Before anyone could say more, Dawk said, "I'll ride with you if you don't mind. Get myself a bike or other means of transport in town."

Drew looked at the kids. "Of course, you're welcome to come. I'm trying to decide whether we should go on toward Cheyenne or come back here for another night. He almost said, *Rosie's gone, and we don't have any grandparents left in the area, so really nothing to hold us here.* But he caught himself. Sometimes the truth was best communicated in small doses.

Carlos took Dawk aside while Drew and the kids were taking turns in the downstairs bathroom. "You're a smart man," Carlos said. "I hope you come back by here in your travels."

Dawk shook his hand. Said he would. "I intended to stay another night," he said. "But if Drew is going to town now, this is probably the best time for me to go, too."

"I need to ask you a question before you go," Carlos said. "It was a bad thing that happened to the kids' mother. Horrible." He made the sign of the cross on his chest. "I want to make sure that never happens again, but I can't think how to know what's on the other side of that door before we open it. You just can't see it from any of the windows." He shuffled his feet, obviously not used to asking for help.

Dawk nodded, understanding the problem immediately. "A mirror," he said. "We can attach a mirror to something, at the proper angle, you know."

Carlos tapped his forehead with his hand. "A mirror! Of course. We could tape a small one on a stick, run it under the crack of the door before opening it up all the way."

They both had a laugh at that. "Old school, right?" Carlos grinned. "We used to tell the girls we were going to do that with selfie sticks when they were wearing their uniform skirts." He laughed. "We didn't of course. The nuns would've had our hides."

Dawk chuckled. "Don't know if we'll ever see those days again." He shook his head. "But that doesn't mean it won't get better."

Carlos nodded. "I like your attitude. Optimistic."

Dawk didn't reply. He was already thinking about the best way to get to the airport in Denver.

Carlos didn't hesitate. He recalled a silver antique reproduction hand mirror that was part of a ladies set on the dressing table in the main bedroom. In addition to the handheld mirror, there was also a silverplated brush and a fancy comb.

Retrieving the mirror, he grabbed a roll of silver duct tape from the kitchen drawer, taped the mirror to a fireplace poker, then hurried down the steps and met the others in the garage. He ran the mirror under the edge of the rollup door, looking for anything out of the ordinary.

By the time he'd done that, Drew and the kids were in the Nissan, ready to roll. It was torture for them to be in the garage. Like being at the murder scene of a loved one. Their loved one.

Carlos understood. He ran the mirror under the door one final time, gave a thumbs-up all clear, then went to the car window and shook Drew's hand. He leaned in to give the kids a half-hug through the open window. "Come back if you need to," he said.

Dawk raised the garage door, and Drew and the kids drove straight out. They paused, waiting, the kids hunkered down behind the seat, just in case.

"It's okay," Drew said. "All's clear, I promise."

They sat up in the seat, looking around suspiciously.

Dawk jumped in the passenger side, gave Carlos a goodbye

wave, and away they went. "You can drop me in town," he said. "I'm sure I can find a bike that will get me on down the road." He smiled a sunny smile, touched the chin patch with his index finger—just a thoughtful caress—and gazed out the window. The sky was bleached blue. The same high thin clouds still stretched away into the distance like a pleasant dream. Even the torn places were near invisible in the pale azure dome. "New Mexico is beautiful—" he said.

"—when monsters aren't around," Milo added.

No one argued with that.

They remained quiet until they came upon the turn off to the horse farm and greenhouse. "Right there," Dawk said. "See the greenhouse?"

"Yes," Drew slowed. "Maybe we should stop and gather some more veggies for the road—"

"Could," Dawk looked at the farm. "I pretty well cleaned out the ripe ones, though. In another day or two there should be more, but—"

"I gotcha," Drew replied. "We'll make certain to stop by there and explore on the way back. If we decide to spend some more time with Carlos." He understood that Dawk felt an urge to go on to Denver and then Cheyenne, since finding the notebook. In fact, he was beginning to feel that same urge. Something was about to change. Or was that just hopeful thinking?

CHAPTER NINETEEN

Helicopters

As they drove, Drew instructed the kids to be his lookout, scanning the horizon all around them continuously. It was a ploy to keep their minds occupied so they wouldn't constantly mull over what they were leaving behind.

To their relief, the area was completely, eerily devoid of monsters.

Drew knew it was a temporary reprieve. The mass that was headed their way—the wavery black line in the south—terrified him.

But we'll be long gone before they get here, he told himself. *We're driving, they're walking.*

He thought of everything they had packed before leaving: an extra gas can plus all the ammunition for the rifle, and a full box of bullets for each pistol. They planned to pick up more ammunition in town if they could find it. Along with food and water, ammunition was now his main concern.

To the west, the smoke from the downed helicopters had grown dim. He wondered, briefly, if any of the 'copters might have weapons. *Nah*, he thought. *Probably not the kind we need. Who knows how far away that smoke is, anyway?* The smooth, flat prairie could be deceptive in terms of distance.

The sign came up suddenly, and he swung the Pathfinder off the highway and onto the exit ramp that would take them into Kansas.

"Small town," Dawk said as they entered the city limits. "Brick streets. I like that."

They found the courthouse sitting in the middle of a square of shops and wrecked cars and trucks. Pickup trucks were big in Kansas.

On the old-fashioned metal signposts at each streetcorner, bodies fluttered in the breeze. Drew tried not to look at them, but when he did, he realized it wasn't the bodies that were fluttering, it was the remains of the hair and clothing, and the strips of skin. The bodies weren't decomposed enough to flutter, yet. *Give it a few more days,* he thought. Then they would be little more than skeletons. *Do bones flutter? Like Halloween decorations on cold October nights?*

He felt his mind wandering, leaving the reality of the moment, and mentally forced himself to focus.

"I've seen this exact thing all over the country," Dawk said. "In every town I've passed through."

From the backseat, a deafening silence permeated the car.

"Kids?" Drew said. And then it hit him. They were seeing the same thing he was. "Don't look, kids. We can't help them." He recalled how Rose wanted to stop every time they passed a car on the highway. At first.

"Hey," Dawk said. "Is that a bike store?" He pointed to a shop on the square. Visible in the cracked window, a mountain bike on a rack.

"Looks like it," Drew said, pulling into a slanted space in front of the shop. "If it's all the same to you, I'll let you go in and check it out while I wait out here with the kids. But we won't leave you, don't worry."

Dawk hopped out. "I'll be quick," he said. "Know just what I need."

The man seemed unafraid of anything. In moments he returned with the window-bike, a backpack with an air pump sticking out of the pocket, and a couple spare tubes folded and showing as well.

"You did know," Drew said.

Dawk laughed. "I've put a few miles on a few different bikes over the years, even before this fiasco." He adjusted the seat for his lanky frame, then tucked his multi-tool into his pack. At last, he turned, held out his hand for Drew to shake, then leaned his head into the Nissan's window. "You kids hang onto each other and your dad. It's going to be all right. I have faith." He squeezed their shoulders, easy to do since they were clinging to each other like conjoined twins, and then pushed his glasses up the bridge of his nose.

"You be careful," Trina called.

"Yeah," Milo said. "Watch out for those monsters."

To keep from prolonging the leaving, Drew backed out and continued the trek through town, looking for a grocery store. Dawk grew small in the rearview mirror as he rode away.

Drew began to feel exposed, on stage, as if the living were all in hiding, watching them.

There were no grocery stores to be seen—*what I wouldn't give for Google Maps about now*—but he knew there had to be a decent sized store here somewhere. Unless they had missed a turn somehow. *Not likely in a place this size.*

Soon, they came to the opposite edge of town where they found themselves entering an empty housing development that had probably been planned and abandoned sometime in the previous decade.

Street signs leaned, and empty lots loomed. There wasn't a single structure built within the already named and divided neighborhoods. The paved road came to a halt and a dirt road meandered away into the shallow hills. It was there Drew could see the smoke still wafting away from the canyon.

"What're we doing, Dad?" Trina's voice was curious, verging on concern.

Drew smiled his best dad smile. "C'mon up front, kiddo. I'm just going to check out a theory right quick." He put both hands on the wheel. "Shouldn't take but a few minutes."

Trina legged over the seat and stared straight ahead. "Going to look at the helicopters, huh?"

Drew patted her knee, tried for a chuckle. "Can't get anything past you, can I?"

Trina gave him a crooked grin. "Not today, Dad."

Drew couldn't help remembering when he'd patted Rose's

knee while she sat in that very seat, trying to convince him to go back to the big house on the hill.

Milo unhooked his seatbelt and stuck his head between the bucket seats. He didn't like being left out.

Trina didn't say a word. She seemed to have developed much more tolerance for her little brother since the horrific death of their mom.

"I've been wondering if anyone in the choppers could have survived," she said, her voice trailing away thoughtfully.

Drew clicked his tongue against the roof of his mouth. "I wondered if any of their ammunition survived." He cocked an eyebrow at Milo, looking for a partner in crime. *Here I've been thinking only of ammunition, and there's my daughter thinking only of the people. Just like her mother.*

"I guess survival would be impossible, wouldn't it?" Trina didn't seem to expect an answer. Her tone of voice said she already knew.

"Yeah, probably," Drew admitted. "In which case I don't think they will care if we look over their weapons. Hoping for machine guns or something we can learn to use. Hand grenades, even." He'd never been in the military, so he really had no idea what might be on a helicopter like that.

Trina frowned. "All the creatures will be gone, right?"

Drew nodded. "After the 'copters went down, Dawk and I saw the monsters marching away, over the prairie. If we even think we see one, we just hightail it out of here. But you know what?"

She looked at him, waiting.

"I really think those whirly birds will have something we can use, or at least some information about what's going on." He hoped he wasn't being completely stupid, convincing the kids it was a good idea to go down to the crash site. Would they freak out if they turned a corner and saw something horrible? Should he even put them through that?

They drove on, his mind not yet made up, but feeling freer as the little town disappeared behind them. Drew hadn't realized how all the death had been pressing down on them. But why wouldn't it?

Especially after losing Rose that way. And that's when they came to the end of the development, and the end of the road.

"Is this what they call a box canyon?" Milo asked.

Drew felt a twinge of fear tickle his spine. "Is it?" Box canyons have only one way out. The same way you come in.

Before he could even change his mind, the road dipped and ended at a thick clump of tall sage, and there they were. Pieces of three or four huge military helicopters scattered across the floor of the shallow canyon like smashed and smoking toys.

His foot automatically found the brake. "My God."

Evidence that at least a few of the people had survived was obvious by the way some carcasses had been dragged out of the wreckage and stabbed onto the spiky broken rotor parts. Other body pieces were scattered around the blackened site as well, either from the crash or from the monsters picking them up and slinging them around.

"Look!" Trina pointed toward a female soldier hanging, bloodied and broken, but not flayed, from one helicopter's smashed window.

Drew had seen enough. He slammed the Pathfinder into reverse, chastising himself mercilessly. *What did you expect? Stupid idiot. What were you thinking bringing your kids here? Did you think the dead would have simply disappeared?*

"Hook your belts!"

Trina yanked the belt across herself and checked that Milo was buckled, too.

Drew planted his foot on the accelerator, and they reversed at light speed and wound-up plowing earth on the opposite side of the dirt road. "Dammit!" He smashed the gear back into Drive, but the rear wheels spun uselessly, creating a cloud of choking, red dust.

Stuck.

"Dad!" Trina yelled.

He forced the shifter back into Reverse to rock the Nissan and break the grip of the earth, but it was no good. He let his foot off the gas, reached into the console, grabbed the two pistols Carlos had given him, and shoved them into the waistband of his jeans. He felt like a wannabe-gangster. It would've been funny if it wasn't real life.

"Dad, look!" Milo smacked him on the shoulder to get his attention.

Drew looked up. The dust was so thick, he wouldn't have seen a monster if one had appeared right in front of them.

"What is it?" he demanded, smashing the gearshift back into Reverse.

Trina pointed out the front window. Both kids seemed to be on the same page. "What is that?"

Drew let off the gas completely.

Some of the dust settled and he was able to see what she was seeing. It was the huge black tail section of one of the helicopters.

Black Hawk Down, he thought. But what the hell *language* is that? Stamped on the panel in military precision were several red letters in a text that appeared, to Drew's uninitiated eye, like something out of a history book. Hieroglyphics, perhaps. Or cuneiform, one of those ancient scripts that exist mostly in museums.

Below that was a triangular symbol that reminded him, on some level, of the radiation-warning icons sometimes seen on placards in X-ray departments or the nuclear medicine section of a hospital. AM RI—was spelled out in weirdly blocked red script just before the break. They were the only letters they could read.

He took another hard look at the bodies hanging from the wrecked chassis of the other 'copters—the people who'd been dragged out of the them were now little more than skeletons—he couldn't tell anything about their features. But the woman, she hadn't been flayed. He had to see the woman again. Closer.

But first, they had to break free. "I've got to push us out," he told Trina. "Can you steer it onto the road when I do?"

She nodded and unhooked her seat belt.

When her dad stepped out, she climbed over into the driver's seat.

Drew grabbed a couple of towels from the back seat and ran to the back of the SUV. He stuffed the towels under the rear tires to give them traction.

"Now," he told Trina when he'd taken his place at the open driver's door again. "Make sure it's in Drive, then step on the gas." He patted the girl's shoulder. "When you feel it turn loose, let off the gas or you'll drag me right off the other side of the road."

Trina clenched her teeth and checked the gear shift.

"Go!" Drew commanded.

She took her foot off the brake and stomped the accelerator. The SUV shot up off the soft shoulder as if from a slingshot.

"Whoa, whoa, whoa!" Drew yelled, falling to the ground.

Trina let off the gas and rolled to a stop. They were almost to the other side, the wreckage of the helicopter directly in front of them. "Stay here," Drew said, struggling to his feet, thankful his head hadn't gone under one of the back tires. "Put the gear in Park," he rasped.

The helicopter with the blonde soldier sat right in front of them.

Drew ran back the other way.

"What're you doing, Dad?" Trina sounded on the edge of panic.

He grabbed the half-buried towels—never knew when they'd need them again—hurried back to the Nissan and threw them in the backseat. He turned and put a finger to his lips. "It's okay, sweetie, I just want a quick look for weapons, supplies, that's all." *And maybe a glance at this woman's face. See if she's human or 3D plastic.*

Trina nodded, but her furrowed brow belied her fear, and her eyes never stopped scanning the surrounding brush for movement. She caught Milo's gaze in the rearview mirror. Something passed between them as they watched their father approach the helicopter with the woman hanging through the front.

After a few seconds, she could stand it no more. "What is it, Dad?" she called softly. "What does she look like?"

Drew hesitated. He couldn't see the woman's face. His own shadow fell across her and kept the sun from illuminating her features.

Apprehensively, ignoring the stench of spilled fuel mixed with fresh blood, he reached out and grasped the blonde by the hair. *Don't I wish for a Covid glove now?* He pulled the woman's head up just enough to see her face. A fly buzzed from away from her nose.

Another from her mouth. It had been less than an hour, but the insects were already laying the eggs that would become maggots.

Bile rose into his throat.

"She looks different, somehow." He let her head back down. One of her eye sockets was crushed, probably due to the broken window, but the other was as round and empty as that of a doll's face. One with the glass eye removed.

In truth, he couldn't place her nationality at all. Broad forehead, strangely flat skull, tiny, round eye socket, bright white-blonde hair. He wished he'd gotten a better look at the nose, but that buzzing fly had thrown him off.

Look into that eye hole, his subconscious whispered. Will there be wheels and cogs, wires and gears, maybe a computer chip or two?

But no, he couldn't make himself peer inside the strange skull. He glanced inside the wreckage behind her instead, in hopes of finding an automatic weapon or at least a pair of binoculars.

He was dumbfounded at what he saw.

The control panel was covered in the same red, ancient-looking script.

Drew shrugged and continued his visual scan of the interior. "Wish I knew what language that was."

His toe struck something protruding from the sand. He bent down and dusted off some sort of weapon partially buried in the dirt. "It must've flown through the window when they crashed."

He held it up for the kids to see. It was matte black, with a bayonet affixed to the business end. "It almost looks like one of those old WWI or WWII weapons, the ones with the stocks made of wood. Except, I've never seen wood like this. Maybe it's been stained to look this way." He ran his hand over the grain and slipped his finger inside the black trigger guard. "I believe I can shoot this—"

"Look!" Trina leaned out the window and pointed at something else on the ground.

"Good eye, kiddo." Drew walked over and bent down to retrieve another weapon, this one with a scope attached. "We can take that off and use it separately, like a—"

"Spyglass!" Milo pulled the word from one of the video games he played.

"Yes," Drew replied. "Now, if we can find some more ammo—"

"Dad!" Trina screamed. "Look out!"

CHAPTER TWENTY

Don't forget the safety!

Drew straightened and whirled around to see a huge garnet-eyed monster coming at him from behind one of the other downed helicopters.

Instinctively, he lunged at the thing with the bayonet hoping to stab it in the throat. But the monster simply grabbed the weapon, wrenched it from Drew's hands, and slung it aside like a toothpick.

"Run, Dad!" Trina yelled, gunning the Nissan's engine. "I'm gonna ram it!"

"No!" Drew shouted. "Stay back!" He took off in the opposite direction so the monster would follow him.

Trina laid on the vehicle's horn. She was still revving the engine even though it was in Park.

All at once, the creature stopped chasing Drew and turned slowly toward the noise coming from the Pathfinder.

"Come on, sucker," Trina yelled. "Come over here!"

The creature's words squirmed beneath its skin like black worms. Its eyes glittered in the sunlight, and then there were two. The other came through the brush toward Drew. He stopped when he saw it. Now he was sandwiched between them.

Trina redoubled her efforts on the horn. Milo screamed and yelled from the backset, waving his arms out the side window, trying to save his dad.

Trina glanced down at the gear shift. At the same time, she twisted her head this way and that to see all around them. She knew there were probably more monsters coming.

With the first creature distracted by Trina's noise, Drew concentrated on the second one. In a move that would have made Dirty Harry proud, he pulled one of the pistols from his waistband and lined up his shot. *Squeeze the trigger, don't jerk it. Get it in the head. Gotta be a headshot.*

He closed one eye and peered down the site. The thing was huge, and it was coming right at him. His heart pounded in his chest. *I can do this.*

He squeezed the trigger gently, almost lovingly.

Nothing happened.

Drew looked at the pistol. He'd forgotten to thumb off the safety.

The second creature reached for him—its blue-black words tumbling beneath its skin. *Kill Kill Kill.*

Drew turned to run and tripped over his own feet. He went down hard. The pistol flew from his grip and landed beneath a broken helicopter blade. Drew went after it on his hands and knees.

The creature swiped the air with its long arms and big, nail-less hands.

Trina, screeching and honking, finally remembered to wrench the gear shifter into Drive.

The heavy vehicle leapt forward and stalled.

"Dad! What do I do? What do I do?"

"Restart it!" Milo screamed. "Re*start!*"

She crushed her left foot down on the brake, pushed the starter button, then smashed her right foot down on the accelerator while letting off the brake with her left.

The SUV roared with power, but Drew wasn't certain it could take out the monster. He scratched the pistol from beneath the 'copter blade, thumbed off the safety, and pointed it at the creature leaning down to scoop him up.

This time when he squeezed the trigger, the bullet tore through the thing's chest. Words poured onto the ground. *Kill Kill Kill* dissolved into clumps of wiggly letters before the monster even realized it had been hit. Drew shoved himself further beneath the giant, 'copter blade and fired again. And again.

The monster went down, but not before it found Drew's foot and yanked him from his hidey-hole like a lost sock.

Trina had been frantically attempting to maneuver the SUV back into position when Drew began firing again. The first monster stopped and turned its head to assess the new threat. The injured monster finally toppled over still grasping Drew's heel. The first one dismissed the threat and turned back toward the SUV.

Drew fired at his captor, but the bullet whizzed past the gray shape and clanged off the front of the blonde's helicopter.

Trina managed to get the SUV lined up. This time, she kept her foot on the brake until the gray creature was directly in front of her.

"Hit it!" Drew screamed, suddenly out of bullets.

He clawed for the other pistol in his jeans, but the barrel seemed to be hung up in the elastic waistband of his jockey shorts.

Trina tromped the accelerator the way she'd seen her father do. She shrieked when it jumped forward, tires spinning for traction.

The giant loomed in front of her as the Pathfinder lurched forward. This time, it hit the creature dead center and knocked it to the ground. Trina crushed the gas pedal to the floor. The Nissan jumped the downed monster, smashing its head like a pumpkin, pinning it to the earth with sheer vehicular weight.

Trina's foot fell away from the pedal.

She looked out the window, dismayed to find they were directly on top of the badly leaking freak. One back wheel pinned its leg to the ground. One of the front wheels was exactly where its head should have been.

"Dad!" she yelled.

But Drew couldn't look.

Cleansing black slime had begun to fall.

The thick droplets coalesced on the ground and headed directly toward the leaking creature still holding Drew's heel in its dying grasp. Just like his Rosie, Drew was in danger of being hoovered up along with the monster. He had to get free at any cost.

Closer and closer the dark syrup flowed, splitting itself into narrow streams as it surged around bushes and scattered helicopter parts.

Drew yanked at the second pistol, ripping it from its unlikely mooring—

And then, once again, he was firing wildly.

He couldn't tell if he hit the thing on the ground or not, but his foot came free. Minus one shoe, he scrambled to get back to the Nissan, glancing around just in time to see the slime climbing the wounded alien's legs as if it were a downed, sap-leaking tree.

"Scoot over!" he shouted at Trina, still frozen in the driver's seat.

The girl fell over the console and into the passenger seat as Drew dove in. He spared a quick look at the remains of the first creature, the one flattened beneath the SUV, but it was no longer a threat. "You did good, Baby Girl," he said, reverting to one of her earliest childhood nicknames. "You saved us all."

"I hate them!" Trina screamed, hysteria taking hold. "I hate them, and I hate this place, and I hate that black stuff, and I hate the way things are now." Tears sprouted from her eyes and tumbled down her cheeks like sudden rain.

Drew saw she was on the verge of a major meltdown. "Hang on, sweetie," he soothed, letting the SUV climb down the other side of the halfway-flattened creature. "We're okay. We'll be all right. We will."

They cleared the monster just as the slime reached it, devoured it, and began breaking into locusts, buzzing as they broke away from the mass and took flight, headed back toward the waiting sky hole.

Repulsed, Drew wanted to say something, anything, to get rid of the image of his Rosie being devoured that way. *She's nothing but a bunch of locusts now.* The thought kept spinning through his head. *It turns into locusts and flies away. How? How can that be? How can that lead to an afterlife?*

His autonomic nervous system took over, and he twisted the steering wheel and reversed toward the spot where it had all begun only minutes earlier. "We've got to get the gun that thing knocked out of my hand. And the one with the scope, too."

From the backseat, a small hand patted his shoulder and the back of his neck. Drew took a deep breath and grasped Milo's fingers briefly. "Thanks, son." He wanted to appear brave and heroic for his boy, but the best he could do was repeat, "Let's get those guns."

Trina swiped at her face with the backs of her hands. Her words had dissolved into sobs much like the creature's words had leaked out and dissolved into spiky blobs on the ground.

Drew reached over and squeezed her shoulder, distracting her from the loud, dark mass buzzing behind them. "It's going to be okay." He felt like an idiot repeating that, when everything in their lives had suddenly gone to hell, but what else could he do? Give up and fall apart? No. That wasn't going to happen. Not as long as he had his kids to protect.

He put the gear shift into Park, hopped out, and retrieved the military rifle, then he dashed over and got the one with the scope, too. At the last second, he peered into a different helicopter and was rewarded with a strangely old-fashioned set of binoculars and a bandolier of shells that he hoped would fit one of the guns. "Maybe we can use these," he said as he hopped into the driver's seat and shoved them at his daughter. "And there are a lot more." His expression darkened. "Maybe we'll come back later."

Trina looked at him.

Drew said, "Someone seems to be trying to help us fight back. It wouldn't surprise me to see military jets streaking overhead at any second—"

"That woman looked alien. And we don't know what kind of language that was." Trina's voice sounded as flat as the stain on the gun's stock. She stared out the front window. "It almost said America, but with those missing letters, it could've been anything."

"That's true," Drew admitted. "It could also be like NATO. Combined forces, or something."

Trina snorted. "They're alien, Dad. Like that black stuff that smothered Mom." She swiped at her cheeks roughly. "Probably the second wave."

"Second wave?"

"Yeah. The monsters were first, like soldiers that go in first and kill everyone so the elite can follow and reap the spoils."

Drew shook his head. "Sounds like a video game."

"Cannon Fodder," Trina mumbled, hunching her shoulders, and staring at the road.

They drove back out of the canyon toward the highway.

Milo made a noise from the backseat. He'd taken the rifle with the scope and leveled it out the window to peer through. "Umm, Dad. I think there's some more cannon fodder coming at us."

Drew fitted the binoculars to his face. "Oh, my God."

Hundreds—maybe thousands—of creatures were marching toward them in a tight, narrow, platoon. The sunlight glimmered off their dark red eyes and bounced off their shiny, gray skin.

"Take this." Drew handed the pistol to Trina and reminded her how Carlos had taught them to reload the bullets from the box in the console. "And make sure the safety is off." He grimaced as he recalled his own close call. He'd lost that gun; this was the one that had hung up in his shorts.

His thumb stroked the strange, blocky writing on the ebony stock of the big gun. "We'll learn how to load this thing when we get back."

"If we get back," Trina muttered.

Drew lowered the binoculars. The creatures were a long way off. "We will," he said, looking at the guns. "At least it wasn't a complete bust."

"We still going into Kansas for food?" Milo asked.

Drew turned the corner. "Yes. We've got to locate the grocery store before we go back."

"This is weird," Trina murmured, chewing at her already short nails.

Drew scanned the area, looking for stray monsters. "What's weird? Do you see something else?"

She shook her head, hair fanning her face, hiding it from his eyes. "No, I mean, all of it." A sob choked off her words, but she had it almost under control when she continued. "I mean, it's weird to talk about stopping for groceries on the way home when we just watched that horrible stuff happen."

Little brother patted her shoulder and chimed in, "It is weird.

Horrible and weird. But what can we do? Mom would say keep on keeping on."

Trina laughed and snorted a bit of mucus out her nose. That made Drew and Milo laugh, too. "She would say that, wouldn't she?" She snuffled back more mucus while wiping her nose on the top of her wrist. "That time Carmen Simper wrote that ugly stuff about me on TikTok, that's what she said."

"And when I had to go to school last year even after Millie Lumis called me *retard* in front of the whole class," Milo said. "Mom told me to keep on keeping on and God would take care of the res—" His face fell. "Do you think God is taking care of Mommy now?"

Drew and Trina looked at each other. Somehow, Trina had aged close to adulthood in the last few hours. "Yes," they said in unison. "He is. All we can do now is keep on keeping on. For her. And for each other."

Milo sighed, silent tears leaving tell-tale tracks through the dirt smearing his face.

CHAPTER TWENTY-ONE

Groceries

They drove on toward Kansas in a stupor. "I'll scout the area first," Drew said. He didn't *want* to go into any stores, but they needed food that wouldn't spoil, and that meant canned meat and veggies. Boxed dinners and noodles. All that packaged stuff they could carry and cook over a campfire or in the wood stove at the Bitty House.

In the back of his mind, though, was the night—only three or four days earlier, he'd lost track of time—when they'd originally driven past the Kansas sign and the cut off. The night he'd taken the short cut and discovered the Bitty Sloan House. The night Rose blew out her flip-flop.

"I'll help you, Dad." Trina cut into his reverie, then glanced back at Milo. "We both will."

Drew felt as if they could read his mind. He didn't mention it, though. Just tried to keep on.

And they finally got lucky.

The one grocery store in Kansas, the Piggly Wiggly, was small, but tidy. It sat at the rear of a large, yellow-striped, asphalt parking lot four times larger than the store itself. The front glass was cracked, not broken. About a dozen empty cars decorated the huge lot.

The scarcity of dead people made Drew debate on whether it would be best to let the kids go in with him or leave them in the car. He decided on a compromise.

He got out and strode around to Trina's passenger window.

"You kids can sit in or get out and stand here." He had pulled right up to the double doors. "You can yell inside to me, if need be," he looked at Trina. "Or if things go wrong, you can high tail it back to the Bitty House. You know the way, right?" He left the engine running and pressed the key fob into her palm.

She looked at him with knowing eyes. *Yes,* she thought. *I can get Milo back to the Bitty House if you get trapped. But Dad, don't get trapped. We can't do without you and Mom.*

As he walked through the cracked glass doors, he heard the soft *ding, ding, ding* of the reminder bell telling him the key was no longer in the vehicle, but the engine was running. They had followed him almost immediately.

"We felt like we were on display," Trina whispered, grabbing his shirt tail.

"It's all right." He pulled up short, both kids nearly crashing into his backside.

"What is—" Trina started to say.

Drew shushed her with a finger to his lips. From the rear of the store, they heard a familiar noise. Someone was pushing a screaky cart.

Drew felt something beginning deep down inside his belly. Hysteria. Hysteria tempered by disbelief. He seemed to want to laugh. But he knew he had to stifle it. Even now, whoever was in the back of the store had obviously chosen a cart with a bad wheel. He could imagine the thing going past the cold cuts, that one front wheel wobbling back and forth like a drunk.

He turned the kids around physically, quietly pointing them back toward the front door through which they'd just come.

They caught the panic bug and broke into a run. At the last second, Drew dashed into the nearest aisle and snatched as many products as he could carry. Cookies. *Naturally it would be cookies. They always put them near the doors.*

Milo and Trina imitated him, snatching anything they could grab.

"What'd you get?" Milo squawked as soon as they jumped back into the car.

Drew laughed and put it in Drive, foot finding the accelerator at the same instant. For the first time in his adult married life, he squealed the tires leaving the parking lot. *Hysteria,* he thought again. *This is what they call hysteria.*

Trina twisted around, looking behind them. "Dad! You laid rubber back there."

Drew glanced in the rearview and grinned. "I did, didn't I?" He had a slight rush, like in his gambling days but without any guilt. It felt good.

"I got M&Ms," Milo said. "And all kinds of squishy candy bars." He dumped it all out on the backseat. "At least the M&Ms aren't melted."

Trina shoved a box of cheese crackers over the seat at him. "Those emmies will go good with these, lil bro."

He grinned, and his face became a small replica of his dad's. "Thanks." He handed her a package of candy. "Mom would kill us if she saw us eating like this, wouldn't she?"

That took some of the joy out of their escape, but it couldn't be helped. The kid missed his mom. She was always at the back of his thoughts.

"What was in there, pushing that cart, Dad?" Trina asked, shoving crackers and candy in her mouth together.

Drew thought of that eerie, squeaky, wheel. It gave him such a creepy feeling, he decided the hell with it, just lie. "I didn't see anything," he admitted. "For all I know it could have been the little ol' lady from Pasadena." When he uttered that line, from the old Beach Boys song, Milo's head popped up, mouth full of candy.

"D'you hear that song?" he asked.

Trina began to hum it. "Is that the one?" She didn't know all the words, but that one line was something their Gran used to say.

Milo nodded.

Drew also nodded. "That's the one," he said. "My mom used to play The Beach Boys in the car when I was growing up. FM radio Golden Oldies." He smiled and sang the actual words in tune. "Man, that takes me back."

If they wondered about why they all suddenly heard the same

nonexistent song in their heads, no one mentioned it. Up ahead. A few monsters trolled the road.

"Uh, oh, Dad," Milo swallowed hard. "Look."

Drew was already slowing the Nissan to swing a U-turn. "I see 'em, Miles. I see 'em."

"No," Milo, said, "Look!" He was pointing the other direction, behind them.

"What the—?" Drew's voice belied his disbelief.

Behind them roared the Harley. Carlos bent low over the handlebars. "Follow me!" he mouthed.

The big bike roared around in front of them, straight toward the oncoming knot of creatures. Their red eyes glittered, and the dark letters swam beneath their skin. They were too far away for the swimmy words to be readable, but they were still visible.

Carlos drove his bike straight at them and then they heard the boom of the small shotgun. The pellets must've hit a couple because a sky hole wavered and in seconds, the dark matter fell in a torrent, directly onto the two injured monsters.

Drew couldn't look away, but Trina and Milo had to close their eyes.

Allowing the Nissan to catch up, slowly, Drew watched as the rest of the monsters gave the black sludge a wide berth. For insurance purposes, Carlos shot a couple more.

Good idea, Drew thought. *Great* idea.

He followed Carlos through the middle of the horde and together they made it back to the house on the hill and drove up to the garage. Carlos hopped off the Harley and rolled open the overhead door, then pushed the bike inside.

Drew followed, right over the top of the shadowy stain. He walled it off in his mind, determined to get past it, but Trina almost killed herself twisting around in her seat to get another glimpse before Carlos closed the door and cut off the daylight from outside.

When Drew glanced in the mirror, Milo had his face pressed to the backdoor glass. He seemed to be reliving the moment as well.

"Okay, kids," he said, to distract them. "C'mon, let's head upstairs to the kitchen."

Ragged sobs filled the car.

"Hey, now," he soothed, not sure what else to say.

"We always drive across the last place we saw Mommy," Milo said.

"Her eyes were huge. So scared," Trina murmured. "And her mouth, her mouth—" she couldn't finish that sentence. She didn't have to.

Drew knew what was bothering her. The black ooze had flowed directly into Rose's screaming mouth, silencing her forever. The images haunted him, too. *Maybe we should go on to Colorado. Put this memory behind us. Not be reminded every time we get in the car to go look for food.*

In a voice that sounded fake even to him, he assured his children things would get better. *Why do I keep saying that?*

Because you must, his subconscious replied. *What's the alternative?*

Carlos came to the car. He pulled Milo out and pressed him into a hug, returning all the sympathy—empathy—the boy had given him after discovering the bodies of his own wife and daughter.

Drew went around and got Trina out and did the same thing with her. Silent hugging, standing in the garage, waiting for feelings to level out enough to move. Again. He tried not to let his mind wander back to the grocery store, to whatever had been pushing the screaky cart. *What if it really had been an old woman? Someone who needed their help, needed to be brought back to the Bitty House?*

"This is how we'll make it, going forward. By leaning on one another," Carlos said, interrupting Drew's reverie.

The simple words and embraces seemed to have a calming effect on the kids. Their sobs quieted, and they all moved up the concrete steps as a group.

Carlos went in the door first. "I'll check the downstairs, make certain all is as we left it."

And that's when reality hit Drew again. *This is our life from now on if we stay. We'll drive over Rose's "grave" each time we leave, and we'll check for monsters each time we return.* He didn't like the sound of that. Not even in his own head.

"All clear," Carlos called out.

I'll ponder the future later, Drew promised himself. But right now, they needed to check the second floor, and then the third. Again.

He clasped his children to his sides and together, they went through the kitchen door to begin their new routine of checking for monsters before going down into the basement rooms.

A screenshot memory of the original *Terminator* movie shot through his head. People in tunnels, coughing, sick, being over-run with Hunter-Killers from above.

Drew had to force himself to find some other thought to replace that one. It was too grim, too depressing. *We'll leave tomorrow,* his mind whispered. *This isn't how I want to live. How I want my kids to live, like rats in tunnels.*

No, not at all.

CHAPTER TWENTY-TWO

Nighttime in the cliff dwelling—Now

Drew closed his eyes, ready to finish his tale, to relinquish the memories of their few days at the Bitty Sloan House. "It didn't take long for us to make a meal of the veggies Dawk had left, plus the things Carlos had brought. We also added the things we'd managed to grab at the Piggly Wiggly," he said. "Carlos even had a pair of sneakers he let me have, to replace the one that saved my life when the monster pulled it off."

"Good thing he always wore his boots when he rode the Harley," Milo said, staring into the tiny fire they'd built.

"Yep," Drew smiled. "He said they didn't quite jibe with his Realtor duds, so he brought along the Nikes, just for that purpose."

I pictured Carlos in his motorcycle boots, shotgun in hand. "He was the best, absolutely."

"I miss him," Milo said. "It was funny that day. The food was like that story our teacher read to us right before school was out. *Stone Soup—*"

"Yeah," Drew said. "The one where the clever travelers convinced everyone that three magic stones would make a delicious soup if they only had a few things to add to it?"

Milo nodded.

"I remember it, too," I said, trying to smile as I recalled the story from my own days in Mom's library. But it was a sad memory. After all, that's how we were living now, traveling around, trying to scrounge up enough food to make a stone soup.

Drew chuckled, bringing me out of my head. "What we really need is a rabbit to put in the pot. We can throw some stones in, too, if you want—"

"*Ewww*," Trina and Milo both found the idea disgusting, but it made the rest of us laugh as well as cutting some of the tension from their long story-sharing time.

At last, we all sat back, digging through our own memories—at least that's what I was doing. It seemed if I ever allowed myself to go down one of those memory trail-rabbit holes, it was hard to get myself back on track.

"I'm so sorry about your wife." Faith's voice carried in the quiet cellar room after Drew's story-laughter died away. "And your mom," she murmured, caressing the kids' hair.

I'd thought the kids might be asleep, but I guess they were like me, just on the verge of it. "I'd like to hear even more about the helicopters," I said.

"They were weird," Drew acknowledged. "Very strange."

Trina opened her eyes, swiped at her cheeks, as if she hadn't been near sleep at all.

"Fascinating," Sam said. "I used to watch a lot of science fiction on TV. Conspiracy stuff. It wouldn't surprise me if some of our higher ups were in cahoots with whomever—or whatever—is behind all this."

"Exactly," Drew said. "When we first found the helicopters, I thought they put that strange writing on there to fool us. Then I saw the blonde woman, and now it's beginning to make sense—"

"How?" I asked. "What made you certain after seeing her?"

Drew said, "Her face was not completely human-shaped. Her head was flat and her eye—the one that I could see—looked like a perfectly round hole."

"A round hole, as if something might have fallen out? Something like a multi-faceted, garnet lens, perhaps?"

That idea made Drew's own gaze widen.

I shook my head. "I don't know, though. I'm still half-stuck on Dr. D's idea that the things came from the dimension of Purgatory."

"I read that in your journal," Trina said. "But we saw what we saw." She looked at her dad for confirmation.

Drew nodded, smoothed her hair the way Faith had done.

"Sounds alien," I said. "Human helicopters flown by aliens." I looked around at the rough cellar room and thought, *and all that high tech stuff has reduced us to this.* I touched the earthen floor outside the edge of our blankets and sleeping bags, then looked at Faith, then Dad, then Sam. "Things have changed so much, I would never discount what anyone says now."

"Yeah," Sam said. "Maybe that's how it all began. Aliens took over our government and the governments of the other big countries."

"No argument from me," I said. "Although before now, the topic of aliens was banned from our dinner table." I glanced at Dad, recalling all the times we'd discussed TV shows and oddities until things would take too much of a weird turn, and Mom would shut down the conversation with bowls of ice cream or hunks of chocolate cake.

Faith must've caught a bit of what transpired between Dad and me because she opened her mouth to say something to the group, but in that instant Snake jerked his head toward the dwelling entrance and began to bark.

A look of terror crossed Faith's face. "What is *that?*" she cried.

Sam was nearest the opening. He jumped up, brushing at his head and shoulders. "What the *hell?*" Bits of black letters showered to the floor.

The small fire threw Sam's shadow-motions against the ceiling and the opposite wall, and something came crawling out of those frantic shadows upside down and clinging to the sandstone like an unholy mutation brought to life by our discussion.

"What *is* it?" Milo screeched.

Snake leapt at the crawling thing, but it clung to the ceiling on its bent spider-like legs, upside down, quite out of the reach of the snapping jaws of the Snake.

"Its face looks like the woman you saw, Drew, almost human but so *flat,*" Sam yelled. "But this one has the words. The inside-out tattoo words."

As suddenly as it had come, the thing whooshed above us and

was gone into the dark reaches of the long dwelling. But not before I saw its twisted face and the many-faceted garnet eyes looking back at us, taking our measure.

"Where is it?" Trina whispered, clinging to Milo and her dad. "Where did it go?"

Before anyone could answer, another one appeared and skittered toward us, falling directly onto my head, wrapping slimy gray legs around my throat in a terrifying death grip. *Faith!* I screamed in my mind.

She appeared. But her strength was no match for the thing's grasping appendages. They tightened mercilessly. My vision blurred out around the edges. I closed my eyes and gritted my teeth, my fingers clawing into my own skin as I fought for a grip around the slippery legs. An unbidden image of Dad tied to Marla's steering wheel wafted across my field of memory.

Hang on! Faith's voice slipped into the images in my brain. And then a machete whickered through the air, severing the tightening limbs, giving me a chance to inhale, choking and sputtering.

Before I could inhale a second time, dozens of glittering garnet eyes filled the far end of the space and scampered toward us—clinging to the ceiling upside down—flat human faces and dark red eyes terrifying as they loomed in and out of the darkness.

Just like before, something began to fall on us.

"What...?" Trina screamed, swiping at herself, dislodging wiggly black letters just like the ones that had fallen on me. And on Sam.

"What's going on? Are they injured?" Faith shouted.

Milo shrieked, batting at his head. "Is it the black rain? Is it come?"

Trina yanked her little brother to her side, combing his hair with her fingers. "It's okay," she said, her voice on the edge of panic. "It's not going to get us. I won't let it." She curved her thin body around his.

Drew observed the scene for a split second, then flung himself up the stout ladder to the outside. He motioned for the kids to follow and then he yanked them up one at a time, shielding them in his embrace. "We're getting to the Nissan," he yelled to the rest of us.

Our little plan about Sam or myself taking watch fell by the wayside. This was an all-out attack. We hadn't expected anything to happen while we were still awake. *Go!* I thought at him.

"We're right behind you," Dad called. "C'mon Jackie, Faith, grab what you can and let's—"

"Dad!" I screamed.

A tangled creature fell upon him. He ducked just in time to avoid all the grasping limbs but one. It snaked around his throat the way the other one had done around mine.

I grabbed the gray appendage before it was able to fully tighten its grip. The tip of the leg was not like a foot, it was more like a tentacle ending in a large, deformed finger, narrow and grasping, doing its best to dig into Dad's flesh.

Try as it might, this one's ugly leg-finger was too new, too weak to have any serious strength. *Oh, my God, is this a creature nursery? This one's like an infant.* Its power—its terror—came from the fact that when you dislodged one, there were several more to take its place. *Eight legs,* I thought. *Like a spider. Or an octopus.*

Arms, Faith spoke in my head. *Arms. Not legs. See that finger?*

Dad dropped to the floor, and I flung the bizarre creature against the wall. Black letters exploded from under each loose and flapping fingernail. *That's an experiment gone wrong,* I sent to Faith. *I don't think they're hurt, just unfinished. Leaking, somehow.*

I couldn't read any of the words pulsing beneath the greasy skin on those arms, or even after they began to float through the air, but they were there, as always. That's how I knew they were connected to the Takers. Or to the *creators* of the Takers.

"Go!" I shoved Dad toward the entrance and Sam grabbed him and fairly tossed him up the ladder to Drew, who had not deserted us.

Faith and I rushed under the hanging monsters now crowding the openings. Their arm-like appendages grasped at the air, their red insectile eyes tried to pin us to the walls.

Snake yelped as one of the things fell to the floor in front of him. The dog's canine reflexes saved it at the last second as the creature half-leapt half-crawled toward him. He snapped it up in his pit bull jaws and shook it like a dead rat.

Droplets of fluid clouded with dark letters flew around the space as Snake's teeth pierced the thing's flesh. The creatures drew their arm-legs into their bodies in preparation for a concerted attack on the dog. That's when I saw the tiny feet on the undersides of their pits—or what *would* be their armpits if they looked more like Takers instead of octo-spiders.

I stood, dumbfounded, as they all turned loose of their moorings and fell to the floor.

"We're trapped," I shouted. "You guys *go*."

Sam was already at the top of the ladder. I tried to pick up Snake—intending to chunk him up the ladder—but that was not happening. The muscular dog slithered out of my grip as if oiled. That's when I realized I had the Chrysler key in my pocket.

"Sam!" I yelled. "Catch!" I tossed the key up and out of the entrance. "You and Dad get inside where it's safe."

"Hang on, Jack!" Sam called back.

I didn't know what he thought I would hang on to. The creatures were everywhere, on the floor, on the ceiling, climbing up the walls.

And then something hit the floor near my feet, and I recognized the sound of metal on stone. I lunged for Sam's machete and started swinging.

The first two I killed were easy, got 'em right in the top of the head before they knew what happened. And even though the black rain might not be aware of the spilled Taker-ish blood, I had an idea of how to gain its help anyway.

Get ready to hit the ladder, I yelled at Faith in my head, and then I followed Snake's lead—he had found his doggy rage, snapping, and biting every twisted creature he could reach—and I began to slice and stab everything that crossed my path, too. Soon, the floor gleamed with fluid. Letters squiggled in the mire. I saw only one word that made any sense. Not surprisingly, the word was *evolve.*

All four of Snake's feet slipped on the slimy floor and saved his life when a mass of the things rushed at him. He literally slipped away.

"Jack!" Sam called from outside. "Throw out some dripping pieces, maybe the rain will come."

My thoughts exactly. I grabbed chunks of severed arms and tossed them up and out the entrance. Eric Clapton's "Let it Rain," slammed into my head just like it had back at the Cheyenne Complex. I think it had been playing in the background for a minute or two.

"Carry on Wayward Son" joined in.

Okay, okay, I thought, *carry on, make it rain. We know how to do that.*

Faith bravely gathered bits and pieces and slung them at the opening, too. I wanted to ask her if she heard the music, but I didn't have to. She said, *Let it rain, Jack!* And we did.

When the creatures saw what kind of damage my machete could do, they backed off a bit. Snake backed off, too, shaking his head. Black letters clung to his tawny fur.

I think it's going to work, I sent to Faith. And then I heard something I hoped I would never hear again. It was the sound of a thousand toeless feet shushing on the asphalt tourist road leading up to the dwellings. *I guess the things do share the same pheromones as the Takers.*

From outside, Dad began to pray, "Our Father, who art in Heaven—"

Before he could utter the next line, I heard Drew's voice join in at the top of his lungs, "Hallowed be Thy Name—"

Then the kids joined in, and I swear my blade began to glow. The faster I swung at the leaping, crawling abominations, the more brightly the edge seemed to blaze. Just like the Mustang key at Cheyenne, the one I used to dispatch the evil Marla, the turquoise-edged machete slid through creature flesh like a hot knife through cold butter.

A Native American flute joined the noise in my head, and I made short work of three crawling horrors and tossed them toward the doorway. The floor had grown so slick I could hardly stand. "Time to *go,*" I yelled to Faith and Snake. "Takers are coming!"

Faith's mental connection, and Snake's snapping jaws, had

turned out to be extremely helpful when it came to staying out from under the crawling ceiling creatures, but how would I ever get Snakeman up the ladder when I could barely take a step without slipping down, and more and more monsters were coming up from the dark length of the dwellings?

The fire was almost out. Soon it would be pitch black except for the shine of the far-off rising moon. *If those marching toward us arrive before we get out of here, we won't have a chance.*

The thoughts zipped through my skull toward Faith and Snake just as I heard another noise, the most beautiful one in the world.

It was the whirring sound of wings whipping the air.

We're saved now, Faith yelled. *Turq is coming. Turq is coming to save us.*

I didn't have to worry about Snake. When he felt the vibration of those wings, he slid across the floor to the ladder and climbed up as easily as he'd climbed down. Together, Faith and I slipped and slid across the floor behind him. Outside, the black rain began to fall, blocking out most of the moonlight.

We scrambled up and out, making our way to the Chrysler under the welcome shelter of our guardian-angel-Turqs.

Sam opened the driver's door, then touched my shoulder almost the same way I often touched Snake on the head to let him know my intentions. The big guy left the Chrysler key fob in the cup holder and dashed across to the tow truck.

Wings parted here and there to allow streams of black rain to rush down and clean up the remains of the hybrid-monstrosities. As before, at Cheyenne, the flock of Turqs sheltered us and our vehicles—along with Snakeman, of course—until we were safely ensconced and on our way.

Small puddles of oily blackness shone in the off-and-on moonlight as the Turqs opened and closed their wings to allow the dark, cleansing rain access to the grisly, butchered pieces.

Only then did I realize we were all still reciting The Lord's Prayer.

Thank you, Lord, I breathed into the midst of the voices. *Thank you for sending these friends to help us again.*

Faith said, *Amen.* And it occurred to me that perhaps we were all conduits, not just me, not just Faith, but all of us Remainders.

Carlos would be proud to hear that, Faith whispered in my head. *Maybe it was always that way, and there was just too much noise for us to hear it.*

Turq 2.0 dipped his wings like a plane, telling us he was aware. Or maybe telling us he agreed with the statement about Carlos.

I inhaled deeply. *Now what?* I asked the group. *Head on to Four Corners?*

Yes, they all agreed, *Four Corners. More important now than ever.*

We drove down the little road, my mind still preoccupied by the creeping, crawling, hybrids. *No wonder Dawk was anxious to begin his experiments,* I thought.

Not experiments, Faith sent back. *Investigations. He would never experiment without a purpose.*

Sorry, I replied. *I was only giving him props for trying to figure things out.*

It's all right, she said. *I just know he wouldn't do anything cruel or unnecessary. Although it appears someone has been doing exactly that.*

They sure have, I sent back. *Someone has.*

Yes, Sam said. *It would be nice to know our enemies.*

We drove back to the highway leaving the black rain to clean up the mess. I hoped Turq and his flock would hang around to clean up the Takers that were marching up from the direction of Cheyenne, too.

When our cutoff road met the highway, we all hesitated, one vehicle at a time, gazing into the distance, listening to the *shush-shush-shush,* looking for the first glint of moonlight on moist, gray, skin.

Even though I never saw anything, the sound carried across the stillness like the after-effects of a loud concert, and I recalled Dawk's comment about stealth technology. *Oh, geez. Have they gone invisible?*

I didn't want to think what that would mean.

It seemed imperative we keep moving, especially with that new thought, so we continued down the highway in a mild state of shock, all of us continuing to whisper our thanks, and our prayers, into the night.

CHAPTER TWENTY-THREE

Four Corners

I was not surprised to see a prominent vein of turquoise highlighting the horizon once we began to encounter the signs indicating the Navajo Nation National Park. The riotous colors of the distant aurora had faded as we left the dwellings behind.

"Is this it?" Milo's voice was so excited I couldn't say if it was aloud or in my head. It was only about the tenth time he'd asked that question in the last half hour.

I was still trying to understand how this hive mentality worked. Quite certain I wasn't privy to every single thought each of the others had—wouldn't that be chaos? So, maybe we only caught each other's excited, or shouted, thoughts.

That sounds about right, Faith said.

Now, there you go, I thought back at her. *I doubt you shouted that at me, right?*

Hmmm, she sent, softly. *I see what you mean. I hear a lot of your thoughts. Not just the ones meant for the whole group.*

Same, I said. *At least I think it's the same.*

"Hey, everyone," Drew called out. "We're making a pit stop up ahead."

He swung into the drive of a roadside rest stop.

We'd driven several hours in the darkness, but there was the moon, and since there were few cars, and we didn't see any bodies, everyone felt it was probably safe. *This is when I really miss our big gray friend,* I thought.

Yes, Faith sent back. *Me, too.*

Apparently, no one else caught our thoughts, because Trina began to speak. "Reminds me of the day we went to see The Bitty Sloan House," she said. "Remember that, Dad?"

We were all getting out, standing near the curb waiting on Sam to pull in.

"I sure do remember, Trina." Drew pulled her to his chest. "It was a good day until the storm, wasn't it?" His voice sounded far away.

I couldn't see his eyes, but I figured they were seeing some other scene. The one they'd told us about that night at the fireside.

"Anyone want to actually go inside this place?" I asked.

"Nah," Faith laughed. "I'm good with going around back."

"I'm glad you said that. It looks pitch-black in there. But I'll stand guard for anyone going around the back."

"Can I go with you, Faith?" Trina asked.

Faith held out her hand. "Of course."

Milo started to speak up, but Drew stopped him by saying, "C'mon, buddy, let's you and I go to the other side of the road."

Sam indicated an eighteen-wheeler parked on the curve. "I'll go check out that tractor-trailer up there. See if it has any diesel left in those big old tanks."

"I'll join you," Dad said.

The moon was high now, edging slowly toward dawn. When crossing the Ute Mountain Reservation in Montezuma County, Colorado, we'd been enthralled by Sam's story about the Great Warrior God who had come to help his people fight evil and was then wounded and lay down to rest. He fell into a deep sleep which became the Sleeping Ute Mountain.

It seems all the gods are with us, I thought. But I didn't shout it out. If Faith heard, she didn't comment.

That had been over an hour ago. Now we were nearing the Four Corners Monument. Once we got there, we would rest up and then continue southwest to San Diego, California. I thought it was the right thing to do, but I also felt a little uncertain.

I think I was waiting on a song to direct me. Which made

no sense. Dad was here now. Why should I expect headtunes to guide us? Those early songs had been straight from Dad. Leading me to find him. I thought they had, anyway.

Maybe it didn't matter, Monument Valley and the famous red rock formations were only an hour away according to the map. We didn't rush at the rest area, but we didn't dawdle either. Soon, we loaded up and hit the road, again.

That hour flew past. I barely noticed the scenery, simply drove, replaying our brief time inside the cliff dwelling over and over in my head. I noted the same going on with Dad and Faith, as well. What were those things? Are we destined to find more of the same, or even worse?

Yeah, Faith's voice appeared in my head. *I wondered the same thing.*

Great minds think alike, I sent back with a mental smile.

Those things were nasty, she thought. *Worse than the big Takers, the way they moved so fast.*

What would we do without Turq 2.0 and his flock?

Faith was silent for a moment. *I pray we never find out,* she thought at last.

That left me speechless because I knew that it was true. We'd be in dire straits without our winged friends.

Yes, I think we'd be dead, she thought.

We might've continued in this vein for another hundred miles, but suddenly, we were there.

Monument Valley. The big sign. The big statues. The red rocks, the works.

We stopped the caravan in a parking area filled with more deserted cars but no people. No bodies anywhere. "Odd," I said to anyone listening. "How about the horizon? Did everyone notice the color?"

Dad gazed around. "I began to notice the color when we blew through that last little town called Turquoise." He chuckled. "It was nice, but not enough to warrant the name. Maybe it's the color of the sky. Sure feels healing, doesn't it? I guess we're now on Navajo land, now."

I looked at the empty vehicles in the waning moonlight. "How can there not be any bodies at all? Does it have something to do with the color of that horizon line? Dad's right, it is beautiful, and kind of amazing."

"Makes me think of Carlos," Faith said. "And our original Turquoise Turq, of course."

Snake chuffed, and we all laughed. He still had the scrap of Turq's old shirt tied into a hard knot on his collar.

"There are a lot of cars here," Sam said. He had parked the tow truck nearby and walked over to the Chrysler. He stretched and rubbed his back. Since his capture, he appeared to always be in a state of discomfort, as if the injuries he'd sustained at Cheyenne still hadn't healed.

"Some schools let out earlier than others," Trina said. "I'll bet lots of people were already on vacation, coming to see the famous Four Corners."

"Yeah," Drew answered. "Or maybe this many people travel all the time. They say our population aged. Lots of retirees on the road, seeing the historical sites."

We all thought about that as we got out and stretched. Snake ran to a car, lifted a leg, then turned and sniffed the air coming from the opposite direction. Before walking away, he did that funny thing dogs often do after marking something. He turned his hindquarters to it and pretended to cover it up *backwards*. I always thought that was hilarious, like a dragster on four legs, trying to grab some traction with his claws on asphalt, maybe to lay down some rubber and take off at top speed.

"Snake approves," Sam said.

We all laughed. It felt good. So good.

Milo charged toward the giant flat monument representing the four corners of the United States. Built on a raised square platform, the circular medallion reminded me of the head of a flat screw with the cross in the center dividing it into the four quadrants. Flowing around the outside edge of the circle were the words:

Here meet, in freedom, under God, four states.
Each quadrant was labeled with one of the state names.
Arizona, New Mexico, Utah, Colorado.
Wow. Very impressive.
No one questioned my statement as we all stood on the circular pad and gazed around at the amazing rock formations and the wide-open sky. Without all the light pollution, the dark sky seemed to be part of us now; part of our world again, not just something to light ourselves against. The moon gave off plenty of light to read the words on the monument. The turquoise glow helped too.

"We read about this place in my geography class section about the Southwest," Trina said, "but there was never a mention of that bluish colored horizon."

"Feels holy," Dad murmured. "Unspoiled. I'm glad it survived the rip."

Milo hopped up the broad, shallow steps to the giant medallion and flopped down on his back.

When we followed him, we saw what he was about. Lying on the monument, on his back, he had one leg in the Utah quadrant, one in the Arizona quadrant, an arm in Colorado, and the other one in New Mexico. His body lay spread eagle on the flat monument with the motto going around him in a circle.

Very fitting, I thought. *Very fitting.*

"This is *sick*," he said.

"I think so, too," Sam laughed, acknowledging the slang. "I've been here before. A little further on, there's a nice restaurant and giftshop run by the Navajo people. Also, a hotel called The View. Stayed there with my wife once." He gazed at the heavens. "The moon and stars are amazing here, aren't they." His laugh turned into a sort of bittersweet chuckle. "I guess that's one good thing about the absence of all other light."

I didn't know about the rest of the group, but that comment just about knocked me for a loop. The absence of all other light. *Every night, now. The absence of light. No more light—*

I might have gone on repeating myself if Faith hadn't interrupted.

But we aren't really in the dark, Jack. Her thoughts entered my head. *Especially not tonight, and never in the daytime.*

We all stared upward the way Sam had done. We had the flat monument at our feet and the miraculous bowl of the sky overhead. One arm of the Milky Way curved over the furthermost rock formation like part of a vast, starry wheel.

"Isn't this wonderful?" Faith inhaled, then exhaled slowly. "How could anyone deny the existence of God when they see something like this?"

"And how did anything break through and cause all the destruction?" That was Sam, always the military man.

Milo spoke up, clearly on a different thought train. "My teacher said Earth is in the Milky Way galaxy, but if that's true, how can we stand on Earth and still see the galaxy out there?" He pointed at the stunning curl of stars overhead.

"Good question, kiddo," Drew began, but Trina interrupted.

"'Cause we live in a spiral galaxy," she said. "Like this." She waved a large swirl in the air with her hand. "Earth is just a tiny planet in one part of it. The whole galaxy curls around and around. It's huge. Made up of more than 200 billion stars. That's why we can see this other part, this arm, curling around us, too. And it's not the only one, there are more."

"That's as good an explanation as I've ever heard," my dad, the music teacher, said.

Drew nodded, and Trina scuffed the concrete platform with the side of her sneaker. "I like science stuff," she said. "I used to anyway."

We all stared upward again, until Sam drew our attention to the telescope at the edge of the viewing platform. We each took a turn peering through it until we finally realized something had knocked it out of whack and none of us knew how to fix it. Everything was blurry.

"We need Dawk," I said, because I knew that's what Faith was thinking.

She laughed, "You're right, he would probably kno—"

But she didn't finish the thought or the sentence.

All at once, something pulled our attention toward the monument. Some sound. An unexpected noise, loud in the mystical desert silence.

It wasn't the sound of shushing feet, thank God. It was a grating sound. Like the sound of metal scraping against rock.

For a moment, I had no idea what could be causing such an abrasive, worse-than-nails-on-chalkboard sound. And then I saw it. I guess we all did.

The brass center of the monument had begun to turn inside its granite mount.

The sound made me want to cover my ears. Instead, I ran toward it to see why it was moving.

"Careful, Jack!" Faith cried, following me.

In a moment, we stood around the thing, around the part with the inscription, and we watched it slowly turning. Even Snake stood beside me, head cocked to one side as if he could hear it. *He feels the vibrations*, I thought.

"Is it sinking?" Milo asked, leaning over, looking closely.

Trina flung one arm sideways against her brother's chest. "Careful, bro!" She reminded me of a small soccer mom throwing out a protective arm in the front seat, but her voice was an almost perfect imitation of Faith's.

"We have to—" Sam started to say, but he didn't finish because at that moment the brass plate stopped turning, and we stopped breathing and just waited to see what had been unlocked.

"What's happening?" Trina whispered.

I shrugged and we all waited some more.

Snake gingerly stretched out one forepaw and bravely touched the edge of the brass plate with his toenails.

Nothing happened.

I looked at the others. "Did you all see it moving?"

Everyone nodded. "Could we be hallucinating?" Faith asked.

"Like the things I saw at the missile silo?" I murmured. "I guess it's possible, but why?"

The stars overhead seemed brighter and brighter. The dark part even darker. The moon, not full but getting close, gazed down. It was on the downward slide now, going to bed, laying stripes across the desert, claiming it before leaving.

"Come on," Faith said, taking my arm, breaking the weird spell. "Let's move on. Go check out The View hotel that Sam mentioned." She tried to make light of the situation. "As for the restaurant … we can only hope they don't require reservations."

With an *aww shucks* look on his face, Sam said, "I called ahead. Got their best table."

"Does this remind you of the place we found the helicopters?" Milo asked.

Drew nodded. "Well, it's remote like that." He hesitated. "But I know what you mean, son. It's surreal. A little bit spooky." He looked at me, then Dad, then down at the ground.

"I agree," Dad said. "I think it's okay, though. Guess we just follow our instincts. And our Faith." He smiled at the retreating form of the girl who had started off down the path toward the parking lot. "And look there," he pointed toward a four-legged form only visible now and then in the moonlight. "There goes Snakeman."

"Well, that settles it for me," I strode back to the Chrysler.

"I'm not trying to be bossy," Faith called. "But this stone in my pocket is growing warmer and warmer." She reached in and brought out the lump of turquoise. "It's telling me to do something, I'm just not sure what it is."

"Maybe that's Carlos," I said aloud. "Maybe he's telling us we're on the right path." I felt a bit of mental weight shift. I'd noticed that often happened when I quit trying to figure things out and simply allowed my subconscious to take over. *Is that it? I wondered. Is that the still, small voice within me?*

"Here we go," I said. "Anyone want to ride with me to The View?"

Everyone hurried back down to the vehicles, bidding good-bye to the Four Corners Monument and the momentary shared hallucination we'd seemed to experience.

Faith and Dad settled into their usual spots and for once, the kids rode with their dad. Snake seemed indecisive. For a moment I thought he was going to jump in the Nissan with the kids, but at the last second, he made a run to the Chrysler. Sam backed out and led the way in the tow truck.

"Gorgeous," Faith said as we drove down the highway, moonlight paving our way. We approached the hotel sooner than expected, time and distance somehow skewed in the desert stillness.

"It is nice," I said, being agreeable.

The place was built to blend into the desert landscape sort of like the cliff dwellings. Desert stone walls interrupted only by the wide glass windows situated behind each private balcony looking over the monument valley. There were also large circular patios built a short distance away from the rooms where folks could sit and drink coffee or have a meal while enjoying the outdoor scenery.

"Oh," Trina said. "It's amazing!" She jumped out and scampered up the walkway to the first patio looking out over the valley. In a moment, she appeared on one of the balconies. "Well, they didn't quite survive intact. All the glass is shattered. It's everywhere." Disappointment cut into her voice, but only for a moment. "It doesn't really matter," she said. "The view is still unbelievable." She leaned against the balcony railing and inhaled deeply. "You know, Navajo people believe they go through three incarnations on their way to this, what they call *The Sparkling World*." Her voice was reverent. "I wonder where they go after this?"

We stopped on the circle patio where she had been. It was easy to see her and to hear her speaking. She seemed to be drinking it all in, absorbing the view and the atmosphere. In a moment, Milo and Snake stood beside her. They also seemed to be in their elements. Snake was more animated than I'd seen him in a while, checking every scent with his super doggy senses.

The area was both captivating and haunting. Eerie and still. Soon we began to see the desert animals that had crawled back out of their holes.

Knew they were here somewhere! I thought triumphantly.

Snake stood like stone as a cottontail crept around a clump of wild grass.

I held my breath, wondering if he would give chase. Then I saw another quick, tiny movement just off the patio. A small, striped ground squirrel dashed a few feet away and stopped to chew something it had picked up.

Snake's hindquarters began to tremble. A whine shivered the air between us. He was so excited he didn't know which way to run. And then a cat slunk out from under the balcony next to ours and made the decision for him.

Did you see it? Faith thought at me, leaning over the rail. *That was a cat, a tabby. The first one I've seen in ages. Maybe this is why we were meant to come here, to see that life is coming back.*

I like that idea, I thought back at her. "And look, out there on the horizon, another rabbit, and maybe even the shape of a coyote."

"Now, all we need is a road runner," she joked.

"Maybe they also live underground," Trina offered. "But to be honest, I have no idea. I agree with Jack, though. That's either a coyote or the scruffiest looking dog I've ever seen."

Dad laughed. "Surely there *are* more dogs around. Snake can't be the only one that was under a house or barn."

"True," I said. "It makes me wonder if one of reasons he survived was because of his deafness. Maybe their extra-sharp canine hearing made the rip affect them even worse than it did humans."

"I say we discuss it over breakfast," Dad said, just as Sam squeezed off a rifle shot and hit the cottontail causing it to jump straight up in the air and fall back to earth with a thud. "Anyone have any objection to fresh meat?"

I thought Trina would object, or maybe even Faith. Truth be told, it startled me so that I almost cried out. From joking about adding a rabbit to the stew pot, to finally seeing one live and then automatically killing it. That seemed cold, extremely harsh.

The rifle report brought Snake back to heel. He had not caught the cat, but he knew the vibration of gunfire when he felt it.

From the patio below us, Drew said, "I'll gather wood for the cookfire." And I realized how practical they were being. Fresh meat. Protein. A precursor of the way things would be once the canned foods went bad. *If we lived that long.*

Milo ran down to his dad's side. "I'll help." He immediately began to gather clumps of dried grass.

"Looks like Sam is the cook," Faith said. I noticed she averted her eyes from the rabbit as Sam strode out toward it, knife in hand.

"I say we choose our rooms," I told Dad, and Faith. "I guess we have our pick." I smiled.

"I'll check out the restaurant," Drew said. "Maybe there's something left in the pantry or at least some pans and cooking utensils." Between the hotel and the spot where the rabbit lay, no longer twitching, Milo had begun to gather rocks to add to the fire pit.

Dad and I started up the path to the rooms where Trina stood, silently watching Sam skin the cotton tail. "What do you think?" I asked Dad as we looked out at the valley. "We can have separate rooms, or we can book together."

He looked back at the Chrysler. "I guess we'd better stay close together," he said. "I'd hate to be too far apart if we needed each other like last night."

I nodded. "Good thought. Exactly right." We went on up and chose the room next to where Trina stood on the balcony, attempting to entice a seemingly fearless lizard to crawl into her palm.

"Dessert!" she said, laughing. And that's when I noticed several other lizards on the walls and on the floor. They were everywhere, taking back what had once been theirs.

"Guess we'd better check the beds for scorpions, too."

That got her attention. She immediately forgot the pretty green and brown lizard and went to the bed, stripping back the perfectly made covers to reveal … nothing. "Whew," she said. "You had me going there for a minute."

I laughed. But Dad said, "Just be sure to check again before you lie down. They do like to crawl into dark places. Along with spiders. And snakes."

Trina gave up and took off outside to help Milo gather more grass for the firepit.

"I didn't mean to scare her," Dad said.

"Me, either." I shrugged. "But if any of us got stung or bitten—"

"Right," he agreed. "Can't be too careful."

We left the rabbit skinning to Sam, but he didn't seem to mind. He even got a second one before we got the fire built. In the restaurant's kitchen, Drew found nothing useful. It had been months already, and mice and rats were thick as thieves in the desert. He said everywhere he looked, bags of cornmeal, flour, and dried corn were chewed open and fouled by the rodents.

"I found nothing but a magnificent view. A big, rounded dining room full of tables all looking out on the scenery." He sounded completely smitten. "I wonder where their water comes from, for this area." His voice still held a note of awe mixed with curiosity. "Wouldn't I love to wake up to this view every morning, go to sleep with it every night?"

We all tramped up to the dining room to see what had him so amazed, and he wasn't exaggerating. "I wouldn't mind this either," I said. "How about you, Dad?"

He nodded. "It's amazing. But I would also worry about water," he said. "That's the only thing I know about where to start over. Make sure we have water."

That was a bit of a downer, but again, it was only the truth.

Just then, Sam called us all to come down to the lowest patio firepit and help him grill the rabbits. "The kids went into the gift shop," he said. "Got into the vending machines. Found some sodas and snacks."

"And tons of pretty jewelry," Milo said. "Look!" he held up his hands to show off a couple of turquoise and silver rings, and then he pointed to a necklace with a turquoise stone as well. "Trina's got some, too," he said. "It's okay, isn't it, Dad? I mean, we're all Takers now, aren't we?"

"Takers and Remainders," I said.

"And Seekers," Faith added. "Always Seekers, until we find our place to start over."

I glanced out at the expanse of the valley and tried to imagine living there year-round. "Maybe we will always be Seekers," I said. "Like those Native American tribes that followed the bison." I remembered the buffalo jump again, but I was the only one of us who had been there besides Snake.

Drew said, "I did find these in the restaurant kitchen." He handed over long shish kebob skewers, long-handled barbecue-type forks, and a couple of pans and other utensils he thought we might need.

We grabbed some canned beans and corn from the food trailer, and in no time, Sam had the fire going and the meat sizzling on the skewers.

It was a wonderful meal with strings of gamey meat that Milo loved but made Trina gag. She did love the canned veggies, though. And the MRE pastas and brownies.

"Let's go explore," Milo said, after we finished eating. We all laughed and sat back in the metal chairs, exhausted, admiring the rock formations and the colorful expanse of the desert sunrise.

"Look at those rocks," Trina said, reading from a plaque beside a built-in telescope. "See them? They're called Mitten Buttes—"

I looked at the prominent formations again. "They do look like mittens, don't they?"

She began to read aloud about how they looked when their shadows were just right, but about then we heard Milo call, "Look at this!"

"What is it?" Drew called, a note of alarm in his voice.

We all took heed and ran toward the sound of Milo's voice.

But we didn't see him anywhere.

"Milo?" Drew called. "Where are you, son?"

Trina cupped her hands around her mouth. "Miles!" she shouted. "You better not be playing tricks!"

Faith pulled the lump of turquoise from her pocket. "It's warm again," she said.

Before I could say anything, Snake dashed up a short path and then we saw them. A cluster of small reddish colored hogans.

"What's that?" Drew yelled. "They look like giant beehives."

"Those are Navajo hogans," Trina said. "Small houses. Each one is a wooden frame covered with mud."

"These are replicas. They rent them out to tourists," Sam said. "I'd forgotten all about them."

Snake ran inside the first dark doorway. For some reason, the door was wide open. The hogan itself was only a small hive-shaped structure. These looked barely large enough to hold a bed.

Sam got there first. He had to duck to look inside.

"Snake?" he called. "Milo?"

When neither appeared, he moved on to the next hogan even though we'd all seen Snake go into that one.

"Snake is deaf," I shouted. "Remember?"

Sam turned around, a sheepish look on his face. He ducked and went all the way inside the tiny house.

"Milo!" Trina yelled again.

By this time, we were all there. I pulled out my little ever-present Dyno flashlight and gave it a few cranks. I couldn't believe we'd left all the battery-operated lanterns back at the firepit. We hadn't needed one with the fire and the rising sun. "Let me look," I told Drew before he could rush inside. I didn't like the way the others had gone in and wouldn't respond. I leaned forward and shined the weak beam inside. The house was facing east so I couldn't understand why the rising sun didn't light up the interior. But it didn't.

The light disappeared at the doorway, sucked up by the darkness. "I can't see anything—" I said.

"Jack!" Faith cried holding out the turquoise.

I couldn't believe it. The lump of cool blue rock was now red hot. Before either of us could react, the stone flew out of her blistered hand and disappeared through the doorway.

"What th—" was all I could say before I felt myself yanked into the hogan by some unseen force.

CHAPTER TWENTY-FOUR

Transported

I came to in total darkness. A void. My body hurt all over, as if my skin had been turned inside out. Or as if I'd been flayed and hung out to dry. *That's it, I'm so dry, my mouth full of sand, my eyes feel as if they haven't been closed, ever. As if they have lost the ability to close.*

I traced my face with my fingers. My eyes *were* open, but I could close them, easily. I blinked several times. The light did not change.

The total darkness reminded me of that first day, in the school basement, when the rip occurred. And the tuba-sounds shook the world.

I swiped my fingers across my mouth. It was also wide open, as if I'd been screaming in my sleep. Wait. *Was I asleep?*

I think we all were, Faith replied. *Or unconscious.*

Ugh, someone moaned. *What happened?* It sounded like one of the kids.

We unlocked the monument and went down the rabbit hole, Dad said. *I felt myself fall through the floor. It just opened up below my feet, right after I was sucked into the hogan. That's the last thing I remember, though.*

Me, too, I thought. *Can anyone see anything?*

Are we still in the hogan?

Drew? I asked.

It's me. His thoughts felt raw, serrated, worried. *Kids, y'all here? I can't see a thing.*

Two thoughts came toward me at the same instant.

Yes, thought one.

Where are we? thought the other.

I don't know what happened in that hogan, Dad shared, *but I feel the way Dorothy must have when she woke up after the tornado.*

At least you haven't lost your sense of humor, I chimed in.

It's black as the bottom of a latrine, Sam thought. *I feel like I've been roasted and toasted, can't tell if I'm standing up, sitting down—*

Or lying down, Faith finished. *I can't even feel my own body much less see it.*

Everyone murmured agreements in our conjoined thoughts, and then fell silent. I thought of Psalm 46:10 in the old King James Version, "Be still and know that I am God." *Now why would I think of that? Sunday school Bible verses hadn't been part of my life.*

"Breathe," a female voice said, out of the darkness. "Inhale slowly, exhale as you count to four. Stars will appear in your vision. Breathe in again, slowly. Exhale as you count to five."

I followed directions. The tone of that automated voice gave me no alternative.

"Now, inhale once more and exhale to the count of six."

I did. Tiny flashes peppered the dark. Gray light slowly began to illuminate the shapes of my companions. The first one I saw was Sam. He was just standing, gazing around. The kids stood near their father, and Faith and Dad stood, side by side, and I … *where was I?*

Oh, my, God. Will you look at that?

I couldn't tell who said it. But suddenly my attention was pulled toward a scene that appeared out of the gloom like a movie fading into view.

It was a faraway beach scene on a cloudy day. I could see what appeared to be a mirrored structure rising out of the ocean like a strange, futuristic pyramid.

The structure itself appeared to be sinking, but the bright apex of the thing still rose above the waves, a mirrored pyramid pointing toward a single brilliant source of light shining down through an ugly sky hole.

"Breathe," said the instructional voice. "Inhale, exhale, count."

We did. Or at least I did. I assumed the others did, too. While I was counting, I could not hear the others' thoughts. But the voice helped me gain consciousness. I imagined sand beneath my feet, shifting my weight, giving me reality with each and every breath, each and every count.

Are we inhaling Joy Juice? I thought-asked the group. *Seems I hear a hissing sound.*

Silence. No one knew. Or they couldn't say. I could see their shapes in the murky gray, but they didn't seem able to move any more than I could. The shifting sand was no more. My feet did not move. Not one bit. We were just *here*.

Where are we? a small someone asked. Before I could respond, the mechanical voice said, "Prepare yourself."

The pyramid exploded and sent shards of mirrored glass flying.

I closed my eyes, tried to duck. Nothing happened. Nothing but silence. The hissing sound had stopped.

Was that pyramid real? I thought at the group. *Or was it just the effects of some drug? Did anyone else see the exploding pyramid, hear that hissing sound? What just happened? Am I tripping? What was that voice?*

I heard the tinkle of glass breaking, Faith thought. *But I couldn't see anything except a gray sort of mist. Yes, I also heard the hissing sound, like fabric sliding on plastic. Gone now, though.*

Snake barked, as if he could explain. If he only had a voice. *Snakeman,* I cried out in my head. *So glad you're here. I can't—*

I can't see anything, Milo said. *Where are we? A funny voice said we're here, but I don't know where here is. Is that a beach?*

Questioning murmurs and murmurs of agreement. Everyone had heard the voice, but no one had any idea why.

Laughter from Dad. "Who said tripping? Tripping sounds about right."

Around us, a new scene became apparent. "I think it's an illusion," Trina said. "I saw sparkles. Heard the hissing sound."

"A mass illusion created inside a tiny hogan. Can we get out of here, back to the monument or the hotel?"

"Back to our vehicles," said Sam, ever the pragmatist.

"I don't think we're anywhere near the hogans," Faith said.

I scanned the area. "I see an immense, silvery canopy. It stretches above us and across a gorgeous beach and out toward that pyramid sticking out of the ocean, which, apparently, did not explode the way I thought. Is this just my personal illusion or—"

"I see it," Sam said. "It's opaque and iridescent, and every time I blink it disappears into the glare of the sun."

The metallic fabric stretched out in all directions, sheltering all of us. The scene was becoming clearer and clearer.

"Ground zero," Sam said.

"Yes," Drew agreed. "This might be where it all began. That pinpoint of light is like the one in the room at the top of the stairs."

"So, this canopy," Dad chimed in, "is attached to that pyramid? Because I see it now. But it isn't shattered, it's whole, and shining. Right below a rip in the sky."

Snake pressed himself in between Faith and me. Both our hands found his soft spot. The sand beneath our feet became real. The sun overhead, warm, with bright rays bouncing off the mirrored panes of the pyramid like soft fish-arrows darting, pushing our vision away from the image.

It all felt real but unreal, *surreal*. Above real. As if we were looking down at it, but in it at the same time.

I could see everyone now, even Dawk.

But that wasn't the strangest part. Aside from the unbelievable pyramid, shapes strolled everywhere. Tall ones, medium ones, and a few shorter ones who had the slightly softened features of females. They weren't people, though. They were Takers. Blocky, gray, iridescent Takers.

But these were different.

"Look!" I pointed toward a knot of them strolling together, actually *looking* at one another as they walked and communicated. Their tattoos roiled—merrily—and the letters were in colors. Reds, yellows, greens, and more. Even some blue edging toward turquoise.

"What on earth?" Trina's voice held a note of awe. "Are those *girls*?"

Just then, one stopped, flung her head back, and flipped an amazingly fine, almost transparent, lock of hair over her shoulder.

"No way," Trina thought. "See-through hair—"

"And look at their tattoos," Milo replied. "I see hearts and flowers."

I laughed, but it was true. "Look at that one!" I pointed at a different gray, translucent-skinned creature strolling along. "He doesn't move like a Taker, at all. Look at *his* tattoos." Beneath his skin I could see the dark shapes of notes and musical staffs.

After watching for a moment, Dad said, "That's part of Bach's Concerto Number 3 in G Major." He got so excited he forgot to be inconspicuous.

Another huge Taker marched past. It was tall like Sam but translucent gray and even more muscular. The thing's spine was ramrod straight, eyes focused forward, black-slash mouth closed, and its tattoos, highly visible, did not roil like the happy hearts and flowers, nor did they leap about like the notes of Bach's concerto, this guy's tats were all business.

Even the fonts were strong and straight. MARCH, one read. OBEY, read another. PROTECT, OBSERVE, PATROL, read the others. The words bobbed in and out, visible, then not visible, here then gone. Just like the pyramid and the canopy. Visible in the sun, then gone when the light changed.

Just about like us, I thought. *At least that's how it felt.*

"Well, I guess we know his job," I said. And then it hit me. *We know his job. We know all their jobs. They are no longer unfinished destructors. That part of their journey must be over. Now they are—*

"—becoming," Faith said aloud, finishing my thought for me. "This is where they are becoming."

"Pod people becoming real," Dad said. "Like that old movie."

"Not exactly," Drew and Dawk spoke at the same time.

I wanted to point out to everyone that Dawk was with us again, but before I could ask him where he'd been—or how he got here—Milo said, "What are pod people?"

"It's from an old movie called *The Body Snatchers*," Dad replied. "Aliens came to Earth and began to abduct people, copying them inside giant seedpods. Only the new people were stiff, indifferent. Automatons. That's how they took over."

Automatons, Carlos's word from the get-go.

"What happened to the real people?" Trina asked.

"I can't recall," Dad said, daring anyone to contradict him.

"Kinda reminds me of metamorphosis, those pods, but not like Turq 2.0. Once he changed, his old form was gone forever." *Way to go, dummy,* I thought, chastising myself. *You just answered Trina's question anyway.*

Thanks, she thought back at me. *That's what I figured.*

I felt my face flame. I'd totally forgotten my thoughts weren't always private.

Trina touched my arm, having received that thought, too. "It's okay," she said aloud. "It's like our combined minds are a new world of knowledge. All the time knowledge. Like the internet is no longer at our fingertips, now it's inside our heads."

"PeoplePedia," Faith added. "We're writing each other's answers in our thoughts."

I shook my head to dislodge them all. "It's much stronger here, under this weird canopy."

"Much stronger," Dawk agreed. "I'll bet it's this funky lid causing it." He took it upon himself to move away, outside the covering.

Hey! I exclaimed. *Am I hallucinating you, Dawk? Like I did that pyramid exploding?* I tried sending the question to Dawk alone in case the others didn't have the same experience.

Nope, he sent back. *I'm here, too. Just trying to figure things out. I heard something about a hogan. I sure don't know about that. Last time I looked, I was trying to escape a lab in Colorado Springs. Somehow wound up in that military base.* He jerked his head toward the undulating dunes behind us.

His thoughts were like his voice, full of wonder, but also full of optimism. I could see why Faith trusted him. But before I could ask about the lab and military base, Milo spoke up.

"How'd we get here?" he asked. "I remember we ate a rabbit and then I went into that little round house." He stopped, obviously thinking back, "And then *poof,* here we are."

I scanned my memory, too. "Does anyone recall the sound of the monument turning?"

Several noises of agreement. "I think that opened something—"

"A portal," Dawk said. "I must have found one, too. But not the same as y'all. You say yours was a round house?"

"Yeah, we all entered a hogan, at Four Corners."

Ahh, he thought. *That makes sense. Such a mystical place.*

Mystical, I thought. *Okay*. I let my mind return to my earlier idea that we were seeing attributes of each of us in the surreal Takers nearby.

Girly for Trina, military/protector for Sam, musical notes for Dad … and yep, there was one like me. Creedence Clearwater Revival's "Up Around the Bend" came floating toward us as the Taker looked my way.

His garnet eyes hadn't changed, and his gray see-through coloring was still the same, the rest of him, though, that was all me. A sandy shock of hair, long knuckly fingers, big, clumsy feet, and CCR. All he needed was rumpled jeans and a black t-shirt.

Come on … rising wind …

"That's me!" I yelped. "They've remade me."

Milo began to cry, and at the same instant, a small Taker across the way began to cry, too. "They're making pod people to replace us," he wailed.

Trina laughed in my head. "No, silly boy. We aren't being replaced." She grabbed her brother in a tight, smothery, hug. "You're still here, and I'm still here." She pushed him slightly away and forced him to look into her face. "We're all still here. Together."

She glanced over at the group of teen-girl Takers. "Look, some of those are like me. And I don't mind. It doesn't even scare me. Heck, I'm impressed someone wanted to copy me."

Faith said, "I've heard imitation is the sincerest form of flattery."

Things were happening too fast. I couldn't tell thoughts from spoken words, not under the roof, or canopy, or whatever this thing was, but I wished it would stop, for just a few minutes. I needed to collect my own thoughts—something about the pod-people really bothered me, like, were they copying us and then taking us someplace else—some other dimension?

Maybe the CCR lyrics were trying to tell me something. I

needed to focus. *Up Around the Bend*. Look for a rising wind. And a big red tree.

"Maybe it's Redwood City," Dawk said, reading my mind. "*Climate Best by Government Test*. City motto from way back when."

"A big red tree," I half mumbled, half sang. "Up Around the Bend. A big red tree."

"Redwood City?" Sam echoed.

"It used to be quite a high-tech place," Dawk added. "Back in the early days."

"Strange," Dad said. "A juxtaposition of our early music and our early technology."

"And our movies," I said. "So many of our old movie-aliens have been jumbled up in these Taker scenarios, but I don't think Redwood City is what it's referring to." I couldn't be certain, but it didn't feel right. "In my head I'm seeing *lots* of big trees. I assume they're redwoods, but I'm a desert rat from Texas. What do I know?"

Faith laughed. "Maybe we *are* creating this whole thing as some kind of mass hysteria episode." She softened her tone. "My mom and I did the drive up the west coast once, just the two of us on a whim." Her voice grew even softer. "Seems like those redwoods were in Northern California." She paused. "I'm looking at this ocean, this beach. Maybe we are there, but I don't see a lot of trees—"

"Right," Dawk agreed. "This is near San Diego. I came through a portal or tunnel or something. Wound up in a lab on the base. Redwood City is much further up the coast."

"That's a lot to unpack there, I said. "Guess it proves the hallucination theory can't be right." I recalled the early days, all the annihilation, mutilations, murder, the gory killings, the sounds, the smells. "Anyway, we all saw people flayed and stabbed onto tree branches … they were real. Especially the one who broke my arm," I remembered how Turq had yanked me away and stuffed me in the Chrysler with Thad. "And the one who saved me."

"You're right," Faith agreed. "Whoever, or whatever, is in charge of the bad stuff probably lifted all these things from our collective consciousness—our books, movies, music—and now they're using them against us."

"That must be it," Drew said. "And maybe not even just *our* collective thoughts, but maybe from the humans working with them. Humans who think they can bargain with aliens, partner with them to take over the world, create a class of human/alien hybrids they can control or use. Like slaves."

"Slaves to be used in another dimension or on another … plane or planet?" I let my imagination speak. Every time I felt I'd figured out how to survive this madness, something new occurred.

"This is sounding more and more probable," Sam said. "And just like we originally thought, we are a lot closer to where the UFOs were filmed under the water. Maybe we should check out this place and then Redwood City like you mentioned."

"Actually," Dawk interrupted. "Redwood City is probably five hundred miles further north, near that, anyway."

"Weird," I said. "Maybe just San Diego then."

Dawk shrugged, touched the chin patch. "Maybe we're meant for both." He glanced around. "I believe we all came through different portals. Y'all from Four Corners, myself from Colorado. I think we missed our chance to connect with Jack at the Bitty House, but we're all together now. Seems meant to be."

Several of us nodded, but I was not certain at all. I had no idea how we'd arrived here. Not really. "Maybe," I said. "I'm not sure, though."

"It's all right," he said. "I think we are all on the path to enlightenment." He grinned when he said that, as if he knew how it sounded. "We are Seekers, you know, like in someone's idea of a video game, so maybe we're meant to find something in each place."

CHAPTER TWENTY-FIVE

Gone

Out of the blue, Drew thought, *What group sang about innocence dying in so many ways?*

That's Kansas, Dad replied in our thought hive. *Why do you ask?*

It's in my head, Drew replied. *And I'm not sure, but I'm afraid it's referring to the lack of people here. There should be lots of innocent people here.*

We all fell silent, trudging across the baking beach sand, wondering if we were in the right place, dumped out here on a beach beside a sparkling pyramid rising out of the water, the ocean lapping at our feet.

We were in Four Corners, how'd we wind up here?

"Slaves for the Beast," Dad murmured. "Souls to feed them."

We all stopped, glanced around. Silent Takers marched in tandem, or seemingly in tandem. Even if they were alone, they seemed in formation. None of the garnet eyed creatures acknowledged us. At all.

"Are we invisible?" I asked the others.

"I hope so," Faith replied. "But I'm afraid it's something more—"

Sam nodded. "I believe we are—"

"The chosen ones," Drew said.

"Chosen?" Milo and Trina spoke together. "For what?"

Drew looked at us over the top of the kids' heads. *We need to be ready for anything. The fact that these Takers stroll around as if we don't exist seems almost worse than when they try to eat us.*

"I agree," I said. "Be ready for anything. This is freaky."

Sam put his hand on his gun.

"Maybe we aren't really here," Faith said. "Maybe we're still back in the hogan at Four Corners." She reached out to put her hand on Snake's head, but the big dog was no longer with us.

I whipped my head around, searching frantically.

Snake was nowhere to be seen.

Alarmed, I sent a direct message to my dog, not at all sure if it would work. *Snakeman, if you can hear me, stay loose. Don't let them get you. We don't know what is going to happen. Stay away, be safe!*

I kept my mind open, hoping for some feeling or some kind of idea of where my four-legged sidekick might be lurking, and almost immediately I was hit with an intense feeling of trust and understanding.

In my mind, Snake's brown marble eyes appeared. *Don't worry,* his expression seemed to say, *I hear ya. I got this.*

But that could be nothing more than my wishful thinking. *He's a dog, after all—*

Wrong! Faith yelled inside my skull. *You know full well he is not just a dog. If there ever was such a thing.*

Dad, quiet until now, touched my shoulder. "Snake must have sensed something."

I nodded. "Makes me double wary—" I looked around. The silver-metal sheath stretched across the beach and across the edge of the waves and out across the ocean to forever.

Even squinting, I couldn't see the far edge of it. It was like the curve of the earth, there, but not there. *How can anything that thin sustain that shape,* I asked the group at large. *And why doesn't it reflect the sunlight.*

"Must be alien strong," Sam said. "Appears to be attached to that cell-tower thing—"

"You mean where that dragonhead is?" Faith asked. "Look at it."

"Wow," Trina said. "It really does look like a dragon's head up there."

"Weird," Faith said. "Are we creating these images as we go? I mean the canopy seems to spread from the pyramid out in the ocean—when I can see it, that is—all the way here to that thing."

She laughed. "Maybe we're making it up as we go, or maybe it's designed to get us to come closer—" her voice cut off as her feet stepped into nothing.

She was gone.

One second there, the next—nowhere.

I fell to my hands and knees. *Faith!* I screamed her name inside my head. *Snake!* I was certain he must've fallen in, too.

"Hold on to me!" I shouted. "There must be a hole." I scrabbled around the sand on my hands and knees.

Sam grabbed my backpack. "I got'cha," he yelled. "You feel anything?"

"Nothing!" I continued digging at the ground beneath the sand. "Seems solid—"

I was about to stand when the ground went out from under me, and I found myself whooshing down a slippery tube. *This is slime,* I thought. *It's the slime the Takers brought in, but it's coating a great tube slide. A huge tube slide coated with slime.*

"Jack!" I heard Sam's shout as he fell in behind me.

I felt my backpack separate from my shoulders, but I couldn't say anything. I was in the tube and the daylight was fading fast as I went deeper and deeper into the earth. And then it hit me. At the angle I seemed to be sliding—flying—I must be going under the ocean. *Had to be!* I could only hope I would go to the same place Faith had gone.

Jack! I heard other voices calling out for me. The sunlight was gone, the darkness pitch black. Again.

I'm here, I called out. *I'm here.* But I was picking up speed. Thank God for the thick coating of slime. If not for that, friction would have worn all my skin away. Turned it inside out. As it was, I began to have trouble breathing. My chest felt tight, constricted, as if my lungs were flattening.

Just when I couldn't take anymore, I began to level out.

Now, I was sliding on my back, but no longer at a downward angle, now parallel. Like a parallel universe, my mind whispered. *Like another por—*

And then I was out.

When I came to, there was light. Gray light like before, reflected from somewhere unseen. I reached out with my mind, *Faith? Dad? Sam? Drew? Kids?* I almost called out for Snake again, but I wanted to avoid that. Wanted to keep him secret from thought-thieves just in case that might be happening.

"Jack?" Faith's voice, nearby.

I spoke in the dim light. "Can you hear my thoughts?"

"No, not anymore."

"Are you hurt?"

"I don't think so," she replied. "You?"

I shook my head. Realized she probably couldn't see me. "I'm okay," I said. "I think we fell into some kind of tube."

And then I could hear *and* see her. Either my eyes were adjusting, or the light was growing brighter. "Where are w—"

My question was interrupted by the scene becoming visible in front of us.

"Oh, Jack," Faith breathed. "Look."

I did. I was. How could I not? Our entire surroundings were nothing but glass, or something like glass. And we were, in fact, down under the sea. The ocean was amazing. Like being inside a giant aquarium. Millions of gallons of water. Amazing. Just like this.

"The twilight zone," Faith said. "Remember the different ocean zones from science class?"

"I do," Trina said. "Look at the whales and the octopuses."

"And the sponges and that tall, wiffly plant," Milo said, becoming visible as he spoke.

"Could that be a plasma wall?" I wondered. "Or is it just glass?" I could see Milo standing in front of it, but not exactly. I could only tell he wasn't part of the water scene because he wasn't wet, and he was breathing.

"Wow," the kid said, craning his neck to look above us. "Up there, look!" He pointed upward, and we all saw a school of fish, colors flashing in the dim light.

"Amazing," I said. "We're in a giant aquarium."

Drew appeared out of the gloom. "I think we *are* prisoners in a giant fish tank," he said. "I don't see any way out."

We all turned in a circle. There were no openings of any kind. It looked just like ocean, blue-black and foreign, all the way around.

"So, we all fell into a hole on the beach?" Faith asked. "Right?"

"I guess we did," I said. "Now, it appears we're in some kind of Sponge Bob bubble under the sea—"

"Sandy," Milo said. "Sandy the squirrel is the one who lived in a bubble in Bikini Bottoms."

He was right, of course. And Sandy was from Texas. *Haha, what is it about Texas. Aren't we in California?* I looked at Faith. *Am I somehow projecting all of this with my mind, my memories? I mean, come on, a plasma bubble under the ocean? Weren't we just in New Mexico, or thereabouts? And what does it matter, we sure aren't there now.*

Faith didn't answer.

Oh, I forgot. Our thoughts were no longer shareable down here. In our bubble. Under the sea.

The lyrics to *The Little Mermaid* song smashed into my brain. "Under the Sea ..." *What the heck is going on? All this childhood stuff. And The Little Mermaid?* That wasn't me. But it *was* my mom. She often read that book to the little kids at the library. Showed the movie on Saturday in the Park sometimes.

That's when it hit me. Thoughts may not be sharable among the living, but this might be Mom chiming in. Telling me not to give up, not to give in.

The library.

The park beside the library. In Texas. In the park where I first saw Turq in his turquoise shirt? *Turquoise, the color of ocean water in a certain zone of light. Is that right?* I rubbed my head.

"Okay, Mom. I think I get it. All is not lost, but we're still dealing with Takers or, more likely, whoever is *controlling* the Takers." I thought of my slave theory. My stomach clenched.

Did they build this? The ones who conquered—maybe even brought—the Takers? Did they create this see-through prison, these ridiculous tunnel-tubes?

There were no answers from Mom, but Drew turned to look at me. "This can't be right. Are we really under the sea, or is this all an illusion?"

"Maybe everything is an illusion," Trina murmured.

Her voice sounded so dreamy, an image of Dorothy in the poppy field flooded my mind. I glanced around for some sort of Joy Juice sprayer built into the wall, or ceiling. But I saw no walls, no ceilings, no place for a sprayer at all.

I reached out to touch the wall, but my hand simply disappeared into it. Like reaching into cold, cold water. When I pulled my hand back, it was dry. Where'd our slimy tunnel go?

Milo watched me. When he saw that it was safe, he stuck his hand in also. A smile lit up his face. He stuck his other hand in, laughing, and soon everyone was doing it.

Dad looked at me. He was the only one not trying the magic walls. "They aren't really walls," I said. "Seems to be plasma or something." I glanced all around the softly lighted enclosure. "Is it a prison cell?"

We all examined our space. When we walked toward the walls, the entire area seemed to grow larger, but if we stopped to touch them, we could put our hands right in.

"It is a prison cell," I said. "There's no way out. It expands with us." I glanced at the others. "What if we just start walking and don't stop?"

"Hey!" Sam yelled, looking upward. "Who are you, what do you want with us?"

That scared Milo and Trina. Their eyes grew wide, the amazement gone, fear taking over.

"Dad?"

I couldn't tell which voice said it.

"It's okay, kids," Drew replied. "We'll figure it out."

To me, that statement was so profoundly sad I felt my mind transported right back to a memory-image of Carlos sitting on a farmhouse floor, clutching a teddy bear and a photo of his little daughter to his chest, tears streaming down his face. Parents try to comfort their children, and we try to comfort each other. That's what we do. Even when all hope seems lost.

Are we all our brothers' keepers? We children of God?

I continued walking toward the invisible wall until I became aware of soft music. Nothing I'd ever heard before, just tones—round, soothing tones. It reminded me of the prequel to my phone alarm. The tones meant to wake you slowly, gently.

"There's our answer," I said. "Those sounds mean something. Not sure what, but I don't think the sounds are coming from the Takers." I paused. "I guess y'all were right. They were automatons, soldier-slaves, the first wave."

"Toeless boots on the ground," Sam added.

"Not Turq and his kind though," Faith said. "They're angels. Guardian Angels."

She was right, of course. "Yes," I agreed. "But where are they now?" I asked. "Where are they now?"

Before I could chastise our angels any further, the floor began to soften, and I was reminded of the old childhood game The Floor is Lava. Everyone began to raise their feet and check the bottoms of their shoes for something sticky.

I thought of the new shoes we'd finally got for Faith after finding her, barefoot and searching, in the Eden High locker room. "Anything?" I asked.

Everyone shook their heads.

I examined mine, anyway. But when I stood on one foot to look at the bottom of the other foot, it threw me off balance. The walls became wavery.

"Like the portal in the old house," Milo said. "Does anyone see a hole?"

"Nothing," I cried. "And hey, where is Dawk?"

No one had seen him, and now, it was too late to wonder.

One by one, the entire crew—myself included—swayed and fell over while staring upward at the wavery walls and watery ceiling.

"What's going on?" I tried to ask. But even though I mouthed the words, no sound came out. First, no thoughts, now no voice.

The entire room began to sway. It grew larger, and larger. Sleep seemed imminent. I forced my half-mast lids to stay open long enough to check each face in my group. Everyone appeared to be fighting the urge to nap.

Joy Juice, I thought. *Happy, sleepy, Joy Juice.* It must be. And the floor is not lava but a cradle, soft and warm, rocking us all to sleep.

I rolled my eyes up one last time, searching.

The ocean walls were gone. Looking down at us were crowds of face-shapes, large and small, fat and thin, parched and sallow, big black eyes and bright blue ones, too. Creatures and beings such as I'd never seen before.

Their features were distorted, stretched, thin-skinned, mesh-skinned, boneless, metallic, translucent. As soon as my half-mast eye examined one, my glance would skate right on to the next, and the next, and the next. Each one stranger than the one before.

They had the skin of the Takers but not the features. The only resemblance between the two groups were the words swimming beneath their shiny, see-through skin.

I blinked, but I couldn't feel my eyes respond. I wanted to read their words. I *needed* to read those strange letters, those words. But my vision was too blurry, and though I tried to raise a hand, to rub my sleepy eyes, my muscles would not comply. It remained beside me on the floating floor.

The things stared down at us as if through theater windows. Operating room theater windows, like those popular hospital shows on TV.

CHAPTER TWENTY-SIX

Inside the pyramid

When I opened my eyes again, narrow black letters were wafting through the air. I could see their reflections in the smooth non-walls. The letters landed on my skin and on the skin and faces of the people around me. "Healthy," I felt one spell out. "Scarred," another set spelled.

The words "Slight damage," appeared on my thigh. The one where I'd taken a bullet. I could feel the letters. They were warm, like rope pulled across bare skin.

"Healthy," landed on Faith, and Trina, and Milo, and Drew.

"Damaged," appeared on Dad's forehead and across Sam's cheek. "Scarred," appeared in several places on both, especially around Dad's neck, and across his restored eye. I didn't have time to ponder the difference between damaged and scarred. But I felt certain there was a difference, somehow, to someone.

But how do they know, these things? Are they psychic? Where are they? Where are we?

Questions crowded my sleepy, paralyzed mind.

Before I drifted away again, I forced my mind to concentrate. The odd faces were still there, peering down at us.

I made myself look through the gaps between the faces, through all the glimmering light, straight up to the narrowing point above.

Is that the tip of the mirrored pyramid, gathering all the sunlight? Are we inside it? Are we rising?

I felt us rising. As if our plasma cell was an elevator moving slowly to the top. The motion put me back to sleep. A babe in a cradle.

I awoke again, alone and paralyzed in a solid white room. It took a great while before I became fully awake. There was no longer anything resembling an aquarium. It was simply a white space filled with dim light. A nothing kind of light. Neither sunlight nor fluorescent nor the soft glow of a library lamp. Nothing. I could discern nothing at all. Not even myself.

It was the most frightening feeling I'd encountered yet. Nothing to fight—or run from. Nor even any strength to fight it. That was the problem.

My eyelids fluttered and closed, then opened, then closed again.

Eventually, I became aware of slight movement near the ceiling.

Colorful, lighted numbers, red, green, blue, and white crawled across the area just inside my field of vision. Tiny numbers, like a ticker tape. Like Wall Street, or Times Square.

What is this? Where are the face-things? The clear walls?

I watched the numbers appear and disappear. Every now and then, a few black letter-parts floated down through the air like spider legs on an invisible breeze. But they didn't land on me, or if they did, I never felt them.

They didn't seem connected to the scrolling numbers. These were just pieces of old letters floating around. The word *detritus* came to mind. Leftover letter parts. Remainders.

Sometimes I recognized the actual letters, other times, they were broken or strange, foreign, and I could not see where they went. I was alone. Were the letters there? Or were they the remains of my strange, unconscious sleep? Another illusion?

Nothing made sense.

I took stock of what I could see. There seemed no rhyme, no reason. Just occasional black spider-leg letters. And now, the numbers. What could the numbers represent? *They aren't vital signs—they aren't birthdates, or social security numbers, they're not phone numbers, not even prime numbers*—I could discern no patterns at all. Just random digits. Sometimes single, sometimes doubles, sometimes long strings that seemed unending—until they did.

Then the spider-legs would begin to fall.

My mind spun, seeking, searching, feeling. Drifting. Coming back. Praying. Hoping for clarity.

Once again, I could not make my body work. Nor could I speak or send a thought to anyone.

A shadow-figure moved across the side of my vision.

It might have been the silhouette figure of a young woman, but it could've been a boy. Or a young man. Or it could've been something altogether different. My mind touched on possibilities, then tossed them aside like used confetti. Or spider legs, floating.

The figure did not look at me, it seemed to be talking to someone on an invisible headset. "One," the odd flat voice said. "One."

Then it disappeared from my field of view. I could not turn my head to look further. I didn't seem to *have* a head. Or a body. Or arms or legs or anything but eyes and a brain. And, I suppose, lungs, for respiration. I couldn't feel myself attached to anything or lying on anything. No tubes, no wires, no breathing apparatus, no bed.

The more conscious I became, the more terrified I felt. Total weightlessness. Lack of substance. I was not touching anything. I could not move anything.

I simply was.

"Jack ..."

I opened my eyes.

"Are you there?"

I could hear the voice inside the room with me.

Or did I imagine it?

Another figure walked across my field of vision. The numbers and letters scrolled randomly. *Did I sleep?*

"Jack ..."

Was the silhouette figure speaking to me? No. It just walked the length of my room and disappeared. Wait. Maybe it *was* speaking to me. *Someone* had said my name.

A voice said something unintelligible, and then an ancient song began to drift through my consciousness. It was a song I'd heard Dad play on the piano. He said the intro was inspired by a different song about someone's father. *Steely Dan.* That was the name of the band. It was a jazzy kind of rock song called "Rikki, Don't Lose That Number." Yes. That was it. That was the name of it.

Dad? Is that you?

No reply, and I didn't get a sense of him the way I did when he sent me the Kansas songs. But the memory blurb about the piano intro being related to someone's father made me think it *must* be Dad, getting a message through. *But why a song about numbers?*

I stared into the blurry atmosphere of the room, straining to see the walking-talking person more clearly, to see if it could be the one sending me this random song remnant, but it was impossible. The figure was a fuzzy silhouette against all the white. I couldn't even determine the source of the light that allowed me to see.

I made myself take stock of what I knew about my surroundings. The entire area was plain, smooth, white, endless.

Like plastic or the inside of a fridge? Maybe not a fridge, not with those colored numbers running around the top of the walls, disappearing into the ether, and the spider-leg letters floating down. But like a fridge or a freezer it seemed airtight, inescapable.

Watching the numbers for a while, I discovered when I counted them, I could never go higher than 42. Even if I multiplied them, or added them together, they would disappear at 42.

That number seemed the apex of something. The beginning, or maybe the end.

Oh. My. God.

Am I dead?

Is this my white high-tech coffin?

"Jack ..."

Dad? Is that you, are you sending me this song about numbers?

No answer, just a blue light and a cool breeze. I must be dead. This must be the afterlife. Or the journey to the afterlife.

Snakeman? I sent the thought out into the void, desperate.

Keep calling him, Jack. I can hear you, maybe he can, too.

Faith? Is that you?

No reply came, but I gradually became aware of feeling. The feel of Snake's rough tongue. Like the cabin at Palo Duro Canyon and Snake licking my face after I'd been shot. The place where Faith was kidnapped, where Carlos was killed. *Are we back there, in the giant canyon? Palo Duro. Is that an Indian word? Oh, wait. We don't say Indian, right Mom? Native American, that's right. Is that a Native—*

Jack ...

The voice again, just a thought-sound this time. A vibration of the air near my ear. *But that's what sound is, right? Vibration of the air, or vibration of the hairs in our ears to produce sound? Well, that's just stupid—*

Jack, open your eyes. The voice interrupted my rambling thoughts again.

And I did it. I opened my eyes. The whiteness came into view. *I don't want to open my eyes. This is like death. It's not Heaven. I don't know what it is, but I can't move, and I can't speak, and I can't—*

They've captured us, Jack, but listen.

A whirring sound. Far off, like a dream. A good dream but fading. Going away. I listened. *Is that you, Faith, talking to me in my head?*

Yes.

And is that Turq 2.0 whirring?

I think so. I think he's helping us, somehow.

Where are you? I asked.

The numbers sped past on the wall. The white room shone from unseen light. The shiny surfaces glimmered. I closed my eyes again.

Don't close your eyes, Jack. We're moving up the levels. Stay awake.

"Carry on Wayward Son," floated into my thoughts.

Dad!

I'm here, you two are chatterboxes. He chuckled in my thoughts. *Snake is nearby, too. I feel him.*

Where are you?

He laughed a bit more. *I'm not sure. Somewhere near this crazy dog. I can't see him but he's whining, wanting me to do something.*

We are in some high-tech prison or hospital, Faith sent.

I tried to focus my thoughts, send them out. *A lab,* I thought. *A pyramid lab. I keep seeing glimpse of the pyramid shape, narrowing to a point.*

Faith and Dad seemed to mull this over.

Tell me what you see, I thought.

Green, Sam chimed in. *Military green numbers scrolling across a white wall, soothing but frightening. Frightening because I can't feel anything. But the numbers are soothing green—*

Hey, Sam, I sent. *Good to hear your voice. Green, huh? My room is white, too. But my numbers are all colors. Scrolling—*

Blue here, Dad replied. *Turquoise blue. Like the light when Turq saved me and wrapped me in his wings.*

Ahh, Faith thought. *I remember that day. My numbers are turquoise, too. With some that are white.*

Who has the Snake? I asked.

I can't see—

By now, we all heard and felt Snake's presence. *Unh, unh, unh.* A deep whine, but with an edge like a growl, like a rumbly engine in a deep, furry chest.

Snakeman! I blared the greeting so he could feel me, not thinking about how animals' senses are so much more acute than humans' senses.

Rauer! he barked. But I'd swear he said Jack. I'd swear it on my hopefully-far-in-the-future grave.

Where are we, Snake? Can you find me? Can you find us all?

I heard the dog's claws scrabble against something slick. Then the noise scrolled off into the distance like the appearing and disappearing numbers.

CHAPTER TWENTY-SEVEN

Colors

Within minutes the barky-whine came again. *I'm so glad to hear you,* I whispered, hugging the stout neck in my mind.

My arms are coming back. I lifted them slightly, looking at them, wondering where they'd been.

Mine, too, Faith said.

Dad laughed, *Same!*

Each time one of us spoke, the lighted numbers changed colors. Mine, white, Dad's turquoise-blue, Faith's light, light turquoise blue outlined in white, and when the voice of Drew spoke out of the dimness, I realized Snake must've awakened him, too.

Milo chirped as his dad's voice called to him and to Trina. Snake must've awakened them all. The kids' voices sounded out, *Dad! Are we alive?* The scrolling numbers appeared red near the ceiling.

When Drew spoke his children's names, the numbers stayed red.

"Hey, gang," I said aloud. "Is everyone here?"

Trina spoke first. "I'm here. Can y'all see those lights? The numbers?"

We all murmured our agreement.

"Can any of you see me? Or Snake? Or each other?" My voice sounded strong, but bland, as if enclosed, prevented from going very far. When that idea crossed my mind, I realized there was also an absence of odor. No smell at all … *or was there?*

I inhaled deeply, felt my chest expand for the first time in ages.

Then I caught it, the soft tang of salt water. *We are under the sea.*

"I can't see anything but the numbers," Trina said.

"Same—"

"Me, too—"

"Same here—"

"Anyone seen the Snake yet?"

We all fell silent, listening.

After a few seconds, his whine told me he was still nearby, almost on top of us it seemed. I pictured his stub tail and tiptoe gait, but I couldn't see him. Didn't know if he could see me, but maybe he could, or at least feel me, somehow. And then I heard the whirring sound again. The one we'd all come to know and love.

"It's Turq," Faith cried, excitement flashing the numbers in cadence with her white-turquoise voice.

"I hear him," I said.

Snake barked, and I laughed. "Maybe things are clearing up. I think he's with Snake." I raised my arms to shoulder level. I still couldn't see anything except the scrolling numbers. I stretched my arms, bent my knees. "I'm becoming a real boy again," I said, twisting my head from side to side.

"I feel floaty," Faith said.

"Maybe we're in a sensory deprivation tank," Sam said. "Some sort of giant sensory dep tank, to keep us under control, gauge our responses for some reason."

"Or to keep us unconscious while they did some tests," Dad said.

"Hey!" I yelled. "Is that your hand, Dad? I see someone's hand with a turquoise number one glowing in the palm."

He waved. "It's me, Jack."

I yelled, "I see you, Dad. You're right here, with me."

"Thank God," he said. Then he dropped his voice as if talking only to himself. "This reminds me of the way we felt immediately after the hogan. Except not quite so toasted."

I laughed, held up my own palm. "My number is also one, but it shines white in this dim light. It's not solid though, it's shot through with turquoise, like yours, Dad." I flexed my fingers, opening and closing my hand. The number appeared and disappeared just as it had in the overhead scroll. "I'm number one," I said.

"Me, too," Dad murmured. "A deep, turquoise blue number one."

I spoke to Snake, again, hoping he could feel the vibrations of my voice. Hoping he really knew where we were and that he wasn't just running around wildly, searching for us.

He rumbled in his chest.

"Turq," I whispered. "Are you out there, with the Snake? Why can't I see y'all?"

There was no answer other than Snake's continuous rumble.

"I'm number two," Sam said, chiming in unexpectedly. "A green number two." He chuckled. "Not sure how I feel about that."

Milo giggled. "What's your number, Dad?" He held up his hand. "I'm a four."

"I see it," I yelled. "I see you, Milo!"

"Me, too," Faith said.

"So do I," Sam said.

"And me," said Dad.

"I'm the same," Drew said. "Red four." He also held up a palm as proof.

"I'm a number one," Faith said. "Turquoise with white outlining. Same color as Jack, but outlined, not marbled."

Trina held up her palm. "Red number four for me," she said. "Like Dad and Milo." Her voice went up a notch. "Hey," she cried. "Do you guys hear that?"

We all went silent, listening. I thought it would be the whirring of wings Trina heard, but then I heard it, too. An actual voice. Calling our names.

I opened my mind and blasted a thought into the void. "Dawk? Is that you? Are you there?" He was the only one we hadn't yet seen or heard. And I really wanted his input on these numbers. I didn't like being marked this way. Too close to those historic concentration camp tattoos.

In moments, a shadowy form appeared outside and beneath the scrolling letters.

"Dawk!" I yelled, "We're in here." I could see his wild-haired silhouette moving across the room. Only now did I realize the white walls were translucent, too.

Is that why I can suddenly see everyone? I would have sworn I was alone.

Dawk's shape went away, and then his face appeared *through* the ceiling. He stuck his head down from above as if through clear corn syrup.

"Hey," he said. "What's going on?"

"Dawk," Faith said. "I can't believe it. How'd you find us?"

Snake barked so we knew he was here, somewhere, even though we still couldn't see him.

"Heads up," Dawk said, dangling the end of a thick, knotted, ship's rope toward me.

I grabbed the first knot with my half-numb hands. "What is this place? Do you know?" I looked around for something to help me pull myself up the rope to the next knot. My body was still numb. *Mostly dead*, I thought. *Like Wesley in The Princess Bride.*

Hang on, Jack, Sam thought at me. *I'm coming.*

I craned my neck, searching for Sam. Black spider legs floated slowly through the air. "Does anyone see the spider legs?" I asked.

"That's me, Jack," Dawk said. "When I broke the seal on this tube, those black pieces floated out." His voice sounded anxious. "I've noticed they speak everything they want done and it appears someplace. Like those internal tattoo instructions."

I laughed self-deprecatingly. "I guess the words then break down into these letter-pieces." I tried to remember when I'd first noticed the floating legs. It seemed a while ago, but everything was fuzzy, just like the legs. "So, Dawk, is this the end of that slimy tube we fell into?"

"This one originates on the beach all right," he said. "I assume it's where y'all fell through the sand. I guess this room is the terminus. Or one of them. We need to avoid those colorful tubes, though. That much I know for certain."

I tried, but I couldn't see any other tubes. My head and neck still didn't work just right. One thing I did learn, there was no salt water. We were *not* floating in a sensory deprivation tank. Not exactly. But we were floating in something. Or trapped in it, perhaps.

As I turned my head to look for Sam again, his tall form came into view. He was blurry. "Sam!" I cried. "Can you see Dawk? He's up there." I indicated the other end of the rope.

A chorus of voices sounded from around me. *Don't worry,* I thought. *Dawk is here to get us.*

I slowly turned my head again. The air swam around me like thick, clear, Karo syrup. Primary colors pushed away from me in wide, wavy lines. *Are we in some kind of preservative?* I felt my hair, but I couldn't *really* feel it. Either my hands were still numb or the syrup—*slime, just call it slime*—had numbed my senses.

I held on to the thick knot tightly.

"C'mon you guys," Dawk said. "Let's get the kids up first." He was looking at us from the observation deck or operating theater, just like the alien faces before.

"Coming," Milo yelled. "Trying to, I mean."

Behind Milo, I finally caught a glimpse of the colorful tubes Dawk had mentioned. They were also translucent, but their colors corresponded with the colors in our palms.

"That's where you were headed," Dawk said, filling us in as we began rubbing at our arms and legs, trying to get enough feeling into them so we could climb. "In fact," he continued. "Time is of the essence. When the vacuum begins again, you will each be transported again, via these tubes, to the appropriate color lab."

"What?" Panic laced Faith's voice.

"From what I saw at the military base," he continued, "each tube delivers subjects to a specific lab once intake is complete. White is genetics, blue has to do with immune systems, green would be musculoskeletal, and red is for blood and organ transference."

"Organ transference? What's that?"

"Nothing good," Dawk said, dodging the question but letting a glimpse of operations being performed by Taker-bots slip into his consciousness—thus, into ours.

He tried to deflect the accidental picture of gore. "C'mon, let's get everyone out of here before the black rain finishes up on the beach. That's the only thing that's interfering with their signals and instructions. Well, maybe that and the fact that some of you have two colors instead of one."

"That's because Turq 2.0 saved us and infused some of us with his blue healing properties," Faith said. "Guess that's what confused their tests. Thank, God."

He seemed to think that over as Sam waded through the syrupy atmosphere with Milo and Trina under his arms. Together we boosted the kids up to the deck via the rope knots, one after the other. Next came Faith, and then Dad.

It was like watching He-Man in slow motion. I knew all along Sam was uber strong, just like the old comic book character, but to watch him lift grown men up so they could get started on the saving climb, that really impressed me.

I helped where I could, rubbing my neck and looking over my shoulder as I held the first knot so the others could put their feet on it.

The now-ominous colored tubes leading away from our strange little prison yawned threateningly. I kept waiting for the sound of the vacuum.

And then it was our turn. Together, Sam, Drew, and I were able to push each other up and out of the slimy, gel-filled white room.

"The rope is so slick," Dawk called down. "Take your shirts off, turn 'em inside out, try to use them like gloves. Y'all were encased in some sort of conductive gunk—"

Just then, Snake set to barking again. But they were happy barks, as if he'd just found the kids or Faith.

"Is Snake on the beach?" I asked.

Dawk appeared at the tube opening again. "Yes," he said. "That's your dog. And I hope the sound of his happy barking means he is done with Takers. He's the one that's been out there causing the black rain to fall and take them out. Which is also what alerted me to where you guys fell into the holes."

Wow, I thought. *That dog. That amazing dog.*

"Yeah," Faith said. "We slid right down into what we thought was some kind of sensory deprivation tank—"

"That's how they run their tests on you," Dawk said. "To see if you're worth keeping alive. They can make you *see* anything. *Feel* anything. Like Joy Juice, but on a much higher level. Probably part of the conductor goo they covered you with."

I wanted to ask how he had learned so much, but we were busy getting Drew up, and then me. I looked around for something to help Sam grasp the knot after he had tossed me up to Drew, but he didn't need anything. Turned out his strength alone was enough.

By now, Dawk had led the kids and Faith on up the rest of the rope from the observation deck toward the beach opening. I followed.

Looking back down into the strange room, I saw we weren't lying on medical beds or anything. There was absolutely nothing else inside the space other than the lighted numbers. We'd all been *standing* in the pod-shaped room immobilized by the slime.

"We were in a preservative," I muttered. "Under the *ocean*." I pulled myself up through the remainder of the long, long tube. *This is old school,* I thought, as claustrophobia began to settle around me. I feared the tube would collapse on us, preventing us from climbing out. But what else could we do?

I distracted my mind with Faith and music as I dragged myself, hand over hand, up the knotted rope, through the person-sized circumference, toward the daylight at the upper end of the tube.

"It was like egg white in there," I heard Milo saying. "Like the inside of an egg. The slimy part. Yuck."

As soon as my upper half cleared the opening in the sand, Snake hit me like a freight train, rumbling in his chest, licking my face, pawing my arms, tumbling me onto the sand as if I were no bigger than a toddler.

Dawk laughed, and his thoughts slipping into my head. *Everything will get better and better as we move away from the opening.*

At last, Sam heaved himself out of the tube and onto the beach. "Talk about one size fits all," he said. "The whole room just deflated like a dead balloon."

Or a dead womb, I thought, my claustrophobic fears resurfacing, but I didn't say that. Instead, I said, "We saw it. Through your eyes, and your thoughts." I looked around at the others standing on the sand. "At least I did ..."

Everyone chimed in that they had been watching through Sam's eyes, too.

"It was just one weird room," I said. "But there *were* numbers, right? We didn't imagine that did we?" I looked down at my palm. It was clear now. As were all the others.

"I'm glad to be rid of it," Dad said, examining his palm. "It was way too reminiscent of Hitler."

"Yeah," I said. "Dawk says they were prepping us for experiments—"

That took us all a moment to work through, then I asked Dawk to tell the rest of how he'd found us.

"Snake," he said. "I couldn't believe it when I heard him barking." He reached down and ruffled the dog's loose neck skin. "I spied him across the beach from the top of that largest dune." He pushed at his glasses, and we followed his gaze toward the dune.

"You know," he said, "I thought he'd disappeared with y'all, so I went to the highest point I could get to, in order to see down the beach."

We all looked down the beach to see what he might have seen, but he wasn't through talking. "As soon as Snake had my attention, he shoved his snout down into this hole like an ostrich sticking its head in the sand."

He gestured at the near-invisible opening, and we all laughed at how funny it must have looked to see Snake with his head gone and only his body showing. "It must have taken a miracle for him not to get sucked in like the rest of us."

I looked down at where the opening had been, imagining those colorful tubes branching off from the egg room. A miracle? Yes, no doubt that's exactly what it was. Either that, or a guardian angel. A chill invaded my body. We'd been a hair's breadth away from annihilation.

We all looked at our furry hero. And his wiry human sidekick.

"It took only a second for me to understand what had happened," Dawk said, continuing his story. "And I thought I knew what they were doing, too."

He jerked a thumb over his shoulder in the direction of the base. "Huge lab back there. Not sure if it was there before the rip, but it's there now." His face lost some of its happy charm. "They've got human body parts. Human blood, Taker blood—the clear stuff full of words and letters—and they've got a genetics department set up to mix elements of the two. That's where I observed all the color-corresponding tubes and numbers."

His mouth was a grim line. "They're exterminating all chosen humans by mixing us with their Takers, which I think they created to be their soldiers and slaves. I believe they're ancient. I'll bet they've been doing this a long, long time, gathering DNA from each successive takeover, cobbling their *soldiers* together according to the needs of each new universe."

I gazed around the dunes, imagining the giant lab Dawk described. "So, they brought these Franken-Takers with them?" I asked, trying the theory on for size.

"Just my idea based on what I've seen," he said. "They use them for everything—"

"But then some of them morphed into angels?" I couldn't let that go. It seemed the most important part of this whole debate.

Dawk pressed his hand onto my shoulder. I knew whatever he was about to say was important. "There's no way of knowing what other genes or DNA is mixed together inside those creatures."

I tried to understand what he meant. Did he mean they had angel DNA thrown into the mix, too? Was that even possible?

He rubbed the soul patch on his chin. "The way I understand it, from the lab tech I encountered, is that they collect all kinds of raw genetic material as they travel the universes, or dimensions, hopping from one place to another in their quest for Utopia."

"So, I was right. Sort of. *They* are also Takers. Not just the creatures themselves, like Turq before he changed, but all of them. Takers, traveling the multiverse, taking what they want while they search for the perfect place. Sort of like I thought all along."

"Whew," Sam wiped at his forehead in mock relief. "This is deep for an old vet like me. A huge concept—"

"But sounds true," Dad interjected. "Or possible, at least."

"*Feels* true," Faith said. "And as for the angels? That wasn't them at all. That was God. Giving us hope and the weapons to survive."

"So, it isn't hopeless. We're not alone?" Trina asked.

"Not by a long shot," Faith said.

"Not even under the sea?" Milo asked, laughing.

We all looked at him, momentarily confused.

"What?" he asked innocently. "Am I the only one who liked that aquarium part at first?"

Suddenly, we understood. Leave it to the kid to find something positive inside the madness.

"That *was* cool, those lights and numbers. Freaky, though," Trina murmured. "Very freaky."

"Yes," I agreed. "There for a second, in all my shiny whiteness, I thought I'd died—"

"One thing's certain," Dawk said. "Snake was brave. He didn't even pause once he got my attention. He was ready to dive into the tube no matter where it led."

I thought back.

"Wasn't Snake the first one to disappear into the tube?" I recalled looking for him, wondering where he'd gone. Maybe he'd sensed the tube beneath the sand just in time to avoid it.

Dawk shook his head. "We'll have to talk about that later. Something tells me they are not going to let any of us simply leave." His feet made deep dimples in the smooth sand as we made our way out from under the stretched overhang toward the dunes.

"Something else I want to talk about is why, if they have this high-tech stuff in the pyramid, would they do anything in a military lab?" I shook my head as I mulled it over. "Seems backward to me."

Dawk shrugged. "I think they were in such a hurry they set up labs everywhere."

"You're right." I thought of the mess inside Cheyenne Mountain. "You are so right."

CHAPTER TWENTY-EIGHT

Theories

We walked on.

We saw no Takers, no creatures, no humans. Nothing. "I don't think we're out yet," I whispered, testing the air around us with my hands, feeling nothing but strangely still California air, but still feeling trapped somehow. *Shouldn't there be a breeze? It is a beach, after all.*

"Do all these tubes lead back to the military lab?" Faith asked.

"Yes, and vice versa," Dawk said.

"Did they lead from the lab and from openings on the beach, too?" Faith asked.

Dawk shrugged. "All I know is what I saw. And what I was told in the lab. I *think* the openings may appear as needed. Or when one of the overlords causes one to open."

"Yeah," I said. "Everything here seems fluid, like the waves. And they know how to manipulate it." I thought for a moment. "The overlords. That's a good name for those beings who seem to be running everything."

"Wow," Milo said. "Check this out." He jumped up and down causing his feet to almost disappear into the fluffy sand. "This feels weird. And why is everything deserted now?"

"Good question, kid," Sam said. "I think we should get off the beach. Why wouldn't another tube open under us at any second. It's giving me the creeps. If we don't fall into another tube, we could be walking right into some other trap. Or an ambush. Maybe even being led there."

Dad voiced his agreement. Then added, "I was *convinced* we were in a spaceship down there. This huge canopy also appears otherworldly. Especially that dragon head leering over everything."

"I thought it was a spacecraft too. I still do." I shot a glance over my shoulder. "Look, the tip of the pyramid is barely visible in the ocean. Can a spacecraft be shaped like a pyramid? What about all those faces staring down at us while we were immobilized ... and where did all the Takers go? Did the dark rain take them all? I don't even see any footprints on this beach. I can understand the black rain taking the creatures themselves, but even their footprints?"

I continued walking, moving closer and closer to the dunes, away from the sand nearest the water. "And where is Turq?" My eyes roved the cloud-bandaged sky. "I know I heard his wings. I believe we all did."

"Most of that, I don't know," Dawk said, glancing over his shoulder, feet picking up speed. "But if that pyramid is real, I believe that's where all the tubes lead. Even those from the labs. And it's probably the place where you all were trapped."

He glanced at the sky, too. "As for the Turqs, as you call them, I've seen them flying in the distance. But around here, it's been strictly run and hide ever since the lab tech clued me in." His stride lengthened as he spoke. "Do the dunes seem to be getting any closer?" His breathing seemed to be coming faster.

"No, they don't," Trina gasped, eyes searching the sands for possible tube openings.

"An illusion?" Dad asked.

No one answered that, so I asked the other burning question. "How'd you get inside the lab without getting caught? And what else did the tech tell you?"

I waited for Dawk to answer, but at the same time I was thinking how nice it would be to just camp out on the beach, build a bonfire, sit around singing "Kumbaya" with my new family.

Maybe there are traces of Joy Juice still in our systems, Faith thought at me.

I shook my head and made myself focus on Dawk's answer as the old "Kumbaya" spiritual continued to drift through my thoughts.

"Look at that thing—it does look like a dragon's head," Dawk gestured toward the dragon-head-on-a-stalk sticking up out of the sand. "I know it's the tether pole for one corner of the canopy, but sure has the look of a small craft of some sort."

"A drone—"

"Or a giant camera watching the entire beach."

A funny look crossed his face. As if he hadn't been able to see the forest for the trees, so to speak.

"That would be the simplest explanation, wouldn't it?"

I nodded. I couldn't quite imagine a flying craft perched up there, but little did I know the things yet to come.

"Look," Sam said. "The long spiny neck sticks up above the surface of the beach a good fifty to seventy feet." He clenched his jaw. "The canopy splays out from it, but the head itself seems to move as if scanning the entire area. Like the eyes in some paintings. The way they follow you everywhere."

"I think it's detachable," Dawk said.

I glanced back at the triangular head flattened to cobra-like points on either side of the face. "Those windows could be the eyes, right? A place for a camera. An overlord's tool, like you said."

"Yep. I'm sure they're watching us right now. So why don't they do something? Why did they let us escape in that way to begin with?"

"Exactly what I wondered," Drew said, appearing on my left. "Talk about old school. I mean, a knotted rope that just happened to be laying there on the sand?"

"Turq," Faith murmured. "We need our Turq."

Dad stopped, his feet also sinking into the too-soft-sand. "He hasn't deserted us, but for now, what's our plan?"

"Sorry," Dawk said. "I've gotten so used to everyone hearing my thoughts, I guess I thought you all knew. Believe it or not, there is another tube, or portal, if you will. I'm pretty sure it goes all the way back to the old Bitty Sloan house."

"Nah," Milo said. "That's hundreds of miles." He thought for a moment. "Probably more."

"He's right," Faith said. "That's just—"

"Crazy?" Dawk laughed. "I know. But I believe, according to what I'm hearing and seeing, that once you hit a certain speed or velocity inside any of the tubes, you are automatically flashed on to the end." He rubbed the back of his head with his fingertips. "I'm just guessing. Could be hokey pokey for all I know ... but I think that's how I wound up here, one of those tubes from the military base at Colorado Springs led to the one at this base—and the lab—and then I escaped to the beach. And Snake."

"Sounds like all these places are connected," Dad said.

"Shoot," Drew said, "after what we saw under the sea, I believe they've got tubes and tunnels all over the Earth. Maybe all over the universe." He looked at me. "Isn't that how we wound up here from that hogan?"

Silent agreement until Faith spoke up again. "Look around us. Maybe we are still in a giant tube of some sort." She dragged a hand through the air around her body. "Why isn't there any breeze?"

She looked to me for affirmation as her feet stopped and began to sink into the sand. "Remember how we were able to walk all directions in the egg room down there, and the walls would just move with us?" She pointed at the dragon's head perched on the nearest column, the canopy splaying out toward the pyramid in the distance. "Maybe we are still trapped."

"One majorly ginormous tube. What a concept." I smiled at her to let her know I also believed anything was possible.

Everyone looked back in the direction from which we had come.

"Maybe," Milo said, still processing Faith's every word. "Maybe they built it for their house, down under the sea, after they arrived here through those tubes, or worm holes or whatever." He hesitated, uncertainly. "Like, we're all out on their patio right now ... about to have a barbecue."

"Could be," I said, to encourage him.

"Maybe it's not a ship at all," he continued.

"You mean you think it might be their actual home? Like they were here all along?" Trina asked.

Milo nodded and Faith pulled her half-buried feet out of the sand and started walking again. Her tennis shoes left dented imprints. Footprints. "I like hearing all the theories." She walked on. "And I know you told us about our different colors down there," she spoke specifically to Dawk. "You saw that. But have *you* experienced anything like the colors or numbers?"

Dawk shook his head, but he seemed on the verge of saying something else. Something he was having trouble getting out.

"Go ahead and tell us," Dad said. "We've all seen horrible things. Nothing you say will bother us now."

Dawk looked at the odd beach, clenched his fists. "The lab tech was dying when I found her." His jaw clenched to match his fists. "She'd been left behind, strapped to a table, an IV catheter still in her vein."

Faith's hand covered her mouth. "She had an IV? I thought you said she was a lab tech. Like one of those *doing* the IVs?"

"She said she used to be, when she was still human."

That stopped us all in our tracks. Even Snake.

We stared at Dawk, awaiting clarification.

CHAPTER TWENTY-NINE

Good dog, Snake!

"She was attached to one of the colored IVs. It was yellow." He ducked his chin. I thought he would touch the soul patch, but he resisted. "But here's the thing ..."

We all leaned forward, just a bit. I kept one eye on the dragon head. *Had it moved? Would it breathe fire like in ancient times?*

Dawk swallowed hard. "It was awful. The IVs were siphoning fluids *from* her." He looked at each of us, to see if we understood. Snake whined, shifted his weight on his paws.

I recalled the blurred faces looking down at us in the egg room under the sea. "I don't recall a yellow tube."

He looked away. "I think it was generic for *take whatever she's got left*."

Faith shivered, clasped her arms around herself.

Fury rose into the back of my throat. "Have you seen them. The overlords?"

"I saw faces looking at us," Milo said. "In that egg white room." He glanced over his shoulder, as if worrying he'd been overheard.

Obviously, we all remembered those faces.

I nodded at Milo. "I saw them, too. Makes me want to get as far away from this place as possible."

The boy's shoulders went down a bit, as if in relief.

"Maybe we take a tunnel to get out," Faith said. "If we can figure out which one goes where." She glanced at Dawk. "How'd you get out of the lab?"

"I didn't see anyone else," he said. "Or anything else, for that matter. It was like they'd abandoned the place. But I did hear something, far away. A familiar sound." His lips crept up at the corners, just a bit. "It was Snake," he said. "After the lab tech woman shriveled like a prune right before my eyes, I began to look for any way possible to get out of there."

His eyes held a look I can only describe as haunted. It was clear he'd been changed by what he witnessed.

He took a good breath. "The lab walls were smooth, seamless, shiny," he said. "I stayed with her, holding her hand. She was awake even after I detached the IVs." He swallowed, straightened his spine, continued, "When her machines went off, they must've been the last ones in the entire lab. There was nothing but devastating silence. Until I heard that wonderful barking."

"Snake!" Of course it was the Snake. What other dog was there? Plus, like the others, I was slowly getting back to reading—maybe I should say sharing—Dawk's mind.

"Yes," he said. "I followed that beautiful doggy voice right to the terminus of an air vent. A regular old air vent. It took me straight out." He pointed at a beige vent sticking up from a rise near the dunes like a large periscope. It was so well camouflaged I never would have noticed if he hadn't shown us.

Then Dawk laughed, and I knew why. I could see the memory in his mind. Him crawling out of the vent, dropping to the sand in a heap.

"When you came out, Snake was surrounded by Takers, right? The original gray ones with the ugly sin words."

"Exactly," he said. "They were doing their best to grab him." He laughed ruefully. "Some of their previous *instructional words* had changed, though. Instead of KILL or DESTROY, the letters said things like CAPTURE, BRING, SEIZE. One simply said TAKE. It was obvious someone wanted ol' Snake alive."

"Not surprising," Faith said. "He is certainly special."

Dawk's mind whooshed like the Nike shoe emblem. He'd seen something. I could sense jumbled words all related to Snake. And then I caught a glimpse of him imagining a table, and Snakeman strapped to it, IVs in both front legs and one in his scalp.

Aww, hell naw, as my old buddy Cade might've said. That's not happening. Not on my watch.

No way, Dawk replied in thought. *Not on my watch, either.* "When I came out of that air-vent, I could see Snake snapping at the monsters lurching around, trying to catch him."

"They're not too smart," I said, "except for the ones who put on clothing, and then—"That gave me an idea. *Were they wearing clothes because they'd had an injection of humanity somewhere along the way? Or because they'd had a shot of angel DNA, or maybe even a bit of dragonfly extract? Could those magnificent, iridescent wings be a combination of angel and dragonfly?*

My eyes immediately went to the odd dragon's head. Maybe it was a dragon*fly*, not a dragon. *Nah, that's just coincidence, right? Dragons, dragonflies? It's the angel question that's more pressing. I mean, are angels real, with bodies that can be poked and probed like ours, or are they just spirits?*

"Not *just* spirits," Sam said, speaking out for the entire group to hear. "Amazing spirits. The way I understand it, they can take on any form."

Everyone looked at Sam. This was a side of him we hadn't seen.

He shortened his stride, so we didn't have to lope to keep up. "Gran liked her Bible Study Group," he said. "She never missed it after I got back to the bar to help her." He grinned.

"I once suggested she hold the weekly meeting in the bar. She popped my rear-end with a wet bar towel. Really zinged me, even through my back pocket." Rubbing a spot on his butt cheek, he joked, "After that, I never mentioned the Bible and the bar in the same sentence again."

We all chuckled. At least he and Faith agreed with me that our flying Turqs *could* be angels. It wasn't just my fanciful thinking.

The miraculous healing at Cheyenne Mountain should have cemented that in my mind, but somehow, I found it easy to let doubt creep in, to unbelieve something wonderful I'd seen with my own two eyes.

I laughed at myself. "Well, that answers my question. Turq 2.0 is our guardian angel." I smiled at the image of a gray-haired granny flicking a wet bar towel at Sam-the-giant. "Now if we only knew how to call our angels when we need them."

Dawk shrugged. Pointed at the sky. "Maybe we just did."

I glanced up. *Maybe they are on our wavelength, too.*

Dawk hurried to finish his tale, "When I heard the barking, and found Snake biting and snapping, sticking his head down into the tube so I'd be sure to understand, I was amazed. I helped him take down a few Takers before I stumbled over the length of ship's rope buried up in the sand." He sounded perplexed at the coincidence. "I dug it out because somehow, I knew we were going to need it. Then I went looking for you guys." He frowned. "It was all I knew to do."

Wanting to know more, I opened my mouth to speak, but he rushed on.

"When Snake and I had the Taker blood flowing—and those spiky black letters flying—the dark rain came down. I swear I'd thought it was gone. Never thought it would come down in that alien landscape with that dragon head watching everything from on high."

We all scoured the oddly distorted sky. But it was gorgeous, a blameless crayon box blue with white strands of stretched clouds unrolling above the waves like gauze all the way to the horizon.

"That dragon head bothers me," I said. "Why don't we climb up there? See what's wha—"

Faith gasped. "No. I say we get as far from here as possible, like you first said, Jack."

I nodded. "Yeah, you're right. I know we should—"

"We have to, Son," Dad said. "There's such a thing as bait, you know. Maybe they're baiting us. Probably the reason they aren't worried about us getting away. I'm not certain, but something seems to be floating in my brain like their sin words—what we now think of as their instructions or orders. Some half-buried idea is nagging at me. There, but not clear. Not yet."

I let that sink in. He was right, of course. There might be a hidden message in the image of the roving dragon head, just like in the words. And in the music.

"What if we go back to that lab?" Drew said. "Would there be a tube to take us back to the Bitty Sloan House?"

Dawk nodded. "There might be one, but how would we know? You guys came from Four Corners, and I came from Colorado." He glanced back at the vent. "There's no way to know except by trying, I guess. And I'm not sure I'm game for that. We could wind up back in the egg room, or even worse. And don't forget, the lab tech was the last human I saw until Snake led me to y'all."

Snake must've tired of our lollygagging. He took off, leading the way. We'd been moving toward the dunes, but still didn't seem any closer.

I noticed Faith scratching at her neck and arms from time to time, and then mine began to itch. *Power of suggestion*, I thought. Until I noticed the slime from the tube and egg room was drying to a crinkly glaze on our skin.

In another second, we were all clawing at ourselves.

Almost as one, we dashed back to the edge of the waves and plunged our hands into the water, splashing it on our skin over and over and over.

I'll bet this stuff really is some kind of conductor, I thought at the group. *Conducting their power over us like—*

Like some kind of Joy Juice, Dad thought. *Although I don't recall it itching this way.* He was scrubbing at his face with sand, rinsing with the saltwater.

That can't be good, I thought. And then I did the same. "This feels like chickenpox," I said aloud. "Maybe we shouldn't be scratching it."

Even Dawk was washing off in the surf, from where he'd climbed down the tube with the rope. But I couldn't worry about that, my skin was beginning to burn.

I stopped scratching and scrubbing and took a deep breath, standing in the foamy water. The sun felt amazing on my wet shoulders. I was tempted to dive under to douse my whole body at once, but I was terrified of what I might see, or what might see me. I stepped out and gathered the rest of the crew. My itch was much better—almost gone. Normal seemed possible again.

CHAPTER THIRTY

Deadly miracles

The cool air felt like a promise, and I realized it wasn't just the water on my skin causing the change in temperature. A breeze had finally kicked up. The gauzy-white clouds had given way to piles of fluff, gray and dusky blue, the color of dust bunnies or a handful of lint pulled from the dryer vent.

Look up, guys! I wanted them to see the darkening clouds.

A bolt of lightning struck the ground near the dunes. Sand flew up in a spray six feet high. When it fell back down, it fused into smoke-colored glass. "Take cover!" I yelled. We couldn't worry about holes opening beneath our feet. We had no choice but to run.

Lightning bolts continued to pierce the veil like electric arrows, scorching the beach, sending up burnt sprays of art one after the other, creating a sort of smoke screen.

We looked at each other, our minds reached out, and the words *Find shelter,* whooshed between us.

Lightning struck the beach over and over, close enough to make the air crackle and the hair stand up on the back of my neck. "Trapped," I yelled.

"Follow your instincts," Sam yelled back. *Pay attention!*

As if on cue, a wall of Takers came over the dunes as one entity. If they had been any closer together, they would have been conjoined.

Red Rover, Red Rover, Sam said in my head. *Who* will *we send over? How about Snakeman?*

Before I could respond, a lightning bolt hit the wall and letter-filled fluid burst into the air.

The ground shivered and shook. Grains of sand scattered away from our feet like bugs running for their lives and then the entire beach rose in a hump and split into pieces, falling away on all sides as a brilliant, mirrored edge split open the waves and rose through the beach in slow motion.

The kids screamed as the sand trickled away and we found ourselves scrabbling to find footing upon the slick, mirrored side of the pyramid. Dry sand mixed with water muddied the surface just enough to slow our rapid descents.

We skidded down the sides as the pyramid ship continued to rise beneath us. In the distance, I glimpsed the point, way out in the deep but higher, that's how wide the thing was, how immense. We were seemingly at the outer edge of it.

It reminded me of how the plasma walls had grown outward us as we moved around down in the egg room. It reminded me of Dawk's statement about the cloak of invisibility.

Could there be other pyramidal craft out in the deep? Or was this all one ginormous craft?

The bolts of lightning slowed to a stop. But it didn't matter, Drew and the kids were sliding down the surface away from the rest of us. The mass of the ship continued to expand. Since it was a pyramid, the base grew wider and wider as it breached the water.

Jump! I called. *Jump!*

But they could not jump. They were sliding. And then the dragon's head detached from the column and flew across the sand toward us like a drone.

"Look out for the head," I screamed.

Everyone turned who could turn.

The dragon's windows had come to life. They were lit up like the eyes we'd known they were. The eye-lights shined across the entire broken length of the beach. It was the only illumination beneath the heavy storm clouds. The canopy broke free and swooshed across the waves on the stormy breeze. It came to rest on the distant point of the pyramid like a shiny nosecone on a rocketship.

The Takers appeared to be headed for the mother ship rising beneath us. It seemed like a bugout in every modern war movie I'd seen. Soldiers running for helicopters leaving battlefields.

But the lightning strikes started up again. As the soldier-Takers crossed over the broken beach, the lighting hit more and more of them. Then the black rain came. It shot down here and there, crashing over the injured, slurping up exploded letters and clear Taker-blood. Preventing the soldier-slaves from rejoining their fold.

"Take cover," I yelled, as we landed hard on the wet sand. The slick sides of the pyramid felt like smooth glass. And the lightning was as deadly to us as the black rain. We didn't know which way to run.

The unbelievable craft continued rising beneath us. It was so wide it had sent us tumbling far from our original point as we slid down its side.

I couldn't even see Dawk's air vent in the dunes anymore and still the thing rose, seemingly ready to take flight. *Are there more of them, or is this the only one?*

Everyone tumbled and scattered as we hit the ground.

"Cover up with sand," I shouted. "Don't let the dragon's eyes find you."

But Snake didn't listen. Thank God. Not even with his doggy mind. And he wasn't about to hide in the sand like the ostrich Dawk had called him earlier.

We can't hide, Jack, Dawk whispered in my head. *We have to—*

His thought was cut short by the sound of Snake snapping and snarling, charging into the quick-marching Takers. *Get 'em, Snake!* I hurled my thoughts at him. Once again, he was our best weapon.

He seemed to have renewed energy. That gave me renewed hope.

As the clear Taker blood flew again, so did the cleansing rain continue to streak down. The line of monsters split apart to avoid the dark fate of their injured peers.

We all cheered when they split, momentarily forgetting the

searching dragon head. But I could feel the vibration from beneath us as a whirring of wings invaded my senses.

Turq! Faith yelled, echoing my thoughts.

Has to be, I yelled back. But then I realized it wasn't just noise. Everything was shifting again. Still shifting to be exact. The pyramidal craft was so immense, it had slowed, but hadn't stopped. One of the four sides faced into the water. Waves smashed into it, climbed, and slipped right back down, unable to breach.

The void began to widen as water filled the cracked earth.

We ran again but couldn't make any headway. I wanted to stop and watch the strange craft rise, but I couldn't. Of course, I couldn't. We had to move or be swallowed.

When the thing cleared the earth, if it ever did, we would likely get sucked under the edge of it by the undertow. A mammoth sinkhole just waiting to gobble us up.

I thought of a giant egg room beneath the sea. *To the dunes,* I shouted in my head. *The rain has cleared the Takers. Head to the dunes!*

So that's why the lightning had come. To clear the Takers from the dunes so we would have a safer place.

Black rain now fell all around the craft, hitting Takers, cleaning up messes. The clutching waves grew oily with the black. Every time we thought we'd cleared the rising craft, the sand would begin to crack open beneath us, sending us scrambling again.

Snake! I called in my mind.

Faith joined in immediately. *Hurry, Snake,* she thought-yelled. *Where are you, Snake man?*

We were both doing our best to avoid the darkened waves seeping around the pyramid edges.

To me, Faith sent, *All the black rain falling in the water. If we fall into it, we'll suffocate, be swallowed up, taken away.*

I glanced back as the oil slicks appeared and disappeared on the surface of the water. The blobs of oil *were* attempting to coalesce. They shined on the waves, each drop seeking the others, running together like the liquid metal of the T-1000 Terminator.

Faith was right. If we fell into that mess, there'd be no way out. I thought of Cade's terrified, rolling eyes when the stuff slurped over his face. I renewed my efforts to keep my footing. The beach was a maze of cracks and gullies. We ran, jumping them, praying, never getting any closer to the dunes. Glancing back at the monstrosity still rising.

Look! I threw out the thought. When the sun hit the surface of the craft just right, I could see fine shadows moving inside the translucent walls. They must be the aliens. The overlords. The faces-looking-down enemies from the egg room. Were they coalescing like the dark drops of rain on the waves? Were they joining together like the Takers in the dunes, individuals apart, but joining together to make something happen … *to make the ship rise?*

No! Faith shouted in my head. *Those aren't alien shapes, look at the wings, Jack. Those are our Turqs. That's what we keep hearing!*

I focused my thoughts on what she could see from her angle. *They are Turqs,* I agreed, amazed at the flapping wing-shapes inside the glimmering walls. *Are they powering the ship? Is that what's bringing it to the surface?*

What's going on? Drew interjected.

Not sure. We think they're holding our Turqs in the pyramid, using them for their flying power.

We have to get completely away, Faith added. *Before this thing clears the sand and we all find ourselves underneath it.*

No one tried to answer. We were all scrambling together behind the dunes, but it was too late. We'd completely forgotten the dragon head spy.

It screeched and homed in on our position.

Watch out for the drone! Dad yelled. Cover your head in case of Joy Juice!

We all heard an uptick in the powerful sound of the wings as the dragon head swooped low, its red eyes casting an evil pall over our hiding spot.

Lightning crackled and struck the head, then it leaped in a mighty arc all the way across to the glittering profile of the pyramid where it sizzled up and down the triangular outlines like white fire.

The tremendous craft appeared to tilt, and the dragon head swung away from us toward the vessel.

Dawk shouted, "It's going over. The lightning damaged something. Look!" He directed our attention back to the shadowy figures fluttering inside the silvered pyramid. *They've broken a panel!*

We all stared at a large dark area where a panel had cracked open above the sliding sand. The ship tilted even more. Instead of the entire thing rising from the water, only the closest edge was now rising. The other sides seemed to be tilting over into the black waves.

Through the sudden opening, I could barely make out what appeared to be an engine room. That was the only thing I could think to call it. But instead of the glowing futuristic engines powering the rise, there were our Turqs, huge wings slowly flapping.

They appeared to be tethered one to the other through the tops of their most delicate sets of wings with some sort of plasma cable.

It reminded me of the collaring process I'd seen inside the Cheyenne Mountain Complex, except this cable pierced at least one wing on each Turq, rather than encircling the necks. And it was translucent and alive with clear fluid and black letters.

I sent those images out to the group in case they weren't able to see from their own viewpoint, and then I dashed out into the open, praying God would protect me long enough to get me inside that opening.

CHAPTER THIRTY-ONE

Escape!

"What's happening?" Trina and Milo screamed.

"The aliens are using our Turqs to power their ship. They've got them tied together. I can't see what's keeping them from flying out—"

"Joy Juice," Dawk cried. "Probably sprayed them and hooked them together like I should have done in the van."

Maybe, I thought. *But whatever it is, we need to get inside and help them so they can help us.*

I closed my mouth and opened my mind.

The gray splotched sand began to shift again. Before I could catch my footing, the whole ground tilted as the close side of the pyramid-ship burst up and the far sides sank under.

Will they drown? Will our Turqs drown all stuck together that way?

I found myself sliding toward the widening channel created as the near edge broke free of the water.

"Guys," I yelled. "What is that?!" Huge, clear, fantastical appendages coiled and dangled from the rising bottom of the pyramid. When they breached the waves, the open ends of the tubes sought the sand.

"Are those the tubes we were in?" Drew asked.

They look like giant roots, Faith thought. *Giant translucent roots. Maybe they are the tubes. Maybe they connect to other spaceships.*

All at once, a giant one flopped down in front of us. On

instinct, I doubled up my fist and attempted to jam it through the see-through skin.

The smashing was extremely soft, unsatisfying. My fist went in deep, but just like the plasma egg room, the covering simply gave with the pressure.

"Stop, Jack!" Faith screamed. "You'll get sucked *inside*."

"I have to," I yelled. "It's just that membrane stuff. I'm going to punch through, get inside, free the Turqs."

The tube didn't like my fist. It stopped flopping around the sand dune and rose above me, the open end questing like a big, round, mouth. My bravery took a hike as the thing yawned toward my head. *What was I thinking? I can't go back in there!*

The pyramid-ship continued to tilt, as if it would eventually fall over in the water, and then the dragon's head reappeared. It was after Snake. The big dog was hightailing it toward me from the dunes.

I bobbed away from the tube at the last second, narrowly avoiding the searching end. Snakeman leapt into the opening instead.

Noooo, I cried. *Snakeman, come baack!*

But it was too late. He had practically flown into the gaping hole. I had no choice but to follow.

And then we knew for certain.

The tube was slick with slime. We slid directly back into the egg room, this time landing on our sides. No faces peered in at the windows, but no hissing issued from the walls, either.

Snake! I called in my mind. *Where are you?*

I landed in another empty room. As before, it was movable, the walls dim and malleable. Why wasn't Snake in here? I'd leapt in right behind him. But where was he, and where are the Turqs?

Jack!

Dad?

Of course, who'd you expect, the Wizard of Oz?

I laughed. *Maybe.*

What do we do now? he asked, landing in a heap beside me.

I don't know. Snake rushed in, I just followed.

With those jaws, he can chew through that clear cord in nothing flat.

Of course! I thought. *If he doesn't get caught or drown first.*

The ship had tilted so much, we were barely able to stand. Now, the floor really was like lava, slippery plasma-lava. There were no real Takers, though. The dark rain had seen to that, mopping them up before they got inside.

This is a pyramid, Dad thought. *It gets smaller and smaller toward the top.*

Sure, I said. *How does that help?*

The pilots must be up there, he indicated that direction with his chin. *And all the important flying stuff is in the center. Let's break through every wall and hope for the best.*

Yeah! I liked this side of my father. *We'll trash it and hope it doesn't sink before we find the Snake and release the Turqs.*

As if in response, I heard the fluttering of many wings. Like moths trapped inside a glass bottle. But the fluttering was not all I heard. I also heard barking, and something else, something I couldn't quite put my finger on. It sounded like John Wayne.

It is John Wayne, Milo yelled in my head. *Hear him? Hear him tellin' us to get ready to ride?*

Yee haw, Sam shouted. *As soon as ol' Snake finds them and chomps through that tube, those Turqs are gonna fly. Y'all be ready.*

Snake's rumble echoed through the thin, strange walls. Dad and I forced our way through the gelatinous, plasma membranes. It felt like fighting through solid spider webs all melted together. The stuff gave and gave and then held tight at the last second. It took both of us to break through.

And then I heard a ruckus.

We've found him, I cried.

And Sam, too, Dad replied. *But I thought he was on the beach. Did he come in the tube before us?*

We broke through the last bit of membrane holding us out, and there was Snake. He'd scaled the back of one of the tethered

Turqs and was chomping at the clear attachment cord. I couldn't believe that slim strand was the only thing keeping them all prisoner. There appeared to be dozens of Turqs, maybe hundreds.

But when Snake finally bit all the way through, the viscous fluid gushed from the ragged ends. The stuff appeared biologic, like amniotic fluid from an umbilical cord. And then we saw the words pouring forth.

OBEY OBEY OBEY

Just like before. Just like every time. Taker word-blood. Just like always.

Had the Turqs absorbed the fluid through their wings? Or was the cord piercing their wings so that if they fluttered too much, they would make the ship rise whether they meant to or not?

I didn't have time to decide because my next worry was that this would bring down the black rain just like Snake had been doing on the beach, but surely it couldn't come inside, could it? Of course it could, remember the cliff dwellings?

Snake backed away from the nasty fluid seeping from the chewed end of the cord. He shook his head, as if the taste was poison, which it may have been. It had landed on him many times, though, through our battles, and it hadn't killed him yet, so I motioned at him to hurry and come to me, although I had no idea what to do next. Especially since I was looking at him from the opposite side of the clustered Turqs.

Jack! Dad yelled in my head.

All at once, the cavernous gray room was filled with the true sound of wings as all the Turqs began to shake free of the broken tether.

Come on, I shouted. *It feels like we're going over. We've got to get out!*

Wings fluttered and bullet shaped bodies arrowed toward the missing window panel.

The black rain began to fall.

Where is Sam? I knew I'd heard him. *Sam!* I yelled into the void. *C'mon, Sam! We're getting out.*

We need a miracle, Lord. I cast that idea toward Faith, a prayer already forming. *God, please give us another miracle like you did on the mountain. Like you did at the cliff dwellings. Like you did on the beach with the lightning.*

Everyone's voices dropped into my head in prayer. "Carry on Wayward Son" played in the background. Then I remembered the pyramid had been using Turq power to stay afloat. Now, that power was gone.

We're going to go over and then straight down, I shouted. *I don't know how to prevent it.*

"Everyone grab a Turq!" Sam yelled.

"There you are!" I yelled back.

"Yeehaw," Milo echoed.

It had grown nearly dark inside the pyramid. The Turq's were covering the opening as they jammed up, trying to escape.

I grabbed a wing, looking for 2.0, but it wasn't turquoise. I let it go. I needed to find 2.0 and Snake. No way I was going without the dog who had just saved us all.

The sound of rain hitting the slick sides of the pyramid meant the black rain was falling. The tethering tube had contained a lot of Taker blood. The rain wanted to get inside to clean it up.

Will the Turq wings shelter us like before?

I wished I could see the beach, see Sam. Why did he seem so close. He wasn't here. No one was here but Dad, Snake, and me.

I flashed a thought at the crew. *We are on a UFO. An alien spacecraft.*

Everyone sent me question marks as if I'd gone nuts. *This whole thing has gotten weirder and weirder. Turq,* I shouted. *Where are you? Where is Sam?*

Before I could say—or even think—anything more, Snakeman lumbered over to lean against my leg, exhausted.

Snakeman, I murmured, bending down to hug him. *Have you seen Sam?* I glanced around to make sure I hadn't lost Dad. The Turqs were thick. They reminded me of giant dragonflies. Gentle, not quite docile, upright, leaning forward, amazing wings humming in the cavernous room.

And there was Dad, standing open-mouthed, eyes fixed on the broken, Turq-jammed window.

Something was preventing the Turqs from getting through the opening. I thought it must be the black rain keeping them blocked, but no. It was Sam. And the drone.

The window was half-filled with the shape of the dragon-head drone. One of its dark, garnet eyes was cracked. The other eye stared into the pyramid room like a spy.

Sam hung off the side of the thing like a big kid with a brand-new toy.

"Sam," I shouted. "What are you doing?"

"I lured the stupid thing down low enough to grab it," he yelled cheerfully.

Up close, I could see a rail running around it like a bumper. I couldn't imagine how he'd forced it to fly him to the opening.

"C'mon, y'all," Sam yelled back. "I've got this head lodged in here, but some kind of invisible panel is trying to close. It's about to cut this thing in half, then I'll have to let go. C'mon, get out while you can!"

His voice reverberated in my mind to the tune of Janis Joplin's old song "Get it While You Can."

I didn't need any further motivation, all I needed was Turq 2.0. I didn't want to leave without him anymore than I wanted to leave without Dad or Snake.

Jack! Faith screamed in my head. *Look out!*

CHAPTER THIRTY-TWO

Trapped!

The pyramid inexplicably righted itself. It threw me off balance. Sam and the captured dragon head were the only things keeping the panel open. I began to suspect we'd been tricked, somehow, and were about to be trapped.

"What's going on?" Sam shouted. "Hurry!"

"Trapped and sinking!" I yelled. "The Turqs are trying to fly out, but they can't and now the ship is righting itself."

"It's the Turqs righting the ship," Dad shouted. "They don't want to drown, and don't want us to drown. That's why they aren't forcing themselves through the opening, they're lifting the ship again."

"Do we tell them to stop and let the thing sink, or do we let them continue rising and see where it takes us?"

Messages began to fly back and forth so fast I couldn't keep up.

Get out! someone thought-shouted. *Don't try to ride it. We know where the aliens want to take us.*

Where? Milo asked, his voice easy to recognize.

The lab, dummy! his sister chided. *They want our DNA—*

Drew cut that thought off. *That's not going to happen.* His mind-voice had a slight edge to it. *What do we do now?*

An idea struck me. *Milo, what would The Duke do?*

He'd take the reins in his teeth and come out shootin', Milo yelled.

I applauded that thought, and at the same time, wondered what had happened to our Turq 2.0. Had he been killed?

Why aren't you here, helping us?

Hurry, Jack, Sam thought. *This thing is being crushed—*

Before I could do anything, Snake scrabbled through the Turq-jam and leapt toward the slowly narrowing opening.

I grabbed for him. Too slow. There was a sliver of stormy sky visible through the gap and my crazy dog sailed right toward it.

Silence prevailed as we waited for the distant splash from what should have been a sliding, multistory fall.

He can't survive that. No one could.

"This thing's not holding—" Sam yelled.

Of course not. Alien technology putting up their shields, who could stop that?

The dragon head's one remaining eye bulged on the verge of exploding.

Sam wasn't giving in. He clung to the crumpled bumper rail like a giant monkey.

I can't believe you grabbed it, I thought at him.

He laughed in his head. *It was the only way I knew to come here and see what you three were up to! I wasn't about to take another tube-ride.*

Where's Snake? I shouted. *Can you see him?*

Sam let go with one hand so he could look down between his feet. *I don't see him!*

Dad and I forced our way through the Turqs, and I shoved my head out the opening, praying it wouldn't crack the drone and decapitate me.

Look, I shouted. *There he is!* I pointed at the muscular mutt paddling around in a circle far below. *He's going to get sucked under the edge,* I cried.

I threw my leg into the opening, forcing my skinny body into the gap. Dad helped by shoving me from behind.

I looked down, judging the leap. *Is that a shark?*

Something large, long, and pale appeared beneath Snake. I could see its shape rising from the depths. Terror struck me like a sledge hammer.

Go, Jack! Dad pushed me on over the edge, and I was sliding down the shiny surface all the way to the water, determined to fight the shark or the whale or whatever ocean creature was about to devour my best pal.

And then the most glorious sound filled the air as the pale thing beneath the waves breached the surface, spread its turquoise wings, and rose beneath our Snake, lifting him from the ocean, cradling our doggy hero in the nest of those miraculous wings.

It was the sweetest sound we'd heard in a long, long while.

Water droplets sluiced off the wings of our turquoise savior as the pair rose out of the wet and into the air.

By the time they cleared the water, I hit it.

Turq got him, Dad sent.

And then it was my turn. I bobbed back up from my plunge just in time to see 2.0 deposit Snake on the torn-up beach. Snake leapt off, and 2.0 turned, reaching me in record time, diving beneath me like a futuristic machine, half-plane, half-submarine.

I found myself nestled in the multitude of wings just like my furry friend before me. Patting Turq's back, I kept repeating my thanks, telling him how grateful we were. And then I realized I was thanking the wrong one and I amended my gratitude, sent it out to the Lord, our God.

From above us came a loud crack as the dragon's head was destroyed. That must have broken the invisible panel, too. The rest of the Turq's began streaming through the window, one carried Dad, another one had zipped beneath Sam like a surgeon, extracting him from his one-armed-dangle with expert precision.

The skies were drenched with clouds. All our thoughts were drenched with gratitude. Now the rain would flow inside the pyramid, clean up the Taker cord-blood just like it was cleaning up more injured Takers who had appeared from I-knew-not-where and were milling about on the remains of the torn-up beach.

Some Takers had not been covered with the black rain. They had fallen into the vortex below the ship—as I had worried we all would do—when it rose on one side and then tilted back. A few were visible in the water, as pale as Turq 2.0 but nowhere near as graceful.

At last, all the Turqs were out of the pyramid, and it slowly sank back into the depths, lightning striking and crackling its outline again and again.

Thank you for not frying us, Lord, I sent toward Heaven.

The pyramid disappeared beneath the waves with a whoosh and then it bobbed back to the surface causing tsunami sized waves to wash toward us.

Turq deposited me beside the others on top of the dunes, the waves crashing all the way to our toes. As the water receded, the pyramid rolled onto one of its sides, the base partially visible in the dim light of the fading storm.

Would you look at that, Drew thought.

More root-like tubes slithered from the bottom and quested in the shallows like mindless worms. I got the idea that some were the roots that anchored it to the ocean floor. I knew the inside of at least one of the other tubes very well. The transporter tube, not the root kind.

As we watched, something exploded from the end of a tube and dozens of tadpoles with arms and legs burst into the swells and disappeared into the deep.

What was that? Dad shouted.

That would have been us, I yelled back.

"Look!" Faith cried.

The surviving Takers began diving into the surf, swimming toward the upended pyramid with all their strength.

We stood together, hands shading our eyes, watching in awe as the once-formidable Takers were reduced to oddly childlike monsters seeking a return to their womb.

"They will drown," Trina said as more monsters dove into the roiling water.

"Yes," I said. "And we will have a chance to get away."

The Turqs flocked around us, flickering their wings, testing their wounds, healing from the inside—where the most delicate wings had been pierced—to the heavy outside layers, their strengths. Our protectors.

"What do we do now?" Milo asked.

"We stay together," Drew said, glancing at the rest of us. "You guys have become our family—"

"Same," Faith said.

"Teach Your Children," the old Crosby, Still, Nash song filtered into our collective consciousness. It was quickly followed by "Down on the Corner," by CCR.

"Well," I said. "Does everyone hear the music?" I was pretty sure they did. Somehow, I could tell when a thing was directed solely to me—just like when I directed some thought or impression solely to one person.

"I hear the music," Faith said, tucking frizzed hair behind her ear. "And I remember the talk about the redwoods. Does that mean we need to keep going?"

"As soon as our Turqs are ready," Sam said, glancing at them tucked up in the beach grass, nursing their injuries. "I hope they will be willing to get us a little closer to our destination."

Trina clung to her dad's hand. "Is that ship alive? I mean that pyramid thing?" She shaded her eyes and watched the gargantuan craft floating in the ocean like an iceberg, ninety percent of it below the water. "It is a ship, right? An alien spaceship?"

No one spoke for a moment. We didn't really know, but what else could it be?

"Looks like it could be the home of the beast," Faith said, glancing at Dad.

"It's obviously alive," I said. *Those roots, or tubes*—I closed my thoughts. *No, they aren't roots. It's a vehicle of some sort, obviously. And those tubes are for sucking up fuel, transporting nourishment, DNA.*

I think it is the lair of The Beast, Dad thought, smiling at Faith.

The Beast from the Bible, Faith thought. *I recall something about it rising from the sea—*

"And being controlled by a dragon," Sam said. Then he chuckled. *But this was the other way around, right?* He shot an apologetic look at me. *Will it sink back into its nest, now? I mean those tubes dangling from beneath it—*

I'll bet those root-tubes cover the entire ocean floor, Drew thought.

I wonder if it is somehow connected to all the oceans? Dawk murmured, deep in his own head.

No one could answer that. We were still learning as Faith always said. Learning as we go.

We watched the mirrored behemoth bobble along, and then slowly begin to sink back into the waves. Without the trapped Turqs, there seemed to be no power in it at all.

You'd think it would have another source of power, I thought at Dawk, but he reminded me the thing had been underwater for no-one-knew how long. Eons, maybe. Maybe it's not a ship at all, but a station for ships, or drones, like the dragon. And the labs, of course. Could be a nursery for all we know.

The pyramid edges were impossible to make out in the deep water, but the reflections of the clouded sky in its mirrored surface were barely visible, incredibly beautiful.

The craft sank slowly, its questing tubes sinking with it, the churned beach sand filling with water, packing itself back into place as if it were healing, like our Turqs.

We all inhaled and relaxed for the first time since we'd arrived. Then I remembered how this had all started with Faith falling into a tube and getting sucked down to the egg room inside that very ship.

CHAPTER THIRTY-THREE

Let's go!

I must've transmitted my fear to the rest of the group for all at once we were running further inland, behind the dunes, toward the military base where the labs were.

Not there! Dawk blasted into our heads. *Not safe!*

As if to emphasize those words, a platoon of Takers appeared in the distance.

They're probably headed to the ship, too, Dad said.

We didn't have time to worry.

Turq 2.0 swooped back down in front of me, opened his strongest wings and created a marvelous sitting space the size of a teenaged boy. I crawled inside the sweet spot and motioned for Snake. Dad came with him. It felt as if we were home.

A second Turq picked up Faith along with Sam.

Drew and the kids got their own flying Uber.

Thank you, God, we all began to babble inside each other's thoughts. And then we were on our way. Flying. It seemed miraculous.

Turq 2.0 shocked me by flying out over the ocean rather than heading immediately inland. Below the surface of the water, I could see the edge of the pyramid. Multiple tubes floated outward from beneath it. I couldn't believe we had been in one of those—more than once. It was crazy. Everything was crazy.

You ain't seen nothing yet, Faith interjected. *Look down there.*

I leaned over to see the other side below the pyramid, between our two Turqs.

Does that look like a nest to you?

It is a nest, Dawk said. *Look at that froth, those bubbles … those are eggs. Just like we thought.*

Remember the tadpole things that burst out of that tube when it was pulled off the bottom? I asked. *I think those are the same things.*

So … the pyramid was sitting on top of the nest?

No one knew or wanted to guess. Once again, our thoughts were jumbled one with the other. But Dawk wasn't through talking.

I suspect the pyramid shape is a shell, he said. *You know a carapace, and the alien lives inside it like an Argonaut Octopus, you know, the one nicknamed the Paper Nautilus because she builds her own shell around herself and her embryos so they can float closer to the surface of the ocean where it's warm.*

So those tubes could be octo-arms or whatever you call'em—

Yes, that's how it feeds and gets more specimens to add to its DNA database. For its future worlds and dimensions.

Trina chimed in: *I saw a TikTok once that said octopuses are really aliens.*

Images of cartoon aliens with hundreds of legs mishmashed through our thoughts. And then 2.0 dipped his wings and indicated we should pay attention to the water below.

It was chilling.

The pyramid was still sinking, growing smaller and smaller as it disappeared into the dark depths.

That's freaky, someone thought.

I couldn't agree more. To see something that huge and shiny reduced to little more than a murky image beneath the waves was like looking at a dead face at the bottom of a pond.

How deep is the ocean? Milo asked.

Miles deep, Dad said.

In places, it hasn't even been measured, Dawk added.

That did not make me feel better, but it did make Turq's insistence on showing it to us more understandable.

We slid over the water. The glimmery image continued to sink into the abyss, its tubular arms trailing, questing, visible only now and then in the shadowy deep.

"We Built this City," an old song by Starship, one of Dad's favorite classic rock groups, wafted through our thoughts.

It is kind of a city I thought, loud enough for everyone to hear. *An alien octopus that made its own shell city and pumped out its new aliens in those arm tubes—*

And then used the same tubes to suck up parts for new babies to keep it alive and help it keep building.

Yeah, I agreed. *That all sounds logical—*

That made Faith giggle. *We threw logic out the window on the first day of the rip.*

2.0 leveled out and we continued our flight path northward, toward Redwood City. At least I hoped he understood that's where we wanted to go. I was so exhausted, all I thought about now was getting a nap. Like Snake who was snoring away under my forearm.

As I dozed, visions of transparent tubes invaded my dreams. *That's how the best parts of the specimens from the lab were transported,* Dawk had said. *The specimens were transported through the chutes like bubbles through straws. This thing, this alien thing, was sucking it all up, constantly feeding all the DNA stuff into its central processing unit. It's how they mixed human DNA with theirs. Like some kind of genetic clearing house.*

It must be, Sam said.

Yeah, my sleepy mind agreed. *It must be.*

The buzzing, whirring sounds grew louder and louder even though they were muted somehow, and then I realized I was looking straight down as we flew over the ocean.

All the colors of the underwater sea—anemones, seagrass, kelp, red algae—all were being reflected by the iridescent walls of the pyramid as it sank all the way down. Even the brightly colored fish darting here and there lent their auras to the trippy palette.

Dad, are you in my head? I've never used the words auras, lent, or palette before in my life.

No answer, but as I watched, the reflected colors began to

merge, changing into a different color, like dumping all your paints into one pot—muddy, brown, ugly. It seemed to be camouflaging itself for some reason.

Do y'all see this? I thought. *The thing is lighting up the entire ocean as it sinks back to the bottom.*

I heard a collective sigh from the rest of the bunch. Then all at once, an army of Turqs bulleted down through the water like torpedoes dropped from low-flying planes. The buzzing, whirring sounds became muted—I'd already grown used to them, didn't even question what they were—and I realized the sound came from the Turqs now streaking through the water toward the pyramid.

Did you call them? I asked Turq 2.0? But as always, he did not answer. And then it occurred to me these must be the other ones who were tethered together, powering the entire thing. The ones we rescued.

Before I could finish the thought, the Turqs began crashing into the reflective surface of the sprawling alien shell. Plasma-like material flew everywhere, immediately melting into miniscule spherules, like lava meeting the sea and morphing into obsidian.

Wave on wave of Turqs blasted the spherules further and further from their underwater nest. The Pat Green country song, "Wave on Wave," accompanied the onslaught like a soundtrack.

But that wasn't the worst.

The worst part was when the colorful explosions lit up the ocean floor and showed it to be nothing more than smooth glass, or likely the same plasma we'd seen all along, and beneath that glass, an entire alien city with tubes flowing this way and that like city sewers connecting one neighborhood with another, all except for one immense, triangular base-plot; empty, ready, and waiting.

I knew I was dreaming—or tripping—when I saw that the spherules were the first stage of the tadpoles, the ones with human arms and legs.

I shook my head, certain I was asleep, but looking back one last time, craning my neck, determined to understand what was happening.

I'll never forget that last image. An immense multi-limbed

creature eerily visible, writhing beneath her pyramid-shell as it fitted itself into the opening in the plasma-glass floor of a once-normal ocean.

Dreaming? I wondered as we sailed along, rising higher and higher above the crackled and curling waves.

Dreaming the alien mother? The alien queen?

"Wave on Wave" melted back into ELO's "In the Beginning," the music permeating the very air that we breathed.

I closed my eyes against the scenery flashing by as The Off-spring's chaotic, melodic, "The Kids Aren't Alright" pushed out ELO's "In the Beginning."

Higher and higher we rose over the Pacific, too high to make out anymore of the strange scenes, but still accompanied by the prophetic background music.

The tubes spread out in every direction, I said, when I could think more clearly. *Like the runners spreading from a clump of grass, or from the fungus-among-us mushroom that lived beneath Oregon and spread every which direction for hundreds of miles. The thing is like nothing we're used to. The pyramid is just its plasma shell.*

Or it's hive, Dawk said. *All the queen does is lay eggs and produce pheromones for the colony.*

Soaring thankfully ever higher, we all ruminated on the length of the gargantuan in its alien nest. This far above the water was like having a drones-eye view.

I was mesmerized, transfixed, sickened beyond belief. I knew in my heart we had just seen the mother of the next race of earthlings.

Sam chimed in, *Am I the only one who wants nothing more than to just kill it, and start all over?*

I feel the same, I sent back, *But I don't think we've got it all figured out, folks. We're forgetting one minor thing.*

The silence was my invitation to continue.

The sky holes, I said. *We've completely forgotten how the Takers fell to earth from the sky. They didn't come up from the ocean.*

The seeds came from the sky, planted themselves in the ocean eons ago. Now, it's time for them to take the whole planet—

Yeah, or the Takers come from some other place—

Voice-thoughts went back and forth.

See what I mean? I asked. *We don't know anything, really.*

Dawk chimed in, *I second that. We are still in the dark about the who and why, but at least we saw the what—some of it at least.*

Just like everything in life, Trina mumbled in a half-formed thought. *So many uncertainties.*

One thing is certain, Dawk replied. *Whatever this species is, wherever it's from, it certainly seems to need water, and lots of it. I wonder how long they had to comb space, before they found our little blue, water-soaked planet?*

We flew closer to the coast, not inland, but not over the deep, either. The length of the creature's tubes was still visible every now and then. The size being both amazing and distressing. *How long had it been here?*

Looks like it's been here a while, Dawk thought back. *And look, there are even more of those dragon heads beneath the waves. I can't figure out why we're just now seeing them.*

I laughed to myself. *No water in West Texas where we came from.*

Not much in New Mexico where we came from either, Drew and Sam both thought. *But seeing them under the water is scary. Seems they can go anywhere, see anything—*

Big Brother, Dad said. *Always watching. Always waiting.*

But Dawk wasn't satisfied. *I've been lots of places,* he began. *And I've not seen anything like th—*

We didn't get to hear the rest of that thought. His attention—and as a result, *our* attention—was yanked away by a dragonhead rising up out of the water. It rose, dripping, garnet eyes shifting, left, right, left, and then it headed straight for our flock.

Kill it, Sam yelled. And the Turq he was riding began to swoop toward it in a steep, downward dive. Immediately, the other Turqs homed in as well.

No! I screamed, but I was too late. Sam and the Turq smashed into the roving craft and disappeared in a cloud of mixed-metallic particles.

"Sam!" We cried as the cloud dispersed into the air.

Another head rose to replace the first. *Don't dive bomb it!* I screamed. *Everyone go around, try to outmaneuver it—*

The moment that thought entered my mind, dozens more began to rise above the waters. Stunned by the sudden throng of heads—and the unexpected loss of the indestructible Sam—I could not think what we should do to avoid the glittering red window eyes.

Snake began to bark. It was obvious he wanted to fight.

Hold him! I yelled. I could imagine him leaping into thin air to attack one of the heads. I didn't think the diaphanous wings could hold him back if he leaped.

Knowing my thoughts, Turq 2.0 closed more of his wings and dove toward the ocean. I had no idea what he planned. *Our Father who art in Heaven ...* I began.

We sliced into the roiling water enclosed in our miraculous flying submersible, and Faith and I were able to see just how many dragon heads there were.

They're innumerable, I thought. *Where are they coming from?*

It's the pheromones, Faith said. *It must be. The injured queen triggered something.*

Is there any trace of Sam down there? Anything at all?

Nothing, I said. *But I will do whatever this big gray torpedo wants us to do. I believe Faith is right. These are our weapons from God.*

Everyone murmured agreement.

2.0 accelerated. In moments, we were going so fast everything was a blur. I wanted to send out, "I don't think we're in Kansas anymore," to my dad, but at the exact same instant a highly-sped-up version of "Carry on Wayward Son" slid into my consciousness.

By then, we were moving so fast my own thoughts couldn't keep up. In seconds, we were approaching the shallow ocean floor. Even here, the plasma floor was visible. Even though there was no sunlight to skate off the mirrored surface.

"We Built this City," became audible again beneath my jumbled thoughts.

Good old Starship, Dad thought.

I probably nodded. I couldn't form actual thoughts anymore.

Turq 2.0 slowed and hovered.

My thought processes returned just in time to be completely shocked by what Turq brought us down here to see.

Tubes crisscrossed the ocean floor stretching all the way into the shallows at the edge of a new beach. Myriad tubes were visible. Everything appeared to be connected, and yet, this seemed more and more un-connected to the Takers that fell to earth through the torn sky.

I thought the Takers were going to the pyramid, I sent to the group. *But here are more tubes and no Takers in sight. Are they connected or not?*

Maybe we were wrong. Maybe the EMP and the rip caused the creature in the ocean to come out for the first time ever. Maybe the Takers were headed to the pyramid to kill the queen, not to join her.

Two different entities taking over our world at the same time?

Stranger things have happened, Dad said.

Snake seemed to agree. He shook his head and began to bark.

What is it? Trina cried. *What's wrong with Snake?*

CHAPTER THIRTY-FOUR

Sea life

Snake saw it first, transmitted his displeasure back to the group by his barking and growling.

From our spot on 2.0's back, we could see it all.

Something had begun to agitate the ocean floor. Silt and sand and all the tiny bits of sea life that normally make up the sandy bottom were being churned into a muddy mix.

Every now and then we could see fins in the mix. Lots of dorsal fins, dozens, maybe hundreds, all swimming the same direction, faster and faster, flying through the water and scooping up the pluff off the bottom with their tails, creating a muddy screen around the end of a tube.

Is that where the drones came from? Dad asked. *Out of the tube?*

Maybe. And maybe that's why the sea life is attacking it. Looks like we aren't the only ones fighting back.

Watch out for those sharks, Trina screamed.

No, Dawk shouted. *Not sharks. Dolphins. That's how they hunt, by making a muddy ring around their prey, then they move in for the kill.*

Yes, Sam said. *Let's get out of here before we get swept into that ring.*

Sam?! You're dead. I saw you and your Turq explode—

His deep laugh was unmistakable. *Look up, Jack.* I did. One of the Turqs hovered just above us.

Sam waved, explained what had happened. *The dragon drone exploded before we reached it. A self-destruct action, I think. It looked bad, though. Especially when we flew through the debris field. Took us a minute to get our bearings and find y'all again.*

Everyone cheered. But the celebration was short lived. The strange vortex setting up below us grew more and more violent by the second.

Somehow, our Turq kept us out of the muddy mix of whales and dolphins. We shot toward the light, and soon we were gliding along the undersurface of the water, looking back at the churning mass in awe.

The Turqs above the waves kept pace with us. *I can only imagine what's happening on the East Coast,* Dawk said.

Or out in the Gulf, Dad added.

Or even further out in the Pacific, I thought.

But I couldn't say anymore, not even in thought. My mind's eye kept going back to the surreal whirlpool created around the end of that tube and the fact that Sam had survived. That—and the actions of the whales and dolphins—was nothing short of a miracle.

We flew on, allowing Turq 2.0 to go where he thought best. By this time, I doubt we could've made any decisions anyway.

As we put the churning water behind us, I got the overwhelming impression we should keep our eyes on the ground. *Are you guys sending me this thought?*

Everyone replied in the negative.

Maybe it's Snake, Dad thought.

I laughed a bit, but it could've been true. I'd caught a few of his canine feels along the way. *Doesn't feel like Snake,* I said. *Maybe it's Turq 2.0, is that you, buddy? Telling us to watch the ground?*

We all waited for some sort of acknowledgement, but nothing came, not even a wing-waggle.

I forced my eyes to stay open, searching the scenery passing below. No more evidence of tubes, thank God. These beaches appeared serene, waves lapping gently at unmarred sand.

Wonder what became of all those Takers on the beach, Trina asked. *You know, the ones like us?*

Maybe they escaped, Faith said.

Probably the black rain got them, Milo thought. And we were all treated to a memory-flash of his mom, screaming in the garage.

How can something so deadly also be our best hope? Dawk wondered.

No one else joined in the sleepy conversation. Things had happened so fast, I felt overwhelmed. Needed time to process. At least for now, we all seemed safe above the waves in our angelic dragonfly cocoons.

My eyes still scanned the beach and the immeasurable ocean. In the distance, I thought I saw large ships. *I'm so tired,* I thought at the group. *I'd swear those are more ships out there. Military looking ships.*

Dawk replied, *Why not? All those lab-complex tubes probably went to the pyramid, but who's to say some of the people didn't go out there to the ships? Maybe that's how they escaped. It wouldn't surprise me to see helicopters taking off from those ships.*

You mean like those black ones, there? Sam asked.

We watched half a dozen 'copters land and discharge people onto the decks. From our vantage point, they looked like red-uniformed dots. A few appeared to have on white coats, and some were gray and naked, glistening like moist-skinned Takers. *Maybe those are the hybrids you were asking about, Trina.*

They look like the ships in my Battleship game, Milo thought.

Sure do, Drew agreed. *Lots of bristly parts sticking out.*

Destroyers, maybe, Sam said. *Wish we had binoculars so we could see more clearly.*

That silenced us for a while. None of us knew what to make of the helicopters and the ships, but we knew we didn't want to hang around any destroyers. No matter who was manning them. Not after what we'd seen at Cheyenne.

We flew on.

CHAPTER THIRTY-FIVE

Remainders

Anyone want to guess where we are now?

We've been flying for hours, Faith thought.

I was awake when we passed over Los Angeles, Dawk replied. *What a mess that was. I saw no activity of any kind.*

You mean that huge city—gone? I couldn't keep the disbelief from my voice.

Oh, the city was still there, I just didn't see any movement. Maybe there are survivors down in the tunnels.

Los Angeles has tunnels? Trina asked.

Miles of them, Dawk said. *Homeless population lived down there once upon a time.*

Dad thought, *Wouldn't it be something if the homeless inherited the earth?*

No one replied.

If I had, I might've said, *We're all homeless now.* But that didn't seem helpful, so I kept it to myself.

We traveled on. Dawk said he thought we were nearing the area where Redwood City was located. *That's the place I visited once, in my early trek up the west coast. Climate Best by Government Test,* he reminded us. *Funky town,* he added now.

I recalled the CCR song that had sparked our curiosity, "Up Around the Bend." I expected to hear it now, since we seemed to be in that area, but nothing came. Nothing at all.

It perked us up, though, and we all began to watch the ground for a good place to land.

Turq 2.0 seemed to be giving us the best-coast tour, not just the West Coast tour. On our left, gorgeous, wind-swept coastline. On our right, areas of rolling hills covered by green grass. Now and then tall dunes of dried and drying seaweed, with oatgrass swaying in our breeze and the breeze from the near silent, at times rumbling, Pacific.

We all wondered if the events that occurred around San Diego had happened here. All those tubes opening and closing like hungry mouths under the sand.

No, Dad said. *That was hundreds of miles away, besides, I don't see any sign of tubes or dragon heads around here.*

My eyes scanned from water to land and back again. We'd drifted lower and lower as we observed the land. Now we weren't high at all, about the same as a crop duster or glider. Cruising altitude for a flock of Turqs.

I found it soothing and slightly terrifying that we'd all been granted flying privileges after everything we'd been through. But then something Faith once said came back to me, "Learning as we go, Jack. Learning as we go." And that pretty much summed it up. All of it. Everything.

I waited on one of the others to chime in, agree or disagree with those thoughts, and that's when it hit me … Maybe I'm learning to couch my thoughts *literally* the way Mom always told me I should. *Not* allow everyone to hear them. "Check those thoughts before you send them into the world, Son," she would often say. "Make sure that's where they belong."

Wow. Mom. Even then you were teaching me how to live in this odd new reality. Learning as we go, as Faith would have said.

We remained quiet for a while longer, watching the amazing vistas below us. The lowering sun over the ocean made everything seem golden again. New. As if none of the bad had ever happened. We'd left the broken southern coast behind and entered the sometimes hilly, often rugged part of the central state. We followed the coastal highway, the dark asphalt our dividing line between the mountains, winelands, and the shore.

After a while, something caught my eye. The sun was nearly gone, and the wooded areas were growing a little thicker. We weren't anywhere near the northern coast yet, where the redwoods grew, but the land was changing. And it was beautiful.

I'd been wondering about what we would do overnight when I spied something through the gaps in the canopy of trees. At first, I couldn't figure out exactly what I was seeing. We'd been loosely following the winding highway. All I could make out as we curved with the dark gray and yellow striped asphalt were bits of color here and there.

What is that? I threw out to the group. *Do y'all see what I'm seeing?* Then it hit me, *Tents. Those are tents! I see orange and blue, maybe a green one, hard to tell through the trees.*

Is that a campfire? Drew blasted back. *Is that a campfire down there, too? Could they be Remainders, like us?*

Yes! Multiple responses. *And look! They're right beside a river just like we said we would do.*

I couldn't tell exactly who was speaking or thinking, but it didn't matter, because all at once, a new voice came through. A trio of new voices, in fact. Each one layered over the other in my head, separated from the others, compartmentalized somehow, as if in different thought tubes. *Hello up there!* the voice-thoughts shouted. *Come on down. You're right. We're Remainders, too.*

And then a new sound was added. A sound that let me know they were, indeed, Remainders and could be trusted. But it wasn't a voice, not at all. It was a shiver of leaves in the trees, a rustle of wings, a whirring sound as *their* protectors roused themselves just enough to let us know they were there.

I scoured the branches, attempting to see inside, or between them, wondering if it was real, and then I saw it, a glimmer, a shimmer, little more than a promise of sunlight bouncing off a clutch of gossamer wings, telling me everything was going to be okay.

We're all right now, Faith said. *God is showing us the path. Showing us his—*

Angels! The rest of our group finished her thought. *He's showing us more of his angels at work.* Tom Petty's song "Angel Dream" floated through our thoughts, and I knew it came from Dad. *"Following an angel?" Yes, I guess we are.*

Turq 2.0 waggled his wings, and from below us there were more thought-shouts of *Come on down, come on down.*

Snake whuffed, and Trina giggled, and the song bloomed, and life was somehow filled with promise again.

I reached over and rubbed Snake's soft head with my thumb. *We're coming,* I replied, and then I sent out a gentle feeler to my group only. *Everyone agree it's safe to set down? Anyone get any bad feelings?*

No bad juju feelings on my part, Son, Dad said.

All the others echoed the reply, and Turq 2.0 immediately began to slow our flight for a landing. If I thought about it, I'd have to laugh at how quickly we'd all adjusted to our new modes of communication and transportation. In fact, I think we were all more than slightly in shock. When I thought about it, I couldn't believe the things we'd been through. And I couldn't wait to compare our stories with those of the folks on the ground.

CHAPTER THIRTY-SIX

Camping

One by one our Turqs began to circle in preparation for setting down near the river, and it occurred to me, a moment too late, that I hadn't actually *seen* any of the people, only heard their thoughts. What if these weren't even people? What if it was another trick, or a trap?

For all I knew someone could be tracking our every move, sending a platoon of Takers to gather us back up even now.

But by then it was too late. We were on the ground.

We tumbled off our flying friends and landed, mostly upright, on the soft, leafy earth. The area on one side of the river was ringed by deciduous trees just changing into their bright golden leaves. I didn't realize we'd flown that far inland from the coast.

Oh, it isn't far as the crow flies, someone laughed.

I looked up to see a group of people standing in the edge of the forest. They were a small group like ours, and several of them held battery operated lanterns like we'd had back before the tubes sluiced away all our belongings.

I looked at them, and then I looked at our motley crew. First things first, I walked over to my dad and wrapped my arms around him. Before I knew what was happening, all the others—Faith, Sam, Dawk, Drew, Milo, and Trina, plus Snakeman—were crowding in for their hugs as well. Even Turq 2.0 fluttered his wings a few extra times as he settled onto a branch above us.

"Welcome," said a gray-haired woman with smooth ivory skin. "Join us in our temporary home."

A country song about a temporary home fluttered past my brain cells. A song by Carrie Underwood. I didn't know the song well, but I'd certainly heard it. And Cade and I had marveled over the singer's legs on the YouTube video.

Now, after we all congratulated one another for having survived the beach and the pyramid, and our escape from the San Diego area, I turned and introduced myself and each member of our crew to this young-looking older woman with the flawless skin and crinkly hair. "I'm Jack," I said. "And we are sure glad to see y'all."

She clasped my hand in both of hers, a big smile lighting her warm brown eyes. "My name is Addie," she said. "Short for Adelaide. I am a nurse and a backpacker. I know this area well, so this is where we came."

She introduced the rest of her group. Chachi, a sinewy gentleman with a sun-burnished complexion; Tandy, a young woman so dainty a strong breeze could carry her away, and finally, Bunny, an adorable brown-haired girl in a pair of jeans with the cuffs rolled up. She didn't seem to be related to any of the others, but she was just about Milo's size.

"Now," Addie said. "Please tell us about your journey so far, and we will tell you ours." She led us to the campground which consisted of a group of tents, a cook fire ringed by rocks, several logs pulled over for sitting, and even a couple of nylon camp chairs that could be rolled up for attaching to a backpack. There were also a few blankets scattered around as if someone had just crawled out of their cozy little nests.

"Nice camp," Dad said. We'd all fallen back into speaking aloud, unsure if everyone could read our thoughts, although we suspected they could since we'd heard them inviting us to come down.

We settled in, close together, looking each other over, making questing small talk, relaying in fits and starts what we had seen and done.

After a bit, Addie indicated three battered pans of varying sizes she had placed on crisscrossed logs over the fire. It reminded me of the *Stone Soup* story. The smell was savory, delicious on the fresh, woodsy air.

"You're welcome to join us," she held up a ladle dripping with thick reddish-brown broth and taste tested it. "Could use a little more salt," she said, adding a dash from a blue cardboard picnic-type cylinder.

Soon, the talk turned to monsters and the things we'd recently witnessed on the beach and in the ocean.

"I can tell you this much," I said. "Whatever it was, we didn't kill it." I looked around the group. "Not sure we even hurt it, to be honest."

"We disturbed it, though," Sam said. "Made it sit up and take notice."

That elicited a nervous giggle from Trina. "Not us," she said. "The whales and dolphins did that."

"Yeah," Milo echoed.

"They sure did," I said, thinking of the underwater war we'd rushed to escape.

I heard a whir of wings overhead and knew Turq 2.0 agreed. He and all our Turqs had taken up residence in the thick canopy of the trees where the others resided. It made me believe they were all connected the way we humans were.

I went on to describe the events of our travels to Addie and her friends. "I hope we didn't just make the alien queen mad."

"We can't worry about that," Sam said. "We did what we had to do. The ocean life helped us, is helping us, and helping themselves, too. Maybe we jumpstarted some sort of recovery."

Addie and Chachi both chimed in. "You've done more than we, that's for sure. All we've done so far is survive and hide."

I smiled. "Everything we did was off the cuff, right Dad?"

He laughed. "Right, wayward son. Just like your Grampa used to say. But in truth, everything we did was directed by someone else …"

"Someone up above," Faith added. And to our surprise, the song, "Carry on Wayward Son," floated into our midst. But this time, it seemed to be coming from on high.

I couldn't argue with that. I wouldn't even try. "You're right." I looked around the fire at all my friends. My family. "Now let's talk about new beginnings. And rivers."

Snake whined. "Yes," I said, stroking his head. "And animals. Let's talk about what animals you all have seen."

Everyone laughed when Snake plopped down on his belly, tongue lolling, head resting on his paws. They probably thought he was all ears. But we knew better. He understood everything, not because he could hear it, but because he could read it in our thoughts the same way we all could.

Turq 2.0 buzzed from the tree nearby.

Every now and then one of my group would chime in, to add details about our experiences, or to ask the new group about theirs. The smallest one of all, the one called Bunny, was the only one who had nothing to add. I began to wonder if she could talk at all. Her face spoke of trauma the like of which some folks never recover.

It was in that way, trading memories and bits of information, that we passed the first hour on the ground with our new Remainders.

Soon, it was time to dish up the stew.

CHAPTER THIRTY-SEVEN

Burnin' Daylight!

We spent a comfortable evening sharing food and campfire chatter with our new friends. They even made room for us to have two whole tents. I'm not sure about the others, but to me it felt like a luxury suite at The Hilton, especially after scraping up drifts of leaves upon which we placed our borrowed blankets.

The mystery stew Addie cooked up was about as fine a meal as any we'd ever eaten. That part was agreed upon by all.

After we'd had our fill, accompanied by delicious hunks of hot corn bread cooked over the coals in a cast iron skillet—I wondered who hefted that thing in their backpack when it was time to go— then the conversation really began in earnest.

"That thing in the pyramid-ship," Addie began. "We have not seen that kind of monster. You called it the queen alien?"

"Yes," Dawk answered. "Like the queen of a hive."

"I thought we were going into the belly of the beast when we went down that tube," Dad added. "But maybe that time hasn't come yet, after all." He rubbed his eye, the one that Turq 2.0 had restored. "I don't know. It seems more complicated—" He touched his forehead above his eye, as if to bring forth a better word, one that made more sense.

I'd noticed him doing that from time to time. It made me wonder if he still had pain there.

"Yep," Sam agreed. "We seem to have uncovered a conspiracy of countries and entities behind all this. Humans and aliens alike."

We all added mental pictures of the strange hybrids we'd seen. And Drew showed us a quick flash of a strange flat-headed blonde. Dawk added the horrid memory of the dying lab tech but cut the thought off immediately when he realized how awful the images must appear to the kids.

"And then there are our angels," I added. My own mind cutting to a close up of jagged silver teeth in a Taker's mouth and the early Turq flinging me into the backseat of Thad's Chrysler to save me.

I killed that train of memory-thought, the same way Dawk had done with his. "Sorry for that," I said. "What you saw was my first up-close-and-personal with one of the original Takers." The memory played on against my better judgement even after I did the public service announcement.

Dad said, "But when we saw that tubular queen inside the pyramid under the waves …"

"It was pure alien," Drew said.

"Yes," Dawk said, taking up the tale. "It was just a silhouette inside the plasma walls. A clear blister of a thing with massive tubular tentacles that had been growing into the ocean floor like a spreading fungus." He paused, showing us images from his mind. "Every now and then the tubular tentacles poked out of the water— and out of the land as well—to gather information and food. We think those were the actual portals as well."

"And don't forget all those weird faces in the egg room," Milo said.

"We can't forget them," Drew said. "Not sure if we were hallucinating after the Joy Juice, or if they were real …"

"It's sounds like that famous fungus in Oregon," Addie said, surprising us all with one of our own theories. "It began from a single spore and wound up covering hundreds, perhaps thousands, of miles under the ground." She nodded, thinking to herself but speaking aloud. "Or the ginormous quivering Aspen forest. Did you know it carries an extra genome so it can xerox itself everywhere it goes?" She looked at us, and I could see she was going to be fast friends with Dawk. They spoke the same sciency language.

"That's exactly what we think is happening with this *being*," I said. "Sounds like we're all on the same wavelength."

Chachi and their other Remainders nodded, but also had questions. All they'd known were the first Takers and the black rain—they had not seen the labs, nor the pyramid, nor the tubes. They hadn't even been into the ocean.

Addie had been a member of two hiking and spelunking clubs, so when the world fell apart, she said she immediately moved inland to the woods and the caves, picking up the other Remainders along the way. None of them had experienced any portals at all.

Everyone grew sleepy, and we all agreed to take turns at watch, feeling better than we had since before the cliff dwellings.

"Is that a bear box?" Sam asked as we cleaned up after the meal.

"It is," Addie said, indicating the metal food container where she stored the oatmeal and other foods. "I used to backpack this entire area with my partner, Slim, and our hiking club." In a melancholy voice, she added, "After the big noise that day, I went to the office and found Slim. He'd been at work when the monsters came."

Chachi smiled and touched her shoulder. "Thanks to God that you found me." He glanced at us. "In her basement, Addie had everything needed for camping. Everything you see here. Almost."

"Slim was a good man." Addie patted Chachi's hand on her shoulder. "We were planning to go hiking near Redwood City the day after all this happened. With our club." She swiped a thumb beneath her eye. "In fact, I was thinking about heading there anyway. Until I came upon Chachi and Tandy."

Dawk looked at me, and I didn't have to read his mind to know he was thinking the same thing I was. *Redwood City. There's the connection. We were meant to find this woman and her friends. If not there, then here.*

"After that," she continued, "I was just in shock." She looked around her group. "I came up from the basement, gathered my supplies, and hit the trail. And that's when I found Chachi, sitting on the side of the road, counting his blessings."

"I was visiting this lovely state from Guatemala," he said.

"Hoping to get a green card." He smiled, showing square, white teeth. "I came to find work. To be American." He patted his chest lightly. "Chapine. The boss." He grinned and continued in near-perfect English. "I came to be the boss of me." He touched his chest again, shook his head sadly, said, "Then everything happen." A look of gloom crossed his face. "Now I am chapine and a cit-i-zen, too. All at once."

My dad gave him a sympathetic look. "Looks like we're all chapines now my friend."

They shook hands in a slightly elaborate more-than-a-shake handshake, an obvious connection being cemented. "Citizens of the world, and chapines of our own destinies," Dad said. "As long as we follow the Lord, that is."

Citizens of the new world by default. Bosses of our own destinies by faith.

"Back to that bear box," Sam said. "Did they survive? The bears? I mean, have y'all seen any around?"

The hair on the back of my neck stood up. "That's right. They sleep in caves, don't they?"

Addie looked at each of us in turn. "We have seen signs, yes. We've been flying with our new birdies—" she glanced at the trees where the Turqs all rested. "A whole other story—"

Birdies, I thought. *Okay. That works.*

"—but when we put down here yesterday evening, before you all landed, we saw scat. And carrion. They are eating something it seems. We saw lots of fish heads and the remains of one deer."

"That gives me hope," Dawk said. "I wonder how many deer survived?"

"Hopefully a bunch," I said. "This area is so different than our desert home. So many more places to go underground."

Addie shrugged. "If Slim had survived, he would know about the wildlife. Slim knew everything about our state." A tear welled in her eye.

"I'm so sorry about your partner," I said. "But I'm glad you guys know about bears." I glanced at our group. "Sam, here, has a lot of camping experience, too."

"Maybe between the lot of us, we can figure out what to do next," Dawk said.

Addie nodded, her crinkly hair bobbing with the motion. "I like the sound of that, and I believe my friends will all agree that we should join with you and yours. If that is what you have in mind."

I didn't wait for anyone else to speak, I could read their thoughts. "Yes," I said. "We believe we were led here for a reason."

"Good," she replied, her voice lighter than before. "Today, we had planned to go further inland toward Mount Shasta, the healing place." She shaded her eyes with her hands. "Our birdies brought us this far, and two nights ago, my Shasta grandmother came to me in a dream. She told me the safety is Mount Shasta."

That was enough for me, and apparently for the others, too. As one, we began to gather the dishes and foodstuff. "Just one question," I said as we worked. "What *do* we do if a bear sneaks up? Anyone carrying bear spray?" I chuckled to let them know I was only half-kidding.

In my head, I heard a very faint voice asking his dad what a Shasta grandmother was. In response, Drew replied, "I think it means she belonged to the Shasta tribe native to the area."

Nod to the healing power of turquoise, I thought. *It's all connected in some way.*

Above my head, I heard a whir and flutter. *Thanks, Turq ol' buddy, glad you agree.*

The night went by without a hitch. I took my turn at watch, as did every other adult in our group, overlapping with one another every couple of hours. I suspected we were all still observing each other, making certain we really were as trustworthy as we seemed.

I think the Turqs in the trees helped temper our fears as far as sleeping in the open in our tents. I know I felt better knowing they were up above, so to speak. And we had ol' Snake, too, of course. His sixth sense, the one that seemed to have taken the place of his hearing, was so well developed he almost always knew things before they happened, even though he couldn't hear them.

"Hey," Milo quipped, when we were all awake and fed. "Let's load up. We're burnin' daylight."

Chachi slapped his knee. "John Wayne," he cried. "*The Cowboys.* I love that movie." He flashed his bright smile, and I found myself hoping everyday would be as easy as this day.

Soon, we were packed. We climbed back aboard our magical flying *birdies* and headed north. I never doubted that Turq 2.0 would know exactly where we needed to go.

Addie's birdie fell in behind us, relinquishing control easily, with no dissension whatsoever. The other Turqs fell into a loose flying V formation, like a flock of geese.

Below us, the early-morning asphalt shone like the pathway we'd been following since San Diego. Just glimpses now and then through gaps in the evergreens. We appeared to be following both the highway and the noisy waters of what Addie called the Salinas River. The same one where we had camped.

CHAPTER THIRTY-EIGHT

San Francisco, here we come!

We flew seamlessly through the morning, quickly losing sight of the Salinas below. Addie said our next big landmark should be The Golden Gate Bridge. I felt as excited as if I were that kid from years past, getting ready for one of our big family vacations.

San Francisco. In the back of my mind, I imagined Mom telling us to be sure and see the famous pastel-colored Victorian houses called the painted ladies.

Right, Sam said. *Did you know they were featured in the movie "Invasion of the Body Snatchers?" That's kind of ironic, isn't it?*

I know those houses, Trina added, *They're in the opening scene of "Full House," the old TV show.*

They're famous all right, Dad said. *Almost as famous as the old hippie enclave in the Haight-Ashbury neighborhood. Wouldn't mind taking a selfie right there on that corner if we could. Impress my friends in the teacher's lounge next year.*

I think he meant to be funny. But it fell a little flat.

Too soon? he asked.

Must be, I thought. *Although Cade and my friend Thad would've appreciated it. That's their kind of humor for sure.*

"Dirty Harry," Chachi thought seriously. *Pretty sure they got houses like that in the "Dirty Harry" movie, too.*

I don't know why, but that cracked us all up. Maybe it was Chachi's knowledge of American movies that seemed so funny.

It was good to laugh.

We flew on, ideas and songs carrying back and forth across both groups. Chachi loved to sing, and my dad knew one Guatemalan folk song.

Faith and I kept each other entertained with classic rock—with a few pop and country songs thrown in for good measure.

Sam and Drew talked sports, which seemed to depress Drew.

It just hit me that there will never be another Major League Baseball game. Ever, he thought.

At that, Milo took it upon himself to change tracks. He started a whistling game. I think he did it to make his dad feel better. Such an empathetic kid.

First, he would whistle a song and challenge the rest of us to "name that tune." It turned out to be great fun, especially since we were all playing telepathically. The challenge for Milo was to whistle the tune without accidentally "thinking" the title beforehand.

He was surprised when Sam told him that another famous film cowboy, Clint Eastwood, had recorded a song with Brad Paisley in which the opening to the song was all Clint just whistling.

We all let down our guards. We felt safe in the air.

After the whistling game grew tiresome, we moved on to games like twenty questions and vocabulary and book-type games in which one person had to make up a group of words or book titles and another had to say which one didn't belong.

Faith was pleasantly surprised when I was a champ at most of them (thanks, Mom). Except for the science words, those always went to Dawk.

Finally, we grew tired of our telepathic word games. We'd all learned how to guard our thoughts and only put forth the ones we intended. Usually, that is.

And even though our birdie seats were amazingly comfortable, it was obvious everyone was growing hungry and thirsty again.

Should we look for a spot to land for the night? Addie asked. *I feel a bit out of my wheelhouse, but I know lots of places in San Francisco will have canned foods if we can hold out a little longer. Assuming the stores haven't been stripped bare.*

We all felt a *lot* of trepidation at going into a big city where

Takers and Marla-types might be hiding, but we needed food. *Maybe we can just camp near a river again,* Trina offered. *Catch some fish or something?*

Everyone seemed to like that idea.

Addie hesitated for a second. *That's okay with me. But I'm low on flour, and I'd like some more cornmeal for battering the fish.* She smacked her lips comically. I could hear them even in her thoughts. *And some beans and rice would be just the thing to complement any fish.*

I laughed and thought, *Beans and rice would be delicious with anything. And while I don't know about rivers, maybe we can locate the San Francisco Bay, if we fly out near the shoreline. I'm assuming we can fish from the shore, right?*

Sure, Addie replied. *I don't even think we need a license right now.* She hesitated for a beat. *I could be wrong though.*

We all laughed at that, especially Dad, but a creepy sensation crawled across my skin. Everyone kept trying to make jokes, but what if we got to San Francisco and found it and The Golden Gate gone, crashed into the ocean from the rip?

Worse yet, what if we got there and found it untouched? Unchanged? People going about their business as if nothing had happened. Wouldn't *that* be a Rod Serling moment?

Only one way to find out ...

Anyone object to San Francisco? I asked.

As if on cue, the sunlight bounced off something in the distance, and even though most of it was shrouded in fog, parts of the bridge stuck out like beacons.

There it is, I thought. *There's the Golden Gate.*

I think you're right, Faith said, her thoughts thin, excited.

It's really orange, Milo said.

It wasn't supposed to be, Trina added. *But the builder liked the color of the primer so much, he talked them into keeping it. It's called International Orange. It's the best color to show up in the fog. Like now.*

You amaze me, Trina, Drew said. *Do you know what primer is for?*

Not really, she admitted.

It's to protect the steel, dummy, Milo said. *Until you get it painted, I mean.*

Trina made an ugly face in her voice. *Don't call me dummy, Dummy,* she thought back at her brother.

I had to laugh. We'd all taken our free educations for granted, although it appears we'd had good ones. Now, those classrooms full of knowledge were a thing of the past. That hit me like a no-baseball-games gut-punch.

I never thought I'd miss the idea of returning to school, Faith thought. *But I just heard what you thought. And I agree. We were the lucky ones, weren't we?*

Cue Sam Riggs, I thought. *"The Lucky Ones." Yes, we really were. No doubt about it.*

Now we are educating each other, Drew said.

Learning as we go, Dad thought.

Learning as we go, Faith echoed.

And without my knowing it was about to happen, "Teach Your Children," the old Crosby, Stills, Nash & Young song, drifted from my mind into the midst of the group. *What's this about?* I wondered. I'd heard this song earlier. Were we missing something? *What are we supposed to be learning?*

Look at this, Addie thought. *There's the bay. We can fish right there.*

We all gazed down at the near-pristine shoreline this side of the bridge. *We'll need more fishing gear,* Addie said. *Guess we can scout out a sporting goods store. Should be some nearby, right?*

Hold on, Faith laughed. *Let me pull it up on Google Maps.*

Turq 2.0 swooped lower so we could see the streets, read the store signs. We'd been avoiding big cities for so long I'd forgotten about the wreckage. There were cars crashed into each other and into the store fronts. Broken glass everywhere, but thankfully, no bodies, no gore.

I can't believe how clean the streets look, Faith said. *Aside from the glass and stuff.*

Yeah. Where are all the dead people? Milo always cut to the point.

Hope they aren't inside the stores. I let that thought slip out accidentally, so went on to clarify. *Snake and I have been in that situation a few times. Barely escaped from Takers, there.* I recalled the sickening odor of all those bodies.

Could be where they are, Sam said. *Guess we'll see. There's something called Sports Basement right down there. Looks huge.*

Turq 2.0 glided down in gentle spirals toward the massive parking lot. Dad and Faith held on. She'd decided to fly with us today.

Snake dug in his claws, too. Trina was with her dad and Milo on their Turq. Sam, and Dawk shared a separate one.

The new Remainders followed on their own birdies.

The parking lot was filled with cars, but still, no bodies. Even the ones I thought should be inside the cars were not there. And where were all the dead animals, the birds, the massive piles of dead insects I'd encountered back in Eden?

The rip occurred in our little Texas town around four or five in the afternoon. That would've been two or three p.m. here—if the rip occurred at the same time all over. Should have had the same effects, right?

I looked at the giant store. *There could be a million bodies in there. We'd better be prepared. I'll go in first and check it out, so we don't all get surprised.*

What if you get trapped? Faith sent back.

Oh, I know how to avoid that, don't worry about me.

I'll go, too, Jack, Sam said. *One thing about it, at least we can all communicate now.*

Turq 2.0 fluttered his small, inner wings, and I appreciated the support.

Okay. I glanced at the bridge rising through the fog like an archaeological relic across the bay. *In a few minutes, we'll be heading over there to drop a hook in the surf.*

Dad laughed in my head. *What will we use for bait? I've never been much of a fisherman.*

Guess we can grab some lures, Sam said. *Don't know where we'd find any live bait, unless we happen upon some crabs in a tidepool or on the beach.* He also laughed. *Obviously, I'm not a shore fisherman. Give me a stream or a river and a worm or minnow—*

Don't worry about the bait, Chachi interjected. *I have surf-fish many time. Crab are many. We dig them out, hook them up, they catch fish for us.*

Addie agreed. *What he says is true. We may become seafood lovers. We've been living off river fish; now we will catch ocean fish.*

That sounds like a good plan, Drew thought.

I had to agree, the stew Addie shared with us had been the first meal we'd had in a day or two. Fresh fish cooked over a beach bonfire sounded phenomenal. Not that I'd ever done that, but I'd seen it in movies.

Here we go, I said, sliding off 2.0's back as we touched down.

We scanned the area as we dismounted. When we saw no movement, the Turqs took up perches in the nearby trees. We walked around, stretching our legs and basking in the afternoon light.

"The air smells like salt," Trina said, inhaling deeply.

"It's a beautiful place," Faith replied, also speaking aloud. I suspected they both spoke aloud mainly to break the eerie silence.

We all stopped and looked out toward the bridge again, but it was no longer visible because of a shift in the fog. I glanced at Sam, and he gave a slight nod. Snake picked up on it, of course, and the three of us strode up to the front doors like any old day of the week.

"It's a big place," I said, to cut the tension.

My voice fell into the gap between us, and Sam said, "Let's stick together, go straight to the fishing poles, grab a few, along with any other fishing gear nearby, then head back." He looked at me, one hand on the glass door. "Don't mean to sound bossy, just a little jumpy. Been a while since I've encountered the bad guys inside enclosed spaces."

"I hear that." Images of my mom's library, the Wal-Mart with Thad, and several convenience stores entered my head.

Snake whined and shifted from one paw to another as if to ask what was holding us up.

"Stick together," Sam repeated as he pushed on the door.

It opened with a squeal, and I was not surprised at the dusty smell of dried death that seeped out. I pulled the collar of my t-shirt up over my nose as in the early days.

Sam, I thought at him. *Let's not speak in here.* I assumed he would understand I meant we needed to be stealthy.

Yes, he thought back. And on we went.

The front of the store was all kayaks and tents and camp chairs and ice chests. It made me long for Aunt Edna's food trailer. The one we'd had before we got sucked into the tube. *I'll grab a couple more tents on the way out,* Sam said, lengthening his stride.

I figured he was telling me not to lollygag.

Being at least six inches taller than me, Sam was able to read all the aisle signs. I knew the moment he spied FISHING GEAR because he headed toward it like a shot.

And there were the bodies. The dusty, dark red odor hit my nose through the cotton fabric of my well-worn shirt. I inhaled without meaning to. It appeared the good Takers had swept through and cleaned up. Bodies were stacked neatly, like they'd been in my mom's library, and in the little library park. *Who cleaned these up? And why?*

Sam shrugged, buried his nose in the crook of his elbow, and charged ahead.

Only Snake held back. And as had been happening lately, I got an image from a doggie perspective. It gave me the idea he was watching the front door to make certain nothing was going to block our exit.

Like the old green Grinch, I felt my heart begin to grow. Bad things had befallen this world, horrible, horrible things, but this one little thing—this extrasensory communication with my furry, four-legged friend—this was good.

I caught up with Sam on the Fishing aisle where he was grabbing poles from a display. Snatching up a tackle box with a selection of brightly colored lures and hooks, I tucked it under my arm, stepped past bodies that had begun to mummify, and nodded toward the front where the Snake waited.

Thank God no one is here ...

The remembered image of a huge dead man blocking the aisle in a Wal-Mart with Thad seemed a lifetime ago. A different me. A different world. A chill overtook me, and I realized Snake was sending me images that let me know he remembered those times, too. He was also urging me to *hurry, hurry, hurry.*

My feet responded immediately.

I passed Sam, bypassed the checkout area, touched Snake on the head, and burst through the front doors to where the Remainders were waiting. All of them. The children cheered when the three of us cleared the threshold again.

Turq 2.0 dropped down, and the others followed suit. In moments we were all airborne, headed back to the inviting beach overlooking the foggy bridge. It looked perfect. No bodies, no people, no dangers at all. Just dinner.

Good place to fish, Addie said in our heads. *Not so good to camp. We can go inland for that.*

There were several murmurs of agreement as the Turqs put us down on the postage stamp beach at the base of the craggy rocks. The red-orange bridge peeked out of the afternoon fog every now and then. It lent an other-worldly atmosphere to the whole area.

I could stay here, Faith said to the group. *I know I said it earlier, but I'm just in love with this place.*

You're not alone, Dad agreed. *It is amazing.*

And that was the last time I saw my dad. The ground opened beneath him the same way it had done all of us on the beach near San Diego, and then he was gone.

CHAPTER THIRTY-NINE

Heaven

It's a tube! Drew yelled, grabbing the kids and flinging them back onto their Turq.

Dad! I screamed. But the only sound I heard was the familiar tune of a band called Kansas.

"Carry on Wayward Son."

I leapt toward the last place I'd seen him standing. But the sand seemed untouched. No sign of disturbance whatsoever.

Every Remainder scrambled toward their Turqs except for Snake and me.

In my head, I heard the Kansas song rise and fall. It was overplayed by a song called "Go Rest High on That Mountain." Dad! I screamed again. I recognized the Vince Gill song from Great Grampa's funeral.

Turq 2.0 swooped in to pick us up. Faith pushed me forward and practically shoved me onto his back. *How could we have forgotten about the tubes on the beach?*

Because they were hundreds of miles from here, Faith said.

Snake dug furiously where Dad had disappeared. He was giving it everything he had, wet sand flying out behind him.

A second tube opened nearby, right where I'd been standing. I screamed for Dad inside my thoughts, but I got no reply. Then I realized we were leaving Snake. He was still there, digging with all his heart. We were leaving him.

Come on, Faith and I screamed in our unified mind-voices.

Snake's doggy head came up, and he came at us on the run.

Turq 2.0 slowed, held off rising, and the big dog made the leap.

The other Turqs and birdies were already up. From the air, we could see tubes opening and closing all over the small beach.

Dad, I sent into the void. *How can this be? I spent all this time searching for you. You can't be gone!*

I raved at the others to turn back, meaning to make Snake stay with Faith and go into a tube myself. *I need to go after him,* I thought at the groups. *I've survived it before. I can find him. I know I can.*

Jack, Faith said in her gentle voice. *We don't know where this one goes—*

I'll find out, I interrupted. *I can't just give up. I've got to find him. That's been my goal this whole time. Since the rip. My only goal—*

Jack. Dad's voice slid into my thoughts on the wings of our Kansas song. *You must carry on, son. My work is through.* The Vince Gill song took over, but before I could comment, that one gave way to Tom Petty's "You and I Will Meet Again."

I can't, Dad, I cried. *I can't do that.*

Trust in the Lord, our God, he said. *"It is not for us to bend God's will to ours; instead, we must be like the willow and allow him to bend our will to His."*

I understand what you're saying, but—

No buts, Sam chimed in. *I felt the same way when I lost Danielle. I cursed God and His will, but your father's right, Jack. It's bigger than us. Much bigger than our feelings. Now is the time to let go and let God.*

If you hadn't searched for me, Jack, Dad said. *You would not have found all these Remainders. They are the building blocks of the future. My part is done. Now you must follow your heart. That's where you will find God.*

I lay back in my Turq's winged embrace. Snake crawled onto my chest, and Faith snuggled carefully into my side, one arm across me. My two best friends.

"It can't be," I said. "It's not supposed to happen like this. We found him; we rescued him. He's supposed to die of old age in three or four decades. Not now. Not trapped down there in the belly of the beast." The idea of it nearly killed me, made my chest ache and burn.

We flew across the bridge, into the fog, through the fog, into the unknown, flying across the bay and across more deceptively pristine-looking beaches. It was only when our shadows crossed the sand, that we would sometimes see tubes opening and closing, looking for live DNA. Looking for us.

And then it happened.

Our Turq flew straight up like a military helicopter. Straight up, not stopping, not moving forward, just rising straight up. We rose through cotton-white clouds as soft and blurry as tomorrow. A sky hole opened above us, and the black rain did not fall.

We flew inside, into the sparkly darkness and further, further, and further until 2.0's wings tightened around us like a tidy space capsule. Breathing was strange, different, gravity took a vacation, and still we flew up, into someone's idea of Heaven. *My* idea of Heaven based on ideas gained from my grandparents and Carlos and my limited church experience.

Heaven. It was everything I thought it would be.

"In the Garden" played through my mind.

I come to The Garden alone,
While the dew is still on the ro-ses …

My Great-Gran's favorite hymn. I'm not certain The Garden meant Heaven, but I guess in my mind, it did. So, I let go of my expectations, and I let God be what I never would have dreamed He could be.

We did not speak. Could not, I think. But I saw *everything*. Every street paved with gold, every loved one I'd ever lost: Carlos, Thad, Aunt Edna, Cade, my grands, and of course, the newest member of Heaven, my dad. He stood there, arm in arm, with Mom, eyes bright, smiling as if they'd just renewed their vows, right inside those amazing pearly gates for which Saint Peter held the key.

We moved through Heaven in our funny space capsule, our tidy, cozy, capsule of wings. Once again, it felt as if we were looking at everything through the plasma walls of the egg room. I saw them, each of my loved ones.

They all stood healthy and erect, arms linked. Mom in her turquoise sweater, gran and gramps in their shorts and sun hats,

Aunt Edna in her jeans and flannel shirt, even my great-grands in their Sunday-go-to-meetin' clothes. And then there was Dad, right there, beaming at me in all his new and Heavenly glory.

It was exactly where he needed to be. The perfect place. The place where angels play harps and only come down when the world needs saving.

Dad didn't speak. Like the egg room, everyone was on display. We didn't seem able to interact. They were beyond the veil. I finally understood what that meant.

But I had no time to ponder, for at that moment I encountered the heavy scent of roses and a multitude of other faces, other shapes, other people's loved ones, right there. With mine. They were all beyond the veil.

We flew out, back through the sparkly black, through the soft clouds, back down to the turquoise-blue sky with the puffy clouds of the earth-world—but I remembered. Easily. The sight of Carlos standing tall beside a beautiful young woman, a precious little girl nestled in the crook of his arm and Cade, straight and happy beside his mom and dad, even Thad, our first hero, standing toward the back, on a hill, grinning. Nearby, stood Mo and Lara with their own families. Two children near Thad with another couple as well.

Oh, my God, I said. *Thank you, thank you, thank you—*

Jack? Faith's thought-voice came into my head.

Wasn't it beautiful, Faith? Heaven. Just like Carlos said it would be with the streets of gold and the pearly gates and—

Jack, what are you talking about? We flew over the Golden Gate. We've been flying for hours and hours. I'm ready to land somewhere. Can't remember the last time we ate, or even drank water.

What are you talking about, Faith? We just got the grand tour of Heaven. Wasn't it amazing? Didn't it change absolutely everything for you, the way it did for me?

There was silence. No one said a word.

In the near distance, we could see the bright, snow-capped peak of Mount Shasta, the keeper. The turquoise healer.

We knew what it was because Addie said, *That's Mount Shasta.*

The healer. That's where we need to start again. The turquoise headwaters of The Sacramento River are there, in the park. Granny showed me.

Of course, Faith thought. *Our healing place, I feel it already. And a river, just like we wanted.*

Wait! I cried. *Did y'all not see what just happened, how we got here? Did you not see Heaven, and the streets of gold, and the cotton-blurred sky where the angels reside with all our loved ones? With my mom and my dad?*

More silence from the group. No one seemed to know what I meant, but I could read their non-thoughts as well as their thoughts. *Hallucination* floated through their collective minds. *Shock of seeing his dad disappear that way.*

No, it's true, I thought at them. *It wasn't a hallucination. We flew into a sky hole. We flew through Heaven, just a little glimpse, but we were there. We were—*

Jack?

Dad! Is that you? Of course, it was him, I knew his voice better than I knew my own.

It was only you, Jack. You were the only one treated to a glimpse. But it isn't your time yet. This is my time. You saved me for this. I am done there, but I'm needed here. Do you understand?

Yes, I said. *At least I'm trying to understand.*

Good. Carry on. That's all you can do. Then you can show the others. By your actions. By your Faith. Teach them to let go of all preconceived notions. Just let God rule. It's time for that. It's time.

CHAPTER FORTY

Mount Shasta

I miss having wheels, I thought, when we were safely back on the ground. *That old Chrysler served us well, didn't it? Both of the Chryslers, actually.* I thought of all the possessions we'd carried with us in the cars, how the battles we'd faced had winnowed them down to this. To nothing. *God will provide*, flashed in my head.

We could get more wheels, Faith thought back at me. *But seriously, Jack. We've got our own private planes now, haven't we? Besides, we're still learning to do without all those luxuries we thought were necessities.*

You're right, I agreed. *We've got to learn to do without a lot of things. Like Dad told me, we must learn to let go.*

Crosby, Stills, Nash, & Young sang about how to teach your children well but it quickly morphed into Neil Young singing "Helpless."

Hey, I know that song, Dawk said. *He's singing about a town in north Ontario—*

*Yellow moons—*Faith said—*And big birds flying, the way we've been doing.*

The haunting tune spun out across our melded minds.

They were left helpless, Dawk finished.

That's it. That's right. We must make ourselves helpless and let The Lord work His wonders through us.

I wondered if Dad was the one sending us these tunes. For once, I couldn't be certain. I shook my head, stretched, and patted the old Snake who had just had the longest doggy nap of his life.

I guess we'll be walking everywhere now, I thought. *And when we can't walk, we'll take a Turq the way some folks used to take an Uber.*

It will work out, Sam said. *We have our Faith.* He chuckled at his own little pun.

We swirled down and down toward the ground. The beautiful mountain rose in the distance, sunlight bouncing off its snow dusted peaks. Down on earth, we landed in a shaded area ringed by gorgeous firs and pines.

Addie and Chachi dismounted and stretched. "Well," she said. "Here we are."

We looked around at the lush foliage and coarse river rocks. Clear water sparkled and tumbled, burbled, and rushed, gushing up from an underground spring to plunge across the stones and spill down the creek bed toward the big river.

A park department sign read, **Mount Shasta Big Springs,** and there was a bit of information printed below the name telling us this wasn't the only creek feeding into the Sacramento, but it was a spring known for its pure water, revered by the First People to settle the area thousands of years earlier, and still honored by the Indigenous People of today.

ELO's "In the Beginning" started up in my head again.

A roughhewn fence graced the soft dirt lane that ran beside the headwaters.

"I love it," Faith breathed, hand caressing the rough bark of a ponderosa pine. "It's like the Garden of Eden," she said. "Can we pitch our tents and stay?"

"It's going to get cold, soon," Dawk said. "Perhaps we could find housing with a full tank of propane—" His face took on a look of consternation.

"And a wood burning stove or fireplace," Faith said. "That sounds cozy." She hugged herself, and Addie laughed.

"Good for cooking, too," the older woman said. "Save the propane for the really cold months."

"Here's a thought," I said, speaking aloud. "What if we stayed here in the warmer months and went south in the colder months." As soon as the words left my mouth, I knew how stupid they sounded.

"Good thoughts, Jack. I think they're those are all good ideas," Sam said.

I watched Snake nose around the base of a fir tree. *I'll bet he thinks he's in Heaven now.*

I'll bet you're right, Faith thought back at me.

I glanced up, glad to see a smile on her face. "It might be stupid for us to turn around and head right back into the mess from which we just escaped—"

"Nah," she walked toward the stream. "We can be nomads. We just won't follow the coastal highway this time." She shot me a look over her shoulder, one eyebrow raised, reminding me of some old actress from way back when, and I had to laugh.

Maybe it wasn't too soon after all to find humor in our unsettled situation. I sent a message to Dad, unsure if we could really communicate now.

"Let's pitch our tents here tonight," Drew said. "Tomorrow we can start house hunting if everyone agrees it's time."

Addie said, "There's an old legend that says somewhere deep beneath the mountain is a system of tunnels leading to an ancient hidden city called Telos, the City of Light."

She looked at the peak. "It's where the Lemurians lived. They were members of the lost continent of Lemuria. They say it drowned in the waves of the Pacific thousands of years ago. The ones who survived the waves settled in Telos." She smoothed her crinkly hair away from her face. "Even now, we might see their offspring wandering around the area."

"Really?" Trina breathed. "What do they look like?"

Addie raised one hand far above her head. "Seven-feet-tall, long flowing hair, and they wear white robes and sandals."

"Wow!" I said. "That's just cool. When you said seven foot tall with long hair, I thought it was going to be Bigfoot. But I don't believe he wears robes or sandals."

"Maybe you can tell us more around the fire. I think everyone is about ready to settle in and talk about everything that's happened. And what we need to do now."

"I'll start a fire pit," Dawk said.

"I'll gather wood," Sam added. The kids and Drew offered to help.

"We can set up the tents," Addie and Chachi said. "Or we could throw our sleeping bags in that nice building just up the lane, there." Addie laughed and pointed. "This big sign," she jerked her chin toward the one partially hidden by tree branches, "says there are several park buildings here. It appears to have been a very popular place. There is one building for weddings and large gatherings, and then there is the office building and even a kitchen."

Chachi grinned. "A kitchen? I've got powdered soup mix. All we need is some of that spring water in our pot." He looked around the area. "And perhaps some fresh greens and mushrooms—"

"Wonder if there's any trout in that stream?" Sam murmured. "Good thing we were able to save a couple of the fishing poles."

Addie grinned. "I'll bet there are. We've been fortunate in our travels. So far, we've found fish in every river and stream. And I'm pretty sure it's only a short hike from here to McCloud Falls. Very beautiful. Hiked it once with Slim." She stopped, kissed her fingertips, and threw the kiss toward the sky, as if toward Heaven. Then she continued, "There are also caves and other places where we would be safe—"

Milo jumped up from the edge of the water where he'd been examining something under a rock. "This is the best place *ever*."

"Let's try out that building," Addie said. "It's called the Upper Lodge according to the sign." She held out her hand as she walked, as if touching the very air. "When we hiked this area, Slim and I, we didn't come down this far." She closed her fingers around a bit of air, as if gathering a feeling into her palm for safekeeping. "I'm so glad we're here."

"Me, too," I looked up at the trees where our Turqs had settled. "I hope no one is already living here. Watching us from one of those buildings. At times like these, I kinda miss the old gray Taker. The one who used to carry Carlos everywhere."

"The one who always checked things out before letting us go barging in?" Faith murmured.

We heard a flutter of wings overhead and a few pine needles floated down. "Maybe he's telling us it's okay to go inside."

Faith nodded and looked at the building. It was dwarfed by trees. "I don't *feel* anyone watching us, do you?"

I shook my head. "No, I don't. But I think there are more Remainders, somewhere. I trust Turq, though. If he says it's okay, I believe him."

Without another word, the two of us strode up to the first building and looked in the windows of the roomy, cabin-like structure.

"Oh, this is fantastic," Faith breathed. "I do see a kitchen over there, and look, canned goods and cooking oil, even a spice rack."

"And a magnificent fireplace—"

At that, the rest of the group stormed the doors.

That night, we sat at a long, L-shaped bar while Chachi cooked up the trout he'd caught with help from the illustrious duo of Sam and Milo. The entrée was accompanied by an amazing loaf of bread baked by Addie in a fantastic wood-fired pizza oven.

Faith, Tandy, and the kids offered to help, fetching and carrying, drinking in the near-holy yeasty smells. It was so wonderful to be inside a real kitchen again, we all crowded around with huge smiles on our faces.

There were several lanterns tucked here and there in the wide-open space, and Sam commented that in some ways it reminded him of his Grampa's old bar. I didn't ask for clarification, but I suspected it was because of the way we were all lined up along one side of the long L awaiting the first *home cooked* indoor meal we'd had in this new lifetime.

It made me think of the rustic cabins we'd stayed in on our family vacations when I was a child. And it made the gap left by my dad even wider and more pronounced. *Wish you were here,* I thought. *Wish you were here to enjoy this. You and Mom ...*

During our meal prep, the talk turned to, *Before.*

"What were you doing, before the world fell in?" Addie asked

Sam. They both seemed quite at ease in the kitchen, thus they chatted while they cooked. "You mentioned a bar?"

"I ran my grandparents' bar," he said. "Quaint little bar and package store right on the Texas-New Mexico border. Sure miss those days." He patted a filet in the pan, judging it's doneness by touch. He'd been delighted to find a pantry still full of items like Butter Flavored Pam cooking spray and jars full of garlic salt and other spices.

The smell of the frying fish was mouth-watering.

Addie touched his shoulder, one touch, lightly. "We will have more memories." She set her jaw, checked the bread. "I will always miss Slim. He was my best friend. But we will have a life, all of us, together, here."

I couldn't help but smile at the way Sam laid his large paw on her shoulder in solidarity. I remembered he had also lost a spouse. Before all this. Sorrow before sorrow.

We enjoyed a wonderful, simple meal of pan-fried trout, fresh baked bread—no butter, but that was a minor annoyance, hardly worth mentioning—canned carrots, and funny looking mushrooms which Addie called chicken-of-the-woods, but which reminded me of brains. It was a feast. No doubt about it.

Afterward, we sat and marveled at our good fortune.

The sun was nearly gone, and the light had taken on the dim quality of an old black and white movie.

"I've always loved this time of day," Faith said. "Before the rip, this time of day was made for walking the neighborhood, texting with my friends, or cooking dinner with my mom if she had the night off." A dark image of her friend, Shan, lying twisted behind a wrecked car, sprang into her thoughts and was immediately shared with the group. "Sorry," she said. "Didn't mean to send that to everyone." She took a deep, calming, breath. "I haven't had time to think of her in a while."

I was about to get up, go to her, comfort her in some way—I wasn't sure how—but Trina beat me to it. She wrapped her thin arms around Faith and hugged her loosely. "I saw my mom die," she said.

That was all it took. Suddenly, everyone was sharing their stories, our stories, one after the other until all at once, we became aware of the coming darkness outside.

"Reminds me of the darkness inside the tube," Milo said.

"What?" Addie's tone was incredulous. "You were in one of those tubes that opened on the beach?"

"Yeah," I said. "We all were. Just like the one that took my dad, except ours didn't go to Heaven. Not at all."

Sam and Dawk looked at each other. "We may be thinking about it all wrong," Dawk said. "The portal in the Bitty Sloan House sounds like the one in the hogan—"

"But they don't sound the same as the tubes under the sea."

At the confused looks on the faces of Addie and Chachi, and the other Remainders, Milo briefly described what we'd all gone through after falling through the hogan-portal in Four Corners. His sister took over to describe the pyramid—what Dad had called The Beast—and told how we'd left it all in the clutches of the whales and dolphins.

"Will it just keep whirling around and around like a giant drain, or a—"

"Black hole?" one of the other Remainders said. "You mean swirling around and around like a black hole?"

"Creating a suction—"

"A vortex?"

We all looked at each other. "Nah," several voices said in unison. "We never would have survived anything that strong."

But we did survive, Faith and I thought at one another.

Drew's thoughts chimed in, *Have we? In my opinion, we aren't nearly far enough away from that thing yet.*

I had to agree with him on that, especially when I became aware of a familiar shushing sound like hundreds of bare feet on asphalt. My head swiveled around as if in slow motion. The bank of windows to my right looked out on the soft dirt lane, there was no asphalt nearby, so what could be making that—

And then I saw it. Barely glimmering in the dimness of the early evening, a wall of Takers, marching. Apparently, there *was* a road, beyond the trees—there had to be to make that familiar sound—and overhead, a low-flying drone with red markings on the wings. The drone appeared to be herding the Takers, probably with the help of Joy Juice. I was surprised it was not a dragon head, but then I remembered the one Snake and I had found crashed in the Palo Duro Canyon. This one looked the same.

"Hey, guys," I said. "We aren't quite as alone as we thought."

Sam put a finger to his lips and slipped out the side door into the woods.

I kept an eye on Snake, certain he would take off as soon as he saw movement. Then Sam sent me a mental picture of hybrid-Taker-humans with clear blisters for heads and tube-like appendages sprouting from their arms in place of hands.

They were marching along, timid and docile, their inside-out tattoos—their sin words, their instructions, whatever the words represented—swimming beneath their skin and now, in and out of their blister-like heads.

This could've been us, Sam thought. *Our parts woven into their parts. And vice versa.*

A chill froze my thoughts. Drew was right. We hadn't escaped them at all—

Without warning, Turq 2.0 streaked down from his tree, plowing into the mass at top speed, bursting bubbles and sending spiky black letters flying.

Is there no way out of this mess? Drew yelled in my head. But this time we were in for a surprise. A wonderful surprise in the form of more Turqs, but instead of just the ones we had flown in on, there suddenly appeared dozens more. It was Cheyenne all over again.

And they didn't just protect us from the Takers, they also took out the drone, and when the saving dark rain had come and gone back into the sky-hole—tiny angelic insects cleaning up another evil mess—we heard a different sort of rustling from the other direction.

At first, I couldn't make out what was causing the noise, but then I did. We all did. It was people. Hurrying toward us from the direction of the mountain. Men, women, and children, wearing clothes like us. No blisters or inside-out tattoos, no wings or any-thing. Just people. More Remainders.

"Hello!" someone shouted.

Inside the lodge, we all began to cheer. People were pouring into the area now, running toward the lodge, laughing, happy.

Snake went crazy, trying to get through the closed door.

Outside the windows, we saw Sam step forward, hand extended, to greet a smiling man wearing a cammo jacket.

"Hello," Sam said. "I am glad to see a friendly face."

They both grinned and shook. "Burleson," the stout man said. "Call me Burl."

Sam threw a glance at us. "Those are my friends. We've come from all over the Southwest, trying to get away from these alien creatures." He seemed unable to stop talking. Something about finding more people just opened him up. "You wouldn't believe the thing we saw out in the ocean near San Diego," he said. "But this is the first time we've seen these hybrid monstrosities up close."

The man nodded. "Yes, sir," he said. "We've seen horrible things, and we've seen miraculous things." He looked skyward. "Those friends that just saved us are what we call our Torpedo Birds." With a grin, he added, "I see you brought your own."

We all heard the wings rustle overhead.

Now it was Sam's turn to nod. "Actually, they brought us. They have saved us over and over. We call them Turqs," he said. "Kind of a long story. One we would love to share with y'all around that nice woodstove."

I walked up then, laughing as I did at old Snakeman. Wonder of wonders, he'd found another dog. A rangy mutt of a thing with floppy ears and a big, doggy grin. They were giving each other the sniff test, and I found myself hoping against hope the mutt was a girl. I couldn't wait to hear more about this wondrous find.

But it might be a moment. The dogs were circling each other happily, prancing stiff legged with joy. I reached Sam and the other man who were chatting like long lost friends.

"Jack," Sam said, "this gentleman's name is Burl. He and his bunch arrived a week ago. They are the reason the lodge is so well stocked."

Burl held out his hand, and we also shook. Then Dawk and Faith, along with Drew and the kids, crowded around. Addie and Chachi also joined in. I introduced them all. Sam had wandered away, shaking hands with other folks who were still coming out of the forest. "We go up to the mountain caves when we hear a platoon coming," someone said. "It's the safe place for us."

I overheard another man telling Sam, "Our little girl, there," he indicated Snake's new four-legged friend with a jut of his chin, "is like a monster barometer. Alerts us when they are coming so we can take cover. We've been expecting them for hours." He looked down at the ground, twisted his head to one side, a big grin on his face. "But we didn't expect all of you, and we sure didn't expect Scruff's new friend."

I knew he meant Snake. He seemed as happy as I was to see how the pair immediately hit it off.

I didn't say anything, because I wasn't in that little knot of campers, but I wondered how they kept from being trapped, or sprayed with Joy Juice, holed up in a cave. Maybe I didn't have the whole picture yet.

"We call ourselves The Remainders," Faith told Burl and a woman he introduced as Leena. "Have there been very many of those troops marching through here?"

Leena shook her head. "That was the second one since we arrived from Arizona." She indicated a couple of other people nearby. "We all flew in on what Burl calls our Torpedo Birds," she smiled gently. "It's such an amazingly peaceful place, we decided to fix it up and stay as long as possible." She waved her hand toward the mountain. "There's something about the mountain …"

She let her gaze fall toward the other people milling around. "Folks have been arriving almost daily," she said. "Flying in on their birds, or walking, a few have even arrived in Jeeps and Land Rovers." She pointed toward a couple of vehicles I hadn't noticed, snugged up under the trees at another lodge.

"I can't believe how we all just wound up here," I said.

Faith laughed. "Jack, you know nothing is by accident." She smiled to take the admonishing tone out of her voice.

I was about to agree with her when a boy about Milo's size came dashing up, socked him in the arm, and said, "Wanna play horseshoes? There's a pit over there, and if you don't know how, I'll teach you."

Milo appeared slightly stunned.

The kid grinned and said, "My name's Jamal, what's yours?"

Before Milo could reply, Jamal was off, racing down the grassy slope toward what appeared to be a playground area tucked among the trees. Several picnic tables graced the spot as well.

A slow smile overtook Milo's features and he glanced at his dad.

Drew nodded, and the boy was off, chasing after the energetic new kid at top speed. After a few beats, Trina and Bunny wandered after them, Bunny silently taking hold of Trina's hand as they walked.

Chachi had made a brief mention of finding Bunny sitting on the steps of an old Baptist church like a little stray. No one had been able to learn anymore about her—yet. But I had a notion Trina and Milo would get her to come around. They were good that way.

Tandy, on the other hand, had no reservations about sharing her back story.

"I was the only survivor," she told them with a shudder. "We were in the basement SUB—"

Addie glanced at us and translated SUB to Student Union Building, Arizona State University. Tandy said, "Yeah, that's where we went to get our books and coffee." She'd faltered, for just a moment, with the memories, and then she'd wiped a tear from below one eye and said, "Mardie and Ginger rushed outside to see what was causing the noise. I heard them through the downstairs bathroom door, but I was too slow." She looked down at her hands. "If I hadn't taken time to wash my hands, I would have gone up, too."

Another tale of basement survival, just like mine and Sam's. Saved by being underground.

Now, I saw a couple more tweens and younger kids break away from the loose knit group assembling outside the Upper Lodge. They trickled down toward the playground where the other kids went. Apparently being cool was still important, even now. Good thing I'd had Snake, I thought. If I'd been with someone my own age back then, things might've worked out quite differently. After all, I wasn't much older than Trina and the other tweens.

"This is amazing," Dawk said.

"Almost too good to be true," I added. And then a thought speared my mind on the wings of a song. It started out as "Carry on Wayward Son," and then a new tune wove its way into the melody.

I began to laugh. It was Eddie Money's old song, "Two Tickets to Paradise," a catchy old tune that Dad once said was about a trip to see California's redwoods. A trip that never happened, according to the song. Just like we never found Redwood City.

"Two Tickets to Paradise," Dad? Good to see you've still got your sense of humor. On the other hand, this certainly could fit the bill.

I glanced around at all the people chatting here and there. From one little knot of people, I overheard Dawk's voice. "So, I guess you haven't seen the thing in the ocean yet, but did you see the mutations on those gray monsters we call the Takers?"

The other person, the owner of the shaggy mutt still dancing around Snakeman, said they were well acquainted with the Takers, although they all called them different things, usually monsters or grays.

"Oh, yes," she said. "We've all seen the way they're changing. We think it has to do with the labs and all those military vehicles we saw going back and forth on our way down from Portland."

"And the drones," Dawk agreed.

She nodded and swiped curly brown bangs off her forehead. "We also saw the clothed monsters morph into Birds, what some call the Flyers—"

"Yes," Dawk said. "We call them Turqs because our Jack befriended one wearing a turquoise shirt even before the thing morphed." He chuckled. "Before they changed, we all called them Takers." Running his fingers over his chin, he said, "What a long, strange trip we've been on."

Of course, I heard The Grateful Dead song when he said those words, and I had to chuckle, a bit.

Then Faith appeared beside me, and even Snake broke away

from his new friend and ran back to us. "It *has* been a long, strange trip," she said, touching my hand lightly. "But at least I found you and Snake." She smiled. "And Dawk, and Sam." She cut her eyes to the side and said, "And Drew and the kids …" Her voice took on her old sing-song storyteller tone as she said, "Not to mention your dad and Carlos."

I gave her an impulsive side-arm hug. "Thank you. And thank God, we did find each other. I know we wouldn't have survived without you."

Snake barked on cue, as if agreeing with the entire conversation.

In my head, Sam said, *He just agreed with you, Jack. I know he did.*

I looked his way, and he had the biggest grin on his face. In my head, I heard his thoughts. *We know there are humans, and we know there are aliens, and we're pretty sure one is controlling the other. Or trying to.* He shrugged. *But we will be all right. We've got God and His angels on our side.*

That's right, I echoed. *We'll be all right now. Everything will be all right,* I recognized a song called "End of the Line" by the Traveling Wilburys.

That's right, Sam said. *It's all gonna be all right now. No matter what happens, we gotta stay grateful. Stay thankful.*

Yep, Faith added. *No matter what happens next, we'll be okay. We're still learning as we go.* She leaned her head over on my shoulder and I was surprised to discover we were no longer nearly the same height. Seems I'd grown another inch or two even in the midst of all our trials.

Yes, ma'am, I said, pulling her closer. *Learning as we go.*

I glanced up at the last of the sun's rays peeking through the dark green canopy of trees. One tiny spot shone exponentially bright, like an entrance. *Was it the opening to one of those tubes, or to Heaven?*

Learning as we go, Jack, Faith said. *But for now … let's give it a rest.*

I laughed, Snake barked, and even Sam chuckled.

From a slight distance, I caught the distinct murmur of conversations going on all about me. I remembered the silence that had surprised and annoyed me in my mad drive across the West Texas prairie. But this was a good sound. The sound of friends, of happiness. The sound of life.

CHAPTER FORTY-ONE

End

Jack, Faith whispered in my head. *What do I see, coming up the road?*

I glanced up just in time to see a trio of red uniforms walking toward us.

"That looks like—" Before I could finish my sentence, the ground opened, and two of the uniforms were gone, just like my dad.

The other uniform came toward us on the run. This time she ran off the road and into the trees. She didn't slow down until she made it all the way to the lodge door where Sam and Burl were once again deep in conversation.

"Hey," I yelled, striding toward the place the other two had disappeared.

"Jack, wait," Faith yelled. "There's a tube!"

I stopped at the edge of the road. The dust was barely disturbed although I could see the footprints of the two people leading up to the place they'd disappeared. One set was large, the other much smaller. *A man and a woman,* I thought.

No, Jack, Faith thought. *Don't even think about going after them. They can find their own way out or go back to where they came from.*

From behind Faith, a woman's voice yelled, "Don't step on the road. Stay where there are tree roots!"

I looked down at the ground. *Okay,* I thought. *Makes sense. Tree roots would interfere with a tunnel or a tube.*

"Come back," Addie called. "The lady says it's too late to help them. The tubes are going straight to the ships now."

That got my attention. *What does she know that we don't?*

Drew gathered the kids, and we all rushed back to the lodge, watching our footing as we went. *Doesn't it seem miraculous that God provided us with flying Turqs so that we don't have to travel on the ground anymore?*

Faith and I both caught his thoughts, and we agreed. *Miraculous, indeed.*

Chachi had already shoveled a plate of our leftover food onto a plate for the woman in red. "These nice people before us provided most of what I am giving you. We just brought in the fresh trout and some mushrooms."

The woman slid onto a high-backed barstool and dug into the fish. There was even a hunk of bread on her plate although I'd thought we'd finished all that earlier. She took two big bites and then leapt off the stool and rushed back to the door, barely getting outside before heaving into the bushes.

"Oh, my God," she moaned, head down. Her cap had fallen by the wayside and her bald head gleamed with sweat. "I'm sorry," she said. "They experimented on us. We thought we could trust them."

That answered a lot of questions we hadn't even asked.

Faith and Addie helped her back inside and sat her in a more comfortable chair. "You poor thing," Addie said, mopping the woman's forehead with the corner of a dishtowel.

Her bloodshot eyes looked up at Addie then at all of us. "We were wrong to join them."

I realized I could not read her thoughts. Not at all. I also realized there was something wrong with her pupils. Instead of the round reactive pupils that should be there, hers were slits, small and steady. I wondered how she could even see.

I tried to look deeper into her eyes, but the daylight was almost gone, and I didn't want to grab a lantern and shine it in her face. She seemed way too ill for that.

"There were more of us," she continued. "Some stole helicopters, tried to escape, but they never got far." She dropped her head into her hands. "So, we waited, bided our time, learned what to do, what to avoid. Then they drugged us, implanted something in our heads, made our hair fall out, our eyes go crazy. I see so much more now." She stopped talking and raised her chin. In the right light, her eyes appeared slightly multifaceted. On the verge of insectile.

She closed her eyelids, and I wondered if she would ever open them again.

Other than the kids, no one got much sleep that night. We didn't even spread out into the other cabins. There were forty of us now, and we all elected to sleep in the big lodge. We dragged up mattresses and sleeping bags and blankets from the other cabins and from Addie and Chachi's belongings. Everyone shared everything.

When we stoked up the fire in the woodstove, I thought about that night we had the campfire on the outskirts of Eden. That had been the night we met Sam. When we still had Carlos and our tattered innocence. Faith had commented then that we had lit a campfire as if in invitation, and I wondered about that now. Were we sending up smoke signals again? Did it make a difference? We had to have fire. This was northern California. Fall was on the horizon.

"It's got to be a new order," I whispered as we discussed things around the stove. "A new government. Maybe they've already done the alien-to-human thing but they're running low on whatever fuels them so they can continue." I looked at the bald woman asleep (unconscious?) on the chair. "Maybe it's our life force that's fueling them. Maybe they didn't even mean to kill off so many with the EMP that let them in … wouldn't that be about par?"

Only Dawk laughed at that statement.

Faith started to send me a thought, I felt it nudge my mind, but then she stopped. I knew what she was going to say, though. She was going to say learning as *they* go, too, maybe. Just like us.

I caught her eye and let her know I understood.

She smiled, just a slight upturn at the corners of her mouth, and then the bald woman's words cut through the gloom.

"At first, we thought they were super intelligent, the next rung on the evolutionary ladder. We weren't the ones who made first contact, those humans are all dead now, their DNA absorbed, used to change or improve the aliens' next incarnation." Her words were spooky in the firelight. Especially since she didn't open her eyes.

"We wondered if that's what they were doing," I said. "Going from place to place, taking what they want, discarding the rest—"

She opened her eyes, looked at the ceiling. "One thing I feel it's important for you all to know is that we didn't invite them here. We only fell in with the rest of the workers in the tunnels below the airport. That's how we survived. For a while." She swallowed. "We never wanted to hurt anyone. We just wanted to live. Can you understand that?"

"Of course, we can," Faith said.

Addie bobbed her head up and down. "It's what we all want. We won't talk about the past unless we can learn from it." She didn't hug the woman, but it wouldn't have surprised me if she had.

"Do you know anything that could help us?" I asked the woman.

"Yes," she said. "We learned that they travel the world, other planets, other planes, other universes, looking for the best genetic material—"

"Seekers," I said. "Takers and Seekers—"

"Do they seek enlightenment," Faith asked. "Like us?"

The woman looked down, then away. The firelight climbed the wall in shadows, rising and falling back down, wavelike, vertical shadow-waves.

I glanced out toward the trees, where our Turqs waited, patiently, then my mind skated back to those horrific scenes of carnage after the initial rip. "No," I said. "I didn't think so."

From out of nowhere an image of a slaughterhouse slid into my mind, cows hanging on hooks, bleeding out, mostly dead, but not all of them. Like us, a few always survived the bolt gun. Remainders, moaning in agony, twisting on the hook.

That unsought mental image was replaced by another. One showing a long line of smooth, black cattle in a tight, curving chute. *A feeder chute*, my mind explained. Feeding them directly into the abattoir. The cattle there were aware of their fate. The scent of it permeated the air. They lowed in terror. And despair.

"Oh, my God," I said. "We're no different, are we?"

Tears in her eyes, Faith shook her head, reached for my hand. "We're trying," she said. "Some of us are trying."

Again, I thought of Turq 2.0 and all the other morphed Takers outside in the trees.

"At least we do try," Sam said. Then something occurred to him. "It's in our makeup, this physical need for protein. We don't do it to be cruel."

That hit me, hard. "Maybe it's the same way with them. Maybe it's just in their makeup to take, and take, and take—"

The bald woman said, "I don't believe we will ever know the why of this thing." She clasped her hands together. "They seem to be a lot like us, doing things on instinct."

"No search for enlightenment?"

"This is the search," Faith said. "It's just another part of it. Like the spiral arms of the Milky Way. We've just entered another arm of the search."

I tried to take that in, to understand what she was saying, but "Carry on Wayward Son" played into our midst, distracting me. "The search for survival is the search for enlightenment. Carry on, Son," Dad's voice whispered. "Carry on."

"But how," I asked. "How do we kill them so we *can* carry on?"

"You don't," the bald woman replied. "You don't kill them. You *outlast* them. The sea life is rousting them from their nests. Destroying their spaceships. There are many, sure. But eventually, they will decide we are too much trouble, and they will move on."

She took a deep, rattling breath. "Until they do, you take your family of Remainders and make a new life, always watching the skies and listening for the sound of feet. And above all else, stay off the sand and the soft paths. They don't like roots, those tubular beings. They don't like roots at all."

Author's Notes

As a child of the sixties my head is stuffed with an untold number of classic rock and pop songs, along with myriad hymns and country tunes as well. I'm including a playlist of all those mentioned in the book on the next page, in case you want to give them a listen. If I've left any out, be sure to let me know. You can email me at the link on my website:

authorAnnSwann.com

Happy Reading, until we meet again.

Playlist

May not be in order of mention.

"Carry on Wayward Son"–Kansas
"On the Road Again"–Willie Nelson
"Love is All Around"–The Troggs
"The Sound of Silence"–Simon and Garfunkel
"The Sound of Silence"–Disturbed
"Fields of Gold"–Sting
"Amazing Grace"–written by John Newton–public domain
"Rebel Yell"–Billy Idol
"Come Together"–The Beatles
"Give Me One Reason"–Tracy Chapman
"I Think it's Gonna Be Alright"–Travelling Wilburys
"The Room at the Top of the Stairs"–Tom Petty
"Time for Me to Fly"–REO Speedwagon
"Hotel California"–The Eagles
"Onward Christian Soldier"–hymn written by Rev. Sabine Baring-Gould–public domain
"Hit the Road, Jack"–Ray Charles
"Well, Alright"–Buddy Holly
"Momentary Lapse of Reason"–Pink Floyd
"Down on the Corner"–Creedence Clearwater Revival
"Margaritaville"–Jimmy Buffett
"Mansion on the Hill"–Bruce Springsteen
"It Came Out of the Sky"–Creedence Clearwater Revival

"Woodstock"–Crosby, Stills, Nash, & Young
"Something in the Way She Moves"–The Beatles
"The Little Old Lady from Pasadena"–The Beach Boys
"Let it Rain"–Eric Clapton
"Hollaback, Girl"–Gwen Stefani
"Hold On"–Kansas
"The End of the World as We Know It"–REM
"Under the Sea"–The Little Mermaid Soundtrack
"Rikki Don't Lose This Number"–Steely Dan
"Spirit in the Sky"–Norman Greenbaum
"Teach Your Children"–Crosby, Stills, Nash, & Young
"Rocket Man"–Elton John
"Fly Away"–Lenny Kravitz
"We Built this City"–Starship
"The Lucky Ones"–Sam Riggs
"Go Rest High on that Mountain"–Vince Gill
"You and I will Meet Again"–Tom Petty and the Heartbreakers
"In the Garden"–written by Charles Austin Miles–public domain
"Helpless"–Neil Young
"Angel Dream"–Tom Petty and the Heartbreakers
"Our Temporary Home"–Carrie Underwood
"Two Tickets to Paradise"–Eddie Money
"Long strange trip"–The Grateful Dead
"End of the Line"–The Traveling Wilburys